A LADY'S REPUTATION

AMY D'ORAZIO

Quills & Quartos
PUBLISHING

Edited by Gail Warner and Ellen Pickels

Proofread by Linda D'Orazio

Cover Design by CloudCat Designs

Front cover:

1. Vittorio Reggianini , An Amusing Letter

2. Balthasar Nebot c 1768, The Dam and Fishing Tabernacles with the Octagon

Tower and Rotunda at Studley Royal

Back cover:

 Vittorio Reggianini, The Recital

ISBN: 978-1-951033-03-3

978-1-951033-02-6 (ebook)

Dedicated to my family, with all my love

TABLE OF CONTENTS

Wednesday, 8 April 1812, Kent

COLONEL FITZWILLIAM SAT WITH HIS MOUTH RATHER unattractively agape for what seemed like a full quarter of an hour before finally repeating, "In love?"

"You have heard of the affliction, I presume?" asked Darcy with a droll smile. He wished desperately that he had chosen to confide in his cousin in different circumstances—perhaps over a billiard table or on horseback, somewhere Fitzwilliam would not be so wholly focused on him—but there was nothing for it now.

"But who is she? I have detected no symptom of peculiar regard by you for anyone. Though now that I think of it, you did speak rather at length to that horse-faced lady from Leeds—or was it Leicester? I cannot recall. Is it her?"

"Heavens no!" Darcy laughed. "I shall tell you, but first, I must plead your assistance in concealing this from our family. For Lady Catherine to know before I tell her myself would be nothing short of disastrous. Likewise, I would not wish to have your father learn of it before I tell him."

"My father will be delighted to see you settled. Unless you think the family might not approve of her?"

"The family surely will not approve of her. It is Miss Elizabeth Bennet."

"Miss Elizabeth Bennet!"

Fitzwilliam's exclamations were becoming tiresome. "You seem rather taken with her yourself," Darcy replied sharply. "I do not think you should find it as astonishing as all of this."

"Indeed not. I find Miss Bennet delightful. Charming, witty, and beautiful...kind too. I do not think I could have any greater hope for your happiness than to see you married to such a lady as Miss Bennet."

Darcy rose from the large wing chair and went to the window of his aunt's library. The window might have boasted a view of the parsonage save for the trees that grew up thick and tall between them. Nevertheless, it was a comfort to know that she was somewhere in that direction.

"But?" he asked.

"Her lack of fortune is an issue, as well as her connexions. Did I hear something about relations in trade?"

Darcy grimaced, knowing he would be giving voice to all that plagued him since first coming to understand his attraction to Miss Elizabeth Bennet. "Her relations on her maternal side are not gentry. One uncle is in trade, and the other is an attorney in a small village called Meryton in Hertfordshire.

"Her mother is a vulgar creature. She is outspoken, illiberal, and bold. She would not be received by anyone of quality. Miss Bennet's father is indolent and lackadaisical. He consistently fails to censure his family for their many mortifying antics. The young ladies are not educated properly nor have they been guided into demure womanhood. The younger three are wholly untamed and even encouraged in impudence. However, Miss Elizabeth and her eldest sister have somehow managed to find elegant restraint."

Fitzwilliam exhaled loudly.

"Do not think me insensible of the evils of my choice. Nevertheless, it cannot signify because, no matter her connexions or her upbringing, I love her. To live my life without her is unthinkable."

"So you intend to declare yourself soon?"

"The parsonage party will dine with us tomorrow evening. I thought I might do it then."

Fitzwilliam's eyes flew wide, and once again, he stared agape. "In our aunt's home? Have you gone stark, raving mad?"

"Do you have a better idea?"

"A better idea than having Lady Catherine witness your engagement in her home to the detriment of her daughter? Yes, I believe I can think of many better ideas than that." Fitzwilliam rose from his seat and paced slowly, rubbing his face in the way he always did when deep in thought.

Darcy watched him for far too long before demanding, "Say something, Fitzwilliam."

"I am concerned. You say this affection of yours is implacable, yet I do not think you fully comprehend the many consequences of your decision. Need I remind you that Lady Catherine expects you will offer for Anne?"

"How could I forget that?" Darcy snorted. "I assure you, I have studied this from every aspect. I have considered every objection."

"Considering something, no matter how exhaustive, does not necessarily prepare you for the reality of it. What if you propose to Miss Bennet and then, in the face of her family's lunatic behaviour, find yourself doubting your actions? What if ostracism from our family—I do not think that would happen, but it cannot be ruled out—makes her charms grow dim? There are a number of obstacles, and you would have them before you all at once. How do you know whether your ardour will outlast it?"

Darcy was silent as he settled back into his chair.

"You must anticipate the consequences of your actions and their effect on both you and Miss Bennet. Will the society of your bride suffice if no one in London will receive you? How will you bear being the subject of tattle, unceasing gossip? What about when the vulgarity and impropriety of her family is permeating the halls of Pemberley?"

"We would not be ostracised," Darcy protested. "Naturally, there will be some who remove me from their list of preferred guests, but I shall seek the assistance of your mother to ensure Elizabeth is not shunned. You saw yourself that she is very agreeable. Few can meet her and remain unmoved. She has that way about her. Even Lady Catherine approves of her, albeit grudgingly."

"True, though I think we can agree that Lady Catherine's approval will end as soon as she knows of the engagement." Fitzwilliam paused to sip his drink.

"As for the Bennets," Darcy continued, "we shall likely see them very little. Mr Bennet dislikes travel and can scarcely be prevailed upon to come to London. I would imagine Derbyshire to be quite out of the question."

Darcy drummed his fingers on the tabletop beside his chair, deep in thought. The hours spent contemplating these obstacles over the past months had taught him they could not be disregarded. Overcoming them, however, was entirely another matter. "Perhaps I should go to our family first."

"What?"

He turned to meet his cousin's gaze. "It might be to our advantage to address these objections before I propose."

Fitzwilliam nodded thoughtfully.

"I shall go to my uncle first. He may rant as much as he likes with no one the wiser but myself. Once he realises I shall not waver, your mother will make him see reason. This will also remove any notion of impropriety or some similar nonsense—lend validity to the whole thing, if you will." His voice grew animated as his idea gained momentum. "Then…then I shall go to Hertfordshire and speak to Elizabeth's father."

Colonel Fitzwilliam gave his cousin a dubious look. "But that is the way of our grandfathers, Darcy. A modern young woman expects to be the first to know of her engagement."

"Elizabeth will approve, I am certain." Darcy dismissed his cousin's concerns with a wave of his hand. "It will show a respect for her family, in particular of her father, of whom she is very fond. Moreover, it will be my test; if I can bear this mortification, surely I can bear anything."

Colonel Fitzwilliam laughed. "Do you truly think it might go so badly?"

Darcy rolled his eyes. "I can hear Mrs Bennet's screeching now, exclaiming over my wealth and Elizabeth's pin money."

"If it is any consolation," Fitzwilliam teased, "the mothers of the *ton* would do the same, albeit quietly and out of your earshot."

Darcy scarcely heard him, still turning the idea over and over in his head and growing more elated with each repetition. "Yes, yes…this is how it must be done. Let us depart tomorrow. I have business in London I must attend with no further delay."

"I have not yet made my tour of the park."

"Hang the park." Darcy's spirits could not be repressed. His dreams were soon coming to fruition, and nothing could deter him. "I have walked it often enough with my love these weeks past. All seemed in order or, at least, close enough."

Fitzwilliam laughed. "Far be it from me to interfere with a

man on a mission. Shall we make for the parsonage now to take our leave?"

Darcy nodded. "We shall need an escape once our aunt learns we are to shorten our visit."

Friday, 10 April 1812, London

"THIS HAS ALL THE FEEL OF A TRIBUNAL," LORD MATLOCK remarked with great joviality. "Such sombre countenances on you both! From Darcy, I expect it, but on you, Son, it is a novelty."

Neither of the younger gentlemen responded to his jest. Fitzwilliam went immediately to his father's cabinet, pouring each of them a glass of port before joining them in sitting.

Darcy was surprisingly unnerved to face his uncle and had to remind himself several times that he was a grown man who did not require his uncle's approval to marry. Nevertheless, he hoped for the blessing and support of all his family, and he could not deny the thrill of setting into motion his dearest wishes.

Lord Matlock peered at him. "You first extend your stay in Kent then return home two days early. Is there something in particular you need to discuss with me?"

"Indeed." Darcy took a drink to fortify his courage. He began by telling his uncle about meeting Miss Bennet in Hertfordshire and being fascinated by her, then the blooming of that fascination into a deep and ardent love. His uncle listened with no expression as Darcy told him that he had returned to London prepared never to see her again, but then she was in Kent, even more beautiful than he remembered, and as impossible as it would seem, his love had deepened further still.

He reviewed the time they spent together in Kent—the walks, her impertinence to Lady Catherine, and her friendship with his cousin. At this time, he looked to Fitzwilliam, hoping for some mention of Miss Elizabeth Bennet's many attributes.

Fitzwilliam did not disappoint. "She is a charming and delightful girl. Witty, well read, and kind, yet by no means a bluestocking. She is the sort of lady who would be a great boon to any drawing room or dinner. You and Mother would be utterly enthralled by her."

Lord Matlock regarded his son and nephew with great scepticism. "I have never heard of any Bennets."

"Her father has a small estate in Hertfordshire worth two thousand a year." Darcy spoke with an assurance he did not feel. "It is entailed upon a cousin, Mr Collins, who coincidentally is Lady Catherine's parson. Miss Bennet's fortune is one thousand pounds. They have no connexions of note, or none of whom I am aware."

Lord Matlock was silent for several long moments, regarding Darcy with an amused sort of pity in his eyes. "Darcy, what is this? You cannot be serious."

"I am absolutely serious." Darcy swallowed. "I intend to marry her."

"You will be a laughingstock! What are you thinking?" With that, Lord Matlock was in for a fight. "You have a duty and an obligation to your estate, to your ancestry, and to your descendants to do what is right, and what is right is for you to make a marriage with one of your kind!"

"One of my kind? Miss Elizabeth is a gentleman's daughter, and I am a gentleman!"

"She is no one! You would not be received nor recognised, and if you think your aunt and I shall help, you are sorely mistaken. You cannot cast off all that is expected of you and think we shall clean up after you!"

The fight raged on for above an hour. Lord Matlock blustered, shouted, pleaded, begged, and swore that he could have no part with his nephew nor countenance such an alliance. As he stormed from the room, he told Darcy that, if he proposed to Miss Elizabeth Bennet, he need never darken his door again. Darcy stomped off just as angrily—though more quietly—muttering to Lord Matlock's back that he had no intention of darkening his door ever again.

SITTING IN THE LIBRARY THAT SHARED A WALL WITH LORD Matlock's study, Viscount Saye, the eldest son and heir to the earldom of Matlock, heard it all. He had poured himself a glass of smuggled brandy to enjoy the diversion. Darcy, of all people, carried away by some sort of lust for a country girl! Moreover, the novelty of *not* being the person making his father angry was most enjoyable. Darcy was usually so tiresomely virtuous that it was amusing to see him behaving from sensibility rather than sense.

When his father slammed the study door behind him with enough force to cause the walls to shake, Saye decided it was time to stop merely enjoying the show. He went to the parlour where his mother liked to sit and found her writing letters in a sunny corner.

"My darling boy," she greeted him with a gentle smile. "Was that your father I heard yelling?"

"He is angry with Darcy." Saye tossed himself onto a sofa.

"With Darcy? Whatever for?"

"Darcy intends to propose to some unsuitable country girl with a fortune of one thousand pounds."

Lady Matlock laughed, her pen still moving over the page in front of her. "You must have misheard him. Darcy would never do any such thing."

"I assure you, Mama—that is precisely what happened. Darcy did not relent, they had a violent row, and my father has cast him off."

Lady Matlock's pen stilled. "Indeed?"

"My father said Darcy was never welcome here again, and Darcy stormed off."

With a sigh, Lady Matlock closed her eyes and pressed her fingers against her forehead. "Nonsense. Fitzwilliams simply do not feud. Where is your father now?"

Saye shrugged. "The courtyard, perhaps?"

"Go find him. Tell him we need to talk."

With a sigh, Saye rose, grumbling, "It is always to me to fix these things."

AN HOUR LATER, SAYE STROLLED TOWARDS DARCY'S HOUSE WITH his father. Lord Matlock had been significantly mollified after conversation with his eldest son and wife. An overture of sorts was formed under the assumption that Darcy, having spoken of his intentions, was unrelentingly firm in his plans.

As they approached Darcy's house, Saye made to turn down a different street. His father observed him with surprise. "You do not wish to see Darcy?"

"I trust you can manage the rest, and Miss Goddard is expecting me."

Lord Matlock smiled. At least, his son had made a proper match. "Yes, perhaps warn her of this business. There is bound to be some talk, and she is almost family. She has a right to know. Just be sure she understands the need for secrecy."

Saye, already with his back to his father, shrugged. "Of course," he replied with nonchalance, continuing towards the house of his intended.

Lord Matlock presented himself at Darcy's home, and he was quickly shown to the library where Darcy sat, glaring at the book on his lap. He regarded his uncle's entry with unmistakable wariness. Lord Matlock smiled in a conciliatory fashion.

"You must have anticipated my concerns, Darcy. I have the best interests of you and your family name at heart."

Darcy sighed and closed the book. "Am I not deserving of the felicity of true affection?"

"Of course, you are," Lord Matlock replied soothingly. "I have spoken to your aunt, and we know just how to manage things."

Should Miss Bennet prove acceptable in manners and appearance, Lord Matlock's plan was to feign a long-standing relationship with Mr Bennet—from their school days, perhaps. No one ever remembered who attended school where or when or with whom. With a claim to friendship with the house of Matlock, as well as the fact that the Bennets had been landed for well over a century (no mention need be made of the profitability of the land or the entailment unless it was absolutely unavoidable), it just might pass. Lady Matlock would lend her assistance and influence to young Mrs Darcy by providing introductions and entry into society.

"Now, you must take care of all the legal matters immediately. Get it done, get a licence, and marry quickly. That way, once the Season is at its height, you and your new wife will be in the midst of it in full sight of anyone with any wish to see you. It will not do to appear ashamed or uncertain as that will just feed the gossips."

"Indeed? I had thought rather the opposite. Perhaps an extended engagement—three or four months or so—and then spend the autumn at Pemberley."

"No, no, no—that is precisely what you must not do." Lord Matlock was definite. "Trust me in this. Marry as soon as things can be arranged, and we shall do our part as well."

"Very well. I certainly have no objection to making her my wife sooner rather than later."

Several streets away, Saye sat with his betrothed, Miss Lillian Goddard. Miss Goddard had many fine qualities that recommended her to her future husband: celestial blue eyes, fair hair, an ample bosom to match her ample fortune, and a father who possessed both a good position in the government and a lovely estate in Staffordshire. Of these assets, it was the bosom that garnered his admiring glances this day, even as he spoke of Darcy's news.

"My parents will advise him to marry soon."

Miss Goddard's eyes were wide with amazement. "What about her clothes? The breakfast?"

Saye waved off such notions. "For such a girl to have secured the likes of Darcy, she will wish it done as soon as possible. Her clothes can be sent later, and as for the breakfast, well, even if it is naught but old biscuits and salted fish, she will still enjoy the status afforded a Mrs Darcy."

He reached out to her, trailing a finger down her face and across her neck. "Send your maid away," he whispered.

With a faint blush, Miss Goddard did just that, succumbing happily to the lips of her betrothed as soon as the tiresome maid had closed the door quietly behind her. As Saye kissed and caressed her, he recalled he had neglected to mention that Miss Goddard should not speak of Darcy's engagement. Pulling back for a moment, he said, "Pray keep the news to yourself. Things are not entirely settled."

"Of course," she murmured as his hands made their way farther up her ribs and across her bosom and his lips found hers once again.

MISS LILLIAN GODDARD, KNOWN FOR HER EASE AND FRIENDLINESS if not for her intelligence or understanding, was delighted by the news that Darcy was engaged. It was a rather toothsome bit of gossip after all. Within moments of bidding her intended adieu, she had forgotten that the information she had heard was not to be repeated, and in any case, with such exciting news, keeping it to herself was out of the question.

Her mother was the first to be told. "Mr Darcy to marry?" Mrs Goddard exclaimed. "I do not think I have heard of any Bennets."

Miss Goddard replied, "Her father's estate is Long...something. I cannot recall, but there is an estate."

"I should hope so!" Her mother shook her head in amazement. "Mr Darcy could have had nearly anyone! I suppose this Miss Bennet must be very wealthy?"

"Saye told me her fortune is only...is merely..." She could not help herself, and uncharitable as it was, she giggled.

"Was what? Say it, child."

"A...a...a thou...a thousand pounds!" Miss Goddard gave way to gales of laughter.

Mrs Goddard's hand flew to cover her mouth. "No! You surely misunderstood."

Calming herself, Miss Goddard replied, "It was too shocking

to be misunderstood! Can you imagine Mr Darcy marrying a lady of such circumstances?"

"He must be in love." Mrs Goddard shook her head. "Why else would he throw himself away in this manner?"

The tale had all the best elements—secrecy, a whiff of scandal, and at its core, true love—and as such, it was irresistible. Mrs Goddard prided herself on not being a gossip and, therefore, intended to tell only her maid.

However, her sister, Mrs Donnelly, visited soon afterwards, and of course, she never kept anything from her; after that, her cousin Lady Belmore called. Each of those ladies had daughters who had been raised with Lillian and had their own visit while their mothers gossiped. In both circles, the incredible tale was told over and over again: Fitzwilliam Darcy was revealed as a man of such intense passion and love that he had thrown prudence and circumspection aside, and he would marry as his heart dictated. It could scarcely be believed.

Saturday, 11 April 1812, Hertfordshire

"OH, WHAT NOW?" MRS BENNET MOANED, STARING AT THE LETTER in her hand. The express had arrived early from London, and Mrs Bennet was nearly eaten up with curiosity over its contents. Mr Bennet, quite vexingly, was gone for nearly the entire day on some matter of the estate. With a sigh, she looked at Hill. "I suppose we shall not know what is in it until dinner." Mrs Hill nodded.

Mrs Bennet then spied Lady Lucas who was hurrying down the lane and arrived quite out of breath in her drawing room minutes later. "I saw the express rider leaving. I pray there is not bad news. I nearly ran here in case you were in need of comfort or consolation."

"I very well could be!" Mrs Bennet exclaimed with a peevish little scowl at the letter. "Indeed, I hardly know. Mr Bennet, that exasperating man, is gone all day. I am left to stare at this thing with no notion what it might contain!"

The ladies regarded the tempting missive with solemnity. It was not a common occurrence for express riders to arrive at Longbourn. The idea that important news was contained therein —news to which they were so near yet so far—was insupportable.

"It is from London and likely very important," Lady Lucas noted.

Mrs Bennet nodded emphatically, wondering silently whether it was something to do with Jane, who had been in London since January. "What if it is some urgent business for Mr Bennet? Tomorrow is Sunday. If he knows nothing of this until late today, he will be unable to address the problem until Monday, nearly three days past when it was sent."

"In general, an express is sent for matters of great urgency."

"That is very true! You know how I suffer from my nerves! I cannot worry over this all the day long! It would be exceedingly bad for my health!"

"That is very true, my dear. Lord knows how you suffer."

The two ladies met each other's gaze for a moment until Mrs Bennet said, "Perhaps it is best if I read it for him just to be sure there is not some illness or a death in the family, heaven forbid."

Lady Lucas nodded eagerly. Mrs Bennet opened the letter and shielded it carefully while she read it. Lady Lucas just barely managed to keep herself from peering over her friend's shoulder as Mrs Bennet, contrary to all expectation, went stock-still and silent; her only concession to the astonishing contents was to clutch the letter to her bosom.

"Mrs Bennet?" Lady Lucas urged. "What is it? You have gone white as a sheet."

Her words moved Mrs Bennet from her stupor, and she turned to Lady Lucas, emitting a loud, unmistakably triumphant shriek. "We are saved! Oh, Lizzy! She will be the greatest, the richest...oh, a house in town and all that is charming and good...what pin money...oh, bless me, I shall go distracted."

Lady Lucas grabbed her arm. "Is it Mr Bingley?"

"Even better! 'Tis Mr Darcy! Oh, I know we have always thought him rather proud and disagreeable—and even a bit dishonourable for his actions against dear Mr Wickham. But he says here that he met Elizabeth in Kent, and they have furthered their acquaintance, and thus, he wishes for a private audience with Mr Bennet. He arrives Monday. Monday!"

"So he has offered for Elizabeth? Is that his meaning? It is worded oddly."

"Of course, he has! What else could it mean? He is coming for Mr Bennet's approval, which will certainly be given, and Lizzy will be Mrs Darcy! Oh! Oh!" She was overcome by her effusions, and for a moment, she could only make wordless, joyful utterances while her friend read the letter and came to the same, obviously correct conclusions.

"I wonder whether Mr Bingley will return as well."

"Naturally! And then he will see Jane and all of this business between them can be settled at last, just as it was meant to be from the beginning. Oh my Lord, bless me! Two daughters married, can anything be so happy?"

The two ladies visited a while longer, chatting happily about wedding plans and arrangements. (Though it vexed Mrs Bennet greatly that Lady Lucas should assume she needed her advice on wedding arrangements. Surely, the wedding of Lizzy to so great a personage as Mr Darcy could bear no resemblance to that of Charlotte and Mr Collins.) At last, Lady Lucas was obliged to go on her way, eager to tell Sir William what she had heard at Longbourn.

Sunday, 12 April 1812, Hertfordshire

Mr and Mrs Bennet, followed by Mary, Kitty, and Lydia, strolled towards the church on Sunday morning, enjoying the warmth of a lovely spring day. As they did, they met Lady Lucas, Sir William Lucas, and their sons. Sir William beamed at them. "Bennet, I understand a certain desirable event is in the making."

Mr Bennet scowled. He was unhappy to learn his wife had read his express, and he would have liked the chance to speak to Mr Darcy before the neighbours had decided on the outcome of their conversation. Though he agreed with his wife that Mr Darcy likely wished to marry Elizabeth, he would be surprised if his favoured daughter wished to marry Mr Darcy.

"Well, she simply must," snapped her mother when Mr Bennet dared to offer that opinion. "We followed the perversity of your whims with Mr Collins, and I am afraid I must hold sway with Mr Darcy whether Miss Lizzy likes it or not. You know I am right."

Mr Bennet sighed. If Sir William knew, chances were that all of Hertfordshire knew, or they certainly would by the time church had ended.

And so it was. Mrs Long was speaking of the felicitous news as they ascended the stairs to the church, and Mrs Goulding immediately went to Mrs Bennet to offer her congratulations on the match. Whispers and murmurs abounded, and Mr Bennet doubted even one person counted the words of the sermon as the most important message delivered in church that day.

Monday, 13 April 1812, London

"MISS DARCY?" MRS HOBBS ENTERED THE MUSIC ROOM, BEARING A calling card. "Miss Bingley has come to see you."

As Georgiana was not yet out, she did not expect to receive callers. However, as Miss Bingley was a relation of her brother's good friend, Georgiana thought it might be rude to refuse her and took the card from the housekeeper's hand. "Did she say why she was calling?"

"Forgive me, but I must say that she seems more than a little upset."

"Upset? Why would she be upset?"

"I cannot say. Shall I summon Mrs Annesley to join you?"

"Please do." Georgiana rose from her seat at the pianoforte.

Although she would never admit it, Georgiana always dreaded time spent with Miss Bingley. It was no secret the lady had been in mad pursuit of Darcy since her coming out nearly four years ago. Nor was it a secret that she believed the way to secure Darcy was through his young sister. Miss Bingley fawned and fussed over her in a way that was completely mortifying and discomfiting.

To say Miss Bingley was upset seemed quite an understatement. Georgiana found her looking almost wild with fury, her face pale save for several unattractive red blotches on her cheeks and chest. "Dear Miss Darcy," Miss Bingley said through gritted teeth. "These…these lies cannot be permitted to stand. I know your brother too well to imagine he would so imperil you and your family's reputation by affiliating himself with such a…such a…oh, such a bunch of nothings!"

Despite her confusion, Georgiana refused to allow Miss Bingley to see any sign of uncertainty. She raised her chin and tried to appear confident. "I beg your pardon, Miss Bingley, but what do you mean?"

"Do not be sly," Miss Bingley hissed, glaring at Georgiana with narrow eyes. "The news of your brother's engagement is all over town! You cannot be ignorant of it."

My brother's engagement? Georgiana was stunned into silence. He surely would not have proposed to a woman with her none the wiser! But evidently he had. Was it someone here in town? Surely, she would have known of that. Had he proposed to Cousin Anne in Kent? Oh, she dearly hoped not. Nevertheless, she had her dignity, and she would not allow Caroline Bingley to see her as a stupid young girl who was not enough in her brother's confidence to know of his engagement.

"I am afraid I am not at liberty to speak of my brother's affairs."

"What is the truth, Miss Darcy? Surely, he is not promised to that horrid Eliza Bennet!"

Miss Elizabeth Bennet from Hertfordshire! Georgiana quickly dropped her eyes, not wanting her visitor to see the surprised delight revealed in them. The lady who had so unexpectedly appeared in Kent while her brother visited—had Fitzwilliam proposed to her? *Oh, how wonderful! How happy we shall all be!*

She surreptitiously bit the inside of her cheek to prevent herself from shrieking madly with joy.

With as much cool hauteur as she could summon, Georgiana said, "They recently spent several weeks together in Kent, and I can say nothing more of the matter than that."

Miss Bingley let out an indelicate growl. She looked to the side and muttered to herself, no part of which made any sense to Georgiana. "Mud…headstrong…excellent walker…thousand pounds…trade…the mother!"

Georgiana decided it was due time to end the visit, particularly as Miss Bingley appeared to have lost her composure. She rose. "If you will excuse me, Miss Bingley, I am obligated to my studies. Do give my regards to your family."

Miss Bingley surged to her feet, gesturing to Georgiana with a furiously pointing hand. "You have my pity, Miss Darcy. The gossips will be merciless."

"My brother's happiness means more to me than that," Georgiana replied. Daringly, she added, "He is very much in love, you know." She hoped it were true. For her cautious brother to have acted so boldly, it certainly must be.

Her composure lasted until the door closed behind her outraged guest. Georgiana turned, seeing her companion at the other end of the long hall. "Miss Bingley did not seem best pleased," Mrs Annesley remarked.

Unable to contain herself any longer, Georgiana closed her eyes and permitted herself a little shriek. "I shall have a sister! My brother is getting married!" She jumped up and down like a gleeful schoolgirl. Mrs Annesley quickly quelled her enthusiasm, but it was too late, as Mrs Hobbs, one footman, and several of the upstairs maids heard her. All were filled with delight and eager to meet their new mistress.

MISS GEORGIANA DARCY, HAVING BEEN ORPHANED SEVERAL YEARS past, was under the guardianship of both her elder brother and her cousin Colonel Richard Fitzwilliam. Neither man liked to leave Georgiana alone for too long, and as they had both been so recently in Kent, Fitzwilliam thought Monday evening an ideal time to visit.

He had scarcely been given a drink before Georgiana swooped in on him, her eyes glowing and her cheeks pink as she demanded, "Tell me all about my new sister!"

Surprise made Fitzwilliam draw back a bit, though he remained calm. "New sister? I have not the pleasure of under-standing— Hey! What the devil!"

Astonishingly, Georgiana had pinched his arm rather painfully. "I know all about it, and I am sure you do too! Pray, do not tease me! I must know everything."

Fitzwilliam rubbed his arm, considering her for a moment. "What have you heard?"

"That my brother has proposed to Miss Elizabeth Bennet and spent his time at Rosings wooing her."

"Who told you that?" Fitzwilliam's mind was racing, trying to apprehend the implications of Georgiana having already heard Darcy's news.

"Does it matter? According to one of my friends, the news is all around town! Oh, I am so happy! When may I meet her? Is she in town or still in Kent? Is she very kind? I do hope she is not already returned to Hertfordshire! My brother said she was kind-hearted and witty. Will she like me, do you think?"

"The news is all around town?" Fitzwilliam echoed faintly. How could this have happened? He and Darcy had not been returned a week, and the news was already all around town? Such that even Georgiana, a girl not yet out, had heard of it?

Georgiana nodded impatiently. "I ordered the maids to air the mistress's bedchamber and to clean it out. I know she will likely change it all, but when she first comes to see the house, I would not like her to meet some dusty old museum of a bedchamber! I believe I shall change the coverlet. That one is rather worn, and there was a newer one in one of the guest chambers with the sweetest little flowers on it. Perhaps I could make a little pillow—"

"Georgiana!" Fitzwilliam exclaimed. "Slow down! Things are not yet entirely settled. I know the news has excited your anticipation, but we must not be hasty."

Georgiana subdued immediately. "Forgive me."

"You must wait for your brother to tell you himself. Miss Bennet is not yet even in town."

Georgiana was immediately abashed. Her cheeks flushed a deep red, and she lowered her head but not before tears sprung into her eyes. "I have behaved foolishly, I fear. I do ask your forgiveness."

"Now, now." Reaching towards her, he hitched one finger under her chin and gave her a little tweak. "It is not as bad as all of that. No harm done."

Georgiana nodded and rose, keeping her eyes lowered. In her customary faint mumble, she said, "Excuse me, I must summon Mrs Hobbs."

She rang for the housekeeper and returned to sit with her cousin, shame marking every line of her being. Fitzwilliam regarded her with dismay, wondering at how quickly her elation had plunged into despair and feeling like the veriest wretch for having upset her so.

Mrs Hobbs entered within minutes, responding to Georgiana's summons. "Yes, Miss Darcy?"

"Forgive me, Mrs Hobbs. My cousin has told me I must not interfere with my brother's plans for his new bride. The orders I gave to clean the bedchamber and so forth—I fear it was not my place."

Mrs Hobbs looked blankly between Georgiana and Fitzwilliam. "I do not understand. You wish the rooms to remain closed? We would not delay on your orders and have begun already to clean."

Fitzwilliam rubbed his temples. Darcy would not be pleased by all that had transpired without his leave, but surely he would want Georgiana to be elated rather than downtrodden and humiliated? "Cleaning never hurts, does it?" he said before he could think better of it.

The smile that returned to Georgiana's face showed him that his instinct had been correct. "No! No, cleaning could not hurt at all! Pray, carry on, Mrs Hobbs." The housekeeper departed, a relieved smile on her face.

Fitzwilliam turned to his young cousin. "Your brother would not like to know, I think, that all of his household has been told news that was rightly his to tell. When he returns, allow him to make his announcement as though you had no suspicion of it. Will you promise me that?"

"Of course," she agreed happily.

"Just feign ignorance," Fitzwilliam advised. "He will never suspect otherwise."

Monday, 13 April 1812, Hertfordshire

Darcy's horse had slowed to a trot by the time he entered the drive to Longbourn, but he did nothing to urge the animal to a faster pace. Anxiety, held at bay for the ride from London, roared at him in full force. What form of indignity awaited? He had seen Mr Bennet at his finest and did not relish the notion of performing as the object of his satire.

The door opened almost immediately following his knock, and he was shown into the parlour directly. Within sat Mrs Bennet and her three youngest daughters with Lady Lucas, Mrs Philips, and Mrs Long. The ladies greeted him with varying degrees of propriety but an almost uniform measure of excessive and open curiosity. Astonishingly, it was Mrs Bennet who spoke the least, appearing dumbstruck by Darcy's presence.

Mr Bennet appeared promptly and took him off to his book room. "Mr Darcy, I trust your journey was easy?"

"Very much so." Hearing a certain stiffness in his tone, Darcy tried to sound friendlier. "I do hope you and your family have been well."

"We are all in excellent health," Mr Bennet said as the two men took their seats. "Sir, as I am almost painfully curious as to the purpose of this call, let us both agree the weather has been fine, the health of our families and acquaintances is good, and our recent travels have been easy and move on to the subject of interest."

Darcy swallowed heavily, the moment of truth before him. "Of course." He took a deep breath. "I am recently returned from Kent where I have had the pleasure of Miss Elizabeth's company on several occasions."

Mr Bennet nodded.

"While I was here in the autumn, I developed a regard for Miss Elizabeth, and on meeting her again in Kent, my regard was no less. Indeed, as the weeks passed and we furthered our acquaintance, it grew substantially. I came to understand that I...I love your daughter, and I wish to make her my wife."

With a barely perceptible raise of one brow, Mr Bennet asked, "You proposed to Lizzy in Kent?"

"Not yet. I daresay, she expects my addresses."

"She does? Why?"

"My attentions, while appropriate, could not have been misunderstood. We walked together nearly daily, I called as often as was proper, and we sat together at my aunt's house."

"Ah…" Mr Bennet looked pensive. Clearing his throat, he leaned forward. "Mr Darcy, you will forgive my confusion. Lizzy, alas, has failed to mention any of this in her letters home. Your letter was the first I had heard of any attachment between you."

"I see."

"I do not fool myself into thinking my grown daughter would regard me as her confidante, particularly in affairs of the heart." Mr Bennet gave an indulgent chuckle.

Darcy forced a slight smile.

"However, all of that aside, I would be remiss if I did not make clear my reservations regarding this match." Mr Bennet smiled kindly when he saw the look on Darcy's face. "No, no, I do not intend to withhold my consent. I only wish to discuss my concerns for this marriage as a father who loves his daughter."

Darcy nodded and cleared his throat. "Such as?"

"Your acquaintance began on unusual footing. I refer to the remark you made at the assembly—not handsome enough to tempt you, something of that nature?"

Darcy felt himself flush red. "I assure you it has been many months that I have considered her the handsomest woman of my acquaintance."

Mr Bennet waved his hand. "Who would wish to marry someone he found disagreeable? But has Lizzy forgiven the slight? A woman's memory is long in such situations, Mr Darcy."

"I shall address this with her immediately."

"Excellent. However, my largest concern remains, and I am afraid it will not be remedied so readily."

Darcy shifted in his seat. "Which is?"

Mr Bennet's face lost its previous geniality. "I am enough of a man of the world to understand that, although I am a gentleman, Lizzy has never been near to the form of society such as she would inhabit as your wife. Her reception among that sphere concerns me."

"My uncle, the Earl of Matlock, has assured me of his and my aunt's support and assistance. Some may not welcome her, but I do believe there are enough sensible people in London to appreciate her wit and her charm. She will have no cause to repine."

Mr Bennet nodded. "Good. To be perfectly frank, Lizzy could never find happiness in wealth or in status. She must have true affection and regard for her felicity."

Darcy felt a brief smile alight upon his usually sombre mien. "She will have true affection and regard in abundance, sir. I shall see to that myself."

The two men spoke for a while longer regarding the more practical aspects of marriage, such as the settlement articles. "When do you wish to marry, Mr Darcy?"

Darcy now permitted himself a full smile. "As soon as is possible, sir."

Mr Bennet chuckled. "I have rarely seen a man, once his mind is set towards matrimony, who wishes to delay. Only in the least auspicious circumstances, I suppose, would a young fellow like his nuptials deferred."

He rose, beckoning Darcy to follow him. "As you might have noticed from your reception in the drawing room, Mrs Bennet has already surmised the purpose of your call today, and I imagine she will have much to say on the subjects of lace and wedding finery. Let us go to her now, but I warn you"—he paused to look at Darcy, his eyes twinkling—"this might become loud."

Wednesday, 15 April 1812, Kent

"Hunsford is such a beautiful place," said Elizabeth as she sat with her friend in her sunny parlour. "I am sorry to be leaving on Saturday."

"No more than I am sorry to see you leave." Charlotte smiled kindly, sipping her tea. "I cannot express how much I have enjoyed these weeks."

"Let us not jump ahead to the melancholy of separation. I have always despised the natural tendency to lament the end of a thing, which takes away a part of the very thing we cherish! Let us think nothing of our parting at least until the morning it happens."

"An excellent thought, though I do think the maids who pack your gowns must do differently," Charlotte replied practically. "I must say, I was surprised that Mr Darcy and his cousin departed with such haste."

"I suppose there was nothing that made them wish to linger."

"And that was the very source of my surprise, for it seemed to me that Mr Darcy liked to linger about you a great deal. Yes, his eyes lingered on you quite often."

Elizabeth rolled her eyes. "This again! I assure you, he looks at me only to find fault."

"And I suppose you must think he came upon you by pure coincidence these many days as you were on your walks? The groves and parks of Rosings are vast, my dear. Two people could wander within them all day, every day and never even catch sight of one another."

"All the perverseness of mischance, then." Elizabeth pursed her lips and shook her head teasingly at her friend. "In any case, he is gone, and I shall return to Longbourn. I doubt I shall ever cross his path again."

The ladies spoke of different plans and schemes for the day. Mr Collins had risen early and gone off to Rosings, obeying an urgent summons from Lady Catherine. Charlotte knew nothing of the matter but was unconcerned. There were many urgent summonses that arose in the course of a week, and she suspected her ladyship simply enjoyed having her parson rush to attend her.

In the midst of their planning, Charlotte paused, her attention suddenly directed at the scene outside her window. "Is that her ladyship now? Look there, coming up the walk with Mr Collins."

It was unmistakably Lady Catherine, Mr Collins fluttering anxiously beside her. "She looks seriously displeased," Elizabeth observed.

"It is likely because she must enter so humble a dwelling as this," Charlotte remarked wryly, surveying her small but neatly appointed parlour. The two ladies rose from their seats as they heard the door open. Mr Collins sounded flustered and upset, and Lady Catherine spoke angrily, but they could not comprehend the words.

Elizabeth turned to her friend, "Perhaps I should leave? Whatever distresses her is best left between those concerned."

"You are likely right," Charlotte agreed.

Elizabeth had not yet reached the door when it was forcefully thrust open. Lady Catherine was framed therein, large and magnificently purple with rage. She thrust one bejewelled hand at Elizabeth, nearly touching her nose as she hissed, "Jezebel!"

Mr Collins hovered behind her like a worried little grouse, muttering things about graciousness and condescension and the unworthiness of the Bennets.

As soon as she recovered from her shock, Elizabeth schooled herself to be pleasant, knowing that to express what she truly wished to say could only lead to ill will towards Charlotte. "I beg your pardon?"

"A report of a most alarming nature reached me this morning. A letter from my brother, the Earl of Matlock, proclaimed that you are soon to be united in matrimony to my own nephew. I summoned Mr Collins at once, imagining such a scandalous report must be immediately contradicted! But no! He too has heard this report, and by a different means than I. I insist on knowing the truth. Are you engaged to my nephew?"

Elizabeth felt a little flutter in her stomach. Colonel Fitzwilliam told his father he was engaged to her? It did not seemed likely, but perhaps his intentions had moved her way? "I am not engaged to your nephew."

The hand with that dreadful pointing finger gradually lowered. "I knew you had far too much sense to reach so far beyond your own station."

Perversely, this rankled. After all, she did not consider Colonel Fitzwilliam so far beyond her reach and, evidently, neither did he or his exalted father. "Your nephew has not yet paid me his addresses. But he is a fine man, and I hold him in the highest esteem. Such sentiments from him must certainly be gratified."

Lady Catherine's eyes narrowed. "I pray you do not speak your true mind, Miss Bennet. Such a match would never be tolerated within either the family or society. You would not be recognised by any who knew him, and you would cause him to be censured and despised."

"I do not agree," Elizabeth retorted. "I am a gentleman's daughter, am I not?"

"Who are you to aspire to such a match? Who is your mother? Do not think me ignorant of your family situation."

"If it is nothing to him, it can be nothing to you."

Throughout this discourse, Mr Collins kept a running monologue, assuring Lady Catherine that she was entirely correct and Elizabeth was entirely wrong. Lady Catherine looked at him and barked, "Mr Collins! Silence, I beseech you."

The room was at once eerily quiet.

She turned her gaze back to Elizabeth. "Perhaps you are unaware, Miss Bennet, of his prior attachment. He is already engaged to my daughter, a union planned by his mother and I while they were in their cradles. Now, what say you to that?"

This statement served the purpose of bringing Elizabeth up short. "Engaged to Miss de Bourgh? But I had heard of an existing attachment between Mr Darcy and your daughter."

Lady Catherine looked as though Elizabeth had lost her wits. "Yes! This match to which you have the presumption to aspire will never occur. I shall not permit the pretensions of an upstart such as yourself to destroy the fondest wishes of myself and my sister for her son."

It was then that Elizabeth finally understood, and the understanding nearly caused her to laugh aloud. Lady Catherine had somehow arrived at the notion she was engaged to Mr Darcy!

Lady Catherine was not happy to see an amused light appear in Elizabeth's eyes and pushed for her assurances. "Miss Bennet, I shall not depart this place until you have given me your word that such an engagement does not and will not ever exist."

Gladly! I shall never marry that odious man! Elizabeth was tempted to respond as such; however, she was still offended by Lady Catherine's insulting speech, and it raised within her a spirit of mischief. She would never dream of marrying Mr Darcy, but that did not mean she had to admit as much to Lady Catherine.

"If Mr Darcy is neither by honour nor inclination confined to his cousin, why is he not permitted to make another choice? And if I am that choice, why may I not accept him?"

Lady Catherine sputtered in indignation. "Because honour, decorum, and prudence forbid it."

Dangerously close to a wicked giggle, Elizabeth said, "I am sorry you feel this way. However, I shall act according to my own heart and my own conscience, not by any other dictate."

"Obstinate, headstrong girl! I had hoped to find a more reasonable young lady." With that, Lady Catherine turned on her heel, departing the parsonage with Mr Collins fluttering behind her anxiously.

Elizabeth felt triumphant for just a moment until she turned and saw Charlotte's worried frown. "Charlotte? Oh no, I have created difficulty for you."

"'Tis of no consequence, I am sure." From Charlotte's pinched smile and worried brow, it was easy to see that she did not believe her own words.

"I shall apologise to her immediately." Elizabeth was embarrassed, understanding that her pride had gotten in the way of her friend's happiness.

"No, no," Charlotte said immediately. "It would likely upset her more. Let us avoid her until Saturday, and all will be well, I am certain of it. But why does she believe you are to be married to Mr Darcy? And to have heard it from her own brother?"

"I cannot imagine." Elizabeth had been so absorbed in the insults being served that she had not considered the implication of Lady Catherine's charges. "She said Mr Collins had heard of it through an independent report as well. What did he hear?"

Charlotte shrugged. "I have not the least idea."

By uneasy dismissal, the ladies agreed to wait until Mr Collins returned to ask him of the specific nature of the reports Lady Catherine had mentioned. However, when Mr Collins returned, his countenance clearly showed the distresses of his past hours. He would brook no opposition and no further discussion to the decisions and plans he had made. Cousin Eliza must leave post-haste, not on Saturday but this very day. Travel by post had been arranged, and she would be in London that evening. An express had already been sent to the Gardiner residence

In shock and dismay, Elizabeth assisted Charlotte's maid in packing her things. Mortification that she had caused such trouble for the Collinses rendered her silent and humble, though she still could not abide Lady Catherine's rudeness or such blatant abuse of one's inferiors. Nevertheless, she would depart quietly and leave it to Mr and Mrs Collins to make amends with their benefactor.

3

Wednesday, 15 April 1812, London

THE GARDINERS RECEIVED THE EXPRESS FROM MR COLLINS AT
approximately the same time as they received the subject of it.
All were gathered in the drawing room when Elizabeth
appeared, and if they were surprised by her arrival, they were
kind enough to put it aside to see to her comfort.

Elizabeth was embarrassed that her impulse to provoke Lady
Catherine resulted in an immediate expulsion from Hunsford. In
some sense, she felt she had been sent home in disgrace, though
she believed it unlikely anyone else would see it so. Upon
entering the Gardiner home, she was eager to explain the absur-
dity of what had happened that morning, hoping the Gardiners
and her dear sister would understand the vices and follies of all
involved—and over the most patently untrue and ridiculous
rumour ever told.

Hugs and exclamations of greeting went all around while
Elizabeth apologised for her precipitous appearance. "Has Mr
Collins afforded you an explanation of the matter?"

Mr Gardiner said, "He did, and I must say—"

"Engaged to Mr Darcy! What a notion! Nevertheless, I

should not have provoked Lady Catherine as I did. I would have done much better to tell her I was not engaged to Mr Darcy!" Elizabeth smiled her thanks at a servant who handed her a glass of wine. "This is all my fault."

There was clear discomfort on Mr Gardiner's face as he hesitantly enquired, "So, you are...not...engaged to Mr Darcy?"

"Of course not!" Elizabeth laughed. "Had I been accused of flying, it could hardly be less likely."

Her aunt and uncle regarded her with a mixture of both puzzlement and uneasiness on their faces. Jane, at their side, twisted her hands anxiously.

Clearing his throat, Mr Gardiner handed her a letter. "Read this letter from your father. We have reason to suspect its contents."

Elizabeth took it from him and, after one last look at Jane, unfolded and read it.

My dear Lizzy,

I was most curious several days ago to receive a request to call from none other than Mr Darcy, but my surprise was quickly made into utter astonishment when he informed me that he had come to request my permission to marry you.

You did not tell me Mr Darcy was in Kent during your visit, and I wish now you had. I might then have been better prepared to address his assertions that you had furthered your acquaintance and have grown attached to one another. His sentiments were a far cry from his insult of you last autumn, and I could only accept his word that his esteem of you had grown. I must assume yours did likewise.

In any case, I have given him my consent and my blessing. Indeed, he is the sort of man I would not like to refuse anything once he had condescended to ask for it. I applaud Mr Darcy for recognising in you the treasure he seeks.

With my best wishes and eagerness to see you returned home, T. Bennet

ELIZABETH READ THE LETTER THREE TIMES THROUGH BEFORE RAISING her eyes from the paper. She looked at Jane and said faintly, "This is a joke, I am sure. Papa is playing one of his silly tricks on me and will likely be awaiting my response with glee."

"If it is a joke," Mr Gardiner said, "then it is at my expense as well. Here is my letter."

Edward,
It seems I am to lose a daughter, and my favourite no less. I was most surprised today to receive a request for Lizzy's hand from Mr Fitzwilliam Darcy, a very distinguished and wealthy gentleman from Derbyshire. Margaret might know of his family from her days in that county.

He is a good man, and he will treat her well. They did not begin their acquaintance on the best footing, but apparently they have resolved their differences. You may expect his call when Lizzy returns to London on Saturday. I am eager to hear your report of how he enjoys Gracechurch Street as, I daresay, it is a new experience for him to find himself so far from Mayfair.

I am sure you can imagine your sister's response to the news. There are one or two families in Hertfordshire who do not yet

know of Lizzy's impending greatness, but I am sure by the time this note reaches you, Fanny will have rectified that situation.
T. Bennet

"I DO NOT UNDERSTAND," ELIZABETH WHISPERED. SHE TOUCHED A hand to her forehead. "I cannot imagine what induced Mr Darcy to go to Hertfordshire and speak to my father. Perhaps my father misunderstood or..." She was unable to summon any other likely explanation.

"Well, you must have courted in Kent," Jane said, with all of the optimism inherent to her character. "Perhaps you did not realise his intentions, but—"

"Are you saying I was courted without my knowledge? That will not do, not even for you." Elizabeth laughed weakly, but it turned into an angry sound even as she did it. "This is ridiculous! We despise each other! There was no regard, no courting, not the slightest measure of esteem, and he decides to go to Hertfordshire and speak of marriage to my father? And my mother knows?"

Mrs Gardiner began to make some sort of soothing remark, but Elizabeth scarcely heard her.

"And clearly his family knows something of it as well!" Elizabeth's provocation gained momentum with each word spoken, her cheeks feeling heated and flushed. "Lady Catherine received a letter from her brother, the Earl of Matlock, after which she came to the parsonage to berate me! How well I understand her distress now, though it must pale in comparison to my own."

"Lizzy, calm yourself." Her aunt, ever the voice of reason, rose to place her hand on Elizabeth's arm. "I am certain there is a reasonable explanation."

"But what?" Elizabeth protested. "How can this possibly be explained? And what does it mean? Shall I be forced to marry Mr Darcy?"

"No, no," Mr Gardiner said. "I am certain it will not go so far as that."

"If only I could tell you how odious a creature he is! Proud, arrogant, and disdaining of all who are beneath him, which in his estimation is nearly everyone!" Elizabeth began to pace and wring her hands. "I could never marry such a man!"

"We must speak to him directly," Mr Gardiner said. "I shall send a man to find his direction and meet with him."

"Should we not wait for his call?" Mrs Gardiner asked.

Elizabeth objected immediately. "I cannot allow this to remain unanswered until he calls on Saturday. No, my uncle is right."

"But, Lizzy," said Jane, "what of your reputation? Papa's letter says Mama has been very industrious in setting the news abroad. You would not wish to be known as a jilt, I think."

"I would rather be a jilt and a spinster than married to such a man!" Elizabeth cried.

"Lizzy," her aunt interjected, her tone worried, "the Darcy family has always been known for an attentiveness to duty, honour, and fairness, and I simply cannot imagine the son would be so far away from these principles."

"I have told you what he has done to poor Mr Wickham. Does that seem like a man of honour?" Elizabeth demanded.

"We do not know his part in that story," Mrs Gardiner admonished.

"Yes, but nevertheless, it cannot be denied that he—"

"Lizzy," Mr Gardiner said calmly. "His dealings with Mr Wickham aside, we must concern ourselves with our own interests for now. We shall call on him tomorrow."

Thursday, 16 April 1812, London

DARCY ENJOYED A BUSY AND PRODUCTIVE MORNING, BEGINNING with a visit to his solicitor followed by the jewellers, where he purchased a beautiful pearl necklace for Elizabeth in honour of their engagement.

He next went to his tailor. He did not truly need new clothing and did not intend to settle on anything; nevertheless, an hour and a half later, he exited the tailor's shop having commissioned a new coat in the latest style, using a very fine fabric the man assured him would be just the thing for his wedding suit.

Darcy entered his club and saw his uncle already at a table with several gentlemen of his acquaintance. His uncle was in the midst of relating some tale of boyhood mischief and had the men doubled over with laughter.

"…so then Bennet sees our headmaster is soon to be upon us and calls out for me to climb over the wall, but I misunderstood and instead went into the hall!" The table erupted with boisterous laughter.

"Lord Matlock." Darcy greeted his uncle with an uneasy look at the men present.

"There's my boy," the earl said fondly as his friends began to congratulate Darcy on his forthcoming nuptials. Darcy said nothing, acknowledging each of them with a mere smile and a tip of his head as they rose one by one, excusing themselves to other conversations and discussions.

"What are you doing?" Darcy hissed at his uncle as soon as they were alone.

Lord Matlock picked up a newspaper and replied blandly, "Reading the news."

"Not that! Why are you speaking of my engagement? Need I remind you it is not yet settled?"

"I told you I would put about some mention of my friendship with Mr Bennet." He lowered the paper, looking rather put upon. "If you wish for my help, Darcy, you should allow me to do as I must."

Through clenched teeth, Darcy reminded him, "I have not yet offered for her, and here I am at my club receiving a table full of congratulations."

Lord Matlock shrugged. "These old badgers will forget they even heard it by the time the next drink is poured. All is as it should be. When they hear of your engagement through the proper channels, they will not truly recall what was said, only that they know of the name Bennet."

"If she says yes!"

"As if any lady would refuse you." Lord Matlock chuckled as he folded his paper. "You worry too much. Trust me; I have been among society for many years now. I know just how these things must be done." He rose. "Your aunt wishes the future Mrs Darcy to call upon her. When shall I tell her to expect the call?"

Darcy stared at his uncle in disbelief. "Perhaps I shall propose first and then speak to her about calling on my relations —what say you to that?"

Lord Matlock scowled. "Monday, then." He rose and departed, passing Bingley on his way in.

Bingley had an unusual, worried look on his face. Spotting Darcy immediately, he went to him and asked to sit. Darcy agreed with a tired wave of his hand at the seat beside him.

"Darcy you cannot imagine the tales I have heard of late!

There is a report in circulation that you are engaged to be married."

"What? But who—?"

"Oh, Caroline told me all about it. Rather, Caroline ranted all about it to the Hursts and her maid, and I overheard her and demanded to know the details."

Darcy felt dazed, wondering how on earth Bingley could know so much of what was not yet a story and reeling from the implications of Caroline Bingley knowing...knowing what? What did she know?

"And what...what did your sister tell you? Where did she hear such a thing?"

"I do not know where she heard it initially, but she confirmed it with Miss Darcy, so—"

"My sister! Miss Bingley spoke of this with my sister?"

"So it is true?"

"Ah...well..." Darcy realised he must get to his sister and find out what she knew and more importantly, what the rest of the *ton* knew. "Bingley, excuse me, I believe I must speak to Georgiana."

Thursday, 16 April 1812, London

As the Gardiners' carriage pulled to the front of an exceedingly grand and imposing house in the exclusive Mayfair district, Mr Gardiner leaned towards Elizabeth.

"Let me to do the talking. I know you are upset, but it is important to learn all the facts of the matter. It would not do for you to lose your temper here."

"I know. I would enjoy nothing more than to reprimand him severely, if indeed it was he who spread these falsehoods. But no. I know Mr Darcy dislikes me as much as I do him. Someone else has spread lies about us, for what purpose I cannot begin to guess. It will anger him even more than it does me. My dearest hope is that we can come to some reasonable resolution to the problem that will importune us both to the least extent possible."

They sat quietly while the coachman went to the door and presented their cards. Both were surprised when the coachman returned and informed them, "Mr Darcy is away from home, but Miss Darcy wishes to receive you."

"Oh!" Mr Gardiner and Elizabeth looked at each other uncertainly. Finally, Elizabeth responded, "We can hardly refuse, can we?"

"Are you acquainted with Miss Darcy?"

"No." Elizabeth shook her head. "She is not yet out, and I am surprised she would receive her brother's callers, but I fear we must oblige her. Perhaps she can tell us when Mr Darcy is expected."

They stepped out of the carriage and entered the stately home, following the butler to a beautifully appointed drawing room wherein sat a young girl and a middle-aged woman. The ladies rose when their guests entered.

Miss Darcy was tall and resembled her brother, though less handsome than he. Her figure was well formed for a girl of her age, and like her brother, pride was evident in her countenance. She looked at Elizabeth with an intent gaze that also brought her brother to mind.

There was a grave silence for a moment while the occupants of the room regarded one another. Then without further thought, word, or deed, Miss Darcy broke into a wide, beaming smile, all evidence of pride disappearing in a trice. She crossed the floor in two quick paces, pulling Elizabeth into an enthusiastic embrace, kissing her cheek, and gasping out eagerly, "A sister! I have always wanted a sister! We shall be the best of friends—I know it! I can scarcely wait!"

They had not been long in the Darcy home before Elizabeth reached two firm conclusions. The first was that Miss Georgiana Darcy had heard from an outside source—not her brother—that Elizabeth would marry Mr Darcy and then had confirmed this "fact" with her cousin Colonel Fitzwilliam. Elizabeth chose not to correct her.

The second conclusion was that Mr Wickham could not have been more incorrect in calling Miss Darcy proud, for by Elizabeth's estimation, she was as delightful a creature as could be imagined. She had no scruple in leaping to call her Elizabeth and insisted immediately that Elizabeth call her Georgiana, and she received Mr Gardiner with eager welcome, evidently unknowing or uncaring of his status as a man of trade.

They did not remain long with Georgiana. Elizabeth suspected Mr Darcy would not have agreed with his sister's decision to receive his callers. Moreover, she felt that the longer they remained, the more likely she was to reveal something of her true feelings for Mr Darcy.

"Pray, do not go! I know Brother must be very eager to see you! Would you like me to show you the house? Oh, but no, that would surely be a pleasure reserved for him. Forgive me. Perhaps just your bedchamber? No, no, I must not presume such a privilege. Would you like to see my bedchamber? I am just so elated!"

Georgiana saw them out, keeping up a steady stream of dear effusions from her thoughts on when the wedding should be held (as soon as possible) to information about Pemberley (the finest place in all the world, though she was sure Hertfordshire was charming as well) and questions about Elizabeth's likes and dislikes (all of which she agreed with emphatically). Elizabeth had to laugh as she and Mr Gardiner gently removed themselves.

"Georgiana, you have indeed been a surprise and a pleasure." She gave the girl a quick embrace.

"A surprise? Oh, you likely imagined I would be quiet like my brother. To speak so much is not my custom, but I am just so happy! I feel so easy with you, as though it was fated to be for us to be sisters!"

Elizabeth laughed again, and after giving Georgiana another quick embrace, she and her uncle departed.

WHEN MISS ELIZABETH AND MR GARDINER HAD GONE, GEORGIANA took her exceedingly high-spirited self into the music room, determined to work on a piece of music to honour her new sister at the wedding breakfast. However, once she got there, she realised her spirits were as yet too high to focus as she needed to, and instead, she began to play a light-hearted little song she knew well. During this song, her brother arrived home, looking somewhat wild. After a perfunctory greeting, he bade her to sit with him.

Georgiana was relieved. She did not wish to confess that she already knew about his engagement, yet their butler would likely have informed him of their recent visitors. She gave him a beaming smile as she moved to sit with him.

"Georgiana, I learnt today that you recently became aware of…of my attachment to a Miss—"

"Miss Elizabeth Bennet!" Georgiana could no longer stand the suspense. "Oh, Brother, I am so sorry! Richard believed it best that I wait for you to tell me, but then she came to the house today, and I just love her! She is just as I imagined from your description, and I am very, very eager to—"

"Here?" Darcy cried out. "What do you mean she was here?"

"She called on me! Well, not specifically on me, she called for you—but I was here! I received her! She and her uncle, I do not know—"

"Her uncle!"

"A very pleasant man and so understanding of the fact that I rattled away like a madwoman! I am sure he left his card, did he not?"

"I do not know." Darcy leaned forward, putting his head into his hands. "Did she…was Elizabeth upset in any way? Did she seem angry or…unsettled?"

"Angry? No, not at all." Georgiana shook her head. It dawned on her that something was wrong. Her brother seemed distressed about something more than missing Miss Bennet's call. "She was very amiable."

Darcy made an odd little strangled sound.

Uncomfortable, Georgiana added, "They were surprised that I received them. Mr Gardiner asked for you, but when I heard who it was, I insisted they see me."

Her brother raised his head, forcing an odd strained smile through the anxious lines of his countenance. "I am sure they were delighted with you. However, I must know who told you of this news."

Georgiana felt a rising sense of worry about her brother's questions and could only hope she had not erred in some way. "Miss Bingley. She was dismayed by the news and came to ask whether it were true."

"And you said?"

Georgiana chewed on the corner of her lip. "I simply could not bear to say I did not know. She treats me as if I need her guidance, and I just could not…I felt like a ninny! I could not admit that I did not know of your engagement."

Darcy winced. "So you told her what?"

"I confirmed you had spent some weeks in Kent with Miss Elizabeth. I did not confirm the rumours she heard, but neither did I deny them."

"I see."

Feeling increasingly as though she had made a significant blunder, Georgiana said, "I am very sorry if I have—"

"No, no. You have done nothing wrong, nothing at all. I only hope that I did not—" He stopped, shaking his head. "Everything is well, perfectly well."

Georgiana added, "I should probably tell you…"

"Yes?"

She swallowed before answering. "I told Mrs Hobbs that it might be a good idea to begin to clean the mistress's bedchamber. It might have been a bit hasty, I grant you, but I did not want the room to look dusty and closed up when Miss Bennet was here."

She paused a few moments and then added, "There is a newer coverlet I asked to be put on the bed as well. I am not fond of the one in there—it is a bit old and grey from too many washings. The newer coverlet has yellow daisies on it. I asked Miss Elizabeth, and she does indeed like daisies—and yellow."

Darcy sighed and closed his eyes. "Did you show her the house while she was here?"

"No, I knew that was best left to you."

"And does anyone else in the house know of…of my, uh… um, my engagement?"

For a moment, Georgiana could not speak. "I was just so happy and…well…rather loud in my exclamations. Several of the upstairs maids heard me and…and likely told the others as soon as they could."

Darcy inhaled deeply, rubbing his hand across his forehead. "Excuse me, I believe I shall go look for that card. I must pay a call to Mr Gardiner."

Thursday, 16 April 1812, London

THEY RETURNED TO GRACECHURCH STREET IN SILENCE. AS THEY neared her uncle's residence, Mr Gardiner leaned forward. "Lizzy, forgive me, but in light of recent events, I must ask. Was there something between you and Mr Darcy that has led him to believe a proposal or an engagement was required of him?"

"Not at all. We disliked each other in Hertfordshire, and our manners were no more than polite amiability in Kent."

"I am sure you realise—or if not, seeing his home today must have informed you—that Mr Darcy is vastly rich and quite highly placed. For such a man to have made you an offer of marriage—"

"Which he did not do."

"Very puzzling, that." Mr Gardiner sat back into the squabs of the carriage. "Yet so many think he did. I cannot account for it."

"Uncle, shall I be obliged to marry him? As my father has given his consent, I worry I am bound."

"Your father will not force you to marry," Mr Gardiner replied assuredly.

"Yes, but what about Mama? She is still angry that I refused Mr Collins." Elizabeth referred to her refusal to marry her cousin and heir to her father's estate the prior autumn. Her mother had been enraged at Elizabeth's "foolish" decision, and only her father's intervention had stopped matters from becoming worse than they were. "What will she do when she learns I refused a man worth ten thousand a year?"

"One step at a time, Lizzy. Mr Darcy will call, or his sister will invite you to call on them. Then we may all discuss what must be done."

Elizabeth inhaled deeply, trying to calm her anxiety. "I am so glad you are here, Uncle. My father would tease me, and Mama would have an attack of her nerves."

"There is a reasonable explanation behind this all, I am sure. Once we know what it is, then we may find some means by which you and he can be extricated from any obligation arising from it. So long as the gossip has not gone too far abroad, all should be well."

"Where could such a tale begin?" Elizabeth asked, not for the first time. "From his cousin? I cannot see why he would initiate such a tale, and it was certainly not from his aunt or Miss de Bourgh. Charlotte is as baffled by it as I am."

They had arrived at the Gardiners' home and continued speaking even as they joined Mrs Gardiner and Jane in the drawing room. After a brief pause to relate to the two ladies all that had transpired in the Darcys' home, they continued their prior conversation from where it had been interrupted.

"Being that Mr Darcy has visited your father, I imagine he was himself the author of these rumours," Mr Gardiner said.

"But why? We despise one another."

"Perhaps he does not despise you," Jane said. "Charlotte wrote me a letter, and she said—"

"Hang Charlotte and her opinions!" Elizabeth fumed. "Charlotte has an entirely different notion of love and romance than I do!"

A servant entered at that moment with a card for Mrs Gardiner. She looked at it for a moment before passing it to her husband. Mr Gardiner read it and nodded to the servant, who departed the room.

"I believe we have exhausted the chance to deliberate on the matter, Lizzy. Mr Darcy has come to call."

DARCY SWALLOWED AGAINST THE BEATING OF HIS HEART, WHICH felt as if it were lodged painfully in his throat. As he followed the manservant to the sitting room, some part of his mind was pleasantly surprised at seeing the elegant manner in which the Gardiners lived. Their house was spacious and well kept, and the servants were clearly accustomed to refined circumstances. The larger part of his mind, however, was attempting to quickly devise a scheme to rectify this odd situation in which he had placed himself.

She cannot be so very angry. It is vexing, of course, that others should have known of her engagement before she herself did, but I do hope that, once I explain, she will laugh over the human folly in it all. Certainly, once I assure her of my feelings, she cannot remain angry. Can she? Surely not. She is, above all, a rational creature.

He decided to first explain why he spoke to others before proposing to her. She would straightaway see the wisdom in what he had done. If others had chosen to take his confidences and bandy them about, he could not be blamed for it, could he?

Darcy pulled himself from his musings, seeing that the door was opening and he was being announced.

A man stepped forward first. "Mr Darcy, I am Edward Gardiner. Welcome to my home."

"Thank you, sir," Darcy immediately spotted Elizabeth standing behind her uncle and a woman Darcy assumed was her aunt. Various pleasantries were exchanged as he was offered a seat, and the housekeeper brought tea. He tried to catch Elizabeth's gaze several times, but she seemed determined to keep her eyes lowered. Just as well. A demure lady was always proper, and perhaps she felt awkward knowing he had condescended greatly to call at Gracechurch Street.

Mr Gardiner was the one to broach the topic of the gossip that had gone about. "Mr Darcy, I suppose you must be aware that my niece and I called at your home earlier today. Your sister received us in your stead."

"Forgive her presumption," Darcy replied. "She was very eager to meet Miss Elizabeth."

"We were honoured," Mr Gardiner assured him. "She is a charming young lady. You must be very proud of her."

Darcy nodded. "I am indeed, sir."

Mr Gardiner pursed his lips a moment before continuing. "We were surprised to learn Miss Darcy believed my niece is engaged to you. We did not correct her misapprehension, but I am eager, sir, to understand what you might know of this matter."

Darcy felt himself flush, which vexed him. When he spoke, he knew he sounded rather stiff, even to his own ears. "I appreciate your discretion."

A painful pause ensued, and Darcy recognised that his time was upon him. "I wonder whether I might speak to Miss Elizabeth in…in private."

Elizabeth's head jerked upwards, her eyes going wide. He

offered her a small smile, but she did not return it. He found such diffidence in her, of all people, enchanting.

Mr Gardiner shot her a quick glance before standing. "Perhaps you would like to speak in my study." Darcy followed Mr Gardiner, not realising until he reached the door that Elizabeth had not moved. Mr Gardiner turned, saying, "Come, Lizzy."

They paused to allow her the lead. When they were in the study, Mr Gardiner offered Darcy another drink, which he declined. Elizabeth went immediately to a chair in the corner.

"Well then." Mr Gardiner chuckled anxiously. "I shall await you in the other room, and perhaps we may all...discuss... everything. Will that do, Lizzy?"

She gave her uncle a nod.

Mr Gardiner leaned in, whispering something to his niece that made her flash him a look of annoyance followed by a resigned nod. He departed, leaving the door slightly ajar behind him.

As Darcy watched, Elizabeth took a deep breath and raised her eyes to meet his. His pulse roared in his ears as he beheld her, and his breath suddenly left him. *She is so beautiful.*

In sedate accents, she said, "Mr Darcy, I am eager to hear your explanation for the fact that quite a few people believe we are engaged."

"Yes...um...forgive me for that. This has all gone rather backwards."

She stared at him.

"I only wished to dispense with some of the obstacles to our union before I offered for you. I had hoped we then might begin our betrothal in true felicity unmarred by the inevitable agitation that would occur in the wake of such an amazing announcement."

"Inevitable agitation?"

"My family, naturally, would not meet the news of my marrying one so far beneath me with approval. Indeed, I struggled mightily with it myself, knowing I was going against every claim of duty that has ever been laid upon me. But once my mind was made up, I could struggle against it no more. I knew my relations would raise the same objections I have long debated in my own mind, and thus, I believed it best to tell them of my plans before they were irrevocably laid. Should my affections for you have proven unable to outlast their censure, further consideration of the scheme would have been best."

She appeared surprised. Surely she must have realised his family had more exalted expectations for his marriage than a girl from the country with a fortune of one thousand pounds and no notable connexions?

"You must understand, my family has always expected me to marry someone of great fortune, someone from an excellent family with which to connect the Darcy name—a lady of the highest circles. For me to degrade my family name and suffer the decrease to my estate by your lack of fortune must concern them mightily. Moreover, there are your ties to trade through your mother's family. All of it is degrading to me, though I must own that the Gardiners are delightful people."

He did not wish to insult her, but honesty was surely required. Married people should not have secrets between them. "And, yes, I would be untruthful if I did not admit that the want of propriety frequently displayed by your mother and your younger sisters is…alarming. Their manners would not permit them entry into many places in better society. It was the reason I was so relieved when you indicated you were desirous of marrying someone who would take you away from Hertfordshire."

"When I did what?" Elizabeth exclaimed.

He smiled, remembering the occasion. "You will recall the day I came upon you alone in the parsonage house? I believe Mrs Collins and Miss Lucas had gone into the village, and you remained, writing a letter to your sister, I believe. We spoke for a little while, and during that conversation, you said you believed it was possible for a woman to be settled too near her family."

That had been a blessed day indeed, for he realised that she knew her family was objectionable and longed for something different. Moreover, he realised how very much he wanted to be the one who took her away, who rescued her from the lowness and vulgarity of her family.

He went to her, kneeling and taking her hands in his. All had been said now, and he was eager to speak of pleasanter concerns, that of making their engagement a reality. He gently kissed her hands. "That is all put aside now. What remains, my dearest, loveliest Elizabeth, is that I ardently admire and love you, and my greatest wish is to be permitted the honour of loving you for the rest of my days."

Darcy glanced up at her face and was surprised to find her mouth agape. He had thought she might cry or at least become teary-eyed, or smile or laugh or something similar. Instead, she seemed rather dumbfounded.

She gently tugged her hands from his grasp. "In such cases as these, it is, I believe, the established mode to express a sense of obligation for the sentiments avowed, however unequally they may be returned. It is natural that obligation should be felt, and if I could feel gratitude, I would now thank you. But I cannot. I have never desired your good opinion, and you have certainly bestowed it most unwillingly. I am sorry to have occasioned pain to anyone. It has been most unconsciously done, however, and I hope will be of short duration. Your feelings, which you tell me have long prevented the acknowledgment of your regard, can have little difficulty in overcoming it after this explanation."

He rose slowly and walked towards Mr Gardiner's fireplace, resting for a moment against the mantel. What did she mean by such a rejoinder? Not to reject his offer, certainly. How on earth could someone in her position refuse an offer from a man such as him? The idea of it was absurd! Had they not gotten on very well in Kent? She seemed receptive to his advances then. He began to feel a sense of stupidity and mortification that he could not like.

A girl with nothing could not reasonably refuse a man who wished to give her everything. Did she not understand all he had to offer? Perhaps she was, in some manner, playing with him? That would be ungenerous, but he knew ladies who would resort to such arts. She did not seem that sort, yet…surely, she could not suggest that she would not marry him…? "Do you mean to say that you refuse me?"

"Yes, sir," she replied calmly.

Mortification flushed his body. "Might I ask why?"

"Why?"

"You must know how much it would raise you and your family were you to marry someone of my position, yet you refuse. I cannot think you so foolish."

"My wishes for matrimony include more than fortune and position."

"Such as?"

"Respect, perhaps even love, for my marriage partner."

"You cannot respect me?" The affront to his character was beginning to enrage him. Mortification was giving way to outrage, and he was grateful for it, much preferring indignation to humiliation.

She crossed her arms and looked away, then spoke in a

dignified tone. "It cannot behove us to discuss the reasons we dislike one another."

"I just told you of my regard. If you would wish to say you dislike me, do not suppose I share in your sentiment. I wish only for an honest answer to my question."

"We have done nothing but argue since the day we met!" she exclaimed, her tone heated. "How can you pretend to like me? You have lost no opportunity to scorn me and vex me in all the days of our acquaintance."

"I believed you sought my notice with your opinions and arguments."

She laughed bitterly. "I did no such thing! You seemed to have some design to offend me in every utterance I have ever heard from you. You have made me feel my inferiority very well, sir."

He paced, his jaw clenched, and his boots rapped smartly on the floor. "So you would have preferred me to play to your vanity then? To flatter and cajole you?"

"I do not want any such thing from you. I say only that to pretend to affection for someone—"

"Pretend to affection!" He turned and looked at her. "Indeed not! Disguise of any sort is my abhorrence."

She fell silent. He watched from the corner of his eye as she took a deep breath, regaining her equanimity. "Mr Darcy, I do not wish to insult you in any manner. I am flattered by your offer, but I regret that I cannot accept you."

He could not let this rest. In later reflection, he would blame his incredulity for continuing to press her, but in the moment, he hardly knew what impelled him.

"Is this because of the assembly? I had not supposed you to be the sort to hold onto a grudge, but in any case, forgive me. I should not have spoken so." Even to his own ear, he spoke carelessly. He knew his words conveyed not a true apology but more a condemnation of her need for an apology.

Elizabeth replied peevishly, "I am not so ungenerous as to refuse an advantageous offer of marriage for a slight given months ago. If you must have an understanding of my refusal, I shall say only that it is exemplified in this situation you have set upon me. Having no notion of my feelings nor any apparent wish to know them, you have set out a plan, a plan that involves my life and my father and my mother—and you have the audacity to assume I should just agree with it. You did involve me, and now it will be my unhappy lot to tell all those people we are not engaged. *I* will be the one facing the mortification and gossip. And why did you do that? Your pride, sir. It knows no bounds."

"Pride?" He was surprised. "How is it proud to assume that a woman with no notable prospects would not wish to—?"

"No prospects? Am I to be judged only on financial considerations? I assure you, I have a solid character, which to me is worth far, far more. I would not wish to offend you, sir, but yes, you are proud and arrogant. You disdain those beneath you, which would be most people, and I cannot like you for your treatment of them as I have seen it."

She warmed to her subject. "From the very beginning, from the first moment, I may almost say, of my acquaintance with you, your manners impressed me with the fullest belief of your arrogance, your conceit, and your selfish disdain of the feelings of others. These were such as to form that groundwork of disapprobation on which succeeding events have built so immoveable a dislike, that I had not known you a month before I felt that you were the last man in the world whom I could ever be prevailed on to marry."

He said nothing through her speech but felt his cheeks grow

warm, and he knew his colour was high. When she was finished, he replied, "You have said quite enough, madam. I perfectly comprehend your feelings and have now only to be ashamed of what my own have been. Forgive me for having taken up so much of your time and accept my best wishes for your health and happiness."

Darcy knew he must flee. It would be rude to exit without taking leave of her aunt and uncle, yet he did it anyway, desperate to be in his carriage and away from her forever.

WHEN HE HAD GONE, ELIZABETH REMAINED FOR SEVERAL MINUTES in her uncle's study. At length, Jane, who had gone to her bedchamber when Darcy arrived, knocked on the door. "Lizzy? Let us join our aunt in her parlour, shall we?"

Resigned, Elizabeth rose and followed her sister to where her aunt and uncle awaited. They looked at her expectantly when she entered. Elizabeth averted her gaze to the ground to avoid meeting the uneasy looks that went about as she and Jane sat.

"Mr Darcy asked me to give you his apologies for having to leave so quickly." He had not, but she did not wish her aunt and uncle to feel slighted in any way.

"Lizzy, what happened?" Mrs Gardiner asked. "We did not wish to eavesdrop, but we did hear raised voices."

Elizabeth could not immediately speak of it. She sat with her eyes lowered and her cheeks warm, fearing to open her mouth lest she sob.

Once her tears had been safely swallowed, she spoke. "Somehow, at Rosings, Mr Darcy formed a design to propose to me. Because he is an exceedingly proud man, he was certain I would agree—if he considered my answer at all—and went about creating a situation in which our friends and relations now believe we are engaged."

Jane asked, "Are you engaged to him?"

Elizabeth raised her head to give Jane an incredulous stare. "No! I refused him in the strongest possible terms."

"Oh, of course." Chastened, Jane turned her eyes to her lap.

Elizabeth felt remorseful for having rebuked her sister so. "Have I not always said I wished to marry for love? How can I turn my back on that principle for the first wealthy man who offers for me? Much less a man I despise with such a passion!"

Mrs Gardiner sighed, a troubled look on her face. "None of us would wish you bound to a man you despise, Lizzy, but I am concerned about your mother's response to this."

"Yet one more thing I must hate him for. He has done this! It is he who spread these tales abroad, and he who exercised poor judgement and false assuredness in his opinion that I would be inclined to marry him. Nevertheless, it is I who shall bear the consequence!"

An ache pulsed through her head, and Elizabeth rubbed her temples. She rose, desperate to escape to a quiet place. "Forgive me, my head is aching. I must retire."

Mrs Gardiner nodded, telling her she would send up the housekeeper with some powders. With that, Elizabeth was off to keep company with her resentment and her aching head.

INDIGNATION PROVED AN INCONSTANT COMPANION AND DID NOT even last the whole of his carriage ride home. He was midway when anger faded into regret, and by the time he alit from his conveyance, outright desolation had set up residence in his bosom. He tried to regain his resentment, telling himself Elizabeth Bennet was a far more ignorant lady than he had realised, but he knew very well that it was not true.

Darcy arrived home to find the solitude he dreamt of was to be denied. Georgiana and Fitzwilliam awaited him in the library. He nearly groaned aloud to see them, particularly his sister. He did not relish the prospect of dashing her hopes or removing the happy, expectant look from her face.

"Brother, Richard and I might ride in the park. What say you to the excursion?"

Darcy could scarcely recall when Georgiana had been so animated or lively as she was at present. "Actually, Georgiana, I had hoped to—"

"You are so dispirited, Brother, and I do not need to wonder why!"

He gave her a grim smile as he marshalled his fortitude to tell her the news. "I need to speak to you—"

Georgiana nodded knowingly. "She must return to Hertford-shire! Oh, but if she could only stay in town! Think of all the clothing she must purchase! It must surely be better to prepare a trousseau in town than in Hertfordshire." She suddenly blushed. "Oh, I beg your pardon. I did not mean that as any sort of slight on Hertfordshire."

"Of course not," Darcy replied. "Allow me a moment—"

"I am sure the dressmakers in Hertfordshire are excellent. In fact, the gown she wore when she called was very pretty! I liked it exceedingly well and wished I had one just like it!"

Darcy sighed, rubbing his hand across his brow as he sank into a chair. "She dresses nicely."

"Pray, do not tell her of my slight, I did not mean it as one. How easy it is to speak amiss! Her taste is exceedingly elegant, and I am sure whatever she picks for her wedding clothes will be just the same whether they are obtained in town or in Hert-fordshire." Georgiana rose from her chair and took one nearer his. "Just think—soon, you will never part again!"

"As a matter of fact—" he began.

"Had she wished to shop in town, I might have been tempted to impose myself on her. I do love to shop, and now that Miss Parham has gone home, I am at ends as to how I might amuse myself."

Miss Parham was one of Georgiana's particular friends, having been at school with her. A few years senior to Georgiana, she had come out this Season. Georgiana had gained much plea-sure over the last month in hearing Miss Parham relate her activ-ities, from dressmakers to balls, breakfasts, and walks, with endless patience to absorb every word.

Fitzwilliam, clearly sensing something afoot, was quick to seize on the change of subject. "Miss Parham has gone home?"

Georgiana nodded. "She is gone into the country and will

not return to town. I am invited to join her in the autumn if my brother and Elizabeth approve."

"But what of her Season?" Darcy's astonishment was equalled in Fitzwilliam's tone, having never heard of any young lady doing such a thing. Too much money was spent in assembling wardrobes and garnering invitations to simply cry off.

"The most dreadful thing happened to her," Georgiana explained. "She was at a ball, and there was a certain gentleman there, Sir Frederick Boyle. He is a wealthy baronet from Kent, I believe."

And a stupid popinjay. Never saw a reflection of himself he did not like. "Yes, I know Sir Frederick," Darcy said.

"Her uncle wished to introduce Miss Parham to Sir Frederick, but he refused. She was not pleased but not too entirely distressed either, for she is aware of her position. She does not like to reach above herself, even in her friendships."

"Aware of her position? And what is that?" As Georgiana's friend from school, Darcy had assumed Miss Parham was from a well-settled and prosperous family.

Georgiana said delicately, "She has no titled relations, and her fortune is not large. In any case, she might have disregarded that slight except that she overheard him in conversation before supper, making some remark on her dancing. Something to the effect that he was pleased to have been able to avoid her, for her dancing brought to mind the hopping of a grouse during mating season, and her figure was much like that of a grouse as well."

Darcy nearly choked, turning it into a cough at the last moment. His surprise was not so much at Sir Frederick's remark —although appalling, it was not a surprise coming from that man—but with the similarity he saw between his conduct at the Meryton assembly and that of Sir Frederick.

Georgiana continued blithely, "Is that not the most ungentlemanly act you have ever heard, Brother? I am sure I cannot blame her for wishing to run off."

"Surely, that alone was not sufficient to send her off to home? He is one man. What should his opinion matter?"

Georgiana replied, "Whether or not people like him, they do hear his opinion, for his wealth and consequence bring him that much. There were many in the area that undoubtedly heard him —she herself was several feet away, and it was a crowded ball. It was exceedingly humiliating and then…well, she had a partner for the next dance but was not asked again. She was forced to sit in mortification with the matrons for the remainder of the evening. After that, she told her mother she had to go home. While at home, she intends to have more dance instruction and give up biscuits and chocolate."

Darcy rose abruptly, almost before he knew what he did. He moved to the window, turning his back on Georgiana. He had never before considered the way his words might have been perceived by Elizabeth's neighbours. If she had heard, so had many in her vicinity, and those who did not hear directly were likely told by others. The Netherfield party was the object of much speculation and comment that night, so a scandalous remark about one of their own would not have gone unreported.

"Her friends must have consoled her," said Fitzwilliam.

"Pity is as heavy a burden as outright scorn," Georgiana replied. "I could not have borne it. I would have run for Pemberley as fast as I could."

Darcy turned from the window and looked at his dear, sweet sister, who was still looking at Fitzwilliam. His chest tightened with remorse. Such an experience would have shattered Georgiana's fragile confidence. She would have avoided London forever had such embarrassment been inflicted upon her.

But Elizabeth was different—she would not be intimidated.

She had risen, giving him that little look to let him know she had heard him in an attempt to rouse his own mortification. However, just because she looked well and brave did not mean that inwardly she did not suffer distress. After all, her father, who was not at the assembly, had been told of it. She had not dismissed it as easily as it seemed.

An unhappy recollection arose. When he had asked her to dance at Bingley's ball, he believed he overheard her say to Miss Lucas, "I promised myself I would never dance with him." He thought he must have misheard her, yet she had declined him twice before. Once with clear disdain and another time with teasing insouciance. At Bingley's ball, however, she could hardly refuse. It was before supper, and she would not have wished to sit out for the rest of the evening. She unwillingly agreed to partner him, and he had gone on his way, revelling in the honour bestowed upon her while she despised him for requiring her to do it.

"Forgive me, Georgiana." He was nearing the door to his study in a moment, desperate for escape. "I have forgotten something I must do."

"Darcy, wait," said Fitzwilliam, hard on his heels. "Georgiana, excuse us please."

AFTER SPENDING NEARLY AN HOUR WITH DARCY, WATCHING HIM pace and rant in his dressing room, Fitzwilliam left for his father's house. As he entered, his father was crossing the entryway and stopped him immediately.

"There you are! Tell me, when do you suppose Darcy's Miss Bennet will be by? I must admit, I am rather keen to get a look at this girl."

"She said *no* to him."

"No? Surely not."

"Oh yes."

"That is the most absurd thing I have ever heard. You must have misunderstood him." Lord Matlock clapped his son on his back, chuckling as they strolled from his book room to the drawing room.

"I understood perfectly. She will not have him. She cannot like him."

His father turned, giving him a bewildered look. "Why on earth not?"

Colonel Fitzwilliam considered it for scarcely a moment before deciding to confide in his father the particulars of the tale Darcy had told him. Lord Matlock winced here and there, obviously surprised by some of what he learnt, but he said relatively little.

"Badly done for sure, but how can she possibly justify refusing him? Does she not understand how wealthy he is? How well placed? He is certainly a catch such as she might never before have imagined."

"She has refused other good possibilities too."

"What?"

"Lady Catherine's parson—the Mr Collins of whom you have heard—offered for her in the autumn. He is, you see, the heir to her father's estate. A distant cousin, I believe. In any case, she refused him too."

"Well, that man seems like an imbecile." Lord Matlock waved it off. "What lady would wish to marry him?"

"Mr Collins, loathsome as he is, is an eligible match. In marrying him, she might have secured the future of her mother and sisters, yet she would not do it."

"Principles are fine things for those who can afford them. However, at some point, principles become foolishness. It seems

Miss Bennet needs someone to explain to her how the world works."

"Prudence does not always beget happiness."

The two men were interrupted by Lady Matlock, who bid her son to follow her, having received a letter she wished to share.

Lord Matlock watched them go, but his mind was still with the amazing story his son had just told him. Shaking his head, he mused aloud, "Prudence might not lead to happiness, but neither are poverty and indignity the harbingers of felicity."

His own words came back to mind. She needed someone to explain to her how the world works.

It is the duty of a father to advise a young lady in such a way. Mr Bennet, after all, had given his support to the union. That gentleman's wishes for his daughter were clear.

However, Bennet is not here, and I am. And if I were, in truth, the friend I claim to be, I might act in his stead. Who could better know what needs to be said to this headstrong miss of his?

With a satisfied nod, he was resolved. He would visit this young lady, whom he firmly believed would yet become his niece, and talk some sense into her.

Friday, 17 April 1812, London

ELIZABETH DEPARTED FOR A WALK JUST AFTER BREAKFAST ON THE day following Darcy's proposal. Slivers of blue peeking from between the clouds gave every indication of an impending turn in the weather and pulled her out of doors. Almost as soon as she reached the park, the clouds proved teasing, gathering and darkening above her as they released a few warning drops of rain. Not wishing to chance a soaking, she turned back, reentering her aunt's house only a quarter of an hour after she had departed it.

She went to the parlour where she was sure to find her aunt and Jane, but before she could enter, she heard them speaking. Although she knew she should not, upon hearing her name, she stopped to listen.

"Now that Lizzy has refused Mr Darcy, I daresay, all hope is gone. But do not think I blame her! Oh no…no, it is likely hope was gone anyway."

Elizabeth heard a sound that could only be a sob along with some gentle murmurs from Mrs Gardiner that she could not make out.

Jane said, "No, I am sure Mr Bingley could never associate himself with a family who had injured his friend in this way."

Silence ensued, and Elizabeth's heart broke. She had seen her sister's distress but tried to persuade herself that Jane was improving. It would seem she had fooled herself.

"We may at least console ourselves with this," said Mrs Gardiner. "The gossips of Meryton will be well occupied with Elizabeth and Mr Darcy this summer."

"That is true. Even if my mother had been silent—but I know she could not help crowing her triumph—they would still have much to speak of."

"They will speak of Elizabeth and forget all about you," said Mrs. Gardiner. "We can only hope that soon their tongues will wear themselves out. And if nothing else, console yourself with the knowledge that there is always a newer, more interesting story just around the bend."

A tear slid down Elizabeth's cheek as she forced herself to move away from the door. Her steps were heavy as she made her way to her bedchamber. Once there, she lay upon her bed, feeling her grief like a blanket upon her.

She had to admit to a shameful sense of ungenerous triumph for having delivered such a set down to Mr Darcy. Now, however, in the light of a new day, who was truly the victor? His charge to her—that she had refused him for a mere grudge—was in error. She had much to hold against him, far more than just that.

She began to think of their conversations—of all of the times they had argued. What if the sentiments behind their arguments were not censure but rather interest? It put a far different light on things.

Then she thought of Mr Wickham. Mr Darcy's actions in that case spoke to a mean spirit. But would she refuse Mr Darcy on the basis of Mr Wickham's testimony?

Her refusal of Mr Darcy materially damaged Jane's hopes. That much could not be denied. Her own wishes might be damaged as well, for somewhere in her mind, Elizabeth had thought she would live with Jane and her family and not need to marry. However, Jane was correct: Bingley would certainly not associate himself with the Bennets after what she had done. So who would be this man—Jane's future husband—who would not only wish to have a Bennet sister live with them but also have ample income to support them all?

And meanwhile, her family would be embarrassed. Although it was her mother's fault for spreading gossip, the world did not require yet another example of Fanny Bennet looking foolish, which she would if Elizabeth jilted Mr Darcy. Her father would also appear ridiculous if it were known that he had given his consent only to have Elizabeth refuse. Once again, the world would see what little influence Mr Bennet exerted over his family.

The unfairness of it burned through her sorrow. For what

cause had Mr Darcy visited this distress upon them? Why? What had he hoped to gain?

"I ardently admire and love you." His words came suddenly to her mind, but she shooed them away irritably.

THE TIME SHE SPENT IN REFLECTION WAS LONG, AND SHE COULD reach no good opinion of herself afterwards. She could not regret refusing Mr Darcy, but she did regret her conduct, and she dreaded—heartily dreaded—what she knew was to come.

She emerged from her bedchamber resolved to find something to do that would distract her from thoughts of Darcy, gossip, and Jane's persistent melancholy. Nothing would do for her: not cards, writing letters, or books. The weather had turned, precluding anything out of doors. Thus, she was fixed in the Gardiners' house.

Finally, Elizabeth joined the children in their schoolroom, much to their delight. She sat with them as they went about their work, offering her assistance as she could. She had just resolved to leave them when she heard a knock at the door.

It opened, revealing her aunt's housekeeper, her eyes wide and her demeanour frightened. "You have a caller, miss."

"A caller? Who is it?"

Silently, the lady handed her a fine, engraved card bearing the crest of the Matlock earldom and the name Henry James Sutton Fitzwilliam, 5th Earl of Matlock. A pulse of alarm went through her. Mr Darcy's uncle, Colonel Fitzwilliam's father—she could not think this call boded well.

She moved quickly with the housekeeper's assistance, hastening to change her gown and fix her hair from where it had fallen during play with the children. Within ten minutes, she was descending the stairs and moving towards the drawing room, her anxiety mounting.

The gentleman she presumed was his lordship sat with her uncle and aunt in what appeared to be a pleasant conversation. Lord Matlock looked like an older version of Colonel Fitzwilliam; his hair was greyed blond, and he had piercing blue eyes. His figure was suggestive of a man who had once been active but was now less so.

Everyone looked up when Elizabeth entered, and Mr Gardiner hastened to make the introduction, telling Elizabeth, "Lord Matlock and I have met before over some business interests."

Lord Matlock, who was busily inspecting Elizabeth, boomed loudly, "I knew as soon as I saw Gardiner here that any lady related to such an astute man of business could surely not have done something so foolish. I knew there must be some mistake!"

Elizabeth felt uncommonly fidgety, but she raised her chin slightly to cover it and laid her hands against her skirt in an effort to blot the light moisture that was suddenly present on them. "I do not understand you, sir."

He looked at her a moment. "My dear, you are full young. Pray, tell me, what is your age?"

Elizabeth sighed. *Oh yes, I forgot for a moment that you are the brother of Lady Catherine.* "I am twenty, sir."

"Ah! Twenty!" Lord Matlock sent sage nods about the room. "A lovely time in life. Though at my age, I can scarcely recall it!"

The Gardiners laughed politely at his little joke. Elizabeth smiled tightly.

"Miss Bennet, you perhaps do not realise the extraordinary nature of the offer you have received from my nephew. Now, I shall admit that I believed he had taken leave of his wits when he first announced this plan to me. 'A lady with no fortune and no claim to any good name! It cannot be borne!' That is what I told him.

"However, when he told me of his affection for you—his love, that is—what could I do but support him? I know Darcy, and when he sets his mind to something, he will not be gainsaid."

"That is all well and good when one is speaking of an object to be won or bought. However, I am neither of those things. Thus, in this case, Mr Darcy will need to accept the novelty of being gainsaid."

Lord Matlock regarded her. "Have you no thought for the compliment of gaining such a man's affections? And if you do not, can you at the least apprehend what it would mean to your family to be elevated in such a way? Here we are, in the fine home of Mr Gardiner, who I know is a hard-working, intelligent man. Would his business not be benefitted by having a relation amongst the highest circles of society? Your sisters—would it not be to their benefit to be the sisters of Mr Darcy?"

He was hitting uncomfortably close to Elizabeth's feelings of guilt, and she felt herself redden as she looked down at her lap. "Sir, I do not think you understand—"

"I do understand," the earl replied with sudden and surprising compassion. "I understand this better than you could imagine. He told me how he slighted you at your first meeting. That must have indeed distressed you, and he should have offered an apology then and there. Abominable behaviour.

"However, do not be so foolish as to allow your pride to cling to some silly grudge against him to the detriment of yourself and your family. You have a highly undeserved proposal of marriage from a fine gentleman who is honourable, good, wealthy, and comes from one of the best families in all of

England. To add to that, he loves you. What more could you wish for?"

It was too much. Elizabeth thought if Lord Matlock had shouted or upbraided her, she might have had more anger from which to draw. As it was, he neatly skirted all of her best courage and went to the home truth. Would everyone believe she had refused Mr Darcy for the sake of a grudge? She thought Mr Darcy proud; instead, was it she who was proud? Would she damage her prospects as well as those of her sisters and ruin her reputation merely for spite?

There was no doubt that for her to marry a man like Mr Darcy would have enormous benefit to every one of her relations: Jane's future with Mr Bingley, her mother's not needing to fret about the loss of Longbourn to Mr Collins, her younger sisters' prospects, and Mr Gardiner's business. She sighed heavily.

Elizabeth felt her hands trembling and clasped them together in her lap. Her voice, when she spoke, sounded much weaker than she might have liked. "I assure you, sir, I do not intend to hold a grudge or to act to the detriment of my family. I am only resolved to act in a manner that will, in my own opinion, constitute my happiness without reference to you or to any person so wholly unconnected with me."

Her words sounded undeniably selfish, particularly as the words of Jane and her aunt echoed through her head. An image of her life after refusing Mr Darcy entered her mind: her parents angered and disgraced, her sisters' futures diminished, and now her uncle possibly harmed in his business interests. She stole a quick look at Mr Gardiner who had said little thus far but appeared concerned.

There had been too much emotion for the day, running from anger to frustration to sadness and back again. As she looked at the rather formidable Lord Matlock, a sense of defeat overwhelmed her and tears rose in her eyes. She attempted to bring herself under regulation, not wishing Lord Matlock to see her cry, but it was a futile effort. Tears began to roll down her face.

She rose hastily. "I beg your pardon." She exited the room with Lord Matlock's expressions of disbelief ringing in her ears.

She threw herself on her bed, tears flowing as she considered her situation. An earl—had she even met an earl? Ever? She could not think that she had, yet today, one came to Gracechurch Street to chastise her for her behaviour. Jane was in deep distress, and her aunt did not disagree that they were due to face gossip for some time to come.

Her father had given his consent, and her mother had spread the word. Even dear Georgiana was delighted by it all. She was ensnared quite neatly by the silken bands of an arrogant man's notion that no lady could resist him.

Saturday, 18 April 1812, London

THE FAMILY WAS ALREADY GATHERED FOR BREAKFAST WHEN SHE descended the next morning, having spent a restless night filled with the anxious ghosts of dreams—Jane in travail, Longbourn in ruin, her younger sisters crying, the shrieks and chastisements of her mother—never had a night's sleep passed in such an exhausting and wretched manner. As she dressed, she had seen her own pale, hollow-eyed countenance staring back at her, worries and distress clearly marked on her features. Somewhere within her was the understanding of what she must do, though her conscious mind was not quite willing to give way to it yet.

"Oh, Lizzy, good morning!" Her aunt's voice made every attempt at cheer though Elizabeth could clearly see some measure of her own worries written on Mrs Gardiner's face. Jane also looked as though she had not slept well, but she attempted to hide it behind a smile.

"Good morning, Aunt." Leaning over, Elizabeth kissed her on the cheek. "Has Uncle already eaten?"

"No, no. Your uncle has run across the street to inform his foreman of something, but he will return in—"

"He is already returned." Her uncle announced himself with the same forced cheer her aunt had used. "Back and ready for a meal!" He rubbed his stomach, looking eagerly at the sideboard.

After serving themselves, Jane, Elizabeth, and their aunt and uncle sat down to breakfast. The Gardiners' two older children were notably absent.

"Where are Edmund and Rosalie?" Elizabeth looked at her aunt.

"They breakfasted earlier."

Knowing how much her young cousins enjoyed being with their elders, Elizabeth feared their absence heralded more conversation centred on the events of the past days.

Mr Gardiner cleared his throat. "I hoped we might speak more about Mr Darcy."

Elizabeth flushed, looking down at her plate. "You cannot know how I regret having brought all of this into your house."

"You did nothing of which to be ashamed," Mr Gardiner said. "I understand that you have a poor opinion of Mr Darcy, and therefore, accepting his offer of marriage was quite out of the question. No one can fault you there."

A pause followed while the weight of what was unspoken filled the room. At last, Elizabeth spoke. "There is clearly more to be said here, Uncle. Please do continue."

Her aunt's gentle voice broke into the conversation. "The situation has unfortunately gone beyond yourself and Mr Darcy."

"Which was his own doing!" Elizabeth exclaimed, but her voice had lost its heat and contained only dejected protest.

Mrs Gardiner said gently, "Regardless of how it began, what matters is where it is now."

"He made an error in how it was handled, to be sure," Mr Gardiner agreed. "Be that as it may, we must now look at the reality of the situation. Laying blame can do no good. We must consider what is best for the future."

Elizabeth attempted to force a smile. "I hear the West Indies are nice. I could go there."

All gave her perfunctory chuckles. "Is it really as bad as all that, Lizzy?" Mrs Gardiner asked. "His family is known for their honour and goodness, and he seems a respectable gentleman. I believe he would treat you very well. In fact, I am sure of it."

"Would you say Mr Wickham would agree?"

"That situation is between Mr Wickham and Mr Darcy," Mr Gardiner interjected. "It says nothing of how a man would treat his wife and her family. Moreover, it was some years past."

Elizabeth did not reply, staring miserably at the half-eaten piece of toast on her plate.

After a pause, Mr Gardiner spoke again. "We must also consider that gossip has already begun to circulate—slanderous stories that could materially damage your reputation should you continue to refuse Mr Darcy."

Elizabeth raised her eyes to stare at Mr Gardiner in disbelief. "Such as what?"

Mr Gardiner shook his head. "The details are not important."

"They are important to me!" Elizabeth cried out.

Her uncle again shook his head. "No, no. Nothing more than the prattle of idle tongues. But one good story begets another, does it not? And that, we cannot have."

With a sigh, Elizabeth returned her gaze to her plate. The fight had left her, and she could not think of anything to say for this disaster that had befallen her.

Mrs Johnson entered, two cards in her hand. "Some callers have arrived, madam."

"So early!" Mrs Gardiner took the cards, her eyebrows rising when she read them. She handed them to her husband. "The entirety of clan Matlock is to be set upon us, I think."

Elizabeth gave a little moan. "Lord Matlock has returned to further chastise me?"

"No," Mr Gardiner answered her, examining the two cards. "His wife has come, along with a Colonel Fitzwilliam, who must be their son."

"I DO HOPE YOU WILL FORGIVE US FOR CALLING SO EARLY." Colonel Fitzwilliam grinned charmingly at Mrs Gardiner.

"Of course." Mrs Gardiner was gracious and kind as always and behaved correctly to the colonel and the countess, beginning an easy conversation while Elizabeth awaited the next round of entreaties and veiled insults.

Lady Matlock leaned towards her and placed her hand atop Elizabeth's. "My dear, you look unwell."

Elizabeth was unsure how to reply and offered only a faint smile.

"Oh, that my husband had exercised greater understanding of the sensitivity of these matters before he came here!" Her ladyship offered genial smiles around the room. "Tact has never been his strength. However, all of us have only the best interests of our nephew as well as you in our hearts. With all that has happened, I think it best for you to marry Darcy. What a match you will have made! You must congratulate yourself, my dear, and understand the compliment of having earned the affections of such a man."

Elizabeth privately revolted against the statement but resolved to speak prudently. Not knowing whether it was wise to take her ladyship into her confidence, Elizabeth explained, "I had not the least idea of marrying, you see. I did not comprehend the significance of Mr Darcy's attentions."

"Your modesty does you credit," said Lady Matlock warmly. "How extraordinary for you to learn of my nephew's intentions in such a roundabout manner!"

Lady Matlock gave Elizabeth's hand a vigorous pat. "Your engagement has not begun as it should have, but I would stake my life that your opinion of my nephew will change. He is a good man and wishes to be a good husband more than anything."

"Our engagement has not begun at all," said Elizabeth firmly. "I have not agreed to marry Mr Darcy."

"But you will?"

"I believe that is a matter best left to Mr Darcy and myself."

There was an uneasy silence until Colonel Fitzwilliam was able to introduce a new topic. "Say there! I have only just recalled that I saw acquaintances whom we share in the park yesterday. They wished to extend their well wishes on your…to you and Darcy."

"Oh?" Elizabeth asked politely. "Who was that?"

"Mr Bingley and his sister."

Elizabeth stiffened and noticed her aunt did the same. In a carefully neutral tone, she replied, "How kind."

"I believe Mr Bingley leased a manor house in Hertfordshire, did he not?" Lady Matlock enquired.

"It was next to my father's estate, just a few miles down the lane."

"That is where you met Darcy?"

"Yes, it was."

Colonel Fitzwilliam chuckled. "Darcy is forever doing favours for Bingley, but in this case, it seems to have redounded to his benefit."

"How true that is!" Lady Matlock exclaimed, evidently wishing to support her earlier assertions of Mr Darcy's goodness. "He is always offering his advice and assistance to Mr Bingley."

Colonel Fitzwilliam obviously understood his mother's purpose and eagerly continued the conversation for Elizabeth's benefit. "I recently learnt of a time when Darcy spared Bingley from a most imprudent attachment. Forgive me, I do not wish to be indiscreet—it could be that the attachment was someone you knew in Hertfordshire."

Elizabeth schooled her countenance into an appearance of complacency. "I did not see Mr Bingley in danger of any imprudent attachment in Hertfordshire."

"No, no, in fact, now that I think on it further," Fitzwilliam mused, "Darcy mentioned something of the lady being someone in London. Bingley's sister paid a call, from what I heard, to cut the acquaintance."

Elizabeth did not move a muscle although it felt as if her stomach had been punched.

"Darcy said the family was entirely unsuitable and Bingley was quite unreserved in his displays of preference. The lady had not much affection for him. It was entirely a mercenary scheme."

"Was it indeed?" Elizabeth felt her hands begin to tremble and clenched them tightly in her lap. She saw from the corner of her eye that Mrs Gardiner was giving her a worried glance. "I suppose Mr Darcy must have been quite intimate with the lady and her family to so fully understand their intentions for his friend."

Fitzwilliam shrugged. "From what I have heard of their behaviour, the family made no secret of their scheme. The lady's mother spoke without reserve of the match, as if it were a done thing. It took some doing—Bingley was quite attached and can be surprisingly intractable when opposed—but my cousin did at last triumph."

"He is so good to his friends," Lady Matlock hurried to add.

Elizabeth clenched her teeth to keep from crying out at the injustice of all they said. She dared not look at Mrs Gardiner knowing that her aunt had likely discerned the full truth of the matter.

Did you ever doubt it? You have suspected this for some months now. It was not the same, however, for inasmuch as she suspected Darcy had a hand in separating Bingley from Jane, it was another matter entirely to know it in truth. And that he had boasted of it to his cousin—appalling!

"Miss Bennet, are you well?"

Elizabeth shook herself, realising she had been lost in her distress and drawn the attention of the room. It was Colonel Fitzwilliam who enquired of her health while Lady Matlock and Mrs Gardiner looked at her with concern.

"Just a slight headache," she replied hastily.

"Have some more tea, Lizzy," Mrs Gardiner advised. "Or perhaps I should open the windows? The room is warm."

Was it the room or was it the warmth of pure rage that afflicted her? She hardly knew. In any case, she commended Mr Darcy for having the excellent fortune to be far, far away from her at this moment. Had he been in front of her, she did not think she would be able to restrain herself. A severe upbraiding would be inevitable; physical violence would be probable.

DARCY SAT IN HIS STUDY WITH THE NEWSPAPER IN HIS HAND, BUT his attention was on his wounded sensibilities. He was unsuccessful in his attempts to regain his resentment towards Elizabeth for her unjust accusations. Instead, he had begun to see the justice in her complaints, and now self-reproach joined sorrow in his bosom along with more than a little mortification for the embarrassment that would follow when the *ton* learnt of her rejection of him. Of these, he had to admit, the latter was of least concern, but nevertheless, the idea of being a laughingstock distressed him.

Even his home was not safe. Georgiana had done nothing but make plans and discuss his forthcoming marriage. Even now, she was off looking at sketches of gowns and imagining what Elizabeth might favour for her trousseau. He could not conceive telling her the truth.

The door to his study opened, and Saye strolled in with no announcement or ceremony. He shook his finger at Darcy. "I must say, Darcy, you do have a way of doing things."

Darcy exhaled forcibly to demonstrate his impatience. "I have no stomach for you today. Pray, go home before we argue."

Saye unstopped the bottle of port and, ignoring Darcy's protests about his unwanted intrusion, poured himself a generous glass. He then sat down in the chair next to Darcy's desk, dribbling a bit of port onto his lap in the process.

"Blast!" Taking out his handkerchief, he dabbed at the stain. "Well, you have my mother down to Gracechurch Street. I cannot imagine how she even found the place. I suppose her coachman must have known the way."

"Gracechurch Street?" A sick feeling entered Darcy's gut. "What is she doing in Gracechurch Street?"

"There! That is not so bad, is it? My man will get the rest of it out. These are my favourite trousers, and I could not bear to see them stained." Saye smiled lovingly at his trousers then leaned back in the chair. "I am not entirely certain my mother has ever wandered away from Mayfair. Oh, the occasional poorhouse visit, I suppose, and naturally she travels through on her way to more rusticated settings—"

"Why did she go to Gracechurch Street?" Darcy was growing increasingly anxious, and to his exceeding displeasure, Saye either did not notice or did not care.

"Then there was that time she heard of some warehouse, fine textiles or something of the sort, and she and Lady Wellcome had a spirit of adventure and decided they must—"

"Saye!" Darcy roared his cousin's name, causing Saye to look up with a peevish expression.

"What?"

"Why. Is. Your. Mother. In. Gracechurch. Street?" Darcy enunciated each word, making certain Saye understood his displeasure.

Saye waved his hand in a carelessly insolent way. "Obviously, she went to see your Miss Bennet. Who else do we know down there?" He sipped his port.

A light-headed sensation came over Darcy. "Please tell me she did not go there to...to..." To what? He could not imagine what his aunt would do at the Gardiner residence. He did not fear she would behave badly, but more imperious behaviour would only worsen Elizabeth's opinion of him.

Of course, that is hardly possible. She thinks you the lowest, most miserable excuse for a man possible. Having a haughty aunt—another haughty aunt, to be more precise—could hardly lower you in her estimation.

Saye saw something floating in his glass and was preoccupied with removing it. "Do you think I am losing my hair? Because I found a bit of it in this glass, and my brush seemed rather full—"

Darcy tried to quash his irritation into something like forbearance. "Saye, please attend this conversation for just a few moments and then you may rattle on as you please. Why did my aunt go to Gracechurch Street?"

With a sigh, Saye pulled his attention away from the distressing notion of possible hair loss. "To apologise for my father. Clearly, it was not his intention to make Miss Elizabeth cry."

"What!" The light-headedness gave way to pure horror. Darcy was so entirely appalled that his words came in a sputter. "He made her cry! What did he…? Why was he even…?"

Saye at last wore a look on his face that was something other than vexing insouciance. "He wanted to talk some sense into her. On behalf of her father, you know, and with regard to their friendship—"

"They are not acquainted!" Darcy shouted, slamming his palm down on his desk. "Am I the only person who recalls that the friendship of Lord Matlock and Mr Bennet is a falsehood?"

Saye, unmoved by his cousin's display, spoke as if Darcy were the one who was daft. "Yes, but if he and Mr Bennet were friends, he would wish to lend his assistance. It is clear Miss Bennet is not thinking reasonably to turn down such a fine catch as you."

Darcy heard himself make a choking sound that even he could not fully apprehend the meaning of—something between annoyance and despair. "Help me understand this," he insisted. "My uncle paid a call on Miss Elizabeth Bennet at her uncle's home."

Saye nodded. "Just to talk to her! But then she began to cry, so he left and went home. And now my mother has gone to Gracechurch Street hoping to repair the damage."

"Merciful God in heaven." Darcy rose quickly. "Simply beyond anything rational…could not have imagined…" He stopped speaking, pulling the bell to summon his butler to bring him his coat.

"Shall I go with you? I think I might like to be introduced to this girl. She has provided me with greater amusement these past days than all the other ladies of my acquaintance combined."

"Do as you wish," Darcy replied brusquely. Saye grinned and stayed hard on Darcy's heels as they went towards the carriage.

THE SCENE WITHIN THE GARDINER RESIDENCE WAS NOT ONE DARCY could have contrived in his wildest imagination.

His aunt sat in a chair next to Elizabeth on a small settee. Colonel Fitzwilliam sat across from them on another sofa with Mr and Mrs Gardiner on either side. As Darcy and Saye were shown in, all save Elizabeth turned to look at them. Uneasiness made Darcy pause, but Saye had no such scruple, all but leaping into the room with eagerness and going directly to Elizabeth.

"So then! This is Miss Elizabeth Bennet, the centre of our most recent Fitzwilliam Family Furore!"

Elizabeth looked at him in shock as he strode towards her, belatedly rising for the introduction. Saye bowed low over Elizabeth's hand, boldly kissing it as she watched with clear amazement.

"*Enchanté*, my dear. Is it too soon to call you Cousin?" Saye settled himself on the settee, still holding Elizabeth's hand, thus forcing her to sit as well.

"Saye," Lady Matlock said, a warning tone in her voice.

He disregarded his mother, leaning so close to Elizabeth it almost appeared he would kiss her. "Fitzwilliam Family Furore…I challenge you to say it twenty times fast. I thought of nothing else but that for the entire journey here. Try it with me. Fitzwilliam Family Furore, Fitzwilliam Family Furore, Fitzwilliam Family Furore—"

He stopped suddenly, leaning back and looking concerned for a moment. "Though to be perfectly just, I must own that perhaps it cannot truly be regarded as a Fitzwilliam Family Furore since Darcy is the originator of all this. Or can it? For we must concede, he is half Fitzwilliam…and his given name is Fitzwilliam…so yes, I must conclude it works, much to the delight of all."

He beamed at Elizabeth as she recovered from her astonishment and, to the great surprise of everyone in the room, began to laugh, her fingers pressed to her lips and her eyes twinkling merrily.

Colonel Fitzwilliam closed his eyes and pinched the bridge of his nose while Lady Matlock admonished, "Saye, stop being ridiculous at once."

"Why should I? I daresay, of us all at this moment, I am likely Miss Elizabeth's favourite Fitzwilliam. Can you deny it?"

He addressed the last to Elizabeth, and she replied with laughter still in her tone, "I have no wish to deny it, sir. This is indeed the most enjoyable five minutes I have had these three days together."

"You see?" Saye gave his relations a smug little smirk.

At this, Mr Gardiner permitted himself to laugh fully, and Mrs Gardiner smiled broadly into her handkerchief.

Darcy had to own an increasing level of regard for the Gardiners. Despite the fact that his error was turning their home inside out with a virtual parade of his relations cutting up their peace with incessant and ill-timed calls, they remained gracious and kind. It occurred to him that his strictures on the Bennet family might have been—nay, certainly were—bold in the light of his own family's actions. *Everyone has relations who cause them to blush.*

Once he had introduced his cousin, Darcy moved to the subject that must concern them all. "Mr and Mrs Gardiner, Miss Bennet, I wish to offer you my deepest apology for the actions of my uncle."

The smiles disappeared from the countenances of all as Mr Gardiner acknowledged Darcy. "Pray, do not think of it. We are exceedingly honoured that you, Lady Matlock, Lord Saye, and Colonel Fitzwilliam have travelled here to mollify our resentment. I assure you, none of us perceive ourselves as injured."

A brief silence fell upon the group. Darcy broke the quiet, addressing Mr Gardiner. "Sir, may I speak to your niece in private for a moment? Perhaps Miss Elizabeth and I might walk out together?" He glanced at Mr Gardiner and then at Elizabeth in the hopes one of them might give him some indication of how best to proceed.

Everyone immediately turned to look at Elizabeth, who remained with her eyes cast down as she rose in silent acquiescence. She walked to the door and, with no further word or look, left the room. Darcy made haste to follow her.

DESPITE HER MOMENTARY AMUSEMENT, DARCY COULD EASILY SEE that Elizabeth remained enraged at him. She held herself stiffly, careful not to look directly at him as they donned their hats and gloves and went out the Gardiners' door. As they reached the street, Elizabeth immediately clasped her hands behind her, dissuading Darcy from taking her arm—not that he would have dared to in any case.

Their silence continued as they strolled down one street and part way up another, reaching a small grassy area where children and their caretakers ran and cavorted. Elizabeth watched them, a faint smile coming to her face. Darcy wished he could make her smile as easily as that.

Elizabeth glanced up to see his gaze upon her before quickly looking away. He knew he needed to say something, and he wanted it to be something that amazed and delighted her, but he could think of nothing. Finally, without further consideration, he spoke of the most obvious, most ordinary of sentiments.

"Miss Elizabeth, I want to offer you my sincerest apologies. They are given belatedly, but nevertheless, I deeply regret my insults to you, particularly the first night I saw you at the assembly in Meryton."

Elizabeth replied, "Let us speak no more of that matter save for me to assure you—and anyone else who might be interested —that I have not refused your offer of marriage on the basis of a grudge. I am not as ungenerous as that.

"Furthermore, do not think me insensible of the deficiencies within my family. Yes, I am aware my father is of little conse- quence in this world. I realise I have no fortune and shall be in dire straits when he passes and Mr Collins inherits Longbourn. I understand that having relations in trade is not to my benefit, no matter how much I love and esteem them, and I recognise my mother and sisters are often ill behaved. These things I have known long before I met you, and believe me when I say, you do not know even the half of it."

Her bearing was calm and her voice assured, but he could see he had affected her. "I should not have spoken as I did, and in any case my relations are...I suppose I must admit that rank does not always indicate superior behaviour—it just means others are forced to tolerate it better."

"Thank you."

They continued to walk, enrobed in their self-imposed

silence. He had hoped that after offering her a sincere apology, there might be some thaw between them, but there was not. She was as she had been for many months, but now he understood it was not modesty but disgust that made her so.

"Miss Elizabeth." He stopped in the path and turned towards her. She halted her steps as well but looked ahead.

"I would also like to offer an apology for the gossip resulting from my indiscretion. However, as much as I am sorry for it, I cannot undo it, and I fear I have caused damage to your reputation such that I feel we must marry."

She turned suddenly and stared at him defiantly. "You seem to have a great deal of concern for reputation now when it suits *you*. Where was this concern last autumn when you thought nothing of the reputation of my sister?"

"Your sister?"

She began to walk at a quick pace and he, after the hesitation of a moment, followed her. Her words were rapid and short.

"Had not my own feelings decided against you, had they been indifferent, or had they even been favourable, do you think that any consideration would tempt me to accept the man who has been the means of ruining, perhaps forever, the happiness of a most beloved sister?"

He was so intent on her, he missed a step and stumbled briefly. "The happiness of a most beloved sister?"

"Yes, your actions in separating Mr Bingley from my sister. As no one could object to Jane, I can only believe it was my family and my family's situation that led to your disgust."

He was sunk in the space of a moment. What could he say but the truth? Would anything he said make any difference in the situation? "I did not think her heart was touched. She received my friend's attentions gladly, but I saw no sign of their return on her part."

"As if you knew her well enough to discern them!"

"You believe she held a tender regard for him?"

"I do not merely believe it. I know it as surely as I know I stand here. She loved him then, and she loves him now. It matters not to her whether he is a pauper or a prince. She believed him the most amiable man of her acquaintance and delighted in his company."

She stopped suddenly, turning to face him, and he wished she did not look so frightfully beautiful with her cheeks in high colour.

"I am not happy that my reputation has been injured and through no fault of my own. However, I am much more capable of withstanding infamy than is my dear Jane. There is no censure I can face, no sorrow I may bear, that will be in any manner like that which my dear sister has already borne by your hand. You have been the principal, if not the only, means of dividing them from each other, of exposing one to the censure of the world for caprice and instability, the other to its derision for disappointed hopes and mislaid affection. You have involved them both in misery of the acutest kind. Am I to congratulate you on your influence over your friend? Shall I admire you for your bold assurance in your discernment?"

Darcy stood motionless, unable to think of the least mollifying syllable. There was nothing he could do but await her final blow.

"Think of it, sir. Could you marry someone who had so affected Miss Darcy? Could you imagine forgiving, much less loving, such a person as that?"

She awaited his answer. Remaining as much master of himself as he could, he finally said, "No."

"Neither can I." After a brief pause, she turned and began again to walk.

Elizabeth could not know how deeply her words struck him, plunging him straightaway into the remembrance of his sister's troubles. Misery of the acutest kind. Yes, Darcy understood this very well, just as much as he understood the helpless bitter rage a person could have watching as a beloved sister endured it. How many nights had he lain awake knowing his sister wept in her bedchamber and wishing he were able to deliver to George Wickham the retribution he deserved?

And it was this that Elizabeth felt for *him*.

A lady who walked three miles to nurse her sister must have an extraordinary bond of sisterly affection. He could not doubt that Elizabeth suffered no less acutely than had Miss Bennet for Bingley's desertion.

They had nearly returned to the Gardiner's home when she stopped again, turning to ask him, "How did you do it?"

"Wha-what?"

"How did you persuade Mr Bingley to remain in London when, by all accounts, he intended to return? How did you persuade him to abandon the house he had let and the lady he— Well, I daresay, he must not have been as attached to her as it seemed. Is that true?"

"No, no. He…he was. He was attached to her."

"Then what?" Elizabeth raised her face to his, her beautiful eyes challenging him. She wanted the truth, and inasmuch as he hated telling her, he knew he must. Once he began, the words could not be stopped, tumbling from him unreservedly.

"He did not want to believe me. We argued—for quite some time, we argued. I told him of all the many ways a match with your sister would degrade him, but he cared nothing for any of my arguments. In any case, he had heard them all many times from his sisters.

"Then I told him"—he swallowed, hard—"I told him that I believed her indifferent. In that, I spoke the truth. I did not say so merely to achieve my purpose. I truly did think her indifferent to him. She seemed to me rather unaffected by his attentions."

His walking stick was in his hand, and he ground it into the road as he spoke. His mind moved to a cold winter day unlike the one in which he now resided. "He was humiliated when I told him that I thought your sister played him for a fool. His face went scarlet with anger and embarrassment, and he would not look at me even as he thanked me for my assistance in the matter. Since then, I have seen him but rarely. I suspect he does as he must to avoid me.

"I remember once in Kent, you mentioned that you believed Bingley would not return to Netherfield. I said he would likely give it up if a purchase offer were made, but the truth was that he had no idea of returning because of what I said. He believed he was the laughingstock of Meryton, thinking all the neighbourhood had witnessed him pining over Miss Bennet only to be misled. He felt stupid."

It filled him with painful remorse to remember that day, to recall the look in Bingley's eyes—so humiliated, so sad. To know he had undertaken his task in error made the recollection even worse. Such a trail of misery he had left in his wake! His friend, Miss Bennet, and most of all, his beloved Elizabeth. *You had good intentions*, his mind whispered, but it offered him no consolation whatsoever.

The look on Elizabeth's face could offer no solace. Her anger was gone, and in its place was abject misery. He ached to see her so, but he knew he had nothing to offer that would remedy any part of it.

Elizabeth heaved an enormous sigh, lowering her gaze to the

ground. "I cannot speak of this anymore today. I think it would be best to return to my uncle's house now."

TEA HAD JUST BEEN SERVED WHEN THEY ENTERED, AND AS MUCH AS Darcy wished to hasten away, he could not. He already had once departed too precipitously and now must offer every civility. He had developed a fond regard for the Gardiners, he realised, and felt ashamed of what his previous notions of them had been. *You are too sure of your opinions, too certain of yourself and your position, and too inclined to overlook those who are not of your circle.*

There were two places remaining to sit in the room: a settee upon which Saye lolled and a chair. Darcy made for the spot with Saye, but Saye shot him a grin and removed to the chair. So it was the settee for them both, and Darcy was mortified knowing that Elizabeth had to hate being in such close quarters with him.

She sat without looking at him. The eyes of the room were on them even as they were determinedly indifferent to their stares.

Lady Matlock had mercy on them and continued a conversation begun in their absence. "You have planned a tour of the northern counties?"

"Yes," said Mrs Gardiner too brightly with an uncertain glance at her niece. "Tewkesbury and the Peak District, as well as some time in Lambton. I spent my girlhood there and still have friends remaining."

"Tewkesbury? Is that not out of your way?"

"A bit," said Mr Gardiner. "But my dear wife has an aunt that will not stand for neglect." The last was said with a genial laugh. The conversation moved easily as Lady Matlock and her sons urged different sights upon the Gardiners. Darcy was relieved that no one seemed to expect either Elizabeth or him to contribute to the conversation. His mind could not rest, berating him unceasingly on behalf of his actions to Elizabeth, Miss Bennet, and Bingley. Along with those thoughts was some anxiety as well; the call soon must end and his time with Elizabeth along with it. Then what? Much as he had pained her, he would not leave with scandal surrounding her.

Minutes later, the time had drawn nigh to end the visit. He saw his aunt glancing at her sons and Mrs Gardiner glancing at her husband. The conversation was dwindling, all subjects common to strangers having been canvassed. Surreptitious looks were cast his way, but he remained mute, unable to offer anything that would prolong the visit.

Elizabeth did not look at him as he rose to bid her farewell, though she did accompany the guests to the front of the house while they awaited the two carriages. He had already motioned to Saye to ride with his brother and mother, intending to go back to his home alone.

"Miss Elizabeth," he began, but she interrupted him.

"We are not finished, I know," she said. "Perhaps some time next week—"

"Monday?"

He saw her sigh, small and concealed though she tried to make it. "Monday," she agreed.

He returned to his house above half an hour later, going directly to his bedchamber to refresh himself. He hoped to avoid Georgiana for now. What he most wished was to hide away in his study, seeing and talking to no one until he figured out how he could make a woman who despised him want to spend her life with him.

IN THE END, HIS COUSINS GAVE HIM LESS THAN AN HOUR OF

solitude and contemplation before once again intruding upon him.

"What a Friday-faced eyesore," Saye said, following his examination of Darcy's countenance. "Brings to mind the Fleet Street doves once their feathers have been ruffled a few times."

Fitzwilliam elbowed his brother, his countenance bespeaking true sympathy for his cousin. "So your walk with Miss Elizabeth was...?"

Darcy drained the glass in his hand. "A fresh source of misery."

"She must have quite a talent for implacable resentment," Saye opined. "To be sure, none of this was well done, but to bear such malice towards you when all you did was—"

"I did far more than you know," Darcy snapped. Briefly, he shared with Saye some of what he had told Fitzwilliam only the day prior of his insults in Hertfordshire and his slights against Elizabeth's family.

"But you apologised for all of that did you not?"

"I did," Darcy confirmed. "And then I learnt the reason she despises me most of all."

"Something more?"

"Something a great deal more. Suppose George Wickham came into this room, wanting to marry your sister. How would you greet that request?"

"Run him through," Saye replied.

"Beat him severely and then run him through," said Fitzwilliam.

"Beat him, run him through, then remove the blade and plunge it in again," Saye added eagerly.

"No!" Fitzwilliam cried. "Use the blade to remove the offending morsels from his breeches and then drag him behind my horse for a while, after which I run him through."

Seeing that the two brothers were just gaining enthusiasm for creating new and inventive methods of torture for George Wickham, Darcy held up his hand. "Exactly. Well, to Elizabeth, I am no better than George Wickham."

"You seduced her sister? I must say, Darcy, that is astonishing." Saye appeared surprised but interested. "How many are there? These Bennets are handsome girls, are they?"

Despite himself, Darcy chuckled. It was the way with Saye: you either found amusement in him or hated him, and as Darcy could not hate him, he had to laugh.

"I did not seduce her sister, but I did contribute to the disappointment of her sister's hopes of Bingley." He told his cousins that Bingley and Miss Bennet had been in love, and he, quite officiously and without scruple, had persuaded Bingley to abandon her. "With only the best intentions, of course," he added without conviction.

"It was her *sister*!" Fitzwilliam cried out in dismay. "Blast! That is entirely my fault."

Darcy waved away his cousin's apology. "No, I did it, and I must accept the consequences: Miss Elizabeth hates me. In any case, I believe she received still more grounds for her bad opinion of me through her friendship with George Wickham."

Hesitantly, Fitzwilliam said, "If she knew Wickham's true character and all that scoundrel has done—" He stopped as Darcy shook his head vehemently.

"I know nothing of the falsehoods he has spread about me in Hertfordshire. Perhaps he did nothing more than confirm the opinions she already held, opinions shaped by my poor behaviour. Yes, it might be useful to enlighten her to Wickham's character—I do wish she would avoid him—but it would not change her opinion of me."

The sound of whistling interrupted them. Saye had withdrawn some little trinket from his pocket and set to work on it. Darcy could not make out what it was, but his cousin's merry tooting was already a vexation.

"What if you went back to her uncle's house…" Fitzwilliam began.

"Her uncle is likely leaving orders with his manservant right now that no Fitzwilliam, Darcy, Matlock, or anyone related in any way to us should be admitted to his home ever again."

"She must marry you. There are rumours all over town about this already, and however obscure her family might be, you are a subject of great interest amongst the *ton*."

Darcy shook his head, trying to focus his attention on Fitzwilliam. Saye's whistling was like a fly buzzing in his ear. "I know, but if her family fails to force the issue, how am I to act?"

Fitzwilliam sat back, clearly pensive, and Darcy assumed that, like himself, he was searching for a solution to this impossible problem. Saye's irritating whistling could not help either of them, and the patience of both failed at the same time.

"Stop that infernal noise!"

"Saye!"

"What!" Saye shot them both a frown.

"What is it you are doing over there?" Fitzwilliam asked. "Embroidering?"

"Fixing a necklace for Lillian. Is it really such a trial to have a bit of music to accompany my work?"

Both men stared at him, simultaneously amused, bemused, and vexed. "What next?" Fitzwilliam asked. "Will you mend her stockings?"

"If I should happen to tear her stockings," Saye said with a little leer, "I would not be opposed to fixing them."

"You broke her necklace?" Darcy asked.

"I did indeed. Take this as a lesson to you both. If you

should anticipate some time spent with your hands near a lady's neck, do not wear lace on your cuffs. Catches on things dreadfully."

"Your hands were near her neck?" Fitzwilliam gave his brother a dubious look.

"Thereabouts."

"Could she not have her maid take care of it for her?" asked Darcy.

Saye shrugged. "Ladies like it when you fix things for them, and in any case, that horrid maid of hers reports directly to her mother about every little thing. Any stray wrinkle on her gown leads to the wildest accusations imaginable."

He rose, taking the necklace to the window to examine his handiwork. "If you ask me, these mothers spend far too much time worrying over reputation when they should be concerned for their daughter's happiness."

With a smirk, he added, "And I assure you, I do leave my Lillian very, very happy."

"I am sure you do," remarked his brother drolly. "Dare we say that more happiness will ensue when you have returned with the jewellery repaired?"

"Such felicity as cannot be described in mere words," Saye said with a chuckle. "And that happiness can only lead to continued happiness." He tugged on his cuffs, which were, as usual, ornately trimmed.

The necklace fixed and his interest in Darcy's troubles exhausted, Saye decided he must depart. With not a dozen words more, he bid them farewell and was off.

There was more conversation about the futile nature of Darcy's love affair, but no good came of it. Fitzwilliam prevailed on Darcy to join him in some fencing or a ride or whatever he thought might be an agreeable means to pass the rest of the day, but Darcy declined, citing obligations to his estate. Fitzwilliam was not fooled but eventually acquiesced.

Georgiana had gone into an adjacent room to play the pianoforte while the gentlemen were talking, and after his cousins departed, Darcy sat for a moment in his study and listened. She had begun a new piece, evidently a complex one, and she struggled through it with no appreciable progress for the better part of an hour. Darcy heard her bumble her way through some passage, stopping and starting no less than five times before she gave up.

He winced in anticipation of what would come, what was usual based on the past months. There would be tears of frustration, possibly self-recrimination. Definitely stomping and a probable door slam. He awaited it with bated breath.

Instead, he heard a little giggle that became full-blown laughter. Then he heard her speaking—to herself no doubt—and although he could not make out the words, he apprehended that the tone was unmistakably teasing. Then she began again. And though it was far from perfect, she made it through, beginning a second pass almost immediately. He had not the least doubt she would soon learn it creditably.

Yes, he well understood how much the happiness of a beloved sister would bring fondness to a person's heart.

The idea struck him like a bolt of lightning, and he was motionless for a moment as a plan, fully formed, presented itself to mind. It was so simple that he nearly laughed for not having thought of it earlier. Saye's words echoed in his mind: *ladies like it when you fix things for them.*

ELIZABETH MANAGED TO FORESTALL ANY QUESTIONS FROM HER family regarding her conversation with Darcy by slipping away during the confusion of farewells. It could not last long, however, and just before dinner, there came a knock on the door to the bedchamber that Elizabeth and Jane shared while staying with their aunt. Elizabeth was alone and bade whomever it was to enter.

It was Jane. "I do not expect you to knock to enter our chamber."

Jane smiled as she sat on the bed, evidently anticipating a sisterly chat. "So, are you…?"

"Am I what?"

"Oh, Lizzy, do not tease—not about this. Are you engaged to Mr Darcy?"

"No," Elizabeth replied blithely. She moved to the dressing table and began unpinning her hair. "At least to my knowledge, I am not. Then again, I have proven rather insensible of the matter."

"I suppose I should be grateful that you at least appear to be in a good humour." Jane looked at Elizabeth expectantly.

Elizabeth said nothing while taking up her brush and

making rapid strokes through her hair. "I am not in a good humour at all."

Jane allowed silence for a bit under five minutes until her patience deserted her. "You walked out for some time with him."

"Not that I wished to. I was compelled."

"Lizzy…" Jane pulled a face that could only mean Elizabeth was due some admonishment. "For my life, I shall never comprehend why you insist on being so spiteful to Mr Darcy. He loves you! Does that not—"

Elizabeth set the brush down with a smart rap. "Oh, he does not love me. I am as certain of that as anything I have ever been!"

"How can you say so? Why else would he spend so much time coming to our uncle's house when—"

"Because he wishes to have his way in the matter!" Elizabeth cried. "For whatever cause, he has decided he must have me, and he does not like to be gainsaid. It is no more than that. What will the *ton* think when they learn a lady of no consequence has declined his offer?"

"You are ungenerous, Lizzy," Jane scolded.

"And you, my dear, are far *too* generous. After what he has done to you—" Elizabeth stopped abruptly, pressing her lips shut. She had not yet fully considered whether she would tell Jane what she knew and certainly did not intend to blurt it out rudely.

It was too late. Jane's brow wrinkled with innocent perplexity. "What has Mr Darcy done to me?"

Elizabeth picked the brush up once more and used it to play with the hair at her temples, avoiding Jane's eyes in the mirror.

"Lizzy? I must know, and you must tell me."

This gained Jane another short silence.

"Please? Do not make me go mad wondering."

Elizabeth sighed and laid down her brush. "Mr Bingley's return to Netherfield in the autumn—rather, his failure to return —was not his fault but rather due to the interference of his friend."

"We do not know—"

"As a matter of fact, I do know. You were not with us earlier in the drawing room when Colonel Fitzwilliam informed us of the truth of that matter."

Jane blanched and dropped her eyes quickly but not quickly enough for Elizabeth to see her pain. "Colonel Fitzwilliam knew?"

"He knew it was Mr Bingley but not who the lady was," Elizabeth said, rising from the table and going to her sister. The remembrance of what the colonel said shot a quick pulse of anger through her. She did her best to remain calm and speak with dignity. "He said only that Mr Darcy congratulated himself on separating Mr Bingley from a most imprudent attachment."

Jane's face smoothed into lines of demure complaisance as was her custom when distressed. "Oh."

Elizabeth reached out, taking Jane's hands. "I do not wish to pain you, but I do wish you might know the truth of these things. Mr Bingley did not leave of his own accord, and it is likely he loves you still."

"I am afraid you are sorely mistaken in that belief."

"Jane, he does, he does love you. Mr Darcy had an excessive amount of influence over him and used it for ill. One cannot deny Mr Darcy enjoys arranging things to suit himself, and this is but another example."

"Oh, Lizzy." Jane shook off Elizabeth's hands and raised one of hers to cover her face. "Now I must ask you to look at the truth of the matter."

"I do!"

"Lizzy, I *am* an imprudent attachment. I am! You cannot deny it. Beauty is not enough. Heaven only knows, there are beautiful ladies in abundance in London."

"But none that can match you in your sweet—"

"It does not signify. The truth of the matter is that only Mr Bingley can be blamed for leaving. I do not hold Mr Darcy to account for Mr Bingley's actions and neither should you."

Elizabeth stared at her, quite surprised. "But Mr Bingley never would have—"

Jane rose, giving an angry little flick of her wrist in Elizabeth's direction. "We do not know what Mr Bingley might or might not have done. All we know is what he did do, which was to leave me for above five months with nary a look back. It is not Mr Darcy's fault, it is his, and you must stop blaming Mr Darcy for it."

"Mr Darcy has admitted himself—"

"What did he do? Did he tie Mr Bingley down? Secure him in a dungeon? No." Jane shook her head. "I do not say that Mr Darcy did not render his opinion and exert whatever influence he has, but it cannot be denied that Mr Bingley acted on his own choice."

Firmly but gently, Elizabeth said, "Mr Darcy told me they argued quite vehemently on the subject. Not until he told Mr Bingley that he thought you were indifferent was he able to persuade him to remain in town."

At this, Jane fell silent, sinking back onto the bed.

"From Mr Darcy's account, Mr Bingley was rather humiliated by thinking himself the fool, and it is this more than anything that has kept him from Netherfield. So you see, once he realises it has all been a misunderstanding, there will be no impediment. You will want only for a bit of time together, and all will be made new again."

Jane's eyes had become rather glossy, but she maintained her equanimity. "I suppose we shall never know," she said softly. "In any case, I think it truly does not matter. He will be forgotten. In this, I am determined."

Elizabeth felt despair, having somehow forgotten that her rejection of Darcy could reduce the likelihood of Mr Bingley ever seeing her sister again. "He will return to Netherfield, I am sure," she said, in a voice that sounded anything but.

"Maybe," Jane said, quite dispirited.

Elizabeth watched her sister for a moment, feeling a weight of guilt grow within her. "Jane…forgive me. I know my rejection of Mr Darcy might mean that—"

"Oh, Lizzy, no!" Jane laughed weakly. "No, no. You must never think that I hold you responsible in any way, no matter how small. Do you think I would wish you married to a man you profess to despise simply for my purposes? I assure you, I do not."

Elizabeth thanked Jane for her assurance although she wished she could wholly believe it was true. If there was one who could truly keep her unaccountable in the matter, it was her sister, yet Elizabeth could not absolve herself quite so easily as she watched the tiny grain of hope remaining in Jane's eyes die a mercilessly slow death.

IT WAS NOT UNCOMMON, WHEN IN TOWN, FOR BINGLEY TO JOIN Darcy for a family dinner on Sunday, and Darcy sent him a note on Saturday bidding him do so. *Sunday. A day of mercy, perhaps? It will suit, I think.*

Bingley did not reply on Saturday, so Darcy sent another

note on Sunday morning to the rooms Bingley kept, including a short sentence to tell him there was a particular matter on which they must speak. If naught else, he hoped curiosity as well as the promise of the excellent fare by Darcy's cook might compel his friend to join him.

Bingley at last replied, saying he would be pleased to attend. He joined Darcy and his sister at the appropriate hour, and within a short time, Darcy wished he had not.

The smell of spirits hung about Bingley in a cloud, and even though he attempted to look cheerful, it was not difficult to discern his misery. Darcy noticed many of the dishes made him swallow hard and look away.

Darcy said nothing of it until the meal was complete and Georgiana had left them. "Bingley, old man, you look like you might rather be home in your bed."

"That I might," Bingley agreed, taking a sip of the hot coffee in front of him. "Ah, but I fear I am getting too old to truly enjoy the amusements of town."

"I daresay, it depends on the nature of the things that amuse you."

Bingley laughed ruefully and placed his hands over his eyes. "That, I cannot deny. You should have joined me though! I declare I have never seen prettier girls or more amiable people than I did last night!"

"Prettier girls?" Darcy asked, feeling a mild twinge of alarm. "Surely none as lovely as Miss Bennet?"

"Miss Bennet..." Bingley heaved one of his characteristic lovelorn sighs, leaning back in his chair to look at the ceiling of the dining room. After a moment, he straightened. "Never mind that. I must say, I find it a bit tiresome here in town with all the strictures one must consider. Permit me to tell you of the party I attended last night. Such fun! There is nothing I find more agreeable than a pleasant evening spent with no regard to status or rank or fortune—just an interesting group of people who wish to enjoy a pleasant evening! Everyone free to be *who* they are instead of *what* they are. Can there be anything finer?"

"Ah," Darcy was uncertain of Bingley's meaning. "No, I suppose not. It is rather refreshing when pretensions are left behind."

"Yes." Bingley nodded vigorously. "Yes, quite right. No pretensions, just good humour, no artifice, and no need whatsoever to stand on ceremony."

"Yes," said Darcy unenthusiastically. "Now, if I may, I must confess something to you."

"I would like it if Caroline's suitor proved faithful too. Once she is settled, I shall have much more liberty to form friendships where I want without consideration for her marriage."

"Miss Bingley has a suitor?" Darcy found himself distracted from his purpose quite against his will, but he could not avoid asking about this unexpected news.

"She does. Nothing is settled yet, but his attentions have been quite marked. If he does not offer for her, I think I am obliged to demand something of him for the cause of her reputation."

"Her marriage would grant you the freedom to marry where you would like without her concern for it."

"Yes." Bingley toyed with his coffee cup.

Darcy took a deep breath. "And that is why I wished to speak to you today. I must tell you something of great import as well as offer my sincerest apologies."

"Apologies for what?"

Darcy now wished to play with *his* coffee cup, but he forced himself to meet his friend's eyes. "When we departed Hertfordshire last autumn, I shall own I was fully persuaded that Miss Bennet was indifferent to you."

"Yes," Bingley said with a sound between a sigh and a groan. "Yes, I am aware of your opinion."

"However, in my recent conversations with Miss Elizabeth Bennet, she has made me—"

"What a surprise that was! You to marry, and into a family that you held in such little regard! Disdained them even!"

Darcy had taken another sip of his coffee, and he sputtered, gasping inelegantly at the last. When he recovered, he protested, "Disdain? That is ungenerous. If nothing else, they are Elizabeth's family, and my love for her must occasion due respect for them."

"You are in love with her? With Miss Elizabeth?" Bingley looked at him intently.

"Why does that shock you?"

"I have never perceived you as a lover." Bingley shrugged carelessly.

Drily, Darcy said, "As one gentleman to another, I would have been alarmed if you had."

"And to Miss Elizabeth, no less! I should not have said you even liked her, much less loved her."

Darcy frowned. "Yes, I am well aware of the failings in my behaviour, but that is not the point of this conversation. The point is that Miss Elizabeth has made me aware of her sister's feelings towards you, and the fact is, Miss Bennet was and remains much attached to you."

"That may be as Miss Elizabeth sees it. For myself, however, I am not quite certain."

Darcy felt the first stirrings of true alarm. Had Bingley fallen out of love with Miss Bennet? "I should think Miss Elizabeth would know the mind of her dearest sister and intimate friend. She spoke with exceeding surety."

Bingley shook his head. "She was likely trying to please you."

Darcy laughed more loudly and heartily than he intended. "No, I do not believe that is the case."

"Regardless, it was just a misunderstanding, no more. I cannot fault you for that."

And now for the next confession, Darcy thought grimly. "There is a bit more to it." He recounted to Bingley the story of Miss Bennet's winter in London and the attempts made by both himself and Bingley's sisters to conceal it from him. When all was done, he and his friend fell silent for a few painful minutes.

"I was wondering when someone would tell me this," Bingley replied at last.

"You knew?"

Bingley nodded once, his eyes narrowed and fixed on his friend. "I was coming up the street and saw her as she was leaving. I am glad you are telling me now"—Bingley pushed back from the table, rising with his refilled coffee cup. He walked slowly to the window, peering out as he murmured almost inaudibly—"above three months later."

"Bingley, it was not well done at all."

"I should not have believed it of you, Darcy. Outright deception—quite beneath you. As conniving as Caroline. This is a shade in your character I could not have imagined."

Darcy swallowed and began to speak but Bingley interrupted him, dismissing further discussion of the subject. "So, when is your happy day?"

"My wha—? Oh yes, you mean my wedding."

Bingley laughed, turning and giving him a pointed look. "Have you forgotten about it already?"

Darcy felt himself redden. "No, it is not that." He gave Bingley a succinct version of what had transpired in recent days. As few details as possible were given. Bingley was told only that Elizabeth had a number of reasons to be upset with Darcy, including the matter with Miss Bennet.

"Took you to task for it, did she?"

"Yes, she did," Darcy agreed. "And that is I why I thought—"

"That is why you asked me here? Because Miss Elizabeth made you?"

"Of course not."

"No?" Bingley took a measured sip from his cup. "It *seems* to be the case."

"I learnt of my error today, and I came to tell you straight-away." Darcy felt himself growing a bit irritated with Bingley; he was behaving so oddly.

Bingley stared at him, an undeniable look of challenge on his countenance. "You first told me that she did not love me, and I should stay away. I believed you, and now, here I am."

"I had your best interests—"

"Of course, you did. But I listened to you the first time, and you were wrong. How do I know you are not wrong this time too? What if Miss Elizabeth is the one who is wrong? Who am I to believe, knowing that those whom I have trusted before were unworthy of my faith?"

"You need not believe me outright," Darcy replied. "Come with me to call on her, and see for yourself."

Bingley wandered away from the window, making a circle of the room, and returning to sink into the seat he had previously vacated. "When will you call again?"

"Tomorrow."

Bingley nodded. "Very well then."

SUNDAY WAS A SLEEPY DAY AS SUNDAYS GENERALLY ARE, BUT Elizabeth was beleaguered with a fitful fever, anxious to avoid any mention of Mr Darcy at one moment and eager to have the business settled in the next. Whenever her eyes fell upon Jane, she was momentarily at peace; for Jane's sake, she would do this. Alas, the relief was always temporary.

He called early on Monday, as she believed he might. She entered the drawing room where he awaited her. By way of greeting, she said, "Mr Darcy, how shocking to find you alone, but I suppose I have already become acquainted with your entire family. Are there any cousins on the Darcy side due to come plague me?"

He neatly skirted her bile by handing her a posy and inviting her to sit. She settled herself gingerly in the seat opposite him. "I do hope none of my relations on any side will plague you ever again."

She lowered her nose to the flowers. They were gardenias, and she had always loved the scent.

"I remembered that you once said gardenias were a favourite."

Elizabeth looked up in surprise. "I did?"

He nodded. "Not to me but to Lady Catherine. You said you loved them, but your mother did not like them in her gardens because they died too soon."

Although she had no recollection of such a conversation, it was true, and she gave him credit for remembering something so trivial about her.

"I believe it must be the soil," he continued.

"The soil?"

"Yes, um…I recently had some planted at Pemberley, and my

gardener informed me that gardenias like things just so. The soil, that is, and…and the rain. It has to be just a certain way, or they will not flower."

"They like to have things their way, do they? They should fit right in at Pemberley, then."

He paused a moment but did not reply. She winced a little, hiding it behind another smell of the gardenias, then resolved to be less bitter. There was nothing to gain in an engagement filled with sarcastic asides and hidden insults. She needed his help to enact her plan and must repay him, at the least, with kindness.

"In any case," he said, clearing his throat, "the gardener says they are doing well. Already quite fragrant."

She forced herself to smile. "How…how nice. Lovely. I am sure they are lovely."

There was a short, pained silence. Although she knew she must, Elizabeth was loath to utter the words that would signal her surrender. With a deep breath, she forced out the speech she had rehearsed in her mind during the night.

"Further reflection has persuaded me to do what must be done. Our past notwithstanding, it is in my best interest, as well as that of my family, to marry you. Therefore I…I accept your offer of marriage." She could not look at him, could not bear to see with what delighted triumph he comprehended his victory.

"Thank you."

After another short silence, she added, "My father indicated that you had a wish to marry soon, but I would request that we—"

"No."

"No? No, you do not want to marry quickly? Or have you decided against the scheme altogether?"

He smiled then, broadly and with true felicity, and she was surprised at the difference in his appearance. "Yes, I wish to marry you, but no, I cannot think it prudent to rush someone to the altar who can scarcely bear to look at me."

His words had the effect of making her drop her eyes immediately. "That...that is not true."

"Look at me, then."

Slowly she forced herself to raise her eyes, first staring at his cravat pin, then his chin, and finally meeting his eyes. It was a struggle not to immediately look away.

"I understand that Mr and Mrs Gardiner intend to travel to Derbyshire in a few weeks and you with them."

"Yes, well, no one had the least idea of me...um, of us... well, you know. So yes, it was planned that I should go with them."

"So perhaps you—all of you—will consent to being my guests at Pemberley. Pemberley would be a fine place for your aunt and uncle to break their journey. Lambton is not five miles away. They might see all the sights they wished, visit all Mrs Gardiner's friends, and enjoy greater comfort than they would at an inn."

Elizabeth formed her lips into a firm line, pressing her hands together tightly. The notion of seeing Pemberley was a temptation. A place that had earned much generous praise from all who had seen it could only entice her. But surely Mr Darcy did not mean to invite her aunt and uncle? If he did, then he was far more generous than she had imagined.

"And do you suppose," Elizabeth asked carefully, "that merely seeing your beautiful grounds at Pemberley will cause me to change my opinion of you? Because I must tell you, it will not. I know already how rich and how grand you are."

"My hope is that spending time together will change your opinion of me. And there is more at Pemberley that I think will interest you than merely the grounds."

"Yes," said Elizabeth lightly. "The library. I confess I am quite mad to see all the books."

He chuckled. "Yes, there is that. Also, I shall have my friend join us."

"Your friend?"

"It has been Mr Bingley's habit of late to spend July and August with me at Pemberley. So if Miss Bennet were to join you and the Gardiners on the journey, I daresay, she and Mr Bingley might reunite at Pemberley. With some time, I do believe the wrongs of the past might be set aright, and in the absence of impediments, their natural fondness would proceed as it should."

"And in return, you will have my hand in marriage."

"If you would like it."

She nearly fell from her chair. "If I would like it? Sir, have you forgot I am the talk of London?"

He rose and went to her, kneeling beside her chair. He took her hands, and she allowed it, too surprised to protest. "Elizabeth, I was completely insensible of all that I had done to hurt you." He looked at her with such beseeching earnestness that she had to look away. "It was rather stupid of me—in retrospect, I find my conduct unforgivable—but now that I know, I wish to make amends. Once we become acquainted under better terms, I really do believe…"

He stopped speaking and looked to the side for a moment. The morning sunlight coming through the windows shone on his noble mien, and she was forced to acknowledge that he truly was a handsome man. She watched him swallow.

"By the end of the time at Pemberley, if you still do not wish to marry me, we shall find a way to break the engagement. I cannot promise that your reputation will not suffer, but somehow, some way, I shall manage it such as to minimise the damage."

It struck her, this mark of generosity, in a way that quite astonished her. He spoke with such gentleness; it was quite at odds with her idea of him. "Your reputation would suffer too," she said, finding she did not quite mind the feel of her hands in his.

"A man's reputation is far sturdier than a lady's. In any case, just know that I shall protect you insofar as I am able. You have my word."

He squeezed her hands lightly then and stood. She had no idea what to say. Far from triumphing in his victory, he seemed caring and concerned for her well-being. "But for now we are engaged."

The look of delight that spread across his face shocked her. She looked away quickly. It was disconcerting, to say the least, to see this boyish, happy Mr Darcy.

"Yes," he said, sounding absurdly joyful. "Yes, for now, we are engaged."

9

IT WAS NEARLY THREE O'CLOCK WHEN BINGLEY AWOKE, HIS HEAD pounding and his mouth tasting of something akin to a burnt horse's mane. His man had left some powders for him, but the mere contemplation of actually swallowing something was too much to bear.

Too much diversion, he thought blearily as he pulled himself from his bed. For a moment after he rose, the room swam, and he considered diving back into the bedclothes at once. However, nature called, and by the time he had heeded to necessity, he decided he might as well go on with the day.

Something tugged at his mind, a recollection of something he needed to do—a letter that needed writing perhaps? He rubbed his temples while he thought, unable to retrieve the slender black thread of memory from the recesses of his aching mind.

A bath and a shave helped a little, though dressing was a trial. Again, he considered the pleasures of his bedchamber— that is, the pleasures of indolence within. He was quite sated of any more recreational diversions for the present. Alas, he could do nothing but long for the night time as his stomach would not be gainsaid. He must eat, and if he must eat, he required some company to do it. He would go to his club.

He espied Darcy immediately when he entered, sitting at a table with his cousin Saye. *Blast!* It came to him at once. Today was the day he was meant to call on the Miss Bennets with Darcy at their uncle's home in Gracechurch Street. This was not good. Darcy was sure to be displeased with him for his absence.

He gave them both a smile that was more like a wince and moved towards them with as much haste as his aching limbs would permit.

"Well," Viscount Saye drawled when he arrived and seated himself. "Seems someone was punched in the neck by Old Tom."

"I believe so," Bingley agreed wearily. "The details escape me at present."

The viscount laughed, but Darcy was not amused, piercing Bingley with an extraordinarily haughty look. There was little doubt that he was in the mood to ring a peal over his friend. Bingley sighed. If there was something he was decidedly *not* in a humour to endure, it was one of Darcy's lectures about gentlemanly honour and responsibility and who knew what else. Blast, but he was tired of it.

Darcy waited. Drinks and directions for a meal were given to the footmen, and after that, Viscount Saye excused himself to speak to someone else. Darcy and Bingley were left alone at the table just as their soup arrived.

Taking a measured and mannered sip, Darcy said calmly, "I expected you this morning."

"You did?" Bingley pretended to think about it. "The call to Miss Bennet and Miss Elizabeth? Was that today?"

"You know very well it was."

"I had not thought we were fixed on a plan."

Darcy scowled in response. Bingley knew not whether it was the effect of the previous night or merely an inexplicable surge of obstinacy, but nevertheless, it could not be denied. He was suddenly heartily sick of being treated as Darcy's errant younger brother. He could not enjoy being called to task in this officious manner. He did not like being treated as less than a friend.

"Oh yes, I had forgotten. Having tied yourself to Miss Elizabeth's apron strings, you wish to please her. Now I am allowed to court her sister because the great Fitzwilliam Darcy has granted it may be so."

The servant arrived to clear their soup and place some meats before them. Both gentlemen fell silent, Darcy eyeing Bingley rather warily as they were served. When the men were again alone, Darcy spoke.

"As I have said before, I do apprehend that my previous actions in this matter were inappropriately officious. Forgive me if I seem to urge you forward precipitously. I only wish to make amends for the months lost to you."

Bingley was remorseful. After all, Darcy had his best interests at heart. So he was a bit meddlesome and too certain of himself; was it a crime? He opened his mouth to offer an apology only to be stopped by the appearance of yet another of his mounting problems.

Mr Alfred Staley was a minor landholder in Lancashire, near Sheffield. Bingley knew him well, their fathers having been acquainted since boyhood. At one time, they had been intimates, but things had grown strained between them.

"Bingley," said Staley, coming near their table.

Bingley rose with exhausted reluctance. He gave his former friend a wan smile. "Staley. I did not know you were in town."

"I left my card for you at the Albany no less than thrice. Perhaps if you are not engaged now…"

"Now?" Bingley forced an easy chuckle. "Well, certainly—

Oh! But there is Sir Albert!" Staley and Darcy looked to where Sir Albert had entered. Bingley waved him over with rather frantic enthusiasm. Sir Albert grinned and made his way across the room.

Darcy, Bingley noticed, immediately looked haughtier as Sir Albert arrived, and he rose and bowed to the man to the slightest degree required by civility. *Now, what? Is Sir Albert not suitable to be my friend?*

He knew it would be best to be away for now. He was in no mood to tolerate Darcy this day, and Staley was nearly insupportable with his demands. Bingley was quite ready to be done with the pair of them.

"Are you taking your leave?" he asked Sir Albert. "I was just about to myself."

Sir Albert was confused for the merest fraction of a second until he caught on to the scheme. Smoothly, he said, "I am here only to meet you my friend and accompany you to—"

"To...to...that place. Where they are having that...that thing."

"Right," agreed Sir Albert. "We must go now; else we shall surely be late."

"Bingley, a minute if you please," Darcy interjected.

"Bingley," said Staley. "I must speak to you. I shall come to your rooms tomorrow at this time. Be there."

"I shall be there," said Bingley, edging away from the table, Sir Albert with him. "And Darcy, I do beg your pardon for being unable to finish our discussion now. Having a bit of trouble with my plans today it seems."

Darcy was having none of it. "I had hoped we could fix our plans for Derbyshire this summer."

"Of course," said Bingley as he moved farther away from the table. Looking around the room, he saw Saye was still a distance away, and he gave him a quick wave. "Depend upon it."

With a grin of relief in Sir Albert's direction, he happily made an escape. Unpleasantness and confrontation were not for him.

DARCY COULD ONLY FROWN, WATCHING HIS FRIEND DEPART WITH such a character. Returning seconds later, Saye shook his head with dubious amusement.

"What has Bingley gotten himself into now?"

"I wish I knew."

Sir Albert Williams-Broad was known to them both. Of an age with Saye, he was handsome with light blond hair and piercing blue eyes that frequently held a certain devilment in them. He was from a well-connected family with a good fortune, but his claims to reputation were uncertain. For whatever vices and follies were common to men of their age and station, Sir Albert was rumoured to indulge in them to excess. It was said that, for every drink other men took, he took three, and if he visited a brothel, he was likely to engage four women instead of one.

According to various reports, his parties were wild orgies of indulgence in any vice to which a person held a proclivity. There was indulgence in drink as well as in potions from the Indies— or so it was said—that would make a man see visions. Of the female and male forms, there was great variety; Sir Albert did not wish to see any guest go away until their darkest wishes and lusts were wholly sated.

"I should hope Bingley has better sense than to associate himself with such goings-on as that," Darcy said.

"Bingley is young," Saye opined. "Young, wealthy, and easily persuaded. 'Tis a dangerous combination."

ALTHOUGH BINGLEY DID HIS BEST TO EVADE HIM, HE WAS FORCED TO receive his friend Staley at his place of residence only a week after seeing him at his club. He received word the man had called and, as he had done in the days prior, returned word that he was not presently receiving. Staley then returned word that he would wait. Bingley said it would be some time. Staley said he awaited Bingley at his leisure. With a sigh, Bingley went to meet him.

Staley stood, holding himself stiffly as Bingley entered. Bingley moved to bow in polite greeting, but Staley stepped forward, embracing him. Bingley smiled and embraced him in return. He supposed Staley expected the privilege and familiarity of kin.

The gentlemen sat. "Millicent sends her regards," said Staley.

"How is she?"

"Very well. Her studies are advancing, and her governess says she is unequalled in her ability to draw landscapes."

"That is welcome news."

There was an uncomfortable pause, though Bingley suspected it was only uncomfortable to him. Staley appeared ready and able to sit quietly for a decade if need be.

The two men sat in silence, staring at each other until Staley said, "You must understand, Bingley, when I came upon you both, it was quite alarming—"

"She is a child," Bingley replied heatedly. "A child who wished to show me her drawings in the nursery."

"You and I both know very well that she neither looks nor acts like a child." Staley frowned at him. "From what I saw, you were not looking at her with the interest of an elder."

"I did nothing—"

"But there is talk," Staley replied. "Pray, let us keep this amiable for the sake of our fathers' friendship."

Bingley had loved his father and knew it was his dearest wish for his son to be a gentleman both in title and in action; thus, Staley's charge silenced him. He certainly did not think himself obligated to Miss Staley, but evidently Staley felt differently.

Staley, with a smile on his lips that seemed a bit triumphant, summoned a manservant and asked for his hat to be brought. The servant did not tarry. Staley rose, donning his gloves.

"Some men do better for themselves if they settle early." Bingley met his gaze squarely. He thought Staley had rather unpleasant eyes—a watery shade of blue that suggested a sort of slyness. "Other men do best to have had their amusements before the responsibilities of home and family."

Staley studied him. "Some men are far too given to their amusements."

They stared at each other, neither willing to concede the point. Finally, Bingley said, "Say there! Why do you not come to a party with me tonight? There is a splendid group of fellows whom I have—"

"No." Staley was reproving. "No, Bingley, your parties do not interest me. I have heard—" He stopped.

Bingley watched him with some confusion. "What have you heard? I assure you, there is nothing amiss in my friends or their parties."

Staley rolled his eyes and snorted, wholly disdainful of his friend. "Someone needs to take you in hand," he said witheringly.

10 June 1812, London

DARCY WAS MADE INCREASINGLY UNEASY DURING HIS WEEKS IN London by the fact that he remained unsuccessful in his endeavours to pin Bingley to a time to go to Pemberley. The underlying contentiousness that pervaded their recent interactions seemed to have dissipated if only because Darcy rarely saw his friend. Bingley was excessively occupied by his new circle, but when the two gentlemen did meet, he was as amiable as ever.

Finally, in early June, they were together at the dinner and theatre party of Lady Barton, and Darcy contrived to sit with Bingley. His hope was that the arrangements for the visit to Derbyshire would be settled—firmly settled—this very night.

"You are not an easy man with whom to gain an audience these days," he remarked as they met in the drawing room after dinner. The room was rather warm, and they sought fresh air by the windows.

"I had always imagined the Season would be less fatiguing once Caroline was settled," admitted Bingley.

"So your sister has accepted her suitor's offer?"

"She has. Marston of Elmar House in Herefordshire."

Darcy thought about that for a moment, trying to recollect what he knew of the man. A good match, he supposed; the family was old with a respectable fortune. Mr Marston was older than himself, perhaps thirty-five or so, but handsome and fashionable. He was not one of the pinks, but Darcy suspected he might like to think himself one. A gossip, Darcy recalled, sometimes a bit mean but, on the whole, easy enough to ignore. In short, he was a male version of Mrs Hurst.

"And she is pleased with the match?"

"He has pursued her for some time. I see a great similarity in their minds. In truth, all that was wanted for his success was that she should finally relinquish her hopes of being Mrs Darcy."

Darcy winced without meaning to, hastily attempting to conceal his distaste. Bingley saw him and laughed, clapping him on the shoulder. "Of course, the rest of us knew long ago that she was without hope in that quarter! It was only Caroline who needed to comprehend it. Even her wishes could not outlast the reports of your affections for Miss Elizabeth."

Darcy felt a bit silly for a moment, knowing he sometimes looked rather besotted when Elizabeth was mentioned, so he turned his face to the window and pretended something outside had caught his interest. Thus, he was unprepared when Bingley changed the subject.

"Do you suppose marriage will be diverting?"

"Diverting?" Darcy turned back to look at his friend.

"Fun," Bingley said by way of clarification. He said no more, seeming to search Darcy's eyes for the answer to something that was evidently puzzling him. Darcy hardly knew what to say, uncertain of Bingley's intention.

Finally, he said, "I enjoy Miss Elizabeth's society a great deal, so yes, I do anticipate a great deal of…of fun."

Bingley sighed noisily and leaned against the wall. "It is quite different, is it not? You see people marry and then they just disappear! It is like they never knew town at all! Or else they come in for a short while, attend the theatre, a few parties…a different life, indeed."

With a wistful smile, he murmured, "Fay ce que tu voudras."

"Do what thou will?" Darcy asked, puzzled and growing more so by the second. There was something weighing on Bingley's mind, and Darcy had no idea what it was but suspected it did not bode well for Miss Bennet.

Bingley chuckled ruefully. "Yes, do what thou wilt. A lofty goal to live in such a way, so freely, but so difficult for most of us to attain."

"No one can always do as they want, Bingley, least of all, those of us who are adults with the claims of duty and responsibility upon them." Darcy spoke with clear warning in his tone.

"So say you," Bingley teased. "You, who have just gone against all expectations of your family and friends to marry a lady such as could barely draw your notice when we last were in Hertfordshire."

I am tired of hearing this. "Yes, I suppose you could say I shall marry in accordance with my own wishes, but my estate will not suffer, nor will my family. Expectation is one thing, but duty is quite another."

"Yes," said Bingley with a beaming smile. "Precisely."

Darcy was discomfited, feeling he had inadvertently supported whatever idea was rattling about in Bingley's head.

Leaning close to his friend, Darcy said, "I do not understand what you are trying to tell me, but if you no longer wish to marry or even pay court to Miss Bennet, I need to know."

"I just want to enjoy life," said Bingley earnestly and expansively. "A life that is rich in laughter, friendship, and love, and the freedom to explore and experience new things. No restrictions, no oppression. Do you apprehend me?"

"Yes," said Darcy patiently. "But you can do all of that and more as a married man just as well as a bachelor."

Bingley merely looked at him.

"I am sure Miss Bennet will be eager to partake of the amusements of town," Darcy said. "She has not been here much. Does she like theatre?"

Bingley looked oddly disappointed for a moment before answering slowly, "I cannot say."

"What of music?"

"Hmm." Bingley considered a moment. "Yes, I believe she must."

"There are always so many parties. Does she enjoy them?"

Bingley pursed his mouth. "In truth, I think she finds parties rather tedious. She told me she has always preferred intimate evenings with a few close friends as she finds strangers rather intimidating." He laughed awkwardly. "She reminds me much of you in that way."

"They say opposites do attract," Darcy answered immediately. "I daresay, she will awaken in you a more sober side, and in her, you may induce greater liveliness and more desire to be in town, enjoying the amusements of your youth."

"Unless she should fall with child," Bingley said, his glum tone not matching the felicity of such a possibility. "Then we would be tied to the country."

"That is not true," Darcy said immediately. "Nothing needs to change just because you have a child. You can still enjoy town and society as much as you ever did."

"That is true," said Bingley. He thought for a moment and then straightened himself, seeming reassured. "Yes, I believe you have the right of it there. In any case, you and Miss Elizabeth will never want for diversion. If all else fails, you can pass the time away in debating…well, whatever it is you two so often found to argue over!"

The mention of Elizabeth recalled Darcy to the task at hand. "Yes, Elizabeth is eager to meet you again at Pemberley this summer—she and her sister." He gave Bingley a significant look.

"They are no more eager than I," cried Bingley.

"First week of July." Darcy pressed him on the date, seizing the advantage of Bingley's present enthusiasm.

"Oh." Bingley paused a moment, sagging again against the wall. "Oh, blast! I am so stupid with these things. You did send a note to me; I recollect it now."

"You did not make another arrangement, surely."

"I am obliged to attend a house party at West Wycombe Park in Buckinghamshire," Bingley explained, looking uneasy. "I shall go next week and stay a week or so with my friends there."

"Come to Derbyshire afterwards, then."

"Hmm." Bingley looked like such complicated arrangements were puzzling to him.

"Bingley…" Darcy spoke with a warning tone in his voice. "Go with your friends, and I shall meet you there and take you to Derbyshire. There now, we have settled it."

Bingley thought for much longer than Darcy deemed necessary, finally agreeing to the scheme.

10

ELIZABETH WAS SCARCELY HOME A DAY BEFORE SHE LONGED TO BE gone again. The time spent away from her home county had taught her to be more aware of the follies within her family circle. The silliness of her younger sisters was now intolerable, and her mother's vulgarity seemed to exceed anything Elizabeth had previously known.

How had she not noticed the almost painful seclusion of Meryton before? All the gossip and talk was so trivial and silly, everyone saying the same things about the same people, all of which already had been said many times over. It was indeed confined and unvarying, as Mr Darcy had once observed, and she was a fool to have thought the people themselves varied enough to make country life interesting. It was not merely uninteresting; it was excruciatingly dull.

The regiment, which had provided such delightful diversion in the autumn, had quite lost its appeal for her. There was one gentleman whose charms had particularly worn thin, namely Mr Wickham. He lost no time in making several sly comments about her engagement to Mr Darcy that ranged from merely annoying to outright vexatious.

By far, however, the most difficult part of being home was

her mother's disbelief regarding her second daughter's disinclination to marry a wealthy gentleman.

Elizabeth never meant to admit to her mother that she had no intention of actually marrying Mr Darcy. She and Jane had rehearsed several explanations for why Elizabeth was not yet prepared to plan a wedding. All of these careful schemes were lost when Mrs Bennet seized Elizabeth the moment she alit from the carriage that brought her home. Scarcely a word could be breathed before the wedding was planned. Elizabeth was only surprised the seamstress who would make her gown was not present to begin measuring.

In the confusion, Elizabeth found herself telling her mother that she should not anticipate a wedding. What followed was exceedingly unpleasant and unstinting. There were threats and harangues in abundance. Mrs Bennet promised eternal silence to her daughter on no less than twenty occasions, but unfortunately, she never held true to her word. Elizabeth endured her mother's harangues in the same way she always had—with equal parts indifference and feigned repentance, reminding her mother and herself that she soon would be away again.

As the days and weeks passed, Elizabeth took solace in forming an acquaintance with Georgiana through the exchange of letters. It was through these letters that Elizabeth began to find a softer, more pleasing side to Mr Darcy than what she had known—or at least imagined she knew—previously.

The most recent missive she held as she strolled the garden around her home. In it, Georgiana referred to her "wild anticipation" to be at Pemberley and see a new instrument that her brother had purchased as a gift.

She read the passage again:

He gave it to me as a gift, a gift for no other reason than he wished to please me, which in my estimation is the best sort of gift to receive! It was meant to be a surprise. Alas, my brother does not excel in the art of concealing happy news. Knowing the pleasure it would bring me, he told me of it when it had not been bought a week. I shall admit that I am glad he did, for the anticipation of pleasure is often nearly as delightful as the pleasure itself, or so I believe.

It was a charming picture Georgiana presented through her stories. There was no doubt she held him slightly in awe, which was only appropriate given that he had been her guardian through most of her formative years. However, he was also playful with her and mindful of her sensibilities.

"I must give him credit for that much," Elizabeth said to a shrub she was passing. "Most gentlemen when presented with the task of rearing a young sister would have hired as many governesses and nursemaids as they could afford and hoped for the best."

Mr Darcy also wrote to her. The very sight of the letter caused her some trepidation, and she could not open it for two full days after its receipt. When at last she did, she was greeted by only a few rows of the neatly masculine, evenly spaced writing that Miss Bingley had so admired at Netherfield. It was a strange picture to imagine him at some unknown desk, pen in hand, thinking of her and writing to her. He said little; it was the sort of letter one might write to a person of short acquaintance.

His conclusion, however, was quite different:

I had, as you might imagine, no little anxiety in taking this liberty of writing to you. Inasmuch as I have always treasured our conversations, I am aware that you do not feel likewise. So pray, forgive my presumption. You honour me in having read

the whole of it. It has been my pleasure to pass the time writing to you, spending some time with you even in my thoughts.
Sincerely yours,
Fitzwilliam Darcy

When she got to that, she dropped it as if the page had ignited itself then pressed her hand to her chest. "Oh," she said to the empty bedchamber where she had taken herself to read. She stood in silence a moment before picking it up and folding it carefully. She had no idea what to do with it after that and finally decided to hide it in the deepest recesses of her closet.

Shall I reply? She had no idea whether it would be too encouraging—whether, indeed, she should be encouraging at all. Was it rude to be silent? She did not wish to be cruel, but neither did she wish to give false hope. It still astonished her that Mr Darcy had somehow come to love her—that he should express such tender sentiments to her.

"One thing is certain," Elizabeth said later, having spoken of the matter with her sister, "I shall never comprehend this man or anything he thinks or does or says. He is ever a mystery."

"I do not think you would like a man who was so easily understood," Jane said. "I think such a person would not interest you."

"Why not?"

"Do you not often say how complex characters fascinate you?"

"Yes, but it does not follow that simpler characters do not draw my attention. I am rarely unable to find something that interests me. I have discovered that people who cannot keep themselves amused are often tiresome themselves."

Jane laughed lightly. "Perhaps so. But Lizzy, imagine that you must spend your entire life with a man. I think it is best to choose one who makes you think at times; otherwise, you will fully comprehend him in the first two months and be thereafter tired by his company."

Elizabeth considered this. Mr Darcy, in the time of their acquaintance, had mostly been a source of vexation and offence. These feelings, she would allow, had overcome any sense of curiosity she might have had in the subjects of his conversation. Now, putting aside her prejudice against him, she must admit he was a person who interested her. She had enjoyed some of their debates and could acknowledge he was often witty. No matter what, she would never accuse him of being dull.

There was one thing certain in Jane's estimation, as well as that of her mother and most of Meryton—she should marry Mr Darcy. His love for Elizabeth was discussed tirelessly in many drawing rooms, and his reserve was quickly determined to have been the result of a young man being in the presence of a lady he admired. Elizabeth rolled her eyes in disbelief at such notions, but as she had no wish to discredit him, she said little of the matter other than she anticipated knowing more of him when the summer was ended.

Mr Wickham's testimony against him had been rapidly forgotten as well, though it still plagued Elizabeth at times. "I wish I might understand his actions against Mr Wickham," she told her sister during one of their late night conversations. "The more I hear of him from his sister, the more generous and good he seems, yet I cannot forget what Mr Wickham has said of his rather infamous behaviour against him.

Jane gave her a quick, censuring glance. "Lizzy, who is Mr Wickham to you that you should defend him so ardently?"

"I am not speaking in defence of Mr Wickham. I am just saying it concerns me to think Mr Darcy would leave an old friend in such poverty as well as deny the wishes of his father. It does not matter to me who he did it to—just that he did it."

"That is good," said Kitty, who had entered the room and drawn near to her elder sisters. "For I have heard recently that Mr Wickham might not be as admirable a character as we had supposed."

"Kitty, we should not gossip," Jane said immediately.

"It is not gossip," Kitty protested. "Mr Banks has spoken it outright! He said that six months of George Wickham's wages would not be sufficient for what he was owed."

"Kitty!" Elizabeth was aghast. Mr Banks was the owner of one of the less reputable alehouses in Hertfordshire, operated at a considerable distance from Meryton. How Kitty would come by such information was beyond her comprehension.

"My Aunt Philips told me. Mr Banks went to my uncle to seek his help. He is not the only one either. There are several who claim Mr Wickham owes them money, merchants of good standing too!"

"We should not speak so," Jane said. "Mr Wickham has been nothing but honourable in our presence. It might all be a misunderstanding."

With this, Kitty was silenced. She and her sisters would disregard such reports against their friend.

21 June 1812, London

"THERE ARE TWO SORTS OF MARRIAGEABLE WOMEN," SAYE OPINED from where he lolled on the settee in Darcy's library. "The witty sort whose society you enjoy and those you wish to bed. For myself, I have chosen a wife I wish to bed. What I shall do with her for the rest of my day, I cannot begin to fathom, but that is a problem for another time. Now Miss Bennet… What?"

Both Fitzwilliam and Darcy were giving him disgusted looks. "You are appalling," Fitzwilliam finally said.

"What? Why? Everyone else thinks it too, but I am the only one brave enough to say so."

"Not true," Fitzwilliam protested warmly with a glance in Darcy's direction.

"Then name me one lady, just one, in whom you have equal interest in bedding and conversing."

Fitzwilliam opened his mouth to reply but got stuck. He finally settled for a stern look in his elder brother's direction.

"In any case, I say this as a compliment to you, Darcy. You are a fortunate man in that Miss Elizabeth Bennet is one of those exceedingly rare creatures whom one would not only like to bed but who will also provide excellent company during the day. Very uncommon, and I must own that… Now why are you both piercing me with your glares?"

"I shall thank you," Darcy began in a haughty tone, "to refrain from speaking of her in that disrespectful manner."

"I beg your pardon," Saye continued blithely, "but it seems to me, that of us all, only *you* have ever truly disrespected her. I speak of her in the most admiring of terms and always have. You need not concern yourself with it, however. My admiration is honourable, and I am well aware that she is your heart's desire. You knew her first."

Darcy was only faintly mollified, but he turned away from his cousin and stared out the window at his lawn.

"No…" Saye sounded a bit pensive and regretful. "No, that will not do."

Darcy and Fitzwilliam immediately looked at him closely.

"If I must be honest—you both know that I despise liars—I

cannot truly say my admiration is wholly honourable. Now, I shall not act on it—you have my word—but I shall admit I have spent a bit of time, quite a lot of time actually, imagining how it might be to take her. 'Tis a captivating idea in truth, to have one's mind equally agreeably engaged with one's body, and not something—

"Bloody idiot! What was that for?" Saye glared at his younger brother who had reached over and punched him on the leg with his knuckle, rather hard.

"You are the idiot," Fitzwilliam muttered under his breath. "Stop talking about Miss Elizabeth."

Saye hissed back, quite loudly enough for Darcy to hear, "You said you found her rather tempting yourself."

"I most certainly did not."

"Yes, you surely did. I recall it quite clearly. You said you were at Rosings, turning the pages for her while she was singing, and you were fearful that she—or even worse, Lady Catherine—would notice that your breeches—"

"It is a natural response to a beautiful woman! It does not mean that I—"

The brothers continued to bicker, but Darcy determinedly paid no attention. Saye, despite his offensive idiocy, had raised in Darcy a compelling thought.

His greatest fear in the entirety of this affair was that Elizabeth would remain steadfast in her refusal. But he had not thought through to the ultimate conclusion of such a failure: if he did not succeed in this, another man would have her. He did not worry about his cousins—even Saye was not so despicable—but another man. Another man would claim her; another would know her as his wife.

He clenched his jaw, more determined than ever to succeed in earning her love. He stopped his cousins in their disagreement. "Enough of that. I have no wish to discuss it further, save to promise you both that, in the future, if either of you so much as look at her for too long, I shall run you through."

"Fair enough," said Saye cheerily with his brother nodding in agreement beside him.

It had been decided—for reasons still unclear to Darcy—that Saye and Fitzwilliam would both be at Pemberley while the Miss Bennets and Bingley visited. "Bingley's society is much more tolerable now that he is not so much in company with his sister," Fitzwilliam explained.

Darcy intended to retrieve Bingley while Saye and Fitzwilliam escorted Georgiana to Pemberley. She was eager to be at home again and prevailed upon them to leave the next day. Darcy, on the other hand, was obliged to remain in town a few more days until the time arrived to meet Bingley in Buckinghamshire. He already regretted the arrangement. Although he knew Elizabeth was not yet at Pemberley, he longed to be there, imagining her with him.

He urged his sensibilities towards reason. *She will not be there until July. No sense in waiting around for her. She will be enjoying, I hope, touring with her aunt and uncle as they make their way to Derbyshire, and they will arrive in due time.*

At last, anticipation of their travel ended and the enjoyment of it began. The Gardiners arrived at Longbourn on the day appointed, and on the very next day, they, along with Jane and Elizabeth, set out.

It had been planned that the first week would be spent seeing the sights along their route to Derbyshire, including Oxford, Blenheim, Warwick, Kenelworth, and Birmingham.

These fine estates with their corresponding charming gardens and parks were given their due by the merry group.

On the whole, their journey was easy. They met with good roads and comfortable inns and experienced none of the delays travellers might encounter on such a trip. They proceeded according to the plan Mr Gardiner had shared with Mr Darcy and arrived at Pemberley early in the afternoon of the fourth of July.

Elizabeth, as they drove along, watched for the first appearance of Pemberley Woods with some perturbation, and when at length they turned in at the lodge, her spirits were in a high flutter. They entered the park at one of its lowest points and drove for some time through a beautiful wood, stretching over a wide extent.

Elizabeth's mind was too full for conversation, but she saw and admired every remarkable spot and point of view. They gradually ascended for half a mile and reached the top of a considerable eminence where the wood ceased. The eye instantly was caught by Pemberley House situated on the opposite side of a valley into which the road wound with some abruptness. It was a large, handsome, stone building, standing well on rising ground and backed by a ridge of high woody hills. In front, a stream of some natural importance was swelled into greater but without any artificial appearance. Its banks were neither formal nor falsely adorned. Elizabeth was delighted. She had never seen a place for which nature had done more, or where natural beauty had been so little counteracted by awkward taste.

It was, to Elizabeth's mind, far grander than even Rosings Park, which had been, until this moment, the grandest residence she had ever beheld. Unlike Rosings Park, however, there was something of ease and friendliness in Pemberley. She supposed it was the fact that it bore little in the way of false ornamentation or elaborately contrived gardens. It presided over its natural environment but in a harmonious manner.

Their party alit from the carriage for a moment, desiring a view of Pemberley and its surrounding lands. The Gardiners walked a little to the right while Jane and Elizabeth went a little to the left, standing side-by-side and quiet in their admiration.

"Pemberley is a beautiful house," Jane spoke at last, her voice revealing her astonishment.

"To say it is beautiful makes me doubt my capacity for speech, for to call it merely beautiful does not do it justice."

"It would be rather remarkable to be mistress of such a house."

Elizabeth paused for a moment, fearing her approbation of the place was too strong and her sensibilities too disordered to speak indifferently. It did astonish her to imagine herself mistress of such a place as she now beheld and made her feel the compliment of Mr Darcy's declarations more fully. "I must admit, I expected Pemberley to be different. I thought it would be elegant but austere, haughty and a bit censuring, glaring forbiddingly at the landscape around it." Elizabeth warmed to her little farce. "With a broad moat to keep far, far away any person who dare trod upon this land uninvited. I imagined Mr Darcy instructing his servants that any who dare approach him unwanted should be tossed into the moat where vicious sea creatures would await the poor fellow."

"Sea creatures in a moat?"

"That will not do, will it? Well then…a gothic sort of place presided over by a tall and formidable manservant…a hulking fellow with a decided limp and the ability to appear silently behind a person's right shoulder as they stroll the damp and gloomy halls looking—"

"Elizabeth!"

"A joke, Jane."

"Forgive me if I do not laugh,"

Elizabeth was amazed by her severity and fell quiet.

"I insist that you are kind to Mr Darcy."

"When am I not kind?" Elizabeth protested. "Of course I shall be kind to him!"

"I wish that you would be charitable despite your many protestations of despising him."

"I do not despise him."

Jane suppressed a little grin, making a sound very much like that of satisfaction. "I am glad to hear you admit at least that much. I feared you would hold tight to your spite as a means of warding off anything else that might frighten you."

"Why should I be frightened of Mr Darcy?"

"The surest way to avoid falling in love with Mr Darcy," said Jane with a maddeningly superior air, "is to persuade yourself you hate him."

Elizabeth rolled her eyes and sighed. "I suppose in some instances such a thing might work, but I assure you that I am not doing that. Whatever grievances I have held against him have been forgot."

"Good."

After a short silence, Elizabeth said, "You think I should marry him."

"I do."

"But why? To secure our futures?"

Jane gave her a little frown that Elizabeth perceived from the corner of her eye. "No, of course not. I think you should marry him because he loves you as I think you deserve to be loved."

"If one person is in love and the other is not, I think it should be miserable for them both."

"I would never wish such a fate on anyone, least of all you. But love does grow, does it not? Sometimes where it is least expected."

After a momentary pause, Jane slid her arm through Elizabeth's. "Offer your friendship to him, and I think you will be surprised where it leads you."

11

THE ROAD-WEARY GROUP WAS RELIEVED TO ENTER PEMBERLEY, whereupon they found Georgiana, Lord Saye, and Colonel Fitzwilliam awaiting them in a lovely sitting room close to the entryway. Georgiana proved a considerate hostess. She did away with any ceremony by urging them to retire to their rooms and see to their comfort before returning to enjoy tea and a proper welcome.

They were happy to do as she suggested. The housekeeper came, and she was a respectable-looking, elderly woman, much less fine and more civil than Elizabeth had any notion of finding her. With considerable warmth—and several discreet but undeniably curious glances in Elizabeth's direction—they were shown to their apartments for their stay. Elizabeth and Jane hastened to refresh themselves and were present in the drawing room after only twenty minutes.

Georgiana greeted the two sisters with a beaming smile that faded into a worried sobriety. "My brother was unavoidably delayed in town. I am sure I do not need to tell you how deeply regretful he is not to be here to welcome you. He has charged me with seeing to your every comfort."

Elizabeth smiled kindly at the girl. "How good that he may rely on you!"

The Gardiners were soon with them, and refreshments followed quickly. When they were done, the housekeeper returned. "I thought Mrs Reynolds might like to help us on our tour," Georgiana explained. It seemed an agreeable idea, so the four ladies and Mr Gardiner followed her.

Inasmuch as the exterior of Mr Darcy's home had surprised, the inside was even more amazing. The rooms were lofty and handsome with furniture suitable to the fortune of their proprietor. Elizabeth saw, in admiration of his taste, that it was neither gaudy nor uselessly fine, with less of splendour and more real elegance than the furniture of Rosings.

In Georgiana, there was a natural reserve matching that of her brother. Mrs Reynolds suffered no such inclination, and it was easy to see why Georgiana had requested her, for she bore all the responsibility for conversation and direction. Mr Gardiner, in his easy and pleasant manner, encouraged her eloquence by his questions and remarks. Mrs Reynolds, either from pride or attachment, obviously took great pleasure in talking of her master. She boasted of his kindness and goodness to his tenants and servants, adding the astonishing news that, "I have never had a cross word from him in my life, and I have known him since he was four years old."

This was even more of a surprise to Elizabeth than her admiration of his furnishings. Central to her beliefs about Mr Darcy was that he was disagreeable and ill tempered. For a woman who had known him since his boyhood to say she had never heard a cross word from him must challenge these notions. *After all, Lizzy, who would have a better understanding of his character? You or this lady?*

She did not doubt the veracity of Mrs Reynolds's words. Had

the lady not believed what she said, she would only have to be silent.

But Mrs Reynolds was not silent and added, "I have always observed that they who are good-natured when children are good-natured when they grow up, and he was always the sweetest-tempered, most generous-hearted boy in the world."

The housekeeper continued her approbation as they travelled through a main hall. Elizabeth could have listened to her all day as she was interested in these ideas of Mr Darcy that were so unlike the ones she believed she knew of him. Mrs Reynolds called him the best landlord and master and praised his charity to the poor. His appearance of pride, she brushed away by saying, "I am sure I never saw anything of it. To my fancy, it is only because he does not rattle away like other young men."

On reaching the spacious lobby above, they were shown into a pretty sitting room, lately fitted up with greater elegance and lightness than the apartments below.

"Do you like this room, Miss Elizabeth?" asked Georgiana, who had been quiet and rather watchful for most of the tour.

"I do," Elizabeth responded honestly. "I like it very much."

Georgiana blushed. "I confess, this is one of my favourite places to read and sit. It was done in an older style, but when I told my brother how much I liked it, he permitted me to redecorate to my own taste. He is so good to me."

The picture gallery and two or three of the principal bedrooms were all that remained to be shown. In the former were many good paintings, but Elizabeth knew nothing of the art and turned to look at some of Georgiana's drawings done in crayons, whose subjects were more interesting to her.

There were also many family portraits, but they could little fix the attention of a stranger. Elizabeth walked on in quest of the only face whose features would be known to her. At last, one painting arrested her attention, and she beheld a striking resemblance of Mr Darcy with such a smile over his face as she remembered to have sometimes seen when he looked at her. She stood several minutes before the picture in earnest contemplation and returned to it again before they quitted the gallery. Mrs Reynolds informed them that it had been taken in his father's lifetime.

Elizabeth had a great many strange thoughts in her mind as she stood regarding him, and these stayed with her as they moved on. There were many things to consider with regard to what she had learnt of Mr Darcy, but chief among them was an odd, unsettled feeling that she had not ever really known him— nay, that she had not *wanted* to know him. She had fixed an idea of him in her mind, and every word, every look, had been calculated to support her notions. It discomposed her to imagine herself the willing servant of such prejudice, silly and unduly sure of her limited opinions.

And if he is so very different than I believed him to be, then what?

For she could not doubt the truth of what she had heard of him—not so much as a word. His home and his people bore testament to his charity and his good character. His servants, his sister, and his friends were all happy and easy—everyone healthy, hardworking, and well tended. Nothing was left uncared for in Mr Darcy's domain, nothing at all.

There is goodness here. At the heart of it all is goodness.

DINNER WAS EXCELLENT, BOTH IN THE FOOD SERVED AS WELL AS THE company. Lord Saye proved an excellent source of outrageous tattle, and his tales soon grew into a game of sorts. His brother accused him of contriving such tales, and Lord Saye unrepentantly admitted he might have. Soon, he was telling them three stories of which one was patently untrue, and they were required to guess the falsity. Elizabeth could scarce believe it when she realised the length of time they spent at such an amusement or how much her sides ached from laughing.

She had thought, after so many days of travel, that she would be asleep before her head hit the pillow. Instead, she lay awake, thinking of their absent host.

Elizabeth did not mistake their intentions for the evening. Darcy's family wished to paint him in an agreeable light. The tales of his boyhood mischief abounded, laced liberally with stories of his kindness.

Before long, she had wished to tell them such exertions were no longer needed. She already had ample evidence that Mr Darcy had not been deserving of her spite. He had made some missteps—it was true—but she could not say he was malicious or cruel. Unthinking perhaps, maybe even unfeeling sometimes, but certainly nothing like what she had previously thought. She knew after not even a full day at Pemberley that she had grossly misunderstood him, and she was resolved to do as she must to know him better.

Had it been at all possible, Elizabeth would like to have viewed his portrait once more. She found herself rather interested in the man that Georgiana, Lord Saye, Colonel Fitzwilliam, and Mrs Reynolds all loved so well. She was even appreciative that he had pursued her so doggedly when he might have just given up and invited her to Pemberley, instead.

It was not necessary to look at his picture to ponder these things. She just wished to anyway. She did not think too long on her inclination but only told herself not to do it then but wait until the morrow.

• • •

THE CHEQUERS IN BUCKINGHAMSHIRE WAS COMFORTABLE AND WELL appointed. The servants knew their business and did it well, the food was hot and plentiful, and the ale was particularly sating to a thirsty traveller. In all, Darcy could find no fault with it save for one—it had a notable absence of Bingley.

He was not there on the appointed day nor the two following. On the fourth day, Darcy decided he could wait no longer and left a note for Bingley with the innkeeper.

Although his appearance was something of a surprise, the servants were unperturbed when their master entered his London home unexpectedly. The housekeeper betrayed only the slightest hint of astonishment when she said, "Forgive us, sir, we had understood you to be continuing on to Pemberley from Buckinghamshire."

"I had planned it so," he informed her, doing his best to speak calmly. "Unforeseen business called me back to town. Excuse me."

He made directly for his study where he anticipated—nay, hoped—to find a letter from Bingley. He shuffled through the neat stack on his desk thrice before admitting that nothing bearing the telltale splotches of Bingley's communications was there.

His temper rising from the slow simmer he had borne for three days, he rang for his housekeeper who appeared within moments, bringing a light meal. With a nod, she set the meats and cheeses in front of him along with a small loaf of bread. "I thought you might be hungry, sir."

"Thank you. Have there been any letters from Mr Bingley during my absence?"

"No, but he did call once. I informed him you were away from home, and he declined to leave his card."

Darcy stared at her, barely concealing his amazement. "Can you recall which day it was?"

"I made a note of it in my book, sir. Shall I retrieve it?"

"Yes, please do."

The housekeeper returned with the information that Bingley had called on the thirtieth of June. It was the day they had fixed to meet in Buckinghamshire, intending to allow time to travel to Pemberley later that week. Could Bingley have confused the arrangements, thinking Darcy wished for them to meet in London?

He dismissed his housekeeper then sat thinking for a moment, his knuckles beating a frustrated cadence against his blotter. Days wasted and now here it was, the second of July, and he was yet three days away from Pemberley and Elizabeth.

He looked at his watch. The dinner hour was nigh, and polite people would not call at such a time. He cared little for that, and within a quarter of an hour, he was presenting himself to the manservant at the Albany and requesting Mr Bingley.

That Bingley was absent no longer had the capacity to surprise him.

He left a terse note along with his card notifying Bingley that he had wasted his time travelling to Buckinghamshire, and he was expected at Pemberley. He would tarry in town no longer and intended to leave early the next morning in hopes of making it to Derbyshire in as short a time as possible. He hoped to have his friend with him.

DARCY AWOKE ON THE MORNING OF HIS DEPARTURE FROM LONDON to find that Bingley had sent a note. It was mostly illegible. Bingley's usual poor penmanship was in no way improved by the hour at which he must have penned the letter. Darcy comprehended only enough to believe that his friend intended to wait upon him that morning. He could only hope Bingley would arrive prepared to depart for Pemberley.

An hour later, Bingley had not yet arrived. Darcy paced, impatient and increasingly resentful, while a footman was dispatched to his apartments bearing a note. It was another hour until the footman returned, breathless and contrite, telling his master that he had been made to wait for an answer while Mr Bingley finished a bath.

Darcy tore the note open, only to find a series of disordered scribbles that appeared to indicate Bingley would be present within the quarter hour. The forward movement of the morning was inexorable. Darcy was reduced to scowling at his mantel clock at increasingly short intervals as his mind tormented him with calculations of how the delay would affect his arrival at Pemberley.

It did not suit him to have Bingley trifling with him, but Bingley was wanted at Pemberley, and to Pemberley, Darcy would deliver him. For Elizabeth, he reminded himself continuously even as her words echoed in his mind: *"Could you imagine forgiving, much less loving, such a person as that?"* Until this matter of Miss Bennet and Bingley was set to rights, he was no better than George Wickham, cruel destroyer of hopes and reputations. He would reunite Miss Bennet and Bingley if it was the last thing he did.

Bingley appeared shortly after noon, entering with a cheerful, "Ho! Darcy! A fine day for travel!" and no apparent discomfiture that he might have disappointed or disadvantaged his friend.

Darcy bit back the words he wanted to say, instead managing in an even tone to voice his agreement. "It is. Dare I hope we might depart straightaway?"

"We may indeed."

After just a few additional minor fits and starts, they were off. Darcy thought he had never before felt such a sense of relief as when they moved through the turnpike gates and they were at last headed into the country.

Bingley fell into a deep sleep before the gentlemen had travelled an hour, snoring at a volume that Darcy could not have imagined possible. Three hours into their journey, they stopped at a coaching inn. Although Bingley appeared disinclined to stretch his legs—he merely curled tighter into his corner and continued his horrible nasal expulsions—Darcy insisted. He poked and prodded until Bingley mumbled and muttered and finally tumbled from the carriage.

They took a short stroll about the yard while the coachmen went about their business. Bingley was drowsy and wild haired, rubbing his eyes and stumbling about. In a short time, they climbed back into the carriage, and as soon as the horses moved, Bingley appeared ready to resume his noises immediately.

"Before you go to sleep again," said Darcy in a voice that was louder and angrier than intended, "perhaps you can tell me whatever became of Buckinghamshire."

"Buckinghamshire?" Bingley looked like he had never heard of any such place.

"We planned to meet in Buckinghamshire, yet you were absent on the appointed day."

Bingley scratched his head. "Buckinghamshire?"

"Yes, Buckinghamshire," Darcy snapped. "I was there. You were not. Where were you? And why did you not tell me before I was sitting at an inn, awaiting you?"

Bingley was the picture of confusion, looking about him as if the answers might be writ upon the squabs of the carriage. Eventually, some light appeared in his eyes. "Oh! Yes, Buckinghamshire! Right! No, Sir Albert said I should not go. Lord Bosworth was having a party…" And with that, Bingley began telling story after deplorable story, often laughing uproariously at his own weakness and vice.

Darcy hardly knew how to reply. "I see Sir Albert's reputation is well founded."

His censure was clearly understood. Bingley's eyes narrowed. "What reputation is that? You hardly know him."

"I have no wish to know him."

Bingley rolled his eyes. "Not everyone needs to be a priggish dullard, Darcy."

"I should far prefer being a priggish dullard to a dissolute reprobate."

"Sir Albert is not—"

"Most of London thinks he is, and if you do not behave with greater prudence, soon they will think you are too."

"Perhaps I do not care what London and the precious *ton* thinks." Bingley scowled, looking like an angry child with his dishevelled hair and pink cheeks. "Sir Albert is a dear friend, and unlike some, he does not confuse friendship with the right to order me about and ruin my life."

"I do not order you about," Darcy retorted.

What followed was beyond Darcy's wildest imaginings. Bingley began an unmitigated recitation of all the things he had ever held against his friend—and there were evidently many. Darcy replied with some of the things he had heard attached to Bingley's name. Bingley cared not a fig for any of it. In the midst of it all, Bingley delivered the cutting remark, "Pemberley would be perfection save for the fact that I am forced to bear the company of its disagreeable owner."

Darcy, deeply stung, could not check himself and permitted

anger to reply for him. "Then, pray, do not discommode your-self. Go back to town with your dear friend, Sir Albert."

As such, Bingley removed from the carriage at the next posting inn and returned to London on his own.

THE MORNING AFTER ELIZABETH'S ARRIVAL AT PEMBERLEY BOASTED glorious weather. A walking party through the park had been arranged, and there was one particularly fine prospect that Georgiana wished to show her.

The group set out with Mrs Gardiner on Lord Saye's arm, her husband beside them, and Jane and Colonel Fitzwilliam behind. Elizabeth walked arm in arm with Georgiana, and soon they lagged a little behind the others. Elizabeth watched as her friend glanced ahead, seeming to gauge the extent of their separation from the group, and she realised it had been by design.

Georgiana spoke just as they went around a curve in the path that shielded them from the others. "Elizabeth, I have wished for some time to speak to you. I wanted to apologise for my part in spreading the gossip about...you and my brother."

"Do not make yourself uneasy," Elizabeth assured her.

"I hope you will be able to forgive him?"

Elizabeth took a moment to carefully consider her words, not wishing to tell anything that Darcy would not want his sister to know. "I trust I am as capable of mercy as any lady."

Georgiana appeared to read her mind. "I know not the particulars of all that has occurred," she confessed, "only that Fitzwilliam spoke out of turn in his announcement of your engagement. Oh, Elizabeth, please do not permit a quarrel to stand in the way of your felicity!"

"It is not as simple as that," Elizabeth said reluctantly. "Not merely a quarrel, you see. But forgive me, I do not wish to speak more than your brother wishes to have known."

"But there you have it! You wish to marry him, and he wishes for you more than anything! What else can there be?"

"I do not...you misapprehend me." Elizabeth felt trapped, held hostage by dear, sweet Georgiana and her inquisitiveness.

"Forgive me. I would not wish to force your confidence." Georgiana watched her foot as she toed a small branch out of the way, her countenance abashed and glum.

"No, no, it is not that. What I meant was that it is not only the situation with the announcement that has affected me."

"Fitzwilliam has told me your acquaintance did not begin as it should. I do not know all the particulars, but he is ashamed of the way he treated you. That, I do know."

Elizabeth felt her cheeks flush. "Did he say so?"

"He told me it was his dearest wish that he might court you properly while you are here in Derbyshire."

She seemed to be expecting a reply, but Elizabeth knew not what to say.

"He is truly the best of men," Georgiana urged. "I do not say it lightly. He is honourable, good, and kind. He will be a splendid husband, I just know it."

In Elizabeth's mind, a tumult was arising. Her sensibilities were overburdened from her musings the evening before and now all of this. There was too much to be contemplated and felt and too little time to do so, particularly as Georgiana continued to look at her, wanting to see that her exhortation was not in vain.

"It is a credit to you both that you should say so," Elizabeth replied mildly.

Georgiana smiled faintly and continued walking, and Elizabeth hoped that would be the end of her intercessions on behalf of her brother. But not five minutes passed before the girl made another attempt.

"Elizabeth?"

"Yes?"

"My brother told me that you met Mr Wickham last autumn."

Elizabeth was immediately wary, wondering whether Darcy had hoped his sister would plead his case in that matter. "I did, yes."

Georgiana did not immediately speak but eventually made a halting offer. "I suppose you must know of his longstanding relationship with our family."

"I do."

"I hope I shall not offend you, then, if I should tell you something of a matter…"

"My dear, pray, do not feel we need to talk about all that has transpired with regard to Mr Wickham."

The girl did not look at her. "So you know about…about…"

Elizabeth sighed. "Yes, I know all about it. I do not think too little may be said on *that* subject."

There was a brief silence. "You are likely right."

Elizabeth did not think it proper that she should be told of Mr Darcy's private business with Mr Wickham, particularly by his sister. However, she did not wish to wound Georgiana and said gently, "I do know—how well do I know!—that there are two sides to every story, and never can the blame of one be irreproachable while the other bears all the shame."

"That is true…that both…both are to blame." The words were spoken in a mere whisper and a quick look showed Elizabeth that Georgiana's chin had nearly sunk into her chest. Elizabeth wondered why she would be so affected by speaking of her brother's quarrels with Mr Wickham.

She reached over and encircled the girl's waist with her arm. "It is water under the bridge. Let us do what we may to forget all about it. Who is Mr Wickham to us after all?"

Miss Darcy appeared heartened by this, giving Elizabeth a quick smile. "He is no one. No one at all."

12

THE SECOND DAY OF DARCY'S TRAVEL WAS SPENT ALMOST WHOLLY in contemplation of his conversation—nay, his argument—with Bingley. That it resulted in disaster was unquestionable. But what he could not determine was what had possessed him to behave as he had towards the man he had once known as a close friend.

Bingley's conduct naturally could not be approved, but neither had Darcy acted in good part for his friend. He had not behaved as a gentleman should. *And you will pay for that.*

They made excellent progress, covering more miles than usual, but this was of little consolation. For although it brought him closer to home and Elizabeth, it also brought him nearer to the moment of reckoning when he would need to explain to his guests what he had done. He was not eager for Elizabeth to see first-hand the effect his anger had wrought. If he had before broken her sister's heart out of good intentions, now he had broken it for sheer pride and ill humour.

For the last miles of travel, he rode, hoping the exercise would quell his agitation. It did not. He arrived at the stables in as much of a lather as his animal, finding there his cousin, who had been about to exercise his own horse.

Fitzwilliam first exclaimed over the surprise of seeing him and then welcomed him in their usual tradition with a handshake and warm smile. It did not require much in the way of wit for Fitzwilliam to apprehend Darcy's dark mood, and he soon had some inkling of its cause.

"Bingley is not here," Fitzwilliam observed as soon as the groom had taken Darcy's horse away.

"So you noticed? Well done, Fitzwilliam. I have always believed you quicker than has been reported."

"That I am." Fitzwilliam chuckled, taking no offence at Darcy's gibe. "What became of him?"

Darcy sighed heavily, removed his hat, and raked his hand through his matted hair. "I wonder the same thing. What became of him, and what will become of him? Nothing good, I fear."

Fitzwilliam gave him a perplexed look. "Come now, Darcy. You remained behind for the express purpose of escorting Bingley to Pemberley from Buckinghamshire. Yet somehow, you are here and Bingley is not. Did he not wish to leave his party?"

"I have not the slightest notion whether he ever was in Buckinghamshire. Leastways, he was not there when I was."

"But no! You must have been enraged! How could he do that? Where was he?"

"I know not, and in any case, it does not signify. After several days, I returned to London and found him there."

"I would have boxed his ears for running me about the countryside in such a way," Fitzwilliam declared. "What was he about, doing such a thing? I hope you gave him the dressing down he deserved."

"I did not. I merely informed him of my intended departure time and that he should present himself if he wished to join me.

He was there, though not precisely at the given hour, and so we departed London well past noon."

"I cannot abide someone who is so careless of the time of another. So what then? Was he so vexatious as to cause you to toss him from your carriage?" Fitzwilliam snickered.

Darcy shook his head and gave his cousin a neat summary of all that had transpired. "I acted in anger. Everything that happened was a result of my annoyance at being delayed, run about, and disrespected."

"And rightly so," Fitzwilliam said, loyal as ever. "I would have done no different except to perhaps knock him on the head soundly as we parted."

"He holds me responsible for his descent into vice. Sir Albert is beheld as all that is good—and I, all that is bad."

"He is a man, grown albeit green, who needs to take responsibility for his own weaknesses and vices."

"He has had no father to guide him," Darcy continued as though he had not heard Fitzwilliam's defence of him. "Not since a young age, and he relies excessively on those of us who are his friends. Having removed my friendship, he will form a greater attachment to Sir Albert and his ilk."

"That is not your fault."

"What shall I tell Elizabeth? That we have come one great step further away from reuniting her sister with Bingley?" He gave a little groan, again raking his hair with his hands. "Failed, right at the outset. Blast it to hell."

"Perhaps she will not notice."

"She may want to leave." It was this fear that had plagued him all the miles since leaving Bingley, that his second chance was gone before it had even begun. He hoped Fitzwilliam would dispute him, but his cousin was never one to give false assurance.

"The purpose of her being here is so I can show her that I am not the excessively proud, officious, resentful-tempered, ill-humoured, and stone-hearted man she thinks I am. I fear these dealings with Bingley will prove quite the opposite."

Fitzwilliam gave him a rueful grin. "Well, if you would like to rid yourself of the task with expedience, I think you will find her alone in the west gardens. She took a book there earlier."

Although Darcy dreaded the task, he did not believe in procrastination. He was not long in finding Elizabeth, and when he did, he was enraptured. Bingley was momentarily forgot in favour of enjoying the tableau before him.

Elizabeth was a picture of domesticity and comfort, looking as she always did whenever he imagined her as his wife. She had chosen a seat on a stone bench in a sunny spot near the middle of the roses. A bonnet and unopened book by her side, her attention was on a cat rustling about in the nearby hedge. She watched its antics with a small smile on her lips.

Inadvertently, he sighed. She heard him, startled violently, and looked in his direction. An instant later, she scrambled to her feet and cried, "Mr Darcy!"

ELIZABETH FOUND HERSELF AT SIXES AND SEVENS EVER SINCE THE announcement of Darcy's intended arrival. She decided she would meet him with amiability, and she was determined to be all ease and friendliness towards him. Alas, as the hour of his arrival approached, she was anything but easy.

Earlier that day, she had waited—as she often did since her arrival at Pemberley—for a clandestine moment to hie away and look at his portrait. Why she kept returning to it, she could not reckon, but it had become something of an obsession. She would stand and look until she thought she might be missed; then she would hasten away, telling herself she need look at it no more. In not so many hours, however, she would find herself wishing to go to it again. *Very silly*, she admonished herself, but it could not make her cease.

Elizabeth spent the day in fidgets, dropping everything she touched. Thus, it was no surprise that his precipitous, unannounced appearance made her leap to her feet in a most undignified manner, knocking her book and bonnet to the ground and scaring off a little kitten she had been watching.

"Mr Darcy!"

"Miss Elizabeth." He had her at a disadvantage as he had seen her when he approached and was able to greet her with greater equanimity. "Welcome to Pemberley."

"Thank you," she stammered, bending to pick up her things. "You are not expected. That is to say, I had understood you to be arriving closer to dinner time."

"That is when my carriage will arrive. I found that, as the time drew near, I was rather restless and so chose to ride ahead. May I sit with you?" He indicated the little bench she had occupied, and she nodded her acquiescence, willing her heart to calm and the flush that was certainly staining her cheeks to abate.

A sudden and intense attack of collywobbles seized Elizabeth as they took a seat, and she cursed herself for it. It was an odd thing to have a man profess his love, and it aroused the same anxieties as if it were she who loved him.

As was her custom when attempting to hide her feelings, she teased him. "Mrs Reynolds was rather unreserved in her commendation of you, sir. In the words of my aunt, the good lady gave you something of a flaming character."

Seriously, he replied, "It is good to know she performed well. I shall have to remember to supplement her wages accordingly."

It took a moment for Elizabeth to recognise the unexpected jest for what it was, and she laughed. Before something else could be said, Mr Darcy admitted, "No, no, you know I do not truly intend to pay her for the compliments she bestowed on my behalf."

"Of course not," Elizabeth said, still smiling.

"What she wished for was a holiday, so she will have that instead." This time, he joined her in laughing.

She knew not what to say after that and made the first, stupidly obvious observation that entered her head. "Mr Bingley has not attended you."

The effect of her statement was immediate. Mr Darcy sobered. "Mr Bingley was unavoidably detained by some matters of business."

"I see," she said quietly. "Perhaps later, then."

"Perhaps," Mr Darcy agreed.

All ease and friendliness vanished in the work of a moment. Mr Darcy was clearly awkward, but she could not see why. She resolved to make him easier again, beginning with a much-deserved compliment. "I am exceedingly enamoured of Pemberley, sir. The descriptions I heard scarce do it justice."

He inclined his head in acknowledgment of her compliment. "I am grateful you think so."

"I would be a simpleton to think otherwise," she replied with what felt like a shy smile.

"How have you occupied yourselves in my absence?"

She told him what they had seen and done in their days at Pemberley, forcing an animation into her tone that she did not feel. A cloud was over his countenance, and she felt she had displeased him. Her anxiety made her feel brittle and false, and she had no doubt that he felt it too.

Their conversation proceeded in fits and starts. She found

herself becoming more reserved even as she tried to summon her customary wit and vivacity. He first gave an appearance of composure but soon revealed that he was likewise discomfited. He asked after her family twice and several times seemed to lose track of the conversation.

After one silence, as is common, both spoke at once.

"I must tell—" said he.

"You no doubt would like—" she said.

Both stopped. He said, "You first, please."

"I only meant to say that the others are likely impatient to see you. Miss Darcy, particularly, was eager for your arrival."

He rose, extending his hand to help her rise. "Let us go to them, then."

She went inside the house with him, noting that, although his welcome of the others was all that was proper, he was decidedly reserved. A troubled feeling crept over her as she wondered whether he regretted inviting them all to his house. *Maybe some time and distance have persuaded him of the folly in proposing to me.* If so, she would beg her aunt and uncle to leave straightaway.

There was nothing in the remainder of the afternoon or evening to persuade her otherwise. Mr Darcy remained quiet and reserved, and she did not once look to find his eyes upon her. He was not unkind. Indeed, he was *very* kind, particularly to the Gardiners. He and Mr Gardiner spent a good portion of the evening discussing the best spots for fishing in his trout stream, much to her uncle's delight.

It was an early night as the rest of the party had no doubt of their host's likely exhaustion, and Elizabeth, having had a mostly sleepless night prior, could not argue. She hoped she would be able to put aside her burgeoning distress to gain a good rest.

He is tired. See how he is tomorrow. It will be soon enough for expectations and conclusions.

"WHERE IS BINGLEY?" VERY NEARLY, THE FIRST WORDS FROM HER *mouth!* Darcy tore the cravat from his neck. *I knew she came for the purpose of reuniting her sister with Bingley, so naturally she is not pleased that he is not present. Should I have told her where he was? Should I have admitted he might not come? Nay, that he likely will not come? That I should, in fact, be quite amazed if he did?*

He fell into a nearby chair, having removed the most binding of his clothing, for a moment of contemplation.

It had been a dream come to life that afternoon. He had ridden hard to get to Pemberley, resenting every moment that Bingley's foolishness had kept him from her and wishing for nothing more but to see her in his home. To arrive as he had and find her sitting so prettily in Pemberley's garden, her book at her side, was everything he had ever imagined it would be. He could almost pretend she awaited him, that she came outside in order to steal a private greeting with him before he was required to attend the others. The recollection of it was heart-warming.

Her question about Bingley's whereabouts was a rude intrusion of reality, and his disappointment had been fierce and unwavering. He had tried to regain happier spirits as the evening wore on, but he knew he was sadly unsuccessful.

A knock sounded, interrupting his melancholy. It was Saye who, uninvited, took a seat on Darcy's bed. "You hied off too quickly, Cousin. I was just about to offer to thrash you at billiards."

"I am not inclined to play just now."

"Darts?"

"I intend to retire."

"Cards? We shall play high. I believe I still need to win my curricle back from you."

Darcy could not help but chuckle. "The curricle remains yours. I offered a trade if you recall."

"Oh," said Saye with some despondence to his tone. "Yes, and I do still miss that waistcoat."

"It never did fit you right, and the colour made you sallow."

"So it did." With determination, Saye offered, "Chess then?"

"Not tonight. Tomorrow will be time enough for amusement."

"Who could be amused with such a glum face across from us at dinner?" said Fitzwilliam, entering the room unannounced.

"Yes, why were you so dull?" Saye enquired. "I should have thought the mere sight of Miss Elizabeth would be sufficient for your raptures."

Darcy groaned and Fitzwilliam asked, "Dare I suppose that telling Miss Elizabeth that Mr Bingley would not be joining us did not go well?"

"Not joining us? Why ever not?" asked Saye as Darcy admitted, "I did not tell her. I could not."

Fitzwilliam groaned as Saye looked back and forth between them, asking again, "Why is Bingley not joining us?"

Fitzwilliam did not reply to his brother. "You had the best of intentions, Darcy, and I think if you would tell—"

Whatever he had been about to say, Darcy checked with a low, bitter chuckle. "Ah yes, me and my meddlesome good intentions."

"Surely you see that, had they married, it would have been sheer folly. Miss Bennet would not like marriage to a scoundrel, I assure you."

"What did I miss?" Saye cried with desperation. "Someone here has not told me something."

"Tell him, Fitzwilliam." Darcy moved to his dressing table, removing his pocket watch and waistcoat and tossing them onto his bed. "Tell him how my intemperance destroyed all hope in the space of thirty-five miles of road."

Darcy stared into the fireplace as Fitzwilliam did as asked, adding, "Bingley becomes the society he keeps. Had he married, he would be happily in Hertfordshire planning his harvest right now. Had he moved to Jamaica, he would be tending his sugar cane or whatever it is they do there. Had he moved to America, he would be fighting the Indians and trying to take Canada."

"Hardly a recommendation," Saye snorted.

Darcy spoke with the sorrow he felt. "I should have kept him close."

"You surely would not have wished him here with three young, unmarried ladies in the house?"

"Three young, unmarried ladies watched over by not only myself but Mr and Mrs Gardiner, Georgiana's companion, the two of you—yes, I think they would have been safe. In any case, I have not the least doubt that a few days immersed in a more upright society would have seen him back to gentlemanly ways."

"Miss Bennet is far too fine a lady for the likes of Bingley."

"Be that as it may," said Darcy. "Miss Bennet would like to have him. It is not for me to decide who Miss Bennet should and should not like, yet I have seen fit to do so twice."

That he was not wholly accurate in his evaluation was not debated for it was immaterial. He knew his cousins understood what was at stake and that neither their opinions nor Darcy's truly mattered. Only Elizabeth's opinion counted, and in Elizabeth's estimation, it should be Miss Bennet and Bingley.

"So I must tell her—" Darcy began, but Saye was quick to stop him.

"Tell her? Absolutely not."

"I cannot deceive her into thinking Bingley is likely to arrive at any moment," Darcy protested.

"No deceit is necessary. You will write to him," Saye ordered. "Tell him that Miss Goddard is coming with my father and mother—"

"She is?"

Saye nodded. "Yes, I believe she will get on famously with these Bennet girls. In any case, they will come, and he is welcome to be one of their party. Nay, you must insist that he is one of the party. Use that very word—*insist*."

"Do not speak too soon," Darcy warned. "He is not in good company these days. Who knows what he has gotten into since I left him."

"The point being that no deception is necessary," Saye said patiently. "You will write to him and apologise for the argument—"

"I am not sorry for what I said," Darcy replied ominously.

"No, not that, just the argument itself." Saye rolled his eyes. "Lord, Darcy, you are such a simpleton about things sometimes. Now, you do that then invite him again, using the most enthusiastic language you can summon. Tell him you expect him to come. Again, *expect*. Make sure you say it just so and then— voilà! No deception, no disguise. You expect Bingley. Done!"

"And then when he fails to arrive?"

Fitzwilliam replied, "Then it is his fault, not yours."

Darcy rubbed his hands over his face. "It is likely due to my exhaustion that this seems a good idea. My exhaustion and my desperation. I just wish for her to stay long enough—"

"Long enough to make her love you," Saye finished for him. "So you buy a bit of time. In the end, all will be known, but for now, do as you must. We know how good you are. Miss Elizabeth merely requires a bit more time and understanding to see it for herself."

THAT SAME EVENING, JANE BENNET, HAVING RETIRED TO HER bedchamber, formed a resolution—nay, two resolutions. The first was the resolution itself, and the second, a resolution to be unmoved from the first resolution. It would not be easy nor would it be quick, but she would do it.

Lizzy had claimed to come to Pemberley for her, but Jane had suspected from the start that Lizzy would receive the most benefit of it. She believed with all her heart that they would not be at Pemberley for long before her sister's opinion of Mr Darcy underwent a substantive change. From there, it would be quick work for Lizzy's thoughts to move from friendship to love to matrimony. Jane would be nothing short of utterly delighted to see that come to pass.

However, she also wished for something for herself.

Jane knew Elizabeth had told Mr Darcy the truth about her feelings for Mr Bingley before they left London, yet Mr Bingley did not call on her. They had remained for several days, and there was ample time to call, but he did not. He did not return to Hertfordshire and call on her there either. And now, in this third indignity, he did not come to Derbyshire when expected.

So maybe it was not Jane's hesitation to show her feelings that kept Mr Bingley away all these months. Perhaps it was Mr Bingley's indifference after all.

It was now nearly eight months since she had seen him, and she was tired of thinking of it—tired of feeling depressed in spirit, tired of looking pale, and tired of having sympathetic glances and murmurs cast her way. This was the end of it.

There was a chance for her in Derbyshire. She was among

better society in a county with many eligible men. She had over-heard some of the plans formed by Mr and Miss Darcy for their stay. There would be dinners and several balls, some card parties, and picnics, and all of it sounded wonderful. At long last, Mr Bingley would be forgotten, and another would take his place in her heart. This was her first resolution.

Hoping her sister remained awake, she stole down the hall to her room. She knocked quickly before entering.

Elizabeth was seated at the dressing table, seeming either lost in thought or exceedingly enamoured of her reflection. She did not hear Jane approach and gasped aloud when she saw her sister reflected in the glass. "Jane, you nearly frightened me out of my wits!"

"Forgive me. I might have spoken to you in the morning, but I wanted to tell you something now before I lose my deter-mination."

"What is it?"

Jane took a deep breath and blurted it out before she could dissuade herself. "I want to fall in love while we are here—fall in love with someone who will want to marry me."

"That is why we are here."

"I do not mean with Mr Bingley."

Elizabeth's eyes went wide. Slowly, she turned on the bench to face her sister. "You no longer love him?"

Jane tugged at a bit of hair at her neck, a habit when she was anxious. "Perhaps I do, but I think I would be happier if I did not."

"Mr Darcy persuaded him that you were indifferent, and that is why—"

"Yes, yes." Jane interrupted, feeling rather impatient. "I know that. And Mr Darcy also corrected it and told him I was *not* indifferent above a month ago."

Elizabeth opened her mouth to speak but said nothing before closing it again.

"He had ample opportunity to call on me in London or Hertfordshire, and he did not. Now, I am in Derbyshire at the house of his oldest friend, and Mr Bingley had an invitation to be here. Mr Darcy even rearranged his plans to bring him here, but he did not come."

"He was detained on business," said Elizabeth, but her voice had lost its certainty.

"Mr Bingley will always have those things that divert him and change his plans and persuade him to go here or there. Such a changeable man can do nothing but cause heartbreak, or so I have learnt.

"I have an unusual advantage during this visit. I shall be afforded the chance to meet gentlemen in the absence of things...scenes that are not to my advantage."

She had no doubt Elizabeth understood her meaning. Her sister said only, "You must think of your future. You will likely meet many amiable gentlemen here."

"Gentlemen that live in this county." Jane forced a light, teasing tone to her voice. "In the event that one of my favourite sisters should find herself in residence."

Elizabeth rolled her eyes, but she did have a light blush that Jane found promising. "But what will you do if Mr Bingley should arrive?"

"He will not. I would wager anything on it."

"This does present a problem."

"You fear I shall begin to go on like Lydia, no doubt, throwing myself on the men I meet."

Elizabeth laughed. "Hardly. No, but having made such a roar to Mr Darcy about your feelings for Mr Bingley, he believes I am here only for you! And now you do not want your share of the favour. It presents a difficulty, particularly as I am not wholly certain he is glad to have me here."

"How can you say so?"

"He was taciturn tonight."

"He is weary from his travels."

"Perhaps."

"In any case, my change of heart—or rather, the change I hope will come in my heart—need not be canvassed abroad."

"No?"

"No," said Jane reassuringly. "You may permit everyone to believe I still wish to marry Mr Bingley. It cannot signify in any case as he will not come, and I am not so forward that my eagerness to meet another would be noted. This will be between you and me."

"Very well." Elizabeth rose and went to her sister, kissing her cheek. "You have surprised me, but I think you are prudent and courageous."

"It is not courageous. I am forcing myself to see a truth I likely should have seen a long time ago. I am three and twenty, and I do not wish to end like Charlotte, married to an idiotic man because I permitted my best days to pass. I want to marry and have children, and I want to have it now, not if and when Mr Bingley should finally decide to be constant."

"I want you to be happy. And if giving up your hopes of Mr Bingley will make you happy, then you should do it."

"Thank you. I believe I shall."

13

DARCY WOKE EARLY ON THE MORNING AFTER HIS ARRIVAL AT
Pemberley, eager to discharge the duty of writing to Bingley.
Two hours later, he was still at it, having produced nothing of
credit. Although he would apologise for their having had the
argument, by no means would he apologise for what he had
said.

Seated at the small desk in his bedchamber, he permitted his
head to drop into his hands. *What am I doing?* He had somehow
managed to persuade Elizabeth to come to Derbyshire under a
pretence that would soon be revealed as nothing more than time
wasted. Bingley would not come, not if he truly believed even
half of what he had said to Darcy. Bingley's spite was not the
work of a moment, but it was deep and festering, and being left
rather unceremoniously at a posting inn no doubt fed it.

Darcy deeply regretted leaving Bingley as he had. He should
have kept him close. They would have spoken in the morning
and no doubt come to some sort of truce. Instead, a wound had
been opened wide and left to bleed.

Darcy found himself drifting ever deeper into guilt-fuelled
melancholy even as he warned himself against it. Elizabeth was
here, and he must make of it what he could. It would not be

easy. He bore the heavy knowledge of what pain he had brought against her, pain that would be worse if she knew what he had done to Bingley.

At least the first time, he could persuade himself that he was unsure of Miss Bennet's affections. This time, he had no such comfort. Knowing her attachment, and having given his word, he still permitted his pride and his anger to hold sway.

With a determined growl, he raised his head. He could not languish in his regrets nor lament his missteps, many though they were. He would fix this, just as he sought to fix his errors with Elizabeth.

He reached for a new sheet of paper. Bingley needed his help, not his censure, and if the cost of providing such help was to swallow a bit of pride, then he would be the better man for it.

Renewed effort was put into the letter, and in a short time, it said what needed to be said. Before he could think of it any further, he signed and sealed it. "Forgive me, Bingley, I have not been the friend to you that I should have been," he murmured to the letter, wishing it Godspeed.

He placed it onto the salver with the other outgoing correspondence on his way to the breakfast room.

WAS NOTHING AS SHE THOUGHT IT WAS?

Although she had been at Pemberley a short time, the duration had been sufficient to turn everything she believed she knew on its head. And now this business of Jane giving up on Mr Bingley! She did not blame her—indeed, she applauded her resolve—but she could not bear to imagine Mr Darcy's countenance on learning of Jane's change of heart. *How stupid he would think me. Wrong about him, wrong about Jane's attachment to Mr Bingley. I would seem as silly and illiterate as my mother. Believing I knew so much, I have proven to know very little save my own ignorant opinions.*

Mr Darcy had arrived at his breakfast table with no evident improvement in his spirits from the evening prior. Jane dismissed it as the continued fatigue of travel, but Elizabeth could not be so certain. The day was spent in pleasant occupation—music, reading, and walks in the gardens—but her growing worries would not leave her mind.

Most troublesome was the fact that Mr Darcy had not behaved as a man in love. He was polite and amiable and provided witty discourse and ample opportunity for diversion, but he did so in the calm, disinterested manner of a host. He had not singled her out above Jane or his sister or even her aunt. She did not find his eyes upon her in quiet moments. She realised now what his attentions to her at Netherfield had meant and fretted over the absence of them here at Pemberley.

It troubled her more than she cared to admit. She watched him as he had watched her on so many occasions, wishing to understand his behaviour and put to rest the damnable uncertainty that plagued her.

I grew accustomed to thinking I was sure in his regard. I liked believing him in my power.

The plan for the evening was to attend a ball, and Elizabeth was glad. Firstly, she greatly enjoyed dancing, but secondly, it gave her the chance to wear one of her new gowns. As she admired it laid out upon the bed, she chided herself. Mr Darcy had surely seen many finer, and in any case, he had seen her six inches deep in mud. His admiration was as much a mystery as he was and hardly dependent upon a new gown.

She had no great opinion of her beauty, but now, preparing to leave the room, she thought she looked as well as she ever could. Did she hope Mr Darcy thought the same? Did she hope to move his eye towards her, perhaps to even see his admiration? No, this much she could not admit, even to herself, but she did find herself wondering whether he liked Pomona green.

THE DAY COULD HARDLY BE COUNTED A SUCCESS, DARCY SCOLDED himself, standing patiently as his man finished with his cravat. He had been dull and stupid, having failed to set aside his concerns over the situation with Bingley and wholly unable to so much as look at Elizabeth, knowing how he must yet again disappoint her. For this evening, at least, it should be easier. They were going to a ball, and perhaps in a livelier setting he would find himself capable of higher spirits.

Darcy was first to be ready, and he stood awaiting the others with some anxiety. It had occurred to him that he did not know where they were going. Saye had received the invitation and accepted it on behalf of their little party. He only hoped the people would be amiable and welcoming to Elizabeth. The last thing he needed at this point was another obstacle to his courtship created by haughty friends or unkind neighbours.

Saye came down the stairs, resplendent in the latest fashion, his hair swept up to an almost ridiculous degree. Darcy regarded him with thinly disguised amusement. "What have you got in that hair of yours, Saye? I believe it must be the same thing the parlour maids use on the furniture."

"Never mind my hair," Saye snapped. "Let me have a look at you."

Darcy stood indifferently while Saye looked him up and down but balked when Saye said, "Turn, please." Darcy merely rolled his eyes.

"Then I shall walk behind you." Saye took two quick paces and, before Darcy knew what he was about, lifted his coat.

"What the devil!" Darcy yanked himself away, anger and embarrassment flushing through him.

"I believe Miss Elizabeth likes that," Saye said, with a little wink and the lift of one brow. "I just wanted to be certain you were showing to advantage. These are not your most flattering breeches—you are drooping a little—but I think they will do well enough."

"Showing to advantage!" Darcy spat the words in disgust. "Of all things." *Drooping? Surely not. Fields would never permit it.*

Saye said nothing, busying himself with adjusting the fob of his watch. Darcy watched him, warring with himself even as curiosity arose within him.

"Why do you think she likes that?"

"All ladies like a gentleman with nice firm buttocks, and I do not feel I speak amiss when I tell you that yours is finer than most." Saye turned, lifting his coat and presenting Darcy with a view of his own posterior. "Not as well-formed as mine, certainly, but yours will do."

Darcy scowled in the direction of his cousin's hindquarters. "All ladies? Or Miss Elizabeth particularly?"

"Come again?"

Darcy sighed, seeing that Saye intended to make him say it even if he had to drag it out of him. "When you said you thought Miss Elizabeth likes that, did you mean you assumed she did based on your observation of ladies in general? Or have you noted Miss Elizabeth especially appreciates…?" He gestured to the back of his breeches.

Saye permitted a secretive little smile to cross his lips. "I have observed Miss Elizabeth is not an exception to the rule."

"But was your observation sufficient to determine only a general interest in the posterior or was a preference shown in some manner?"

"Good lord, Darcy," Saye cried out in mock distress. "What on earth are you asking me? You say things in such a round-about manner, I can hardly make sense of you."

"Nothing. Forget it. Forget I asked."

Saye nodded and began a senseless little stroll about the hall, looking in a mirror here or adjusting a flower there. Darcy could only watch him for a moment before feeling compelled to seek further understanding. "What I am saying is…have you noticed…that is to say, do you think that…when you observed her, did she…"

"Darcy…" Saye stopped his rambles about the place and spoke patiently but with a decided twinkle in his eye. "Are you asking me whether Miss Elizabeth Bennet admired your arse?"

"Lord, you are a vulgar creature." Darcy put as much contempt as he could into the words.

Saye gave a little humph and turned his attention to some little knickknack on the hall table, straightening and examining it with seeming absorption. His stoicism had the desired effect. Darcy could tolerate no more than a minute of watching him before asking, "So did she? Does she?"

"Does she what?" Saye raised innocent eyes to his cousin's face.

Darcy closed his eyes a moment. Being the object of Saye's ridicule was worth it—worth it and then some—if only he could learn that Elizabeth admired something about him, even if it was his arse. With gritted teeth, he said, "Tell me right now whether you saw Elizabeth—"

"Yes, I see Miss Elizabeth." Saye spoke jovially, stopping him mid-sentence and taking several steps to stand shoulder to shoulder with his cousin. "And Miss Bennet too! Visions of love-liness, both of you."

Darcy started, noticing the ladies were descending, and he

sent up a silent prayer of thanks that he had not said what he was about to say. He smiled at the ladies, who had gained the last landing even as Saye leaned into him, hissing, "Yes. I saw her, and her admiration was quite plain, so make of it what you can."

He was so much in charity with Saye for offering up this small bit of pleasure that he almost forgave him his next great affront.

Their party fully assembled, all moved to the awaiting carriages. Mr Gardiner handed his nieces and wife into his carriage while Darcy and his cousins entered Saye's conveyance. As Darcy climbed in, he asked, "Whose ball is this now?"

"It is not so much a ball," said Saye, "as it is an assembly."

"An assembly?" Darcy asked as Fitzwilliam chuckled. "Not a…"

"A public assembly," said Saye with relish. "I have already paid for our admissions."

Darcy tossed his head back, groaning loudly. "A country assembly, open to any and all—"

"A public assembly," said Saye firmly. "Just as public as the one at which you insulted her."

"Ah! Yes!" Fitzwilliam cried. "A reminder of their first meeting."

"No!" Darcy protested. "I want her to *forget* our first meeting."

"So you rewrite it," said Saye. "Wipe off the slate, and try again to do it properly. Yes? I think it is a wonderful idea." Fitzwilliam seconded him.

"But who will be there?" Darcy asked with dismay. "My tenants? I hardly think I need to tell you that I do not wish to make a cake of myself in front of the tradespeople and farmers of the area."

Saye laughed. "Do not fear, Darcy. I daresay, it will be the gentry. The tradespeople and farmers are too exhausted from their labour this time of year to dance through the night, not to mention that the cost of admittance is prohibitive to those without means."

"They will wish to dance with her," said Darcy glumly.

"Of course, they will dance with her," said Fitzwilliam. "I intend to dance with both of them myself."

"As do I."

"But she will enjoy herself," said Fitzwilliam, "and that is what is important above all."

To that, Darcy could offer no disagreement.

14

"So many people," Elizabeth exclaimed with surprise. They had not yet arrived at the assembly rooms, the street clogged with coaches and horses, but it was abundantly clear where everyone was going. "How big are these rooms, do you suppose?"

"Let us hope the rooms are large," said Mrs Gardiner. "And have many, many open windows."

"I have never been to such a crush," Jane said. Elizabeth looked at her, enjoying the pink flush of anticipation in her cheeks. Jane caught her glance and lowered her eyes demurely. How good it was to see her dear sister so well in looks and eager to enjoy herself! It was a marked contrast to her former spirits, and Elizabeth silently thanked Mr Darcy for affording them this opportunity. Surely a summer in Hertfordshire could not have done Jane half as well.

There was a stir amongst those at the assembly at the arrival of the sons of the Earl of Matlock as well as Mr Darcy, one of the principal landowners in the area. The fact that the gentleman attended rarely could only raise interest. That they had brought ladies with them, one of whom was rumoured to be betrothed to one of them, was more provocative still. As a matter of chance, it was Saye who escorted her into the assembly with Jane on Darcy's arm behind them, followed by Fitzwilliam and the Gardiners. Their entry was something of a sensation. Elizabeth felt as if the music stopped, though later reflection persuaded her it surely had not. All eyes went to them, and the whispers began almost immediately. Although she had never been a person who was shy or easily intimidated, it was rather daunting to be the object of such intense scrutiny. The subjects of the whispers were no great surprise: her fortune—or lack thereof—and her person, which was met with varying degrees of approbation or disapprobation depending on whether the speaker was male or female.

It was mortifying although there was part of her that found it diverting as well. *How he must have felt it in Hertfordshire!* She glanced at Darcy. He looked like he bore it here in his home county only slightly better than he had in hers.

Their party moved into the throng carefully. Jane, as expected, was drawing notice. Elizabeth had no doubt her sister's hand would be sought quickly to join the dances.

It was evident that those present were awed by the appearance of the exalted gentlemen. The crowd parted as they moved through, and ladies and gentlemen alike straightened, arranging themselves to advantage and hoping for some sign of favour.

Their movement through the crowd had the effect of pushing their little party into a single line. Their near quarters provided an ideal opportunity for Mr Darcy to lean into Elizabeth and murmur his request for her first set. With a little smile over her shoulder, she acquiesced, feeling relieved.

They did not have long to observe the others dancing, for a set ended just then, and the next set formed almost immediately. Elizabeth smiled, seeing Colonel Fitzwilliam leading Jane onto the floor as Saye, evidently determined to be gallant, asked Mrs Gardiner to dance.

Mr Darcy began just as he had during their dance at Mr Bingley's ball at Netherfield—silently. She bore it for a little while, even introducing one or two topics of no consequence, which met with no success in drawing him out. At last, she could bear it no more.

"I must say, sir, this is reminding me of the first time we danced. Do you agree?"

Since it was neither the same dance, the same ballroom, nor the same people, he could not possibly agree. He said only, "How so?"

She smiled at him. "In that we are both gravely moving through the patterns, quite lost within our own musings."

"Forgive me if I am a negligent partner. There seems an embargo on every subject I think of."

"An embargo on every subject! Why?"

"So much has passed between us, our history runs quite deep, yet...yet my understanding of you remains so poor that I cannot...I have much in my mind that I would like to say to you, but I find I cannot. And these weightier concerns make it seem that I would be rather stupid to begin in the usual way with the trite pleasantries and inconsequential discourse that make up most first dances."

His candour shocked her but evidently no more than he had shocked himself. Elizabeth was treated to the unanticipated and strange sight of Mr Darcy blushing. He murmured, "Forgive me," but the pattern soon turned him away, and he had recovered himself when he turned back.

Now their silence could only grow more anxious, for they both wished to find a subject for conversation. At length, Elizabeth decided the topic that made them anxious must be addressed. "Ours has been an unusual acquaintance, it is true. By some accounting, we might be said to be well acquainted, and in others, I feel we scarcely know one another at all. I think it is this that inhibits our ease."

When he looked at her, she made sure to smile at him in a friendly manner.

"I believe it must be because we have never been properly acquainted," Darcy suggested.

"Not properly acquainted? How so?"

"The fault is entirely mine. One night at Rosings when I tried to excuse my poor behaviour at the Meryton assembly by saying I did not know anyone beyond my party, you said 'nobody can ever be introduced in a ball room.' I understood you meant it as a rebuke on my poor behaviour the night we first met."

Elizabeth laughed lightly, turning her head from him. "I should not have said anything of the sort, Mr Darcy. I must beg your apology. You need not answer for your conduct to me."

"You were entirely correct," he assured her. "I could not dispute you. In fact, I tried to offer something of an apology to you. Do you recall me saying, 'I should have judged better, had I sought an introduction?' It was a weak apology to be sure. I would not be surprised if you did not understand it to be one."

He watched her closely, clearly expecting an answer. She gave him one. "I did not."

"I meant it to tell you I wished I had done differently that night, because I did. I regretted my rudeness even that night, but since that time, my regrets could only multiply. In any case, that is why I say our acquaintance was not properly begun."

She raised her eyes to his. "Perhaps we should begin anew."

His eyes widened slightly as he searched her face. Would he doubt her sincerity? Slowly he said, "I would like that very much."

A small, shy smile, incongruous with respect to her boldness of seconds before, was her only reply.

"Tell me instead what you hope to see in Derbyshire, what sights you wish to view, and what paths you wish to tread."

She looked up at him, a strange and incandescent feeling arising in her chest. She could not give it a name, not yet, but it was warm and undeniably thrilling. "Derbyshire is yielding many surprises. I believe I wish to see it all."

WHEN HIS DANCE WITH ELIZABETH HAD CONCLUDED, DARCY'S mind was too unsettled to think of dancing with another, not even Miss Bennet, so he took himself into the card room. Therein was a group of gentlemen, most of whom he had met previously, just beginning to form their table for speculation. One of them asked him to join them, and he did.

As the game began, a great deal of the conversation was aimed at acquainting one another with the recent goings-on in each man's life. Some had been in town, and some had stayed in Derbyshire; it was something of a reunion.

There was much to say on someone who had lost a fortune and someone who had gained, and the gentlemen talked about recent news items and the politics of both the county and the country. A local man wished to sell off some of his horses, and the quality of the animals was a subject of much interest.

When these things had been adequately canvassed, the conversation turned to Darcy's guests.

The first man to seek more information was one Mr Robert Abell. Among those at the table, Mr Abell was a respectable gentleman who was a year or two younger than Darcy. He was heir to an estate worth about 3500 pounds a year, though he had not yet inherited. Darcy thought him kind enough, if a bit dull.

"The Miss Bennets are charming girls. From Hertfordshire, are they?"

Although Abell introduced his subject in a nonchalant manner, Darcy did not mistake his interest and responded with a slight dip of his head.

"Bennet..." mused another man, a Mr Stoner. He was a short, dark, hirsute fellow who always appeared too eager to Darcy's eyes. Stoner had always reminded him of a particularly aggressive pug. "Cannot say I have heard of the family."

"Their estate is called Longbourn," said Darcy.

"Ah. Good estate? Profitable?"

This was why he had never liked Stoner although he was of use in certain circumstances. He was unafraid of being thought impolite and asked what everyone wished to know.

It was Darcy's turn to lay a card, and he snapped it down onto the pile with a decisive motion. "It is entailed upon a distant cousin but has afforded them a comfortable life. It is unencumbered by debt, which is more than may be said by many these days."

He knew that, by their association to him, Miss Bennet and Elizabeth would be presumed to have more of "comfort" than their present circumstance truly afforded, but he did not care. As much as he might wish to frighten away prospective suitors, he would not. He wished to bring Elizabeth some acclaim, amends for the embarrassment he had wrought upon her.

"You are their acquaintance of some years then?"

Darcy had to admit that the questions were vexing, particularly as the interest of these gentlemen was thinly disguised. "Months," he replied. "My friend Mr Bingley has let an estate next to that of their father. I attended him there last autumn and met the young ladies at an assembly such as this."

Sir Edmund asked, "So their father is a gentleman, yes?"

Stoner reached over, laughing loudly and rapping his knuckles lightly against Sir Edmund's head. "Estate! Longbourn! Pay attention, sir, or remain silent."

Sir Edmund batted him away with scarcely a notice.

"Mr Bennet is one of the principal landowners in that area. His was not the finest estate," Darcy forced another smile, "but inarguably, he had the most beautiful daughters."

A roar of delight went around the table. "How many of them are there, Darcy?"

"Five," said Darcy. "None married as yet."

"And you have offered us only two! For shame, man!"

A prickling flush made Darcy yearn to squirm in his seat. It went against his grain to be so candid—to sit and be questioned like a prisoner of war. But these men, the people who, with good fortune, would one day be Elizabeth's neighbours, would never doubt his affection for her. He had humiliated her in front of her neighbours, but he would glorify her to his. They would know from the start where she stood in his esteem.

Forcing himself to sound genial and easy, Darcy replied, "Two? I am afraid not. I offer you but one."

"So the rumours are true."

"Which rumours are those?" Darcy asked.

"That you are engaged," said Abell. "Nay—that you lost your mind for love."

"So that is how they say it, eh?" Darcy forced a grin to his face, still taking care to seem unperturbed. "I cannot deny that I have lost my heart, my mind, and my soul to her, and deuced if it is not the most splendid thing I have ever done."

His words sent the men into a paroxysm of questions and exclamations. Darcy felt his back slapped, someone offered him their snuffbox, and plans were thrust forth, inviting him to bring the Miss Bennets to dine, to dance, to play cards, to picnic—a feast of diversion shoved under his nose.

"But why are you wasting your time in here?" Stoner asked. "I should think you would be playing the lovesick suitor by her side!"

Because she does not wish me at her side. All the ease and friendliness that Darcy had managed to summon was gone in an instant. "An excellent point," he said, rising and leaving his cards and money on the table. "I shall do that now."

LITTLE DARCY SAID COULD HAVE AROUSED MORE INTEREST IN THE two Miss Bennets than what he did. As soon as he quit the card table and the door closed behind him, Abell chuckled. "Darcy is in love!"

His words released a torrent of discussion and speculation among the other gentlemen at the table.

"But with which one?"

"The eldest Miss Bennet is beautiful."

"I heard in town that he was engaged, but he did not exactly say he was."

"He did."

"No, not quite. Perhaps he has not yet proposed?"

"For an acquaintance of so many months? Good lord, man, get to it then!"

"I danced with Miss Elizabeth Bennet, and I daresay, I have rarely had a more enjoyable dance."

"Miss Elizabeth Bennet?"

"The younger one." The speaker was a new arrival to the table called Mr Ellis, and he had that unique capability of being influential without much effort. He was tall but not unusually so, handsome but not excessively so, and, wealthy but not so much as to arouse undue jealousy. Everyone liked him, and most wished to be like him.

"She is not quite so lovely as her sister," opined Abell. "But she is handsome in her own right."

"She has a quality," said Ellis. "A quality that prevails over beauty."

"What might that be?" The person who asked this question was a lad of only two and twenty, newly down from Oxford and as green as green could be.

Ellis smirked at him. "A beautiful woman is a delight. She is made to be admired by her suitor and all who see her. Some ladies, however, have something beyond mere beauty, something that drives a man to fever—a quality that makes him burn to possess that which can never truly be owned. Oh yes, I have no doubt that, of the two Miss Bennets, it is the younger who stirs Darcy's blood. I would wager all I have on it."

There was much further conversation, conjecture that grew wilder as a few more games were played. Other gentlemen, coming in and about, heard the tale of Darcy's restraint and impassioned declaration. As the tale moved through the room, the restraint grew more restrained and the declaration ever more impassioned. Gentlemen left the room nearly desperate to secure a place on the dance cards of these extraordinary ladies who had so enraptured Mr Darcy.

"What in the blazing bunghole of Napoleon are you doing?" Fitzwilliam gave Darcy a sharp little shove as he joined him near the drinks table nearly two hours later.

Darcy had spent hours watching Elizabeth be courted by what seemed like every single man in the place. There was surely no shortage of gentlemen as there had been in Meryton in the autumn. He found himself longing for *that* circumstance.

Elizabeth had scarcely been able to catch her breath between dances, for when she was not dancing, she was being introduced to person after person who wished to secure her regard. While many initially sought her for the purpose of novelty, Elizabeth was, as always, charming and pretty and filled with good conversation. It seemed to Darcy that people flocked to her, male and female alike, wishing to know more, and those who did not surround her went about singing her praises. He was wearied to the point of despondence by the very sight of it.

"Leave me alone, Fitzwilliam. Can you not see I am busy watching the woman I love enjoying the attentions of every gentleman in the room save for myself?"

"If that is so, you can blame no one but yourself," Fitzwilliam chided.

"It is her due. If I shamed her at an assembly in her home county, I must at least afford her the chance to bask in the admiration of those in attendance here tonight."

"You might do better to admire her more yourself."

Darcy waved him off. "Never mind me. What about you? I saw Miss Clark over there."

Fitzwilliam groaned, but Darcy knew his little gibe had landed. Miss Clark was a lady who had set her cap for Fitzwilliam when they were both full young, not even out. Despite a good fortune, Miss Clark was decidedly not Fitzwilliam's sort of lady, being ill humoured, sickly, and rather cross. She reminded Darcy of his cousin Anne, including being able to boast of a similarly overbearing mother. "I, too, saw Miss Clark—fortunately, before she saw me."

The two gentlemen talked for a short while, discussing Fitzwilliam's conquests or lack thereof. Eventually Fitzwilliam strolled away in search of a pretty lady to keep him in adequate style, and Darcy was able to return to his thoughts.

He had considered asking Elizabeth for a second dance but persuaded himself against it. Having already acted in London in a manner that led people to believe them betrothed, he did not wish to make the same mistake here—not for his sake, but for hers. Moreover, he saw how much she was enjoying herself, and he would not take that from her. "See there," he said softly as he watched her move through a pattern. "I am not always selfish."

Their dance had been a satisfying beginning, but he ever wanted more where Elizabeth Bennet was concerned. Nevertheless, for tonight, he would make himself be satisfied or, if not that, then at least be resolved to bear dissatisfaction.

ELIZABETH WAS NEARLY INSENSIBLE WITH FATIGUE AS THE NIGHT drew on. Never before had she been at an assembly with such a surfeit of dance partners and all of them agreeable and kind. She had, on the whole, a most enjoyable evening.

There was only one part of the night in which she would claim dissatisfaction. She had believed—nay, hoped—that Mr Darcy would ask her to dance a second time. He did not. Indeed, she had scarcely any idea what had become of him, for after their first, early dance and his dance with Jane, he had very nearly disappeared.

She saw him leaning against the wall looking rather unhappy. He had not seemed so after their dance, but he surely was now. She could read it in the set of his mouth and the disinterested look in his eyes.

Mr Tomlinson came to request the last set of the evening, but she demurred with another glance towards the place where Mr

Darcy stood. Although her time dancing had been agreeable, she now preferred a more sedate occupation.

Yielding to an impulse she did not wholly understand, she stared at Mr Darcy, willing him to look at her.

THE DANCE HAD ENDED, AND THE COUPLES MOVED AND SHIFTED, changing partners and so forth. In the bustle, he lost sight of her, but it did not worry him. He was patient, resolving to find her once the next set had begun.

But when it started to form, she was still not to be found. Trying to be as unobtrusive as possible, he looked about, seeking her without appearing to do so. It took some time, but he finally located her in the chairs off to the side where some of the chaperons sat. To his shock, he saw that she was watching him.

His gaze locked with hers as he took a moment to determine that she was truly looking at him and not merely gazing in his direction.

However, she smiled—just a little smile but a charming one —then, for just a moment, she dropped her eyes. Then her eyes were back on him.

She glanced at the empty chair beside her and moved her eyes back to his. *An invitation?*

He waited. She did it again, this time allowing her arm to drop and surreptitiously tap the chair with her fan. An impish sort of look at him followed.

I have been summoned, he thought with delight. He made haste across the floor, careful not to beam like a love-struck idiot but unable to conceal the lightness of his step occasioned by the intense pleasure in his heart.

When he reached her, she rose, and he bowed. Not knowing

what to say, he settled for the obvious. "Miss Elizabeth, I would be pleased if you would dance the next with me."

"Thank you," she said, with a little twinkle in her eye. "I had believed you not fond of dancing, sir, and now you would dance with me twice in one night?"

How lovely it was to be teased by her! "I am fond of dancing with you."

"In any case, I shall spare you," she said with a smile. "I had another enjoyable pursuit in mind."

"What is that?"

He watched as a blush crept up her neck and stained her cheeks. She appeared ignorant of it although she could not quite look at him when she said, "I enjoyed our earlier conversation and hoped to have more of it."

Darcy agreed, his tone in no way matching the sense of exultation within him. She sat, and he took the seat she had offered, thinking that the night was ending far better than he had dared hope.

They had agreed to begin anew, yet he struggled, not really knowing how to do so. How did one begin anew with a woman who knew of his love and with whom so much had been shared?

It seemed she read his mind. "Let us put aside more weighty issues," she said in a low tone. "Let us speak of nothing and everything, shall we?"

"Gladly," he told her, much relieved.

15

It was somewhat depressing for Georgiana to be left behind the group who attended the assembly, and Elizabeth noticed it even as Georgiana did her best to appear unaffected. In an impulse of sisterly kindness, Elizabeth had said to her, "You must be present for what I consider the best part of any such amusement."

"What is that?"

Elizabeth put her arm around Georgiana's waist. "Why, the discussion of it, of course. My sisters and I sit up after every ball, telling one another who wore what, who danced with whom, and why this person was absent while another person was present. I am sure I would not even bother going to balls if I could not talk them over with my sisters afterward."

Georgiana was delighted by the idea and, later that night, appeared at Elizabeth's bedchamber door with a tray of much-appreciated refreshments. The two ladies were soon joined by Jane, who announced, "I declare, I did not sit once the whole night!" She extended her foot, which was a bit swollen from her exertions.

The ladies settled onto the bed, eating and talking of the assembly. Elizabeth began, recounting her dance partners and regaling Georgiana with tales of the more notable gowns they had seen.

"I met a Miss Abell. Very pretty girl and amiable too."

"Oh yes," said Georgiana. "Our fathers used to shoot together, and she would come to visit although she was older than me."

Elizabeth smiled. "I do not think my sister found her brother displeasing."

"Lizzy," Jane hushed her. "All the gentlemen I danced with were kind and welcoming."

This led to a discussion of their various dances. Elizabeth allowed most of it to come from Jane as she did not feel she could discuss dancing with other men in the presence of Mr Darcy's sister.

Georgiana would not allow her complete silence, however. "Did you dance with my brother?"

Elizabeth nodded. "I did."

"Oh?" Georgiana leaned closer, her eyes wide and unmoving. "How was it?"

Elizabeth looked down. "It was nice."

"Was it?"

"Yes," Elizabeth said, suffusing her words with warmth and finality. "Very nice indeed."

A silence fell, but it was brief, broken quickly by Jane's laughter. "Miss Darcy, you must know my sister's reserve is a desirable thing. That which she prizes is held close. If she thought your brother disagreeable or vexatious, I assure you, we would hear it all."

Elizabeth tried to protest over Georgiana's giggles but found she could not.

Jane, clearly repentant of her little joke on her sister's character, was quick to change the topic. She mentioned a Miss Clark, which made Georgiana laugh and ask whether the colonel had danced with her. He had not, not insofar as either Jane or Elizabeth noticed.

"Are my brother and cousins all good dancers?" Georgiana asked. "I have danced with them at home for practice and so forth, but I do not know whether they are good or terrible or merely average."

This led to a conversation of dances that had come before: the good, the not so good, and the dreadful. Jane and Elizabeth, having been out for some years, had an ample supply of tales for Georgiana, including a generous allotment of those in the dreadful category.

It was likely the sharing of these confidences that led to Georgiana's impulse to share something as well. As she had little of gossip or stories of her own to share, it fell to her to speak of someone else. It began innocently enough with Jane asking of the plans for the days ahead. Georgiana had a fondness for games and picnics, it would seem, and had planned many of them. "I do not know when Mr Bingley will join us," she said contracting her brow. "Perhaps he will not come after all."

Jane went unnaturally still as Elizabeth remarked, "Oh? I had understood his attendance here to be rather certain."

Georgiana said, "Evidently, he and my brother had a terrible argument."

"About what?" Jane's voice seemed high-pitched and a bit wavering.

"He does not like Mr Bingley's friends of late. They are somewhat wild or at least more wild than my brother thinks is good."

Elizabeth was looking at the coverlet. "Mr Darcy is attentive to the good character of his friends."

"That is true," Georgiana said. "He does not associate with the dissolute. He and Saye have had several arguments over Saye's behaviour as well, though Saye is a great deal more settled since becoming betrothed to Miss Goddard."

A sudden pall was cast over their little party. Georgiana looked at the other two ladies, concerned she had offended them with her gossip. She apologised immediately, begging them to say nothing of the matter to her brother. "To overhear what he says in the privacy of his rooms is not honourable, I know, particularly when one casts his communication abroad as I have done."

Both ladies assured her the secret was safe with them just as they heard a rooster crowing in the distance. Georgiana gasped when she heard it. "We shall all be abed until noon!"

"Perhaps we shall," Elizabeth agreed with a little laugh as the others moved to take their leave. Jane would not look at her as she departed, and Elizabeth's spirit groaned to see her sister already downcast over this latest disappointment. Elizabeth was sorry to have heard what she had of Bingley even as she wondered at it. Her first inclination had been vexation at Mr Darcy until she recalled Kitty's report of Mr Wickham and his debts. Was that it? Had Mr Bingley found himself in arrears, perhaps even asked Mr Darcy for a loan?

She would never know, it seemed. Mr Darcy gave no indication that Mr Bingley was no longer expected, nor did she think he would. If nothing else, his dealings with Mr Wickham had shown that Mr Darcy did not feel he needed to answer to anyone about his private actions.

THE DAY AFTER THE ASSEMBLY BEGAN LATE AND CARRIED ON AT A drooping pace. Darcy soon learnt that even after the exertions of the assembly, the Bennet ladies had declined to retire, instead staying up half the night talking to Georgiana. It pleased him as much as it surprised him.

He wished to assume their languor was wholly due to lack of sleep, but it was not long into the day before he feared it was not. He had hoped his new beginning with Elizabeth would mean greater ease and friendliness, but it did not. Elizabeth seemed somewhat wary, almost withdrawn. He noticed her watching him several times, particularly when Georgiana asked when Mr Bingley was expected.

"His plans are not yet fixed, dear. Soon, I should hope."

Across the room, Elizabeth lowered her eyes to the book on her lap. She did not appear to be particularly engaged in it, glancing about frequently and often shifting in her chair.

He found himself standing before her with no recollection of having moved there nor any idea what he meant to say. Thus, he surprised himself as much as her when he said, "I wonder, Miss Elizabeth, whether you would accompany me on a short walk."

She jumped a little. Her eyes were wide and her lips parted, she stared a moment before gently closing her book. "It might rain."

"It might," he agreed with a cursory look at the window. "I think not though. There is a charming stream I would like to show you. I think you will like it."

She placed the book beside her with slow, deliberate movements as she appeared to give careful consideration to his invitation. Finally, she said in a tone of admission, "I need a minute to get my things."

In due time, they were out of doors. The air held an unusual hint of coolness, which persuaded Darcy to introduce her to a favourite spot of his. She agreed although it was something of a distance from the house, and they set off.

Their conversation was inconsequential as they went. Elizabeth was quieter than usual. After some time, he remarked on it.

"You are not in your usual lively spirits today, Miss Elizabeth."

"Forgive me if I am poor company."

"Not at all," he said reassuringly. "But if there is anything that plagues your mind, I am an able listener."

They came to the little stream of which he had spoken. It was charming, shallow, and bubbling merrily over rocks time had worn into smooth ovals. Farther down was a deeper pool that was almost perfectly round—an ideal swimming hole. She knelt down beside it, removing her glove and running her fingers in the cool water at the edge.

Darcy knelt beside her. "Fitzwilliam and I used to think if we swam deep enough, we would find ourselves emerged into the Orient or perhaps the American colonies."

She laughed lightly, looking at him with merry eyes. "And did you?"

"No. We nearly drowned on many occasions, but we never came close to the bottom."

"So the question remains unanswered, then. It is still entirely possible this is the doorway to another kingdom."

He chuckled and rose, holding out his hand to assist her. She stood and turned to face him. "If I am quiet, sir, I must admit that I find myself frequently lapsing into thought today—partly, I must own, from my fatigue of last night."

"And the other part?" He had a sense he must tread carefully, though he knew not why.

"I am pondering the meaning of friendship. I believe you and I have become friends, after a fashion."

"Yes, we have." He did not move his gaze from hers when he

added with some boldness, "You do surely know that to be merely your friend is not my true wish."

She inclined her head slightly in acknowledgment. "It seems, however, your friendship is easily removed."

Not Wickham again! He barely restrained a groan. "My attachment to those I count as friends is implacable."

With a pert smile and a swish of her skirts, she turned away, returning down the path they had come by. "An unforgiving temper and implacable attachment. I wonder, then, under what circumstances will one triumph over the other?"

He made two quick paces to draw beside her. "I told you I had an unyielding temper during your stay at Netherfield, I believe."

"You did."

"Since that time, I have been given to understand that much of what I knew about my conduct might require evaluation and change to become a man worthy of…worthy of love."

She said nothing, lowering her head so her bonnet would obscure her face.

He touched her lightly on the arm without speaking. When she looked, he gestured to her left. She turned towards a small, narrow path. It was not easy terrain, and she shot him a questioning look.

"The way is a bit uneven, but the vista it will afford us is worth the struggle."

She silently acquiesced, beginning to pick her way up the path slowly and carefully. The terrain required their close attention for a time. It was rocky and quite steep in places, but at last, they arrived. The narrow path opened onto the flat edge of a large precipice overlooking both a rocky ravine and the stream they had dabbled in previously. On such a day as they had, the view went on for miles.

Elizabeth exclaimed in delight at the prospect before her. To Darcy, it was as charming as could be imagined, with black rock jutting forth over the water. The stream babbled along over a series of low waterfalls. On the other side was a lovely dense wood, the leaves looking green and cool in the dappled sunlight. Elizabeth sighed, visibly rapt with pleasure in the scene.

"This is indeed a charming place," she effused. "Thank you for showing it to me."

"The pleasure is mine." He watched her, revelling in her felicity. "I am glad you see it was worth the difficulty in getting to it."

There was a brief silence between them. "I recall, Miss Elizabeth, one discussion at Netherfield during which you mentioned that you enjoyed studying the characters of those around you. You said that, as few as they were, they nevertheless had infinite variety and thus provided you endless interest for study."

She nodded.

"Do you not wonder what changes your reproofs might have wrought in me?"

She laughed a little nervously, folding her arms across her chest. "I would hope my reproofs could not have been so severe as to lead you to believe you must change yourself on my account."

"It was not the severity of your reproofs that proved persuasive."

She looked at him, an expectant and quizzical expression on her face.

"I have another recollection from an evening at Netherfield that serves me here. You and I were speaking of Bingley's character in terms of the ease with which he is persuaded by his friends. Do you remember it?"

She thought for a moment. "Not in every particular, no."

"You accused me of saying that to yield readily, easily, to the persuasion of a friend has no merit with you. I said to yield without conviction is no compliment to the understanding of either. You said I allowed nothing for the influence of friendship and affection, that if there was a regard for the requester, a person will often yield on the basis of their affection rather than be argued into it."

"I remember it vaguely," she admitted. "How did we leave it? Did we decide affection or reason was most important in such matters?"

"We decided nothing." Darcy stepped over a protruding root after guiding Elizabeth carefully around the obstacle. "Bingley asked us to cease our conversation, fearing it was too much like a dispute."

Elizabeth smiled faintly, glancing up at him. "Mr Bingley dislikes argument."

He could not answer for that, not when he knew quite well how vigorously Bingley could argue when provoked. "I suppose you must wonder what this has to do with us. Only that I did not require excessive argument to persuade me into attending to your reproofs."

He paused and then added, "The influence of esteem was sufficient."

She silently stared down at the path that was obligingly uneven so as to make her study of it seem reasonable. When at last she spoke, she said, "You should not alter your character to suit me, sir."

"In essentials, I am much as I ever was. However, in seeing the picture of the man I presented to you—in seeing myself through your eyes—I have learnt some lessons of great value. I have been a selfish being all my life, in practice, though not in principle. As a child, I was taught what was right, but I was not taught to correct my temper. I was given good principles but left to follow them in pride and conceit. Unfortunately an only son (for many years an only child), I was spoilt by my parents, who, though good themselves (my father, particularly, all that was benevolent and amiable), allowed, encouraged, almost taught me to be selfish and overbearing; to care for none beyond my own family circle; to think meanly of all the rest of the world; to wish at least to think meanly of their sense and worth compared with my own."

His candour was rewarded. Elizabeth had a soft look in her eye when she raised her head and laid her hand upon his arm. "I fear you do yourself too much discredit."

He laid his hand atop hers. "I likely remain far too prideful even with my reforms. However, I have at least learnt that implacable resentment is nothing of which to boast and friendship must be valued most of all."

She smiled at him in response, and he added, "For someone I love, truly love, I would do anything."

SHE FOUND JANE IN THE APARTMENT SHE HAD BEEN GIVEN FOR HER stay, mending a gown that had suffered some little damage on its journey to Derbyshire.

Jane looked up with a smile. "I thought Mr Darcy had stolen away with you."

Elizabeth laughed absently. "There was a delightful prospect he wished me to see above a mile from the house."

Jane moved her things aside so Elizabeth could join her. Elizabeth sat, her eyes still fixed on a far off place in her mind. When she spoke, she spoke as if Jane was privy to all the thoughts that had been wild in her mind since Mr Darcy's startling and deeply felt confessions. "I believe when a person holds themselves to an exacting standard, it becomes almost natural to hold others to the same high standard."

Jane glanced up from her sewing and nodded.

"Is that what it is to be self-righteous? I suppose it must be, yet it is almost impossible to avoid it. Someone who prizes honour enough to have it themselves will also value it in others."

Jane nodded again.

"I do not think Mr Darcy approves of many of the activities common to many gentlemen of his station, such as excessive drinking and gambling."

"I do not approve of those things either," Jane replied.

"One night at Netherfield—I do not think you were present —Mr Darcy teased Mr Bingley for being too easily persuaded by his friends. I took Mr Bingley's part in it, saying there was nothing amiss in yielding to the persuasion of one who was esteemed, but Mr Darcy said to yield without conviction was no compliment to either the doer or the one who had made the suggestion."

"Those seem like things they both would say."

"Now I wonder," said Elizabeth, smoothing the muslin from Jane's mending, "did Mr Darcy mean to put me on guard for you that night? Was he trying to tell me something of Mr Bingley's character so I could persuade you against building up hope for him?"

Jane frowned at her mending. "I am sure I could not say."

"Now, we see that Mr Bingley is not here, and we have heard —though perhaps we should not have heard—that Mr Darcy does not like the society he keeps. I think it is entirely possible Mr Bingley is indulging in some behaviour that neither Mr Darcy nor we should approve."

Elizabeth leaned closer and put her arm around her sister's

shoulders. "Forgive me if I pain you. I merely cannot imagine what is happening that he stays away and—"

"Lizzy." Impatiently, Jane pushed her sister's arm away and rose, turning from her. "I am sick of Mr Bingley. I wish not to hear another word of him. I have been jilted creditably, as our father might tease. Now, I would like the possibility of a husband and a home—not further heartbreak. Mr Abell is very nice."

This sudden shift took Elizabeth by surprise. "You are not in love with Mr Abell? Surely not yet?"

"No, but neither am I opposed to the notion. I hope more than anything that Mr Bingley will stay away. His coming here could only confuse me."

16

IN LONDON ONE FAIR MORNING, BINGLEY WAS IN RECEIPT OF A letter. That it was from Darcy was immediately plain. No one could mistake the painstakingly even lines or the firm, bold strokes of the letters. Bingley scowled at it petulantly.

Memories of their quarrel floated back to him. A fever of peevishness seized him, and he took up the letter, intending it for his fire.

Just as he outstretched his arm, however, reason intruded. Darcy would not know, would he? He might assume Bingley had read his words and, instead of heeding them at once, had been distracted by another friend, thus proving his point once more. Nay, this would not do. Would not it vex Darcy more to know his letter, so diligently laboured over, had been discarded? Not read but disregarded, dismissed.

With a smile, he went to his desk and took up his pen. He scribbled right across the franking and added several blots simply because he knew it would irk his one-time friend.

IT WAS DARCY'S HABIT TO RECEIVE HIS MAIL WHILE AT BREAKFAST. IT was a habit he deeply regretted a few mornings after the assembly when he was handed his unopened letter to Bingley with the direction to return to sender scribbled carelessly (with blots) across the front. He felt himself redden and hurriedly shuffled it into the bottom of the stack with the intention to dispose of it later.

He glanced around the table. Elizabeth was speaking with Georgiana, and Jane was listening intently as her aunt and uncle gave an account of their prior day's visit to some old friend in Bakewell. Saye was not yet down, and Fitzwilliam had been abroad hours earlier and was already off exercising his horse. It would seem Darcy's discomposure would be unnoticed.

He would rewrite the letter later.

ELIZABETH DID NOTICE.

She had not meant to intrude upon his private matters, but one could not miss the alteration in his countenance as he went from disinterestedly flicking through his correspondence to sitting up a bit straighter, reddening just slightly, then frowning severely as he viewed an unmistakably blotched letter. From Mr Bingley? One could only guess as Mr Darcy did not volunteer further information.

It was becoming something of a puzzle. Had the two gentlemen argued, and if so, was Mr Bingley coming to Pemberley? Or was he not? And what did Mr Darcy prefer? That Mr Bingley should come for Jane, or that he should come to repair their friendship? Or did Mr Darcy merely wish him to stay away?

For the sake of Jane, she hoped he would remain in London, though it could not be known that she wished it so. *If I know for certain that Mr Bingley will not come, must I leave? Do I want to leave if there is no hope for Jane and Mr Bingley? Of course not, for*

Jane is hoping to meet another—to fall in love in Derbyshire. And perhaps I am hoping for the same.

THEIR AMUSEMENTS HAVING BEEN LEFT TO GEORGIANA, DARCY supposed it should be no great surprise that she had planned a picnic. The weather treated them well. The day was fair but boasted a refreshing breeze. It was an ideal day for being out of doors.

Darcy knew not what to make of his progress with Elizabeth. It was several days since they had walked and talked together, and he felt they had established an amiable relationship if naught else. However, she was not unduly friendly, nor did she flirt. If anything, one might describe her demeanour as carefully watchful. It was an improvement of sorts in that whatever spite she held for his past slights was gone. But what he most missed was her teasing and even their occasional arguments. He knew Georgiana had planned some little game for the afternoon, and he hoped that, in this, Elizabeth's more lively spirits might be renewed.

Mr and Mrs Gardiner would join them, as would Mrs Annesley, Georgiana's companion, who had prepared the game's clues. "It is something we used to do at school," Georgiana explained, her fingers twisting themselves about one another as she spoke. "A seek and find sort of game. Each team gets a set of clues, and you must decipher them and then go find the object described."

"How many to a team?" Fitzwilliam enquired.

"Only two," Mrs Annesley replied. "The first couple to return with all their objects will win a prize. We shall sound a bell then, and everyone else should return with whatever they have."

"One gentleman and one lady on each team," said Georgiana. "Because we planned the prizes accordingly."

It was decided the gentlemen would select their partners. Mrs Annesley held out four twigs to the four gentlemen to determine who had first choice. Saye got the longest, followed by Mr Gardiner, Fitzwilliam, and lastly, Darcy.

"So the first choice is mine," said Saye, rubbing his hands together to demonstrate his glee. "I must say, I always choose the most beautiful woman in the room." He took a step in Jane's direction, then moved towards Elizabeth while casting a sly glance at Darcy. Darcy stood unmoving, silently beseeching him to leave Elizabeth for him.

"Yes, yes," said Saye. "Always the loveliest woman…" He extended his hand into the space between the two Bennet sisters, still looking askance at Darcy. Darcy remained stoic, refusing to succumb to Saye's teasing.

Saye whirled with a flourish, turning away from both Bennets, and extended his hand to Mrs Gardiner. "Madam, will you do me the honour?"

Mrs Gardiner was surprised but gracious. "The honour is mine, my lord."

All eyes turned to Mr Gardiner who started a bit, glancing down at his twig. "Oh, me! Well, since my lovely bride has been taken, I suppose I shall resort to my niece." Darcy looked at him sharply just as he grinned and said, "Jane?"

"Of course, Uncle," said Jane demurely.

"And then the choice is mine," said Fitzwilliam. "Georgie, I am no poet, but perhaps between the two of us, it will all work for good." With a smile, Georgiana nodded.

"Miss Elizabeth, it seems you are stuck with me," Darcy said, affecting a nonchalant tone. He hoped his exultation was not too plainly evident, but he was feeling rather triumphant.

"I am honoured, sir."

"Very well then," said Mrs Annesley. "Here are your lists." Four sheets of folded paper were distributed to the teams. "The object is to find as many of these things as you can in as short a time as possible and bring a token of them to me."

"Oh!" Georgiana interjected. "If an item is too large to be brought back here—say a tree, for example—one may render a hasty sketch along with the location of the item and use that for the token. However, the item must be able to be located by the group in case of a dispute." She provided each team with a bundle containing extra paper and a crayon for the purpose.

The group broke into little knots, each duo eagerly opening their lists and scanning the clues therein. There were a few groans of dismay and some brief discussion on how best to approach the task—solve the clues all at once or one at a time while beginning immediately to seek?—but soon enough all was decided. and the game began.

Elizabeth held their paper as they moved away in pursuit of their first object. She looked at the page intently as they walked. "The first is Aristotle," she said. "The _____ of education are bitter but the _____ is sweet."

"Easy enough," said Darcy. "Roots and fruit."

"So quickly! I am impressed, sir. You are a scholar of poetry."

"Hardly." He laughed lightly as he pointed the way towards the apple orchard wherein they would obtain their fruit. "I must say, I do have an advantage here. I would assume most of the clues were taken from books in Pemberley's library, and among these, I likely have more knowledge than the others. And what about you? Do you favour poetry?"

"Some," she admitted. "My father does not prefer it, however, so the library at Longbourn is rather bereft."

"Well, that is why, then."

"Why what?"

"Why you do not think poetry is the food of love. Clearly, your father has only given you the most prosaic sort of poetry to educate you. 'Tis likely a sound notion—young ladies' heads are easily enough turned to fanciful notions without such influences." He hoped she understood that he was teasing her.

It seemed she did. "And a gentleman's is not?" She replied with one eyebrow raised as she cast a mocking look at him.

They had entered the apple orchard as a breeze brushed the leaves of the trees and wafted towards them the tangy scent of ripening apples. He saw her close her eyes a moment and inhale before she answered, smiling as she did. "I do think my father likes to discourage extravagant flights of emotion in whatever way possible, and in any case, he chooses the books he likes most of all."

"A sound policy."

"But what of you, Mr Darcy? Is that truly what you think—that poetry is the food of love? If so, you are more a romantic than I ever should have believed."

Absently, he bent, picking up an apple that had fallen too soon. It was unripe, small, hard, and green—unsuitable for its intended purpose but good enough for theirs. He handed it to Elizabeth who placed it into the reticule she had brought per Georgiana's instruction.

"I have given you the notion that I am rather unfeeling," he said.

"No, not that. Not unfeeling precisely, but yes, my idea of you is of a more practical nature."

"And you? Do you consider yourself of a practical nature?"

She laughed. "If I were, I would be comfortably installed in the parsonage at Hunsford by now."

"You cannot mean…"

"Yes," she admitted as she bent to tug at a blade of grass. It gave way, bringing with it a nice bit of root. She showed it to Darcy, and he nodded his approval. "Wife to Mr Collins."

For a moment, a dreadful vision of going into Kent and finding his Elizabeth in the Hunsford parsonage assailed him. He barely suppressed a shudder.

Elizabeth had continued speaking. "So no, I am not wholly practical in matters of the heart, though I do hope I am prudent. Or mayhap a romantic with a practical bent?"

"I would say the same of myself," he said, speaking cautiously. They were treading rather dangerous ground now, circling the area in which his feelings for her were laid, and it would not do to blunder or be careless. "I have always thought myself rather practical, but I do not think love can ever be truly practical. One must be senseless to truly love, or so I have come to believe."

"One cannot love that which is practical?" She gave him a look he loved: teasing, with just a dash of challenge in it.

"You can," he answered. "Certainly, you can. I would only say that *being* in love is impractical, but the object of the attachment need not be so. I have always believed that to love someone beyond one's reason is a great compliment."

He watched her as he added, "Particularly for a man like myself, a mostly prosaic, practical sort."

She flushed a little, but as the day was warm and they were exerting themselves, he could not know whether it was his words causing her to blush. Briskly, he asked, "I believe we must be on to the next clue then?"

"Correct." She looked at the paper in her hand. "Ah, Shakespeare. If this be the food of love—"

"Poetry," he said immediately. "We have just spoken of it. It is almost as though Mrs Annesley designed this with our conversation in mind."

"I fear you are not correct, sir." With her arms folded behind her back, Elizabeth looked up at him with sparkling eyes. "Music."

"No… Is that true?"

"'If music be the food of love, play on; Give me excess of it, that, surfeiting, the appetite may sicken, and so die,'" she quoted. "*Twelfth Night*, when Orsino is lamenting his lack of success in courting Countess Olivia. He wishes for his musicians to play until he can bear no more, hoping it will cure him of useless love."

Never. A man can never be cured from such as this. He held his hand to his bosom and dramatically said, "A fair strike. You are correct, and I am not."

"Very sweet words, but I must say it is not a contest between *us*," she said with a little grin. "But we must find some music, or shall I write a bit on the back of this paper?"

"We could go back to the house. I am certain Georgiana would not mind us stealing a sheet or two."

She agreed, and they set off at an easy pace. By now, they were a fair distance away, but Elizabeth was accustomed to walking, and he did not mind the exercise. He suggested they talk about more clues as they went.

"The next is Lord Byron's," Elizabeth said. "I fear we must rely on you for this for I have not been allowed to read his writings. My father has deemed it inappropriate, and he refuses to purchase it although I do suspect he has read it himself. The clue is: 'Love will find a way through this _____.'"

Darcy had to contemplate. He did like most of Lord Byron's work and thought that too much was made of its supposed scandalous nature. "Let us go on to the next. I fear I do not have a quick answer for this one. We shall leave it to the end."

The next was easier for them, a quote from Oliver Goldsmith. "'Be not affronted at a joke. If one throw this at thee, thou wilt receive no harm, unless thou art raw.'"

"Salt," she answered at the same time he did.

"Another item to obtain from the house. It should not take us long."

She permitted their page of clues to dangle at her side as she looked around. They were on a path she had not trod before, and seeing her curiosity, he pointed out various things that he believed might be of interest. He took note of her spirits as they went. There was something in her air suggesting discomfort, and he feared he might have offended her during their discussion of love versus practicality.

As will sometimes happen, the quote he had been searching his mind for came when least bidden. "'Love will find a way through paths where wolves fear to prey.'"

"What?"

"The Byron quote I could not recall earlier. It is that—a path where wolves fear to prey. This is our answer."

She appeared thoughtful. They had come to the gardens near the house, and she absently rifled her hand through a shrub as they passed. "So much poetry is about love," she said. "Love unrequited, love fulfilled, love lost... It is a subject that inspires."

"That is true."

"I cannot own that I have ever thought much about love: the nature of it, the feeling of it."

This surprised him. "No? That is curious. If you do not believe in love, I should have guessed you would settle for a prudent marriage."

"Such as with Mr Collins? But no, that would not do. It is not that I do not believe in love, but I had not ever expected to find it for myself." Her gaze was fixed in front of her. She had removed her bonnet, and it swung from her hand at her side with the reticule and the pages of clues. "I merely hoped for respect and mutual regard in my partner in matrimony. Anything more, I believe I dismissed as too impossible given my circumstances."

"Your circumstances?"

She gave him a droll look. "We need not have that conversation again. In any case, I knew I could not truly look to Mr Collins as my superior, as the head of our household, and in marrying him, I should have done him a grave injustice."

How good she was! Though some might have seen a refusal of Mr Collins as silly or selfish—for, character aside, he was deemed an eligible match—it was instead rather noble.

An impulse seized him, and he wished for a moment to say it, to confess once again his love for her. He had not proposed well. This, he now understood. The things he had wished to say —that his love for her had overcome his practical reservations— were said in a manner that was entirely wrong. Now, he wished he might explain it to her better in the way she deserved to hear it. But he could not do it. It was not the right moment; to tell her now could only further her discomfort. Instead, he motioned towards the house. "I shall go in and get the salt and music. Will you accompany me? Or perhaps you would rather wait here and review our remaining clues?"

She elected to wait and took a seat on one of the little benches, the same one where she had met him on his return from London. He strode towards the house and entered, making short work of finding what they needed. He returned to her, approaching from behind.

Elizabeth was staring into the distance, her attitude one of deep thought. The paper with their clues lay by her side, and he doubted she had looked at it in his absence. It maddened him slightly, wondering what she was thinking of.

He approached slowly, the snapping of a twig underneath his foot warning her of his presence. Elizabeth jumped, uttering a little gasp. She looked over her shoulder, holding her hand to her chest while she laughed at herself. "I did not hear your return, sir."

She took up the sheet of paper quickly, peering at it intently. "I am afraid I did not make much headway while you were gone."

"I afforded you little time in my haste to return." Darcy sat down next to her.

"I was lost in my own thoughts," she admitted. "I fear I did not even look at the next clue."

How much did he long to know the subject of her reverie! He could not ask, and she offered him nothing though something of a significant feeling lay in the air between them. Did she think of love? Did she think specifically of *his* love?

Or did he imagine it? Perhaps her thoughts tended no more deeply than to wonder what might be served at dinner.

"Your reconnaissance was successful, I hope?"

"It was." Darcy handed her a sheet of music and a little twist of paper containing the salt. Elizabeth tucked the salt into her reticule and put the sheet of music behind their clues.

"Shall I read the next?" She began without waiting for his response. "She walks in beauty like the night—"

He interrupted her at once, his gaze hungrily poring over her sun-dappled countenance bent towards the page. "'She walks in beauty, like the night / Of cloudless climes and starry skies / And all that's best of dark and bright'"—Elizabeth raised her head and met his gaze, and he faltered for a moment—"'Meet in her aspect and her eyes.'"

He saw her swallow. "Eyes," she said softly. "The word 'eyes' was missing."

"We have with us the most beautiful eyes I have ever beheld," said Darcy, noting his voice was a bit hoarse. "So we need look for nothing this time."

She was silent, her eyes locked on his face.

"Any man could become a poet who beheld the beauty of your eyes."

There was no sound in the garden save for that of a buzzing insect near them. He scarcely heard it; it was merely counterpoint to the pounding of his heart.

"It astonishes me," she said at last, "how little I knew you. I believe everything I *thought* I knew is, in truth, quite the opposite."

This was a great deal more than he could have hoped for at the outset of the day. He was struck mute by her and could do no more than revel in it, staring at her as she looked at him.

Darcy noticed an eyelash had separated from the others and was about to drop into her left eye. He motioned towards it. "You have a lash there."

"Can you…?" She tilted her face, closing her eyes, and he reached out, taking the pad of his thumb to brush along her lashes until the errant lash was freed.

She opened her eyes and saw it resting on his thumb. He watched, surprised, as she removed her glove and pressed her thumb onto his. "Make a wish."

"Is this how you do it? You do not blow it away?"

She shook her head. "We both make wishes, and whosoever has the lash when we are through gets their wish. If the lash is gone, then neither of us does."

There was a momentary pause as they made their wishes. Darcy was not a superstitious man and, in fact, found many of these little customs on the border of sacrilegious. However, this he would not scorn. He made a hasty wish to whatever force of nature might be interested in helping him, that whatever was begun between them would continue to grow.

She took her thumb away, and the lash had adhered to hers. She blew it away with a delicate pursing of her lips, making him briefly imagine kissing her.

In the distance, they heard the bell ringing, Mrs Annesley announcing a winner had been declared. The rest of the party had already gathered where they had begun. Darcy and Elizabeth were visible to the others and were called to return. "We had better go back," Elizabeth said, gesturing towards them.

"Yes," he agreed. They began to walk up the hill towards the picnic area where Darcy saw his servants bringing a light repast for the hungry searchers.

"Shall I know your wish, sir?" she asked, swinging her reticule as they walked at a quick pace. "It is not sound, I know, but I do enjoy hearing such things."

"And deprive me of my chance to have a wish granted?" He affected an incredulous tone. "Never! I am already in arrears because you stole my lash."

She laughed, and they walked a short distance more. When they had nearly gained the others, he spoke rather more quietly than before, "In any case, I believe you already know my wishes."

"I might," she said lightly. "But I do believe mine would take you by surprise."

ELIZABETH SEATED HERSELF ON A BLANKET, A GLASS OF BARLEY

water in her hand and a cake on a plate in front of her. She had no intention of eating it but took something so as not to appear conspicuous. She was undone by the time she had spent with Mr Darcy and needed some moments of peace to attempt to regain her equanimity.

Mr Darcy was inveigling his way into her heart. There was no doubt of that. It frightened her—the speed with which her heart was overtaking her reason. One must be senseless to truly love. Alas, senselessness was rather terrifying, particularly when one's lover was a person who had been formerly despised. *I never really knew him at all.*

Each team had been assigned ten clues. Lord Saye and Mrs Gardiner had been first to return with all ten objects successfully located. Likewise, Colonel Fitzwilliam and Georgiana had found all ten, but Lord Saye and Mrs Gardiner were quicker.

Mr Gardiner and Jane were less fortunate. "First, we were lost," Mr Gardiner explained, "but we reckoned our mistake soon enough. Cost us some time though, and we were only able to find nine of the ten items."

It came then to Mr Darcy and Elizabeth. Lord Saye pounced on the reticule, withdrawing the salt and the apple. He gave Mr Darcy a dubious look, one brow raised. "You did understand the purpose of this, did you not? You were not merely to walk about all afternoon; it was a quest."

"This sheet of music too," Elizabeth offered, stretching out her hand to show it to the others. "And my eyes."

"Yes," said Mr Darcy. "Her eyes."

"No, that will not do," Colonel Fitzwilliam protested. "It should have been a drawing. We all have eyes with us. 'Tis nothing we sought or found."

"It never said we had to draw the eyes," said Mr Darcy. "Only that they be brought before the group."

"Does it matter?" Lord Saye was already disinterested. "This is a miserable showing. I am quite disappointed in the pair of you. What caused you to lag so behind?"

He looked expectantly at Mr Darcy, and Mr Darcy's eyes slid towards Elizabeth. She met his look and held it, at once finding herself in something of a private moment with him. It was like a delicious joke between them, and they savoured it in front of everyone. Elizabeth almost giggled with her shamelessness in it but settled for offering Mr Darcy a tiny grin. He gave the same in return.

"We did our best," he said brusquely, not removing his eyes from Elizabeth.

17

FOR AS MUCH SATISFACTION AS DARCY GAINED ON THE DAY OF
Georgiana's little picnic and poetry game, the days to follow
were disappointing.

On the day immediately after, the Gardiners planned to see a
particular friend to whom they wished to introduce their nieces,
and thus, Elizabeth and Miss Bennet accompanied them on that
day's excursion. The day that followed was similarly unsatisfy-
ing, though that day, it was Georgiana who commanded the
time and attention of the Bennet sisters. He could not protest,
not when he saw his sister so happy in the society of her new
friends.

"I hope it will suit you," he told the ladies at breakfast the
next morning, "I have accepted an invitation from the Abells for
an evening of music and entertainment."

"Their home is rather near, is it not?" asked Elizabeth.

"They are at an easy distance."

"An easy distance you say?" Elizabeth responded with a
little smile over her teacup. "I am not sure your word may be
trusted on that, sir. After all, our feelings on the easiness of
travel have been known to differ."

He was puzzled. "Have they?"

She lowered the teacup, giving him a full smile. "I believe you once told me that you considered fifty miles an easy distance. Much as I found Mr Abell agreeable, I cannot happily anticipate a journey of fifty miles merely for an evening of music."

He laughed. "It is too much to have to account for all the ridiculous things I have said to you. In any case, it is much less than fifty miles. I cannot think why I ever said such a thing."

From the corner of his eye, he observed as Georgiana and Miss Bennet rose to quit the room. Elizabeth, he noted, had no such urgency. She sat comfortably, sipping at what appeared to be a full cup of tea. He reached for his coffee and took a tiny taste.

She reminded him, "I believe it was when we spoke of Charlotte's marriage to Mr Collins, and I said it was possible for a woman to be settled too near her family."

Oh yes—that. Darcy was uneasy although Elizabeth remained smiling. No doubt, she also recalled his stupid presumption during that discussion when he foolishly thought that she wished for him to remove her from her objectionable family.

"Fifty miles is not an easy distance for anyone," he said, keeping his gaze steady on her. "And I know it must seem much farther for a lady who is removed from the bosom of a loving family and happy home."

Elizabeth pulled her napkin from her lap and gently touched the sides of her lips while averting her eyes. "That is true, but it is the way of the world. Ladies are meant to marry and leave their families."

"While something is expected, it does not necessarily mean it is easy." He paused a moment then ventured to say, "I believe it would be particularly difficult for one accustomed to a lively house with many sisters to the change of living with just one husband." *One husband given to reserve,* he thought but dared not voice it.

"Marriage is always an adjustment for both parties, is it not?"

"I daresay it is."

"Eventually, my sisters will marry and leave, and Longbourn will no longer be as it was."

"Not like it was, but what is different is not necessarily worse. Only think how enjoyable it will be on family visits. Your sisters and you will have children, and those cousins will learn to play and grow together. The addition of more persons to the family party will make any occasion a merry one."

A faint smile touched her lips. "That does sound agreeable—though at times, if her husband does not like his wife's family, then the visits are short and infrequent. Soon enough, they are all strangers—whether intended or not—and pleasures seen in their youth are soon forgot."

There was a silence then, heavy with the weight of things unsaid. She clearly believed that marriage to him would necessitate the cutting of her family ties—estrangement from those she held dear. He had not before thought how alarming his words against her family must have been.

She rose. "If you will excuse me."

"Just a moment, if you please." He rose quickly, stopping her. She halted, standing by the table. He studied her for a moment, seeing diffidence in her attitude. He did not know what to say—only the ideas he wished her to know.

"I have been ungenerous," he told her. "And I have looked with disdain on some of your family members—"

"Who were likely deserving of it," she said quickly, colour staining her cheeks. "Do not think me insensible of that."

"I respect your family." She glanced up at him, a quick darting glance. "I do. And it is not my intention simply to tear you away from them. I have given you leave to imagine quite the opposite, but I assure you that you will never be a stranger to your sisters and parents on my account."

"You have been so generous in inviting my sister and my aunt and uncle to your home—"

"All of them," he hastened to say. "Your family will always be welcome at Pemberley and in London, and we shall visit them as much as you like. You have my word."

She did not look at him, offering a little nod and half-smile in his general direction. With a barely audible "thank you," she hurriedly departed the room.

As Mrs Gardiner was too fatigued to contemplate an evening from home, it was decided that Mrs Annesley would act as chaperon for the party going to the Abell's: Colonel Fitzwilliam, Darcy, and the Bennet ladies. Saye had gone to London to retrieve Miss Goddard and take her to Matlock.

Lessing Grange, home of the Abell family for seven generations, was one of the most picturesque places Elizabeth had ever seen. The lane meandered up towards the house, passing through a canopy of old elms. The house itself, although nothing to the scale of Pemberley, was commodious and elegant. A pond lined with rushes sat just so, and the lawns were well tended. The picture it presented was one of happy prosperity.

It was a group of a middling size that gathered at Lessing Grange early that evening, about forty persons altogether. Many of them were the contemporaries of the elder Mr and Mrs Abell, but there were still a fair number of younger people as well. Elizabeth found several ladies she thought she might eventually count among her friends, particularly Miss Abell, who was a sweet girl, and Miss Godfrey, who was of lively spirits, much like Elizabeth herself.

There was one lady, a Miss Olivia Altman, who greeted Elizabeth with cool interest. She was an undeniably beautiful lady with chestnut-hued ringlets, large blue eyes, and the sort of figure Elizabeth had always wanted. Her gown was the latest style and suited her admirably. Elizabeth looked at bit askance at her, wondering whether she would prove to be like Miss Bingley; however, further conversation showed she was polite but reserved.

Their party entered the music room, which was bright in the late-day sun and open with comfortable furniture arranged to view the instruments. Mr Robert Abell came to them immediately. "Miss Bennet, Miss Elizabeth, how good of you to join us this evening."

"We are glad to be here, sir," said Jane, and they spoke easily from there. Mr Abell introduced them to his mother and her guests as they continued to enter. It was not long until Elizabeth and Jane felt at ease among the group, laughing and chatting as if they had long been friends.

Elizabeth soon saw Jane drawn aside by Mr Abell. She turned her head, biting back a smile at her sister's blush. Jane was no doubt pleased by the attention. Elizabeth did not mean to eavesdrop, but she did manage to hear Mr Abell's compliments to her sister's beauty as well as his desire to show her the rest of his home so she might feel as comfortable as if it were hers. The meaning in such a statement was not lost on Elizabeth, and she thrilled on her sister's behalf at such boldness.

"Miss Elizabeth, I understand you are engaged," Miss Godfrey remarked with a smile on her face and artlessness in her manner.

Elizabeth immediately turned her head back to the group of

ladies with whom she was sitting. Her inattentiveness made her stammer a bit. "Oh, ah…I… No. Well, yes. Yes, I am."

It was a peculiar response, and she knew it. The ladies sitting with Elizabeth and Miss Godfrey all lowered their eyes to their laps, shooting quick, embarrassed looks at one another. Elizabeth sighed. That she had been a subject of conversation among the group was no surprise, but she did not wish to tell them of the particulars. When she spoke, she was careful in choosing her words.

"Forgive me. It is all still rather new to me."

"I understand he courted you in Kent." This was from Miss Altman, who had just arrived and was still standing.

Did he? If so, I was unaware of it. Brightly, Elizabeth said, "I was staying for a time with my friend in Kent while he saw his aunt at her estate, Rosings Park."

"You must mean Lady Catherine de Bourgh."

"Why, yes." Elizabeth looked up at her. "Are you acquainted with her ladyship?"

"Yes, I am," said Miss Altman. "I, too, am from Kent. My family's estate is near to Rosings Park. I met Mr Darcy there on many occasions. Our families are quite intimate. Is your family closely acquainted with Lady Catherine as well?"

Elizabeth almost laughed until she realised it was not funny at all. The other ladies were looking at her with unwavering interest, and not knowing what else to say, she admitted the truth. "No, um…my friend is married to Mr Collins who lives in Hunsford. He is Lady Catherine's parson and, um…my cousin as well."

Elizabeth knew she could not be mistaken in seeing a smile move across Miss Altman's lips, a smile that was immediately suppressed and hidden from the view of the rest of the group. She did not like the look of it one bit.

IT IS NO EASY FEAT TO WATCH SOMEONE WITHOUT APPEARING TO DO so, but Elizabeth knew she did not speak amiss when she claimed a mastery of the art. After all, she had a lifetime of seeming wholly engaged in one conversation while carefully ensuring that her mother did not humiliate her in another. And for years, she had watched her father work in his study while she appeared engrossed in a book and sat whispering with Charlotte in church while her eyes never left the preacher and her mouth scarcely moved.

So it was no great difficulty for her to see—though many times she wished she could not—as Miss Altman sought every available moment to attach herself to Mr Darcy. Miss Altman had the good fortune to be escorted into dinner by him. She made good use of that bit of luck, talking to him and having great success in keeping his attention. She was not a coquette by any means, but she did know how to keep a man's interest.

She is the worst sort of rival—wholly unable to be discredited. For once, Elizabeth longed for a lady like Miss Bingley who made herself ridiculous with her airs. Miss Altman did no such thing. She was everything a lady ought to be and behaved accordingly.

Miss Altman was further graced by good fortune after dinner, having risen from her seat just as the gentlemen entered the drawing room after their port and cigars. This time, she had the attention of both Colonel Fitzwilliam and Mr Darcy, and she gave up neither of them. What she could find to speak on at such length, Elizabeth could not know. What she did know, however, was that Mr Darcy was intent upon her words and smiled and laughed often. *He likes her.* Elizabeth pressed her lips together and looked at her lap a moment, hating her feelings about such a realisation.

Colonel Fitzwilliam left the little tête-à-tête, leaving Mr Darcy with Miss Altman, who once again earned a laugh from him. Elizabeth kept her eyes on her group, but her attention was on them. She did not miss it when Miss Altman put her fan over her face a little, lowering her lashes in a demure way, then she closed the fan, using it to tap her bosom in a clear indication of her interest. Elizabeth turned her head away at once.

She swallowed hard, sternly admonishing herself against any show of distress. With a determinedly bright smile, she turned to Miss Abell. "Pray, tell me about the musicians we shall hear tonight."

"It is a group from London," Miss Abell began eagerly. She went on, describing the various talents and achievements of the musicians and adding that they had played not only once but several times at Carlton House. "One is Miss Altman's master, and she has graciously agreed to be a part of our little programme this evening."

Again—Miss Altman! Feeling herself rather excessively distressed and growing more so by the moment, Elizabeth decided to turn her attention to Jane, who was having a good night. She sat next to Mr Abell at dinner, and they appeared to be chatting rather easily. Elizabeth believed she might even have seen Jane flirting once or twice.

Mr Abell was not as handsome as Mr Bingley, nor did he appear as gregarious, but he had kindness in his countenance and a steadiness about him that Elizabeth found pleasing for her sister.

"May I sit here?"

Elizabeth started, having not seen Mr Darcy approach. "Of course." He settled himself just as their host rose to introduce the musicians.

Elizabeth hoped that her feelings of vexation would abate

under the influence of beautiful music played by such proficient performers, and to some extent, it did. However, just as she persuaded herself that she should not feel as she did, Miss Altman rose, modestly taking her seat at the pianoforte amid the cries of delight from those who had heard her previously, and all reason was gone.

Elizabeth was humiliated within the first notes Miss Altman played. It was the same song she had muddled through at Lucas Lodge one evening with Mr Darcy and his party present. She wondered whether he would recall it, or worse, recall what a tangle she had made of it, fudging and slurring and singing over the rough spots.

Miss Altman proved highly proficient, further shaming Elizabeth. She leaned over to Mr Darcy, who appeared to be listening with rapt attention, and murmured, "Miss Altman is very accomplished."

"It is clear she practises diligently." He moved slightly in his seat, angling his head, and Elizabeth realised he was seeking the best position to see Miss Altman. "And she has an able master."

"Miss Abell told me it was that gentleman there." Elizabeth subtly indicated the man said to be Miss Altman's music teacher.

"Yes." He moved again slightly. "I consulted her once I saw Georgiana growing more devoted to her music. She recommended her master to me, and he has been good for my sister."

Elizabeth pursed her lips together, forcing the appearance of rapt attention to her countenance. When some minutes had passed, she, in a carefully indifferent tone, remarked, "Oh! Now this is quite a coincidence, but I do believe I once exhibited this very song in your presence."

"I remember it quite clearly, in fact." Mr Darcy glanced over at her. "At Lucas Lodge."

"Yes." Elizabeth flushed, looking down at her hands. She had hoped he did not remember, but he did—and quite clearly, by his own account. *What must he be thinking of me!* Her inadequacies felt glaringly obvious. "I was quite vexed at Charlotte for forcing me to exhibit that night. I had not practised for some time, though I must admit, I have never been diligent."

He chuckled a bit. "Yes, I do remember thinking that you were not pleased when she prevailed upon you. It was good of you to oblige her."

"You are too kind," Elizabeth replied, almost by rote. They sat quietly for a moment, Elizabeth hearing the flawless execution of a passage that she had never quite mastered. "Her fingering was near perfection on that."

"It was good, I shall grant you that."

Thereafter, Elizabeth was uncommonly silent. A sinking feeling pervaded her being, some combination of sorrow and vexation mixed with envy. *I want to escape*, she thought miserably, but where she would go, she could not say.

A LETTER FROM HER MOTHER HAD COME EARLIER THAT DAY, AND evidently meaning to stir up as much distress within herself as possible, Elizabeth waited to read it until she returned from Lessing Grange. Mrs Bennet had little more than disinterested gossip to relate. It seemed that, with the regiment departed, there was nothing worth noting in Meryton.

Alas, the dullness of Meryton meant that Mrs Bennet's conversation regarding Elizabeth and Mr Darcy was still prized. That Elizabeth would return with her wedding day set was of no doubt to Mrs Bennet. She was quite dismayed upon learning from Elizabeth's previous letter that she was whiling away her days on silly games and walking the countryside rather than planning her trousseau. Her mother advised in no uncertain terms that Mr Darcy would likely lose interest in her quickly, and she should secure him as soon as may be. She ended with the information that Elizabeth's reputation was most certainly ruined if she did not marry Mr Darcy, and she was sure to die a spinster.

A gentle knock was heard at her door. It was Jane, seeking the bedtime conversation the two sisters always enjoyed. In an abstracted fashion, Elizabeth observed that her sister appeared happier than she had been in some months and offered her a tired smile.

"Your night went off well."

Jane sighed. "I like Mr Abell very much, and I do think he likes me too. His mother took particular care in knowing me. She invited me to return for a day's visit."

"I hope you will go."

"I shall make what I can of it," Jane assured her.

It was then that Jane noticed the letter in familiar writing sitting on Elizabeth's side table. "Is that from my mother? How is she?"

"Oh! Very well. She has much of which to boast, and Charlotte still is not increasing, so she can triumph over Lady Lucas yet. She is positively gleeful about it."

"Lizzy," Jane scolded, "do not speak so."

"Forgive me." Elizabeth shook her head tiredly. "I am exceedingly out of sorts."

"But why?" Jane asked, sitting next to her sister. "Did you not enjoy the evening?"

"Oh no, I did, I enjoyed it excessively," said Elizabeth warmly. "I cannot think what I liked best. When Miss Altman flirted shamelessly with Mr Darcy? Or was it when she showed how talented she was at the instrument? Or when she walked about in front of him with her perfect figure? No, I believe I liked watching him talk to her at the dinner table the best. Such fun they had!" Elizabeth crossed her arms in front of her chest and huffed a bit.

Jane surprised her by laughing. "Oh, Lizzy, you are a silly thing sometimes."

"What?"

"I believe you are falling in love with him," said Jane, a devilish smile on her lips.

"That would be my way, would it not? Wait until a man has lost interest in me to decide to love him back."

"All you have said is that she flirted with him. Did he flirt with her too?"

"No."

"I shall tell you what has been told to me many times. Few people have the courage to be really in love without a little encouragement. If your feelings have changed about Mr Darcy, then help him along a little. Flirt with him! The poor man probably thinks you still hate him."

"Surely not. We have spoken of our past often enough by now that I should think—"

"Flirt with him," Jane repeated firmly.

"I am not a flirt," Elizabeth protested. "I would not know how to go about it. This business with fans and gloves...I would draw it across my cheek and likely take my eye out."

Jane laughed. "Mr Darcy did a fine job of falling in love with you without any of that. Just pay him a bit of particular attention. I think he would like that most of all.

18

THE DAY AFTER THE PARTY AT LESSING GRANGE DAWNED SLOWLY, gathering clouds obscuring much of the burgeoning light. Elizabeth woke early and took a brief stroll through the cutting garden, a place she had quickly come to regard as a particular favourite.

The distance covered was minimal, and her pace was slow. She often found herself not moving at all, doing nothing more than staring at some flower or the ground beneath her. Her thoughts tended to the previous night. She needed to determine why it had vexed her so and what she might do about it. That her feelings for Mr Darcy were changing—nay, had already changed—could not be disputed. But was it mere possessiveness, some odd sense of ownership over Mr Darcy's smiles and stares, or could it be something more?

Thoughts of flirting with Mr Darcy came to mind. Should she flutter her eyelashes at him over breakfast? Drop her handkerchief perhaps and touch his arm in a familiar manner? The mere idea made her laugh and no doubt would make him laugh too.

She did not know how to flirt. Was smiling sufficient? Should she flatter him and make comments on Pemberley? Oh, it all sounded so wretched and false! These were the very things she had always prided herself for not doing.

I trust it will come to me in the impulse of the moment. On that weak resolution, she returned to the house, her stomach reminding her she had eaten little the night before.

Scattered raindrops promising many more to come began to hit the windows of the breakfast room when Elizabeth entered. Darcy was found within, looking outside. He turned at the sound of her entry and gave her a smile.

For some strange reason, his evident gladness to see her sent panic coursing through her. Her gut clenched, and she was suddenly unaccountably breathless. For a moment, she clasped her hands together tightly, stopping just short of wringing them. When she realised what she was doing, she quickly dropped her hands to her sides as they commonly were. But somehow, they felt strange hanging there, too loose and too…hanging.

"Good morning. I trust you slept well."

"I did." She attempted a smile, but it felt rather forced, and she still had not the least notion what to do with her arms, hanging there so stupidly. She brought her right hand up to touch her hair. "And you, sir?"

He gestured towards the sideboard where a number of tempting choices awaited. She went over and selected a few items for her plate, grateful to have some occupation for her troublesome limbs.

Mr Darcy said, "As is my rather unfortunate habit, I found that retiring late caused me to sleep restlessly and wake early. I expect it will be some time before the others stir from their chambers."

He pulled a chair out for her, the one immediately next to his at the head of the table. She sat, and he did likewise. His plate was empty, though the coffee cup appeared newly filled.

"I have rarely spent so enjoyable an evening." The taste of the lie was bitter in her mouth as she could not reflect on the party without thinking of Miss Altman's pretty smiles for Mr Darcy's benefit.

"Nor I," he agreed in a most aggravating fashion. "I have never had much aptitude for music. However, I believe my inability to grace myself with a tune has made me more appreciative of that talent in others."

Elizabeth bit the inside of her lip and looked away. Her nerves felt like worms, crawling and twisting inside her as she remembered his appreciation of Miss Altman's talent. She could not blame him; the lady was beautiful and accomplished, everything a lady of higher society ought to be.

She took a deep breath. "You were not diligent in your practice of music? I am surprised."

Mr Darcy did not appear to notice her change in mood. Instead, he spoke with rather more animation than usual of the various songs he appreciated hearing and the manner in which they were played. Elizabeth only partly attended him. Her mind was occupied by distress and her dismay at being distressed.

She made the appropriate comments and murmurings, all the while remembering the mortification of the previous night. She had never been a lady to doubt herself. It felt like a useless occupation to regret the essence of oneself in wistful contemplation of what might have been. Why should she now feel the weight of her inadequacies?

"...do you think?"

She started. "What do I think?"

He smiled at her. "I remember you once saying at Rosings that you were not proficient because you did not take the trouble of practicing. But what do you suppose is more important: natural capacity for the activity or the guidance of a master and diligence in practice?"

"I think there must be both. To be a true proficient, one must unite a natural capacity with diligence and a desire to excel."

"I agree, but I wonder which one you consider most important? I find that someone with a natural capacity for music is always superior to one who has merely practised a great deal."

This, too, brought Miss Altman to mind though Elizabeth would not behave in a manner to betray it. "But without a great deal of practice, the natural capacity remains unseen and unknown. There must be instruction and the diligence in applying oneself to learning to perfect the natural capacity."

"So do you say, then, that one might become a great musician, a proficient, without having any true natural talent?"

"I am saying that diligence, instruction, and practice are necessary no matter what. In the absence of aptitude, diligence will still produce a creditable result. With aptitude, diligence will produce a superior result. Either way, however, there is nothing without practice."

He leaned back, a slight smile on his face. "I cannot agree with you."

"I should have been quite surprised if you had," she said quietly.

"One who is merely practiced may play the notes just as they are written, but the spirit of the piece, I am afraid, is lost."

"To play with spirit but not proficiency will produce nothing more than noise."

"To play proficiently but in a manner lacking expression is also just noise, for is not art meant to convey a feeling?"

Elizabeth pressed her lips together tightly for a moment before saying, "In any case, I think we must agree that to truly succeed, to be truly accomplished in music, one must have both."

"Yet to have both is exceedingly uncommon."

"It is indeed a special and fortunate person who marries both talent and application." *A person like Miss Altman.* She congratulated herself on her composure, particularly as her need to escape this horrid conversation was rising precipitously. She knew full well her inferiority in this matter; she had neither talent nor application, as Miss Altman's exhibiting of the very same song made abundantly evident.

Mr Darcy continued to speak—about what or who she knew not. Elizabeth cast about for something to say for only a moment before she stood rather suddenly, the desire to flee overwhelming her.

The movement of her chair backwards was rather more violent and certainly louder than she intended. "Oh, forgive me, I just remembered..." She was unable to think of anything that would excuse her. She ceased trying and turned quickly towards the door, the linen that had been on her lap fluttering uselessly behind her.

Elizabeth had placed her hand on the door handle when a long arm reached over her shoulder. Darcy laid the palm of his hand flat against the door, neatly preventing her escape. Elizabeth turned, finding herself nearly within his embrace. He did not move, so she retreated as far as she could, her back pressed tightly against the door.

His eyes moved over her face. "Have I upset you?"

"Of course not."

"I can see I have. Please forgive me."

"No offence was taken, I assure you." Her eyes slid away from his searching gaze.

He was so near to her! She could sense his warmth and smell

the light scent of cedar wood and leather emanating from him. She raised her eyes, forcing herself to meet his gaze squarely.

"Are you certain?"

"Quite certain." She laid her hand against his chest, just over the button of his waistcoat, and lightly pushed. He stepped back immediately. His eyes searched her face. Surely, he could not find it so entirely unexpected that she would despise being compared unfavourably to another lady?

"Forgive me."

A litany ran through her head—her mother's voice telling her not to run on with her useless opinions and that she would never be as pretty as Jane, Jane's voice telling her to flirt, her own voice teasing about the probability of being a spinster, and even his voice, saying things that she could not say were untrue. It was all so overwhelming. She did not usually doubt herself or think of herself so severely, but once she had begun, all of it came to the fore.

What was worse than these feelings, however, was the understanding that accompanied them: she cared what he thought. She was aware of her insufficiencies as seen through his eyes, and that was quite the most terrible thing she had ever imagined. His opinion of her suddenly mattered a great deal.

Her sensibilities, impassioned and wholly alit within her, rose in her breast. It was never her intention to speak a word of any of it, yet somehow, quite precipitously, she did. "Do you think I do not know? I know. I assure you, *I know*."

His eyes followed as she stepped aside, extricating herself from his reach. She turned her back on him as words began to spill from her lips. She was unable to stop them though she grew increasingly embarrassed with each utterance.

"You cannot know—indeed, you could not know—what it was like to be raised in such...such a way, where there was no weight given to anything of importance—not accomplishment, not character, not modesty, not gentility. Jane and I have been spoilt by the compliments of those who love us, such as Sir William Lucas, who called us 'the brightest jewels of the county.' We went so far as to dare to believe it."

Having gained sufficient distance to be immune to his nearness, she turned. "Once, after dinner at Netherfield, I left everyone to attend my sister. But then I turned back, thinking I forgot something. Before I could enter again, however, I overheard the conversation in the room. There was a great deal said of me and I heard you say, 'It must materially lessen their chance of marrying men of any consideration in the world,' referring to our parents and how we had been raised."

Mr Darcy started and flushed at her repetition of his remark, but she did not permit him the chance to speak.

"Do you know that, until that moment, I had never thought of it in such a way? I had not truly felt my inferiority until then, not until I understood how I must be seen by those of you at Netherfield, and…and for anyone else who had been raised as they ought, as any other gently bred lady is raised."

The sense of being near tears brought a fresh wave of mortification, and her face, already warm, flushed scarlet. She refused to cry in front of him and steeled herself with a deep breath. "Yes, I understand that most of the ladies you know have applied themselves diligently to music, drawing, languages, singing, and the like. I have not. I have done as well as I could with the limited talents I boast and the erratic attempts at education and mastery I was given. I can never match someone like her."

"Someone like who?"

"Miss Altman."

"Miss Altman?" He asked, his confusion plain.

"I have never wished to raise my station through marriage." Her breath came fast as she faced him. "Although I wish to marry a man to whom I can look as my superior, it does not follow that I wish to marry where I feel inferior. I have witnessed that sort of marriage, and it is not for me."

For a moment, they stood silently regarding one another. That she perplexed him was plain, and she chastised herself. Did they not agree to begin anew? Why did she need to bring the happenings of autumn between them yet again? *You have made an excellent business of flirting, Lizzy. You would have done better with your fan.*

He took a step closer. "It has been my dearest wish that, in having you here in Derbyshire, I might atone for the things—"

"No." She half moaned her interruption with chagrin. "No, that is not my meaning, you need not—"

"I had not realised the quantity of stupid and mean things that I have said, and it speaks poorly of my manners—"

"No, no. This is not about you. I do not blame you." She took a step towards him. "Sir, we have agreed to a new start, have we not?"

"We have, but if I behaved inappropriately last night and—"

She took another step and went so far as to lay her hand on his arm. "No, that is not it at all. You did nothing wrong."

His brow was furrowed with concern. "Was someone at the party unkind?"

She shook her head. "Not in the least, I assure you."

He covered her hand with his, gently insisting, "Tell me, then. There is a great deal on your mind, it would seem. I would be honoured if you would consider me a confidante."

She hoped she might come away from this without having to offer more explanation, for what further explanation for her silly and immature behaviour could she give? It would seem Mr

Darcy would not go away unsatisfied, however. His countenance bore a troubled expression, and she felt he was owed a bit of reason.

"I think I am as reasonable as any of my sex, sir, but I would be untruthful if I did not admit that I am also as capable of being affected by..." By what? Could she admit to the utterly unreasonable and stupid jealousy that seized her upon seeing a lady so clearly better suited to be the wife of Mr Darcy?

"By what?"

"Flights of pettiness. Silliness and...and absurd...absurdity. Forgive me, and pray, forgive my candour in speaking as I did of...you know."

He studied her closely. "I cannot understand."

"Oh! This is impossible, and I am ridiculous!" she cried, flinging her hands up to cover her face. After a deep sigh, she dropped her hands. "Miss Altman would make you an excellent wife."

"What would make you think—?"

"She has beauty and good conversation, and she has applied herself to her music. I do not think anyone in London would be surprised to find you betrothed to Miss Altman." *And I cannot compare to her. Not in looks, education, conversation, and certainly not in accomplishment.*

He stared at her for a moment then held out his hand. She took it, allowing him to lead her to the table, where they both sat. They were facing one another though Elizabeth could not bear to look at him.

Gently he said, "Elizabeth, I am eight-and-twenty, and I have met ladies whom I admire. I shall admit to having met one or two whom I thought I could probably marry and have a reasonably happy life."

She kept her eyes fixed on her lap.

"But never have I known the depth of feeling that I feel for you. I never expected to love, never thought I was in love, and never, not once, have I told any lady I loved her—no one but you."

After a short pause, he added, "And I do. I do love you."

Elizabeth could not speak.

"Has something I did cause you to think otherwise? Something recent, that is?"

Meekly, she whispered, "No."

There was a brief silence during which he continued to stare at her. Elizabeth looked at him for but a moment before moving her eyes back to her lap, aware that a great deal was being said between them although they did not speak.

"Do you recall at Netherfield," he said, "when we spoke of a lady's accomplishments?"

Ah, but I do. She recalled quite clearly how he and Miss Bingley had gone on with their extensive list of what was required to meet their definition of accomplishment, and she believed they had meant to point out her inferiority.

"To Miss Bingley's rather exalted list, I added that a lady must improve her mind with extensive reading. In so doing, I intended you to understand that I thought you had much of which to boast." He gave her a brief smile. "I was referring to the book in your hand. I thought myself rather bold, though I think you must have understood me differently."

"Yes, I did." She forced herself to give him the satisfaction of a light laugh. "I thought it a slight upon me."

"Then permit me to be clearer in what I say to you now." He reached towards her but stopped, leaving his hand to rest on the table beside her.

"That night, the night we were at Lucas Lodge, and you were prevailed upon to exhibit, 'twas a night I can never forget.

Almost from the first note, the first breath, I was utterly enraptured by how you sang—by you. There was no time, no season. There was only you and me and the beautiful sound of your voice. I hardly knew what I did as I listened. Afterwards, I prayed no one had seen me, for surely all that I felt was writ large upon my countenance. But at that moment, the only thing I was aware of was you and the beauty of the song as you sang and played it."

She raised a hand from her lap and laid it next to his with little space between them.

"So, yes, proficiency is a fine thing, and to exhibit flawlessly is good too, but it cannot compare to the feeling of your heart awakening or your soul rejoicing. It cannot compare to the enchanting thrill of finding love where you least expect it to be."

He glanced at her face before gently sliding his fingers atop hers. "It was that night and your rendering of the song that so ably put me under your power, though I would not acknowledge it for some time afterwards."

His hand was heavy and comfortable on hers, and she was caught between a strange desire to cry and to laugh.

"Elizabeth." He touched her lightly beneath her chin then dropped his hand away when she raised her eyes to meet his. His eyes were unclothed, naked with what he felt for her, and she understood anew how much he was truly in her power.

"Do not forget that or think I have failed to realise your worth. If I did not see it then, I surely do now, many times over."

Quietly, she said, "I am ashamed of my jealousy."

"There is too much left unsaid between us. I would prefer to know your mind."

All at once, Jane's words came to her. "*You should marry him because he loves you as I think you deserve to be loved.*" Oh, but I am not sure I do deserve such a love as this.

"I could never marry you until I knew I could love you the way you deserve to be loved."

He seemed to consider this a moment before asking, "Is such a thing possible?"

Her eyes on his, she nodded. His fingers caressed hers slowly as he smiled broadly in a manner she had not seen before, not at her and not, she thought gladly, at any other lady. *I alone can make him happy.* It was a bewildering, strange, and altogether wonderful thought.

"I am of a mind to do some fishing later," he told her. "Will you accompany me?"

"Yes. Shall we make a party of it?"

He shook his head decisively. "No. You and me. The rest may shift for themselves."

She nodded in agreement, but such was the inopportune moment that she noticed the sound of the rain growing stronger. It was the sort of rain that appeared ready to settle in—not a storm but a steady drenching. They both looked at the window, seeing the droplets fall, then looked at each other.

"Tomorrow?" he asked.

"You may depend upon it."

ON LATER REFLECTION, DARCY HAD NO RECOLLECTION OF LEAVING the breakfast room or of retiring to his study where he sat grinning like a fool in the general direction of the window. It was now marked by rivulets of steady rain, precluding any fishing expedition, but it mattered not. He had her agreement to an excursion on the morrow and that, coupled with the hope of today, was surely enough to satisfy him.

His eyes fell on his correspondence, letters he had no inclination to peruse but knew he must. The one on top was a note from Bingley, mostly illegible but managing to be scornful nevertheless. Bingley was for Sheffield, Sir Albert with him, to see his friend Staley. He made a disinterested promise at the end of the letter to visit Pemberley—perhaps—when he was finished in Sheffield. Darcy grimaced, hoping Bingley did not presume to think Sir Albert was welcome at Pemberley.

There was a knock, and Georgiana entered. "Brother, you have eaten breakfast, I hope?" There was an impish light in her eyes, and Darcy suspected she was fully aware of his morning's activities.

He frowned at her teasingly. "I have. Have you? Have our guests?"

"The breakfast room was rather occupied at the usual hour," she told him with an innocent air. "So I asked Mrs Reynolds to serve us in the dining room. We enjoyed ourselves but naturally wished you could have joined us. Miss Elizabeth was absent too! Do you think I should send a tray to her room?"

How lovely it was to see her so gay and light-hearted! She would not have dared to tease him in the months past. She was so sure that she had failed him and their family that she tiptoed about like an unwelcome stranger. He smiled at her. "No, I have it on good authority that Miss Elizabeth has eaten."

"Oh, good." Georgiana directed a look to the window. "As it is raining, I fear we shall have to amuse ourselves indoors today. Some parlour games perhaps? I do hope Saye can return from Matlock today."

"If it were Saye alone, I would depend upon it. However, he brings Miss Goddard and our aunt and uncle with him, so for their sake, he might wish to wait until the weather has cleared. In any case, parlour games will be amusing. I shall join you within the hour."

BINGLEY'S MIND WAS EXCESSIVELY MUDDLED BY THE EFFECTS OF A near-sleepless night at some inn in a town whose name escaped him. One thing Darcy was always useful for was guidance on which places to stay when travelling northwards. Left to his own devices, Bingley had merely taken the first likely looking place, only to find terrible food and noise far into the night.

But that was yesterday's problem! Such a relief it was to be escaping town! Inasmuch as he enjoyed the diversions, there were times when the obligations grew wearisome. Caroline and her demands, Louisa and her husband—too much by half.

He did spare a meagre thought for Darcy when they reached the point in the road where one could turn towards Pemberley or continue to Sheffield. It was regrettable what Darcy had done to him when Bingley had always thought him a true friend.

It seemed Staley would prove truer than any, Bingley having forgotten whatever grievance had lain between them. He had invited Bingley to join a house party, promising good sport, pretty girls, and fine ale, and he had included Sir Albert in the invitation to boot!

Two days later, he applauded himself for his complaisance. Worry and strife were the objects of others. Bingley believed himself formed for good humour and diversion, and those were found in abundance at Staley's house. The ladies were perhaps not so fine as Staley had promised; his baby sister outshone the lot in Sir Albert's opinion. Nevertheless, the other fellows were liberal at the game tables, and the ale flowed from morning until night. All in all, it was not a bad way to spend a fortnight.

19

DARCY ENTERED THE DRAWING ROOM, FINDING EVERYONE BUT MR and Mrs Gardiner therein. They had retired to the library for the afternoon, leaving the younger folk to games and frivolity.

By the time Darcy joined them, there had already been a great deal of debate about which games might be played as they whiled away the rainy afternoon. Georgiana firmly set herself against cards, and Fitzwilliam was rather adamantly opposed to charades.

"A bullet pudding, then?" Georgiana asked hopefully. Of all games, she found this most amusing. Surprisingly, the two Miss Bennets seconded her.

"We are never permitted it at home," Jane explained. "Our mother finds it undignified."

On his own, Darcy never would have expressed any degree of emotion for such an extraordinary statement. Elizabeth, however, slid her eyes towards his, seeing how he bore it. He remained impassive but only as long as it took for her to quirk her eyebrows at him and press her lips together in a suppressed laugh.

With a sly look at Jane, Elizabeth offered, "My sisters and I have a favourite game at Longbourn. We call it Commands and Consequences."

Georgiana was immediately charmed by the intimation of sisterly bonding. "How do you play?"

Jane protested immediately, "That is a game best played among sisters. I do not think it a good parlour game at all."

Georgiana gave Jane and Elizabeth rather beseeching looks. "It sounds ever so fun. Could we just play for a bit?"

Darcy decided to intervene. "I must say, I like the sounds of it myself. What is the object of the game?"

Elizabeth replied, "It is a game of knowing the truth. We each put a token into a bag, and the first questioner withdraws one to see who will be questioned. For each round, a person has the choice of asking a question or giving a command to the other person."

"We may ask anything?"

Elizabeth nodded. "Anything at all. However, the person can refuse to answer, which means they must do the command."

"Who decides on the commands?" Fitzwilliam asked.

"We all do," said Elizabeth. "We put them on bits of paper in another reticule, and the person withdraws one at random. The commands are sometimes silly, sometimes…scandalous."

"Scandalous?" Fitzwilliam sat up a bit straighter in his chair. "Sounds like the very best sort of game to me. Let us play now, shall we?"

"We cannot play with gentlemen," Jane cried, but the others paid no attention.

"And what are the usual sorts of commands?"

Elizabeth giggled. "I have only played with my sisters, so the commands were largely such things as having to curl the hair of another or being forced to loan a certain gown or reticule."

Darcy nodded. "And the questions?"

"Well, you will wish them to be as revealing as possible—not an easy task when you play with those with whom you live and have known since birth. Most of the questions concerned dance partners and suspected misbehaviours."

"Misbehaviours?" Georgiana suddenly shrank back. "Oh! Well...I do not know about that."

"Do you have a great many misbehaviours to conceal, Georgiana?" Elizabeth asked, her brow arched and her tone teasing.

Georgiana laughed uneasily, shifting her gaze to the floor before her. "No, not exactly, no."

Darcy shot Fitzwilliam a quick look. Fitzwilliam, understanding immediately, said, "Perhaps another game will be better suited to the group?"

"Yes," said Jane emphatically. "Something such as alphabet blocks perhaps. I do love alpha—"

"Nonsense." Georgiana straightened her shoulders and schooled her countenance into placidity. "We are playing this game. It sounds exceedingly amusing, and what could be better for a rainy day?"

"There is one thing more," offered Elizabeth. "If it is doubted the truth was told as decided by the group at large, the offending player will be smudged. Mercilessly."

"Mercilessly smudged?" Fitzwilliam appeared to like this idea even more. "What does that mean?"

"Their faces are rubbed with something vile, and they must keep it on until...well, until the group votes they may remove it."

"Yes!" Fitzwilliam clapped his hands together once, rubbing them gleefully. "I love this game already! Excellent indeed! Now, who is playing?"

In the end, it was decided all were playing. Jane was least enthusiastic, which Elizabeth assured the group was her sister's wont. Jane responded by pulling a silly little face at her sister, making them all laugh heartily.

Two reticules were obtained for the purpose. Into one was placed the slips of paper describing the commands for those not wishing to answer questions. The other held the tokens used to select the players for questioning. Lengths of ribbon were used for the tokens: lavender for Elizabeth, pink for her sister, white for Georgiana, and red for Fitzwilliam. Darcy had green.

A servant was summoned to select a ribbon from the reticule, determining who would go first. "It is how we always did it," Elizabeth explained. "For in a household of five young ladies, things must be fair."

Fitzwilliam was delighted to see his ribbon pulled out. "Yes! Now who will be my victim?" He placed his hand into the reticule, mixing the ribbons about vigorously for several minutes until he was satisfied. He withdrew pink. "Miss Bennet!"

Jane groaned, placing her hands over her face for a moment then dropping them with a sigh. "Very well."

Fitzwilliam could not be accused of treating their game lightly. The chairs had been drawn together in something of a circle; however, to simply observe Jane would not do for him. He rose and paced in a circle around the group, his boots rapping a stern report against the floor.

"Any day now," Darcy teased him. "The rest of us might like a turn before we are too old to care."

Fitzwilliam stopped, levelling a piercing glare at Jane. "Question or command, madam."

Jane raised her chin slightly and squarely met his gaze. "Question, sir. I have nothing to hide."

Fitzwilliam resumed a deliberate, measured pace, moving behind Jane and placing his hands on the chair beside her shoulders. "Miss Bennet, there is something I have noticed about you.

You have a decided tendency to disregard that which is most vexatious about people."

Elizabeth laughed as Jane replied rather primly, "I believe in seeing people in the best light."

"Ah yes. Perhaps you do. This game, however, is about truth, and truth I must have. So Miss Bennet, tell me…" Fitzwilliam moved in front of her, glaring sternly.

"You must tell me the absolute truth of what you think of your cousin Mr Collins."

Elizabeth laughed loudly before clapping her hand over her mouth.

"I—" Jane stopped. "He is a fine… He… When he reads…" She thought for a moment. "He is not vicious or cruel."

Fitzwilliam was not satisfied. "But…"

"But nothing. Is that not recommendation enough?"

"The truth, Miss Bennet, or you will be smudged."

Jane turned pink. "But I *am* telling the truth! I do believe he is not vicious or cruel!"

"And what do you think of his wit, Jane?" Elizabeth asked drolly. "What of his table manners? His person?"

The group, each of them now wholly enthusiastic for the game, watched as Jane moved uncomfortably in her seat.

"What is the smudging to be done with?" Elizabeth asked innocently. "We used the soot from the chimneys at Longbourn. Some use mud, but only those who keep pigs."

"Very well," Jane snapped. "He is…not a witty man, and I…I do not like the manner in which he chews. The food is rather too…visible and…sometimes loose."

"Loose?" Georgiana asked. "I do not understand."

Elizabeth had her fist shoved tightly against her lips, but it failed to wholly suppress her mirth. "It means the food displayed a marked tendency to escape the confines of his mouth and go anywhere and everywhere."

"Oh." Georgiana made a slight frown.

"It once landed on my bosom," said Jane, the remembered misery creasing her brow while the group around her dissolved into hilarity, Darcy included. "I never came to the table again without a shawl around me. I cannot think when I have had a more disagreeable sensation than chewed fish on my...my skin."

The group could not calm their laughter after such an admission, and it took some time until a semblance of decorum was restored. Jane, having endured her turn, was the next to serve the question. She withdrew Elizabeth's lavender ribbon.

"Be kind, Jane," Elizabeth warned immediately.

"Do not lose heart for the game now, Sister," Jane replied with a saucy little look. "Not when you displayed such marked enthusiasm for the playing of it. Now, question or command?"

"Question," Elizabeth answered warily.

"What is the absolute worst thing you have ever done? And I am aware you have a great many to choose from, so limit it to this year alone."

Elizabeth shook her head at her sister. "You misrepresent me! Very well, the worst thing I have ever done..."

She began with a fleeting glance at Darcy after which she moved her eyes to the carpet beneath her. "I once injured a friend by expressing some very...condemning opinions that, on further reflection, appear to be quite unjust."

There was silence among the group. Darcy lowered his eyes, unable to watch her make a confession that he understood was for him.

"I have been told I am quite decided in my opinions, and it is true. However, before giving my opinion so freely, I ought to be sure I am correct, and in this case…in this case, I certainly was not."

He chanced to look at her just as she glanced at him. She quickly looked away and fell silent.

Just as the quiet grew uncomfortable, Jane spoke again. "No, it will not do. She must be smudged."

"What!" Elizabeth looked up. "It is true! It is!"

"I have no doubt—but what friend? What opinions?" Jane shook her head. "This is nothing at all. You have confessed to nothing."

"There is some flour over there," Fitzwilliam informed them gleefully. "In case we had wished to play bullet pudding."

"No! Just a moment! You asked a question, and I answered it!"

Jane had already risen and taken up the plate. "Lizzy, you know the rules. Now there are four of us voting so—"

"I shall abstain from the vote," said Darcy immediately.

"Very well," said Jane. "Obviously, I have voted yes to the smudging. Colonel Fitzwilliam?"

"Yes," he said enthusiastically.

"I used to think you amiable," Elizabeth told him. He grinned in reply.

"Miss Darcy?"

"Oh, I…umm…well…" Georgiana looked anxiously in Elizabeth's direction. "No, I cannot excuse…"

"That is two votes in favour and one against," Fitzwilliam said. "Smudge her!"

Elizabeth tried to protest as her sister gathered flour in her hand. With a grand flourish, Jane leaned in, looking as if she had every intention of smearing Elizabeth's entire face with it. However, at the last, she did not. With her forefinger, she drew a delicate line on Elizabeth's nose, after which she kissed her cheek.

"There you are, miss."

"I vote she may remove it," said Darcy at once. Georgiana followed closely with her vote for the same.

"And I shall provide my vote for removal of my smudge," said Elizabeth with a little laugh. "Although I am sure I look quite charming with it! Oh, that Miss Bingley could see me now! My petticoats would likely be less troubling to her."

Elizabeth rose and went to the side of the room where the window, by virtue of the angle of the light, served as a weakly reflective mirror. She raised her sleeve to wipe the smudge, but Darcy was behind her, offering his handkerchief.

"Oh! Yes, thank you." She took it and wiped at her nose, glancing in the window. She asked, "Am I presentable now?"

He took the handkerchief from her. "Not quite," he murmured. A small amount had smeared onto her cheek, and he removed it gently. He ought not to have done it, such an intimate gesture and among company, no less, but she was too tempting. She did not pull away, however, but merely looked at him steadily as he did it, then thanked him quietly before turning back towards her seat.

Elizabeth had just begun to sift through the ribbons when Darcy followed and sat down. She removed her hand from the reticule with two ribbons: those of Darcy and Georgiana.

"Hmm," Elizabeth said teasingly. "Now, I believe I must choose."

Georgiana appeared discomfited, so Darcy offered himself. "You may ask me with impunity, Miss Elizabeth."

"May I?" She regarded him with sparkling eyes and pursed lips. "So I might. However, it is my experience that the secrets of ladies are far more interesting than those of gentlemen." Decisively, she put Darcy's ribbon back in the reticule. "Georgiana, I fear it falls to you."

"I shall take a command," Georgiana said immediately.

Elizabeth's eyes went wide with surprise. "Do you not wish to hear the question first?"

Georgiana shook her head rather adamantly. "No. We have had no one yet who is willing to submit to a command, so I shall be the first."

Elizabeth nodded. "As you wish." She held out the bag of commands, and Georgiana reached in and selected one.

"Read it aloud," suggested Fitzwilliam.

"Give someone a kiss, and tell them what you love most about them," Georgiana read.

"Oh, that is mine," Jane cried with delight. "I wrote that command."

"It is a good one." Georgiana looked thoughtful for a moment before rising from her seat. Darcy thought it a given that she would come to him, but much to his surprise, she went to Elizabeth. She gave Elizabeth a kiss on the cheek and whispered something in her ear. Darcy watched, his pleasure in the scene becoming a warmth within his breast as Elizabeth grew pink and soft-eyed.

When Georgiana went to straighten, Elizabeth did not permit her and held her close for a moment while she returned the kiss and whispers. The ladies then embraced.

"This is all very sweet, I am sure," Fitzwilliam complained. "However, in the interest of the game, might we go on?"

The game provided them with a nearly endless source of amusement and diversion for the remainder of the afternoon. Fitzwilliam was forced to admit he was deathly afraid of spiders, and Elizabeth was required to shove an entire cake in her mouth and eat it in one bite. She nearly failed at this, laughter welling up within her at the worst moment, and for a time, it appeared she might be in some danger of choking to death. She fought it, however, and managed to get enough cake down to recover her dignity.

Georgiana's next command was far less tender than her first, having been supplied by her cousin. He insisted she shoot a pea at a target. She did it with poise and acquitted herself admirably.

Inasmuch as they found much to laugh at in the game and each other, there were also sober moments. Jane admitted to fearing she might never marry. "At times, I suspect I am the sort of lady who is unlucky in affairs of the heart."

Jane's confession pained her sister. When Darcy chanced a quick look, the sorrow was writ plainly on Elizabeth's face. *I shall fix this*, he promised her silently.

The game ended when, surprisingly, it was time to dress for dinner. They would be a quiet party that evening, though Darcy hoped to prevail upon Elizabeth to play for them.

As ELIZABETH DRESSED FOR DINNER, SHE RECALLED GEORGIANA'S words from the game. *"I already love you for the happiness you have brought to my brother as well as the kindness and acceptance you have shown to me."*

Acceptance? Odd choice of a word. Georgiana displayed remarkable diffidence for a lady of her station and fortune. Before knowing her, Elizabeth expected to find someone like Miss Bingley; instead, she found someone more like her sister Kitty.

Further reflection persuaded her that Georgiana had some past misbehaviour she wished to conceal. While Elizabeth was certain it was nothing, clearly it was something that brought the girl some degree of shame. Elizabeth heartily regretted causing anxiety or uneasiness by her suggestion to play Questions and Commands.

I must apologise to her—not to seek her confidence or press her for her secrets but only to beg her pardon for my thoughtlessness and reassure her of my affection.

Elizabeth went to the girl's bedchamber, knocking lightly before being admitted and directed into the dressing room. The maid remained, and Elizabeth told Georgiana to continue with her preparations.

"I wished to congratulate you on a most entertaining afternoon," Elizabeth said. "I have rarely spent such an enjoyable time."

"Thank you. You and your sister have proven the most welcome sort of guests—easy to please and wanting for little."

"You are too kind, but I fear I was rather too outspoken in my choice of game. It did not escape my notice that you appeared to be uneasy."

Georgiana shrugged, looking down at the little bracelet she had been playing with. "Only a little. I had a great deal of enjoyment once we began, but yes, I was a bit anxious. You know what I must conceal from the world and will understand why I was nervous."

"What you must conceal? I fear I do not know what you mean."

Georgiana raised her eyes to her maid using the reflection in her mirror. The maid understood immediately and bobbed a quick curtsey before departing. When the door closed behind her, Georgiana turned to Elizabeth. "What Fitzwilliam has told you about George Wickham and me."

"George Wickham and you?" Elizabeth sank down onto the chair next to Georgiana. "I am afraid I do not understand, but I do not wish to force your confidence."

A red shade, slow and determined, crept from Georgiana's chest up to her neck, finally staining her cheeks crimson. "Ramsgate. I am speaking of Ramsgate."

Elizabeth shook her head, not missing the tremor in Georgiana's voice. "I know nothing of that."

Georgiana raised her hands to her face and rubbed it roughly before sighing heavily. "I thought you already knew."

"No, no, do not worry. I am sure I need not—"

"Yes," she said firmly. "You do need to know. I am just...oh! I despise the thought of telling you!"

Elizabeth reached over and lightly rubbed Georgiana's shoulder. "Nothing can be so bad, I am sure."

"Oh, no, it certainly can. Pray, do not despise me, and do not hold it against my brother. I could not forgive myself if I were to ruin his chances with you."

Elizabeth leaned over, placing her hand atop Georgiana's. "Tell me."

Georgiana stunned her with a recitation the likes of which Elizabeth had never suspected.

She began with the story of Wickham's history with her brother. That Wickham had so shamelessly lied was not entirely shocking. Most of his lies were those of omission. Yes, Darcy refused him the curacy of Kympton, but Mr Wickham neglected to mention he was compensated for it. He was given the value and a legacy from the will of Darcy's father—in all, a tidy sum of four thousand pounds—the whole of it wasted within a few years. The debts Darcy paid on his behalf were more surprising. Elizabeth was appalled to learn Mr Wickham had not completed his schooling, turning his back on honourable professions for the sake of gambling away his money. His tenure in the militia, Elizabeth guessed, was an act of desperation.

But then came the truly astonishing disclosure. Elizabeth

listened in horror as Georgiana recounted what had happened at Ramsgate, telling of her misplaced trust in her companion and her mistaken belief that George Wickham loved her.

When she ended, the two ladies sat in silence. Elizabeth willed herself to speak though she did not know what to say.

"So if your brother had not...one more day and..."

"And I would have been gone," Georgiana said softly. She made an absent wipe at her eyes. "Off to Scotland to ruin my life. I thought it quite the romantic adventure: a girl who has been given everything and is willing to throw it away on nothing. I suppose I was hopelessly vain."

"If you are, then so too am I." Elizabeth reached over, taking Georgiana's hands in hers. "I have believed—how foolishly I have believed!—in some tales that man told me about your brother. He took great pleasure in speaking to me of the wrongs your brother did to him—things that held no truth. He left out, of course, all that *he* had done."

She certainly did not admit to Georgiana that she had plagued and vexed Mr Darcy with the matter and taken Mr Wickham's part against him. And she could not confess to furthering the talk against him. The weight of her guilt was heavy, but she could not think of it at present. For now, all thought must be for poor, dear Georgiana, who was miserable with sorrow.

"I pray you will forgive me, for you once tried to speak of it, and I fear my reply must have made you think I censured you."

Georgiana nodded with a loud sniff that showed she sought to control her emotions. "I did—yes. I believed you thought I had done such an abhorrent thing that you could not even speak of it."

"No, no. I had no idea of any of this, I assure you."

"And now that you do?" Georgiana turned to look directly at

Elizabeth. Her expression was brave, but fear rested in her eyes. "Do you hate me?"

"Hate you? Of course not!"

A shadow of remorse crept across her countenance. "Will you despise my brother though?"

"Despise your brother?"

Georgiana pursed her lips. "He would admit to none of this being my doing, and that pained me far more than his censure. His censure I deserved, but to see his misery, his sure belief in his own culpability—that was too much to be borne."

Thinking of Darcy's feelings brought Elizabeth a fresh pang of guilt though she knew more must come. "He took a great deal of it upon himself then?"

"He took it all upon himself. He would accept no less than full guilt, saying he had not done well by me although he has— he truly has! He felt he had failed me, our parents...but he did not. I knew it was wrong, what I agreed to, yet I...I... It cannot be his fault. He has tried with everything in his power to give me the same principles our parents gave him. I was young—and young am I still—but I was also very stupid."

There was a silence between them, both ladies lost in this moment of sorrow until Georgiana added, "I hardly knew the depth of his misery until I came upon a letter he wrote to our father."

"Your father? But was he not...?"

"Yes, he was long since deceased. Fitzwilliam wrote him anyway. It was a letter of apology." Georgiana could not continue, choosing instead to attempt to control her emotion.

Elizabeth squeezed her hands tightly, hoping to calm and console.

Georgiana drew a breath, continuing to speak when she could. "I should not have read it, I know, and he has no idea I did. It was wrong, but by then I had done much that was so very wrong. What was one more sin added to my burden? I could not bear to witness his grief after that, and I begged him to go to Hertfordshire with Mr Bingley. I could see him no more, cowardly girl that I am. At that time, we were both heavily aware of our failures, and the weight of our combined agony was too much. At last, we agreed he would leave and I would stay at the house in London.

"And there he met you. I remember the happiness I felt when he began to mention you in his letters, for he wrote to me nearly daily. Miss Elizabeth Bennet—he always wrote your full name. Miss Elizabeth Bennet did this, and Miss Elizabeth Bennet thought that. It was positively extraordinary. He had never done so before about a lady, and it made me think he rather liked writing your name."

She sighed. "In some small way, I wondered whether there could be good to come of my tragedy."

"How so?"

"If I had not stayed in London, he would not have gone to Hertfordshire but to Pemberley—he is always there in the autumn—but he wanted to be within an easy distance of me."

She raised her head to Elizabeth and pulled her face into a wavering smile. "So it was Hertfordshire, and there he met you. Almost as if Fate had a hand in it all."

DINNER WAS ONE OF THE LONGEST TRIALS SHE EVER ENDURED, AND Elizabeth was well aware that her dejection was a marked contrast to the gaiety of the afternoon just passed.

Lord Saye surprised them by arriving just in time to dine, bringing with him his parents and his betrothed, Miss Lillian Goddard. They provided a diversion—Lord Matlock enjoyed the sound of his own voice, and his sons enjoyed provoking him into harangues on whatever subjects occurred to them—but Elizabeth knew her melancholy was not unobserved.

Wickham had fed her lies—outrageous lies, it was true—but she had taken them in eagerly against the warnings of her father, Jane, and even Miss Bingley! She was stupid, foolish, and blind. A girl of twenty, she had behaved much, much younger.

"I hear such different accounts of you as puzzle me exceedingly."

And that was because I listened to a lying scoundrel and spurned the truly honourable gentleman who tried to tell me otherwise. She swallowed against the tears that threatened and looked down at her soup. Mr Darcy's eyes were upon her, and she wished she could beg him to look away, to see someone who was worthy of his affection, someone who was not prejudiced and mean and illiterate nor proud of her own cleverness in hating and taunting him.

Miss Goddard was asking her something, and Elizabeth roused herself from her wretched recollections enough to respond. She knew she was poor company, dull and low in spirits, but it was all she could do to stop herself from sobbing.

Mr Darcy frequently had his eyes upon her, and Georgiana did too. Elizabeth did all she could to avoid meeting their eyes. She spoke mostly to Lord Saye and Miss Goddard, both of whom wanted little from her in the way of conversation. Lord Saye was content to rattle on about anything and everything, and Miss Goddard was content to sit and smile at him as he did it.

Her mind returned to that day on the street in Meryton when Darcy unexpectedly came face to face with Wickham. How fraught with anguish and anger he must have been! Yet Darcy remained the gentleman, merely absenting himself from the situation. How difficult it must have been to do so.

The soup course was cleared, though Elizabeth could not recall touching it.

The next course was brought to the table: quail. Although she commonly enjoyed it, her stomach now revolted against the very thought of it. Bile rose in her throat, and she thought she might be sick right then and there.

Even though she could not bear the idea of being still more rude to Mr Darcy and Georgiana, she was on her feet almost unconsciously. "Pray, forgive me," she said, her voice uncommonly timorous. "I beg you to excuse me. I am feeling rather unwell and must retire."

Mr Darcy said nothing but studied her closely. She turned slightly so she would not have to meet his searching gaze. Georgiana was aware of the source of her distress, and while Jane, Mrs Gardiner, and the other ladies at the table expressed concern and offered assistance, Georgiana said, "Of course, Miss Elizabeth. I shall have a tray sent to you later if you would like."

Elizabeth murmured something in return and fled the table.

Once in her room, she tossed herself onto the bed, throwing her arm over her eyes. The tears that threatened for hours were now permitted to fall, but did not. Elizabeth lay cross and dry-eyed, doing no more than thinking of what a fool she had been and wondering why Mr Darcy did not despise her as he ought to.

20

Quite heartily did Bingley wish that Sir Albert did not find his misfortune such a source of hilarity. From the first moment he beheld Bingley's rather battered countenance—one eye nearly swollen shut—he had been in some stage of mirth, from hidden chuckles to outright guffaws.

"Stop laughing at me," Bingley hissed. "The man is an absolute savage, and he wishes for nothing more than to finish me off!"

"You simply must stop sniffing after the man's sister," said Sir Albert, having extracted a handkerchief from his pocket. He used it to dab away the tears of laughter from his eyes.

"He wants to see me married to her!"

Sir Albert again shook with laughter. "Yes, well, from the state I saw you in, I daresay, you might like that too!"

"She has nothing to reproach me for!" Bingley protested, the strength of his objection causing a stab of pain in his head. He closed his eyes a moment and pressed his fingers to his forehead. "I am certain I did not have relations of any sort with her."

"You were so drunk you could barely walk," agreed Sir

Albert. "I should have been surprised if you were able to engage in anything more vigorous than sleep."

"Exactly. Staley put something in the ale, I am sure of it. In any case, I refuse to marry her!"

"I cannot think what you will do to avoid it," Sir Albert replied, finally in earnest. "It is clear he intends to have his way."

"I cannot. I cannot, and I shall not."

"Offer to pay him, then."

"I tried." Bingley sighed. "He is determined to be unreasonable."

"Sisters are expensive and often troublesome. One cannot put a fair price on being rid of them."

The two sat in silence for a moment until Sir Albert sat up, snapping his fingers. "I have it! No man settles for a small fish when he can hook a larger one, does he?"

"I do not know," Bingley replied. "In truth, I do not much care for fish."

Sir Albert rolled his eyes. "Beef then. Why take a small piece when a larger one is given to you?"

Bingley had the worried feeling that Sir Albert was too much interested in his next meal to extricate him from his dilemma. "I am not hungry right now, so the smaller bit would do for me."

Sir Albert inhaled deeply and closed his eyes for a moment. Opening them, he said, "Let us say you have two ladies before you. One has a fortune of ten thousand and the other has twenty. Which would you dance with first?"

"Are they both pretty?"

"Both pretty," agreed Sir Albert. "And you like each as well as the other."

"And what about their families? Surely one must be better

connected than the other?" Bingley thought he had made a good point, but Sir Albert looked merely frustrated.

"You know, Bingley, I think it would be best if I managed this business of Miss Staley myself. I need only for you to do as I say —will you?"

"Really?" Bingley felt immediate elation jolt through him. "You would do that? You are such a friend to me!"

"And pray, do not ever forget it. Now we need to send a note to Darcy—express."

WHEN ELIZABETH WOKE, DARKNESS HAD FALLEN AROUND HER. A servant must have entered at some point, for a lamp was lit and burnt low on the fireplace mantel. A look at the clock showed it was nearly midnight. She had slept for almost five hours.

With a sigh, she realised she was quite awake and likely due a long night. Her sense of absolute shame was not finished, Even now, the remembrance of her folly assailed her. *I have long prided myself on my discernment and quickness, yet I am now revealed for what I truly am: blind, partial, prejudiced, and absurd. Pleased with the preference of one and offended by the neglect of the other at the beginning of our acquaintance, I have courted prepossession and igno-rance, and driven reason away where either was concerned. Till this moment, I never knew myself.*

And what had he done in return? He had proposed marriage to her. He had brought her to his home, shown kindness to her family, and courted her. Just as he turned from Wickham on the streets of Meryton, he could have walked away and never seen her again.

If Mr Darcy were truly the haughty, proud man she had believed him to be, the man who claimed unappeasable resent-ment as his greatest failing, then he never could have forgiven her for all she had done and said to him—not her impertinence to him in Hertfordshire, not her refusal of him in London, and certainly not her slights upon him here. Yet he had done nothing to her that was not kind. His affection, his regard had been steadfast and sure though she little deserved it. Why had he done it? What could make a man behave in such a manner as this? To love, ardent love, it must be attributed.

Elizabeth rose from the bed, thinking how she could occupy herself through the long, lonely hours ahead. She deserved every bit of the recrimination that would plague her, but she could not face it. A book? What bit of fiction might distract her from the painful truth of what she had learnt?

It was then that she noticed a small, folded piece of paper lying close to her door. She picked it up and opened it, reading, in a man's firm, decisive handwriting, "Question or Command?"

She wondered when he slid it under her door. Likely it was several hours ago, for surely he had long since retired. On a whim, she opened the door. As she suspected, the hall was deserted and dimly lit. She closed it again.

Her aunt had purchased a new book for her on one of their excursions. After lighting another lamp, she settled herself by the fireplace to read it. It was one she had wished for, but she found herself lost in thinking of nothing, her mind a chagrined muddle that could do nothing but visit again and again her many sins and insults against Mr Darcy.

A sound stopped the useless litany in her mind—the quiet brush of paper against the floor. She looked up just as another paper appeared under her door. She hurried to snatch it up, and opened it to find the same message: "Question or Command?"

In a trice, she threw open the door to reveal no one. No one was in the hall.

She closed the door rather more gently than she had opened it, pensive as she rested her finger against her chin. In the next moment, she took the note inside her apartment to the small escritoire. With all haste due to great anticipation, she opened the container of ink, barely managing not to upset it, and scribbled "Command" on the note underneath the question. A quick wave was all the drying it received before she slid it under the door and into the hall.

Elizabeth stayed close, listening intently, expecting footsteps or some indication of movement. There came none. After a full quarter of an hour (or perhaps only five minutes, but it seemed longer), she opened the door again. Her note was gone.

She closed the door and waited. Before long, another note was slid under the door. It read: "Back stair. Come now."

It was not wholly proper, what he suggested, this clandestine meeting in the middle of the night, but she did not care. Filled with a sense of adventure that happily replaced the shame and guilt she had felt before, she hurriedly put on slippers and went to meet him.

The light had been extinguished, and she nearly shrieked when he revealed himself. "You expected someone else?" he asked with a mockingly stern countenance.

"No," she said, still smiling faintly, her hand pressed to her bosom. "I expected you."

That made him smile. "I am sorry dinner did not suit you. I hope I have a solution for what must surely be excessive hunger by now."

"No, dinner was delicious. I had a headache."

There was a brief silence. "Alas, my friend, you have chosen to take the command. I am afraid you are bound."

"Bound?"

He nodded gravely. "Solemnly bound. So let us get to it,

shall we? If you are not hungry, you need not eat, but I have made a charming little supper for us—a picnic."

She raised both brows. "You have?"

"Yes. Will you accompany me?"

She hesitated, and he pressed her with a look that was rather beguiling. She should at least oblige him in this.

"A picnic, you say? So shall we be out of doors? Shall I need a sturdier shoe?" She held out her foot for him to see her slippers.

He considered it. "Can you climb something in those?"

"Climb? Climb what?"

"A wall."

She laughed. "A wall?"

"You can do it, I am sure."

She glanced down at her feet once again. "What will you wear on this excursion? Your boots?"

"Years of experience have taught me that this climb is best made unshod."

"Unshod!" Elizabeth felt herself blush. "Is that not...that may be exceedingly improper."

"Perhaps so." Darcy gave her an unexpectedly roguish little grin. "The truth of it is, I have only ever made this particular climb with my cousins, the male ones."

You can hardly lower yourself further in his estimation. Why protest? It will please him, and surely you have done enough to displease him. "Very well then."

She said nothing when he took her hand, leading her down one long hall and into another. She barely had time to glance around before they entered a bedchamber. She stiffened and hesitated, glancing at the furnishings.

"Georgiana's old room," he told her, tugging her forward.

He led her to a side door opening into a short hall and then to a stairway.

"Sir, I do hope you will not leave me, for if you do, I fear I might never be seen again."

Darcy laughed. "I would find you."

They entered a room Elizabeth realised immediately was the nursery. The moon had risen, making ethereal beings of the covered furnishings, but she hardly had time to note it, for Darcy continued to hurry her through.

Another room adjoined—the schoolroom, she supposed. They were soon through it as well, Darcy going to the far side and throwing the windows—that creaked in protest—wide open. "Come," he beckoned her.

She stopped, seeing that he intended to go out the window. "Oh, I cannot think it wise..." She leaned over the sill, seeing the ground many, many feet below. It made her a bit dizzy.

Darcy leaned close, pointing at the wall opposite. "You see there? Fitzwilliam and I chipped small grooves in the wall. Put your toes in the grooves and you can climb to the roof."

"The roof?" Elizabeth gasped as fear seized her. "You cannot intend me to climb to the roof!"

"Surely, the intrepid Elizabeth Bennet is not afraid?" He teased her with a dare. "I once heard you say your courage rises with each attempt to intimidate you."

"My courage is presently contemplating a drop that would kill me and has gone into repose."

"If you go on the roof at just this spot, you can see for miles."

She looked up at him, seeing an eager light, an animation in his features not often seen. He seemed quite boyish, and it filled her with an odd tenderness. *How it would please him to share this with me!*

He took a step closer. "I would never permit you to fall."

She offered him a small smile of agreement, feeling her knees tremble. "I shall need you to turn your back that I may remove my stockings and slippers."

He turned immediately, tending to his own shoes, and Elizabeth bent to her task, accomplishing it quickly. When he turned to her again, he gestured to the window. "If you will go first, I shall watch you ascend and direct you."

Darcy paused a moment to demonstrate their movements to get to the roof. "Whatever you do, you must not look down. It will make you dizzy. Only look up."

Her heart had gone into a mad rhythm, beating frantically in a vain attempt to stop her.

My hands are shaking. Surely, I shall fall if my hands shake? The thought of her hands trembling and causing her to fall made her knees shiver harder, but she forced herself to swing her legs over the windowsill. *Just a tree, Lizzy. Think of it as a tree you have climbed, not scary at all.* She took a quick peek down. The height was terrifying. She swallowed, her throat suddenly parched.

"Very good. Now reach out with your hand and grasp that little stone piece that juts out. Right there." He called out instructions until she was pressed against the wall. She imagined that she looked like a spider and almost laughed through her fear.

He urged her higher, and she reached for the next groove, but her hand slipped. It was of no consequence, just her hand moving slightly, but she was suddenly terrified. Her fear rendered her immobile. She clung to the handhold, her heart roaring in her ears and bile churning in her stomach. She shook, and it required all her strength to hug to the wall.

"Reach for the next," Mr Darcy urged, but she could not answer. Her breath came heavy and fast, and a cold sweat broke over her. She pressed her face against the wall, praying to God to extricate her from her plight.

"Elizabeth?" Mr Darcy's voice seemed to be coming from a far distance, and she did not answer him but closed her eyes tightly.

"Elizabeth!" He sounded alarmed, and she knew she must speak.

"I feel," she whispered, wetting her parched lips with her tongue. "I feel like I might fall."

"Stay there," he said, his voice commanding. In the work of a moment, he swung to the wall, coming up behind her with sure movements. "Come. Let us get you down."

"No." She shook her head. Her breathing was slowing and the sweat that had broken out was nearly dried. She took several deep breaths, forcing herself to calm. "No, I...I think that was the worst of it."

"There is no shame in going back."

"No." She was moved by the wish not to disappoint him. Intrepid he believed her, and intrepid she must be. "No, I can do it if you will help me."

"Certainly. Now move your hand up to that..." He gestured. "Your feet will follow."

She was still unable to move but for a far different reason now. Her fear having abated somewhat, other ideas intruded. She felt an odd flush come over her, brought on by Darcy's proximity. He was pressed against her back, ensuring her safety, and she could feel every muscle, every bone, every sinew of him. She tried to disregard it, but she could not. To make matters worse, he was exceedingly warm. How could one take no notice of such a pleasing warmth pressed along the length of one's body?

He reached for her hand, moving it for her while his other touched her leg lightly, showing her which way to move her foot. She did as he bid, her breath still coming fast, though it was no longer fear that drove it. She shifted subtly, telling herself it was in preparation for the next move, but in truth...in truth she wanted to feel more of him. It was oddly exciting and intimate.

Elizabeth made a feeble attempt to reach for the next holds as her mind moved towards improper topics inspired by the feel of his arms around her. His fingers were entwined with hers, moving their hands together, and she wondered how it would be to have those hands, those strong arms, holding her tight in a lover's clasp. She imagined Darcy's body stretched over hers in such a way when they were both clad in nothing but light sleeping attire...or in nothing at all. The idea made a hot blush course through her body, and she silently chastised herself. *You are going to fall to your death and all because your mind has chosen this exceedingly inopportune moment to go wanton.*

He reached to help her again, his body remaining in contact with hers, directing her where to put her hands. As he did, his leg slid between hers, and suddenly, she felt him, felt the maleness of him, and her blush turned into wildfire. She had no notion how she must look but did not doubt it was very red. She tried to release a gasp of breath silently, turning her head so he would not hear her.

All at once, a wave of hilarity swept her, and she fought against the rising tide of laughter, focusing her efforts on going over the roof as he was directing her. To assist at the last part, he placed his hand on her hip, and it nearly made her swoon. *You are terrible,* she scolded as she fell over the crest of the roof onto her back. Darcy joined her moments later.

She immediately began laughing, the heady combination of relief, exultation, and unmaidenly interests fuelling her giggles.

Darcy simply looked at her, which made her laugh harder, and tears leaked from her eyes.

"To think"—she giggled—"I was concerned"—more laughter—"for how it must seem to permit you to see my feet!"

"I beg your pardon," said Mr Darcy gravely. "It was not my intention to frighten you. I feared you would not be able to go either up or down."

His gravity increased her laughter, and she struggled mightily to gain control of herself, tears rolling down her cheeks. Her stomach ached with the effort while Mr Darcy gave her a strange look.

"You appear to have recovered nicely."

That sent her off into another round of giggles, but he chuckled too, so it was well enough for them both. At last, they recovered their wits, and he pulled her to her feet, leading her a bit farther across the roof to enjoy the view he so wanted her to see.

The crescent moon lent an almost spectral quality to his land, which was unfurled beneath her like an enchanted map. The stream wound its way prettily through the fields and around the park, and the farms that dotted the landscape at regular intervals looked neat and charming. Darcy pointed out various landmarks: the town of Lambton, the river, and the trout pond. A sense of awe stole over her, thinking of the responsibility he bore for all she saw. *It is a magical kingdom, and it is his kingdom.* It filled her with still greater wonder to consider he had wished to share it with her. He was master of all she surveyed and wanted her to be its mistress, to join with him in the care of this land and these people.

Her awe was replaced with a multiplied sense of unworthiness and renewed shame for her treatment of him in favour of Mr Wickham. She felt stupid, understanding Mr Darcy in the way she did now, to ever have given any credit to the ramblings of such a person as Mr Wickham. She snuck a glance at Mr Darcy. He was staring off into the distance, and she admired his profile, the strength and nobility in his countenance.

"And there is our little picnic." He pointed to a blanket laid out with a basket and a decanter of wine.

"A midnight picnic on a roof. Surely something I have not done before."

"Neither have I, and I have always wished to do so."

They seated themselves as Elizabeth enquired, "Then why have you not?"

"Too romantic a setting to share with Fitzwilliam and Saye?"

That made her laugh again as she sorted through the offerings he had brought. The picnic contained a good deal of food, more than enough for twice the size of their party, but they nevertheless did it justice. Elizabeth, seeing how heartily Darcy ate, thought to ask him another question. "Question or command?"

"It is your turn, is it not?" He wiped his mouth carefully with his serviette while he thought. "Question."

"Do you always eat so much in the middle of the night?"

He laughed at the question but sobered quickly. "If the truth must be told—"

"It must," Elizabeth told him immediately. "I have nothing immediately on hand to smudge you with, but I am resourceful when I need be."

"Very well, then." He held up his hands. "I confess, I found myself with little appetite after you left the table."

"Forgive me," she said at once. "I was very rude—"

"No, no." He shook his head. "I suspected something had happened to upset you. Georgiana told me of your conversation."

Elizabeth felt her cheeks grow hot. "Yes," was all she could manage as she stared down at the blanket upon which she sat.

"It has pained you to learn what manner of man George Wickham truly is."

She looked up, and he was regarding her soberly, a hint of pain on his countenance. Startled, she realised he must attribute her distress to having loved George Wickham. She nearly groaned aloud with the idea, but instead set about correcting his understanding.

"Do not think learning the truth of Mr Wickham has so overset me. That is not the cause of my anguish. I never did love him, even when I still believed he had goodness in him."

"You did not." It was a question though spoken as a statement.

"No." She shook her head slowly and emphatically. "Mr Wickham never did touch my heart. I felt nothing more than compassion for him. Christian charity for one who had been—from what he told me—grievously wronged. I know now that it was nothing but lies."

After a thought, she added, "I pitied him."

Darcy's face barely changed, but somehow, almost imperceptibly, it bore a tinge of satisfaction. He sat back a little, looking up at the stars.

She knew she must admit more. "I was upset because of what I did." Her voice broke as she said it, but she calmed herself, wishing to appear a rational creature even if she did not feel like one.

He turned his attention from the stars and asked her, in a voice low and comforting, "What did you do?"

"Believed him. I cannot bear to think of how I taunted and teased you and believed the worst of you, all on behalf of that scoundrel. You must surely despise me for being so stupid." The night air was turning cool, and she shivered a little.

His voice was kind. "How could I think you stupid for believing as so many have before you? Need I remind you that my sister, my father, and I are all among that number? As for despising you, I never could."

She shook her head, remorse sinking her. "Pray, believe me when I tell you how deeply I regret every unkind word I have uttered, every untruth I have heard, and every false thing I have believed. How unkindly I teased you…"

He moved closer and put his large warm hand on her shoulder, speaking softly and caressing her gently as if to soothe her. "I hold nothing against you, Elizabeth. It is all in the past. Let us allow it to remain there."

She inhaled deeply; she had come close to losing her composure moments before and did not wish to do so again. "Thank you," she said softly. "Thank you for not turning away from me and for bringing me here and allowing me to know you better, even though I believe there is much more for me to comprehend."

A brief smile graced his serious mien. "As I must continue in my endeavour to understand you. I cannot think of a time when I have accurately predicted what you must think or feel on any topic."

He paused a moment then added softly, "One must take a lifetime to know these things, I imagine."

21

"*A LIFETIME TO KNOW THESE THINGS...*"

Does he still wish for a lifetime with me? Will he renew his addresses? Elizabeth did not know what she would say if he did. It was all so fast, this shift from utter misery to the delight of being on the roof and enjoying time with him. Her reason could not stay apace of her feelings.

She began to speak but fell silent. Too many thoughts ran wild in her mind to be sorted. She leaned towards Mr Darcy, pointing to the stars. "Vega has come to greet us,"

"Vega along with Deneb and Altair. You are fond of astronomy?"

"I confess I am. My favourite constellation is of Gemini, though we do not see it now. My birthday is at the end of June, and when I was young, my father told me those stars were for me. I am afraid I took him quite at his word and was disappointed when I learnt others could see them too."

As she spoke, Mr Darcy lay back, looking up at the constellations. A moment's hesitation was all it took before she lay down beside him, not touching him but very close.

They spent time pointing to constellations and discussing the writings of the various astronomers and philosophers of the heavens. It was during this discussion that Mr Darcy's hand drifted towards hers, and two of his fingers eventually found their way atop hers. His caress began with hesitation, small and infrequent. It was just enough that she could persuade herself it was accidental—until it came again. Eventually, it grew to a slow gentle touch, her fingers enjoying what the rest of her might have liked too.

They were silent for the better part of five minutes when Mr Darcy said, "I believe, having nicely answered my command, it is now your turn to make a request of me."

His touch distracted her sufficiently that she required a moment to consider what he meant. "Oh! Ah…question or command?"

"Question," he answered firmly.

"You are quite certain!" She laughed. "I think you fear what I might order you to do!"

"A bit, yes." He chuckled with her. "I have much to answer for in your eyes. Your question, madam?"

"I have wondered ever since I was in London how this all came to pass." She glanced over at the noble profile fixed on his view of the sky. "Pray, tell me what happened that there were so many who believed I was engaged to you."

He closed his eyes. "My first thought was to propose to you when your party dined at Rosings."

"In your aunt's house?" She gasped. "Well…I suppose I do not wholly shock you when I say that I do not believe she would have been the first to congratulate me."

"Forgive her poor treatment of you in Kent," he said gravely. "I am aware of her presumption in ending your visit there and her abuse of you when she heard…when she heard what she had."

"And pray, who did she hear it from?"

"Lord Matlock. I must say, I never knew what a pack of gossips my family are. I had gone to him, you see, because I believed his initial response to the news might not be...not quite as I might wish."

Gently, Elizabeth said, "No, I imagine not."

"I was far too confident in my belief that you would say yes, but my original intention was only to ensure that no one would mar what was meant to be a time of joy with a response that would injure either of us. So I went to my uncle and your father and then—"

"Then my mother read the express meant for my father." She gave him a wry grin. "Unfortunately, true."

He nodded. "And Lord Matlock saw fit to tell Saye who told Miss Goddard. And so it went from there."

"So it did."

"Forgive me?" His voice was low in the darkness.

"I already have," she replied lightly. "Did not we agree to begin anew?"

"Yes, we did. I thank you."

The stars above glowed peacefully, and Elizabeth, lying on her back, took a moment to watch them. The night had come alive. An owl hooted, and the frogs warbled their love songs by the pond. It was altogether rather enchanting.

Mr Darcy had stopped his little caress, and his hand stilled beside hers. After a moment of deliberation, Elizabeth reached for him, laying her hand atop his.

Mr Darcy cleared his throat. "Question or command?" He shifted his hand so it was palm up, touching hers. His fingers curled slightly, inserting between her fingertips in the loosest sort of handhold worthy of the description.

"Question," she whispered.

He did not speak for a moment. "It is rather an impertinent query."

"Very well." She stole a look at him, but his eyes were trained on the night sky, and he did not look at her as he spoke. "Have you ever kissed anyone?"

"Kissed anyone? No, of course not!" Elizabeth felt her face grow hot. "That is to say, I had always assumed, naturally, that my husband would be the only man ever to kiss me."

He said nothing, and she wondered whether he wished to kiss her. She peeked at him, her eyes drawn to his lips. They were rather full and slightly parted. Although they looked soft, they also seemed strong. What would it be like to feel Mr Darcy's kiss?

The heat in her cheeks seemed unrelenting. Indeed, it grew hotter on her face and then over her entire body. In an attempt to distract herself from her prior wanton thoughts, she asked, "Have you?"

"Have I?" Darcy sounded surprised.

"Yes, have you kissed anyone?"

For several long moments, nothing could be heard but the sounds of the night around them. "Yes, I have."

"How many ladies have you kissed?"

He laughed, a sharp bark of surprised laughter. "Elizabeth!"

"I am sorry. My curiosity gets the better of me sometimes. Forgive me." She felt chagrined to have asked him, but she truly was unrepentantly curious.

They lay a few minutes longer, the tension pressing down thick around them until Darcy spoke again. "One person, in a... in what was meant to be a romantic sort of way."

"I am afraid I do not understand you."

"Anne." He shook his head at the sky. "She was sixteen, I was seventeen, and we had heard very often by then how we were meant to marry one another. We decided one afternoon to give it a go and see whether we wished to marry."

Elizabeth laughed—a little scandalised—and was relieved when he chuckled too.

"It was then that we both decided we could never marry each other, though as you have noticed yourself, Lady Catherine refuses to abandon the notion. I can hardly say to her, 'No, Aunt, we tried kissing, and it simply will not do.'"

Elizabeth laughed again and then they fell silent. She stared at the sky, as did he. After a moment, she felt his thumb gently caressing the outer part of her hand. It emboldened her to ask more of him. "Are you good at it?"

"Elizabeth!" Darcy made a laughing exclamation, taking his opposite hand and pressing it to his eyes for a moment. "You will be the death of me, I think." He cleared his throat and continued. "I suppose it is not a thing one can judge of themselves." He paused before adding quietly, "I do hope one day to have your opinion on the matter."

The intimation of a kiss brought a new sort of tension, and they fell silent contemplating it, both unsure how to move past the awkwardness. *I want him to kiss me. Do I just ask?*

"Do you want to kiss me?"

She could barely hear his response. "Yes."

The sounds of the night silenced as if the woodland creatures themselves awaited what would transpire. "If you want to, you may," she whispered. "If you wish to. I mean...you may if you would like."

He turned towards her. "I may...kiss you? Now?"

Her heart pounded, and she wondered whether he could hear it. Her voice was faint, and she could not so much as glance at him. "Only if you want to..."

"I want to." Slowly he turned, rising on his side to face her. He propped his head up using one hand.

The moon, alas, was behind him, giving him an advantage. She could not see his face although he likely could see hers. He did not touch her. Using slow, deliberate motions, he leaned towards her, placing his lips gently against hers and bestowing upon them her first kiss.

It was over far too soon. She had scarcely tasted him before he pulled away and looked at her. She could not imagine what he saw, but in scarcely a moment, he was back to kissing her, his lips growing stronger and more persistent by the moment.

She gathered enough courage to reach for him, putting her hand on his shoulder—his strong, warm shoulder—that felt oddly alive to her touch. Hesitantly, he raised his free hand, laying it lightly on her shoulder. They moved closer to one another, their bodies very nearly in alignment.

The kiss deepened. She was surprised at first when his tongue touched her lips and then entered her mouth. It was astonishing, both the sensation of another person in one's mouth and the feelings it created—the yearning for something more. She slid her hand up his back and pulled him down atop her, wanting to feel him—all of him—over her.

He pulled away after a few moments. A shift in their positions permitted the moonlight to touch him, and she opened her eyes to see him looking at her with an indefinable expression. She watched him watching her and thought he had never looked so young or so open. There was an unusual tenderness in his looks.

"Is something wrong?"

He shook his head slowly, his eyes unmoving from her.

"Shall we stop?"

"Never."

"What then?"

He murmured, "I just needed to look at you for a moment. I had nearly persuaded myself this was not real and wanted to be sure that it was."

Something in his tone of voice made her heart pound, and she lowered her eyes. He reached for her, placing his finger under her chin and turning her face to him, and he resumed the kiss at once.

They kissed for both a moment and an eternity. His hand was again on her side, and she felt it begin to shake a bit.

At last, he wrenched away, laying his head back, his eyes closed and his breathing rapid. After a minute, he opened his eyes. "I fear that was too ardent."

She smiled, hoping she seemed reassuring. "Not at all. It was exactly the right degree of ardency."

He smiled faintly.

Elizabeth leaned back and lowered her eyes, still tasting him on her lips. She knew she needed time to reflect upon what had just happened and what it meant. There was one thing she did wish to say. "Mr Darcy?"

"Yes?"

She paused a moment. "You *are* good at it."

This brought forth a deep chuckle along with another kiss. It was quick, but overwhelming in its ability to entice her. It was a temptation for him as well. She saw it in the way he wrenched himself away from her and groaned before saying, "Talk to me, Elizabeth. Tell me of something, of anything, that is not kissing and love and romance."

She began by asking him about Pemberley—a topic sure to induce conversation—and once started, their talk flowed easily.

The discussion moved without direction, a tête-à-tête between old friends, varying between ordinary, light, and sober subjects. There was no more kissing, which both disappointed and relieved her.

Eventually, they paused, aware that considerable time had passed. "We must get you back to your bedchamber," said Mr Darcy. "It would not do for the maids to notice your absence."

It was the moment she had been dreading. Inasmuch as she despised climbing up, going down was likely to be far worse. He was assisting her to her feet when he noted the concern on her features.

"You are nervous about our descent."

"No, not nervous," she said, with an ashamed little chuckle. "Only absolutely terrified."

"There is an easier way. One need only go to the edge of the roof and drop your legs onto a window sill. It is nearly impossible to go up that way, but to go down is no great difficulty."

"Yes," she cried at once. "Let's do that!"

He dropped his gaze, appearing uncertain. "It's the window into my bedchamber."

"Oh." Going into his bedchamber, wherein resided his bed, was surely above and beyond even the rather scandalous behaviour she had indulged in already. If anyone knew, she would be made to marry him immediately. She found she rather liked that idea.

"What if your man is there?"

He brightened, seemingly relieved. "I shall enter first to be certain he is not and to aid you in coming through. Will that do?"

Trepidation tightened in her chest, quickening her pulse and causing her stomach to clench, but she forced a brave smile. "I believe it must."

HAVING PRACTICED THE MOVE MANY TIMES BEFORE, IT WAS AN EASY business for Darcy to lower himself off the roof, dangling his legs over the ledge and then edging backwards until his feet touched his window. His windows were always open in the summer; thus, he could rest his feet on the sill while he called to Elizabeth to begin a similar descent.

He had promised that, as he aided her, he would hold her skirts fast around her ankles, and this he did, even while part of him marvelled at the delicacy of her feet and the daintiness of the bones beneath his hands.

While that part of his mind was thus engaged, a similar part was seeking cause for another kiss, and yet another part would only be encouraged by the feel of her skin beneath his hands. He thought of many other ways in which he might contrive it, but in the end, he resorted to their silly little game to ask her for another kiss once her feet touched the floor. He thought it through carefully, not wanting to coerce a kiss. She had an easy escape if she wished it, but he dearly hoped she would not.

Soon, she was in his bedchamber and stood a moment, leaning against the frame while breathing a sigh of relief.

Before she ran off, he put his hand on her arm. "Question or command?"

Her eyes, which had been skittering over the floor in an effort to avoid alighting on the bed, rose to his. It took a moment before her naturally teasing inclination took over. "Forgive me, sir, but was not yours the last answered? I fear you are out of turn."

"Not at all. You followed my question with several of your own if my memory serves me. You are in my debt."

She laughed. "So I am. Very well, then. I suppose you are ready with your question?"

He studied her a moment, enjoying her beauty heightened by their informal, intimate setting. Her hair was in disarray from their climb and the time spent stargazing. He longed to run his fingers into it, to make it fall completely from its moorings, but knew he should not.

"Perhaps I shall relate your choices to you, and you will be able to decide." He took a deep breath, summoning his courage.

She nodded.

"The command, should you choose it, will be…" He faltered, losing courage in the face of her unwavering gaze, but then he saw it. She was quick and surreptitious, but not enough that he did not see her glance at his mouth. It emboldened him, though he still spoke quietly and with hesitance. "The command is for you to kiss me."

Her eyes went wide for a brief moment before she looked down, briefly touching her fingertips to her cheek. He presumed she must be blushing, but his room was too shadowed to know for certain. She did not falter, however, so he continued, "My question is: do you prefer a plain dish or a ragout?"

"What?"

"I wondered whether you prefer a plain dish or a ragout." It was in the air now, both his stupid question and his deepest wish. She must surely understand the veiled request he made. If she wished to avoid the kiss, she needed only to answer the question. He prayed fervently that would not be her choice.

She tilted her head, not quite hiding a smile. "A plain dish or a ragout?"

He nodded, wondering vaguely whether she could hear the beating of his heart.

"That is indeed a deeply revealing question. I am not sure I am willing to gratify such brazen enquiry."

When he responded, his voice was calmer than it ought to have been, both deep and sure. "If you wish to avoid my penance, you must answer, madam."

Very slowly, she shook her head. "No, sir, I shall not. You must remain ignorant of my preferences in dining."

"Well, then?" He opened his arms wide.

She took a step closer, rising on her toes and putting her arms around his neck. His arms moved about her, pulling her close. He adored her more than ever for the tentative and uncertain manner with which she undertook kissing him—soft, hesitant touches of her lips to his.

Darcy permitted her to direct it as long as he could, but soon he could not resist the temptation to kiss her more deeply, and he pulled her tighter against him, uncaring whether she noticed how much he wanted her. He felt his desire building to dangerous levels and knew he must somehow stop himself even as a part of him calculated the nearness of his bed. He wondered whether it would be terrible to suggest they merely sit upon it.

Just as he recognised his desperation, she slowed, making a transition to small, closed-mouth kisses and pulling back a little, so he had to relinquish his hold. When she stopped, he rested his forehead on hers, keeping his hand behind her head to stop her from moving away although she did not. She too was affected, her delicate sighs music to his ears.

"I need to go," she whispered.

"No." He moaned good-naturedly, knowing how ridiculous and ungentlemanly his behaviour was.

She only laughed at his distress, giving him a last, quick kiss. "Yes. I fear I have gone far beyond the bounds of what is good and proper. I would not wish it known throughout the house."

Marry me, then. Nay, let us pretend we are already married. Fortunately, he did not give voice to his thoughts. Instead, he nodded, resigned to his fate, and watched her with longing as she slipped out the door.

He glanced at the clock on his mantel as the door closed behind her. It had just gone past four in the morning, and although the parlour and kitchen maids would already be busy at their work, no one would be above stairs, at least not in the apartments where the family and guests slept. She would go undetected, he was sure of it. She must, for surely the evidence would be condemning: unshod, her hair in disarray, and leaving his bedchamber. No, it was certainly nothing he would wish either of them to answer for.

SAYE LAY IN HIS BED STARING AT THE CANOPY. PETULANCE HAD dissipated into regret in the long hours he had so lain this night, though he was not yet ready to take the whole of their argument on himself. *Lillian can be positively shrewish at times. Ringing that clapper of hers for all she is worth. Must be female troubles.*

Except it had not been wholly Lillian's fault. No, he had been a bit intemperate, that could not be denied. In fact, the more he thought of their argument, the more he had to concede that, in truth, it had been mostly his fault.

He glanced at the clock, wondering whether she might be lying awake, perhaps also regretting the dreadful waste of an opportunity for a clandestine tête-à-tête.

Deciding a visit to the chamber pot was necessary, he flung his bed linens aside and rose.

"Poor fellow," he said, looking down at his faithful servant. "It is you who suffered most miserably, and through no fault of your own. You were ready to do as you must, were you not?"

He gave his dear friend a little scratch, just as one would a beloved pet, and stood considering for a moment. It was half four in the morning. If he returned to Lillian's chambers suitably penitent, he could still enjoy several lovely hours with her before they were required to present themselves at the breakfast table.

His man knew not to raise any alarms looking for him as Darcy at times suffered insomnia. But things seemed to be proceeding apace with Miss Elizabeth, so surely, he must now be far more understanding of the trials of a prolonged engagement. "Knowing Darcy, he will have her at the altar before Michaelmas," he said with a little chuckle.

He tossed his nightshirt to the side, went into his dressing room, and pulled on a pair of breeches and a fine lawn shirt. It was enough; with good fortune, he would need far less than that ere long.

In her bedchamber, Mrs Gardiner looked longingly at the clock. Breakfast at Pemberley was served at ten, meaning she had above six long hours until any sustenance would be given. Given the excellent hospitality they had been shown thus far, she had not the least doubt that any request of hers would be honoured, but she was too well mannered to ask for anything at this early hour.

"My dear, you do not sleep." Her husband's voice came from the darkness.

"Forgive me, love. Did my restless tossing wake you?"

"No, it was the sonorous rumblings from your stomach that did it." Mr Gardiner chuckled. "I believe we have the answer to our question, do we not?"

Mrs Gardiner laughed and gave him a little poke. "Not yet,

not with certainty. Though I must say, I do not believe I have ever awoken from hunger save for the times when I carried our children."

With a little sigh, Mr Gardiner rose from the bed and donned his dressing gown.

"Where are you going?"

"To get you something to eat. I cannot have the mother of my children left wanting. What would please you, my dear?"

"Oh no, you need not..." Seeing he was approaching the door, she said quickly, "Perhaps bacon?"

"Bacon? Just bacon?"

"Mm...and perhaps some jam to dip it in?"

"Jam? In which to dip your bacon?"

Mrs Gardiner nodded, hoping the gesture was seen from the scant light provided by the candle.

Mr Gardiner raised his eyebrows, stopping just short of rolling his eyes. "A fifth it is, then," he muttered, wondering how the balance of his two daughters and two sons might be changed.

To sleep was impossible, so Darcy made a quick business of dressing, intending to go to his study and read. At least he told himself he would read. In truth, he wished for nothing more than to ponder the rather astonishing occurrences having just transpired. He had kissed Elizabeth, and Elizabeth had kissed him after saying she had always believed she would kiss only her husband. Ergo, he would be her husband! Could he believe it?

He had nearly declared himself but refrained. There was one part of the business in which he could not be satisfied.

"Had not my own feelings decided against you, had they been indifferent, or had they even been favourable, do you think that any consideration would tempt me to accept the man who has been the means of ruining, perhaps forever, the happiness of a most beloved sister?"

He believed she looked on him with favour now. Much of the distress of their past, the misunderstandings, the insults, had been laid to rest and even, in some cases, been rectified. This, however, had not. Miss Jane Bennet remained unhappy. She remained in love with Bingley, and the whole of it remained in Elizabeth's remembrance as her sister's hopes slain by his hand. It could not stand.

"Think of it, sir. Could you marry someone who had so affected Miss Darcy? Could you imagine forgiving, much less loving, such a person as that?"

He had given his word. He said he would be the means of reuniting her sister with his friend. Had he done that? No, he had not. He had tried but then lost his temper and all but tossed Bingley from his carriage.

He must try again. Even if she accepted him—and he was not yet certain of that outcome—he could not be the man, husband or not, who had ruined the hopes of a beloved sister. It was too much George Wickham and too little of what he wished himself to be: an honourable gentleman.

His study faced eastward and was ideal for capturing the earliest light of day. He settled into his chair, belatedly noticing a letter.

He frowned, presuming it must have arrived by express, and thus, it should have been brought to him immediately. Then again, if it had arrived during the dinner hour, it might have been mislaid during his flight from the drawing room. He had been rather abrupt in his leave-taking, telling no one of his intention to retire for the night. He had simply left Saye and Fitzwilliam with Mr Gardiner and his best port, and off he went.

In any case, no matter how the missive came to be there, it must be read with the hope that late would do better than never.

22

Elizabeth was ashamed of herself, creeping from Darcy's chambers like a thief in the night. Pausing in the hall outside his door, she listened carefully for any sound of the household coming to life, such as the maids going about their work. But no, it was yet too early for that, and all was quiet and still.

And what if I am discovered? Marriage was both the worst and best that could happen, though she would not like the scandal of it.

"More scandal, rather," she murmured. "Let us not forget that, in London, we have been engaged since May."

To know her mind, as she now did, had a powerful effect. Not only was she loath to leave him, she longed to fling open the door behind her, rush back into the room she had just left, and throw herself right into his arms.

No, it would not do. She forced herself away from the door, turning into the hall and continuing towards her apartment.

She had just reached the area that divided the family wing from the guest wing when a slight sound, a rustling, made her freeze in her steps. She listened, every sense on alert, ready for the slightest sight or sound. A footstep—was there someone ascending the stair?

Elizabeth froze, not breathing, not walking, still and silent in the shadows of the dark hall. Every sense went on alert, listening for someone else who was out of bed. When she was satisfied that the noise had been mere imagination, she fled, closing the remaining distance to her bedchamber on her tiptoes, silent but light-footed. She closed the door carefully, but it sounded like a gunshot echoing through the hall.

Elizabeth stood again just inside her bedchamber listening. She heard nothing and sighed over her own silliness. *Go get some sleep. He is likely doing so, and you should too.*

WELL, HOW ABOUT THAT?

Saye, who had instinctively pressed himself into the shadows by the wall when he heard the telltale click of a door opening, watched with an indulgent grin as Elizabeth left Darcy's bedchamber. There was no doubt in his mind what had gone on though he also deduced that the final deed was likely yet undone. He had been at this game far too long not to notice the disarrangement of her hair, the lingering hesitation of her hand on the door, and the resolution with which she continued her clandestine journey to her apartment. Some kissing, he concluded with a little nod, and perhaps a hand up the skirts. He smirked. Or perhaps Darcy would be mending a necklace today.

"Nicely done, Darcy," he whispered in the general direction of his cousin's room. "The lady appears remarkably reluctant to return to her own bedchamber."

For a brief moment, he considered frightening her, playing the disappointed and scandalised elder cousin appearing to enforce morality and chastity. Such fun that would be!

He could never manage it though, not when he himself was

barely clothed and standing in the hall aimed towards his betrothed's chamber. In any case, if there was anyone who desperately needed the enjoyment of a few liberties before marriage, it was Darcy. It would hardly be prudent to scare off Miss Elizabeth's provision of them.

So decided, he traced Miss Elizabeth's footsteps, Lillian being in the room across and just up the hall from her. *A wedding by Michaelmas—I should guarantee it.*

ELIZABETH'S HEART LEAPT WHEN SHE HEARD THE SOUND OF footsteps outside her door. It was Darcy, she was sure, and she immediately opened her door.

It was not Darcy, or if it was, she did not see him. She stepped carefully into the hall, looking cautiously about her and advancing slowly in the direction of the family wing. "Fitzwilliam," she said in the barest hint of a whisper.

There was no answer, so she repeated herself, moving forward a bit more. Half a second later, she nearly leapt from her skin as her uncle entered the hall. He moved sleepily in the direction of a back staircase, which fortunately put his back to her. She took immediate advantage of this, scurrying back into her bedchamber. With scarcely a moment to spare, she entered her room, carefully closing the door (but not quite engaging the latch to avoid drawing notice). For a moment, she leaned against the wall, her heart pounding and her face, she was sure, quite flushed. She could not breathe until her uncle, slow moving and heavy-footed, moved out of earshot.

Thank goodness, my uncle did not see me.

"MARGARET," SAID MR GARDINER AS SOON AS HE RETURNED TO

their apartment. "You will not believe what I saw when I left the room."

Mrs Gardiner, happily engaged in satisfying her growing child with some bacon, merely raised her eyebrows at her husband.

"Our niece, creeping down the hall."

Mrs Gardiner winced. "Which one?"

"You need ask?" Mr Gardiner began removing the attire he had donned to go to the kitchens.

"Lizzy? What was she doing? Who was she with?"

"She was alone." Mr Gardiner gave his wife a significant look. "Or at least she was by the time I saw her."

Mrs Gardiner was pensive as she slid her finger through the jam. "I shall speak to her about it tomorrow. Lizzy often has difficulty sleeping. I am sure it was nothing more."

Mr Gardiner snorted. "You evidently recall very little of our engagement."

"Oh dear." The smile was removed from Mrs Gardiner's face in an instant. "That is alarming; nevertheless, Lizzy has always behaved well. We have nothing to reproach her for, I am sure."

"I pray that is true. Love, particularly new love, does not often heed the call of reason, and it does not suit my fancy to imagine having to scold my host for inappropriate behaviour towards my niece."

"No, that would be poor indeed. What do you suggest we should do? I shall speak to her, but Lizzy does keep her own counsel in these matters."

Mr Gardiner settled himself back into bed with a little thud and a sigh. He considered for a moment. "I think it is time that she makes a decision. He has courted her nicely and paid her every regard during our visit."

"Perhaps paid too much regard. I do not like the idea of

returning her to her father..." She did not complete the thought, but her husband understood her well enough.

"I think it might be prudent to cut our visit a little short. She will not like it, but we must not permit her to lose her head here and do something she ought not. Tell her that business calls me back to town. We shall plan to depart a few days hence—long enough for them to decide on a wedding date."

ELIZABETH WAS SCARCELY IN HER ROOM A MINUTE BEFORE THE phantasms of the hall were forgotten. She had hit upon an idea she thought would please Mr Darcy. She would write a love letter to him—just a short note—and slip it under his door for him to find in the morning.

The task proved far more difficult than she had imagined. As she crumpled her third attempt and tossed it into the unlit fireplace for later burning, she muttered, "I am perfectly terrible at this."

She sat back, twirling a lock of hair in her fingers, an old habit from girlhood that occurred whenever she was deep in thought. *What shall I say to him? What can I say that will demonstrate the change in my feelings?*

What about a simple, "I love you"?

Because she did. She had fallen in love with him. She loved him for his goodness, for his character, and for the passionate man who lay beneath the impassive exterior. She loved him for his wry sense of humour and for the manner in which he bore her teasing. She loved him for the way he would talk to her for hours, for the way he would argue with her on matters of interest to her, and she loved him for being willing to change his mind when so persuaded.

Most of all, however, she loved him for his wish to take what was wrong and make it right. So many situations—Georgiana and Mr Wickham, Bingley and Jane—not only did he help, he bore responsibility, and he bore consequences that were not always of his making. He made them his own, doing all he could to prevent those he loved from suffering.

Inspiration came hard on the heels of this understanding, and her pen moved quickly, scarcely able to keep apace of her recent understanding of her feelings for Mr Darcy.

It was around six in the morning when she finished. *And pray to God, Lizzy, that this is never seen by any eyes but his.* But it was nothing to concern her overmuch. Mr Darcy was nothing if not the soul of discretion.

She dried and folded the note, intending to slip it beneath his door and then, with some good fortune, have a few hours rest. Sleep would be impossible; this she already knew. She was too elated, her mind too full of him.

Once again, she tiptoed down the hall, relieved that no one—neither servant nor family nor guest—seemed to be stirring. She went to the outer door of his apartment, the one that she recalled led to a sitting room. After a scant moment of deliberation, she eased open the door, whispering, "Mr Darcy?" into the darkness before proceeding.

Outside the door to his bedchamber, she paused again before laying the pads of her fingers against the wood. She knocked as loudly as would be afforded by fingertips on thick oak yet was unsurprised there was no response. No doubt, he slept, just as she should. She bent, sliding her note under the door.

"What are you doing?" A whisper, low and masculine came from behind her.

Elizabeth started, straightened, and turned in nearly one motion, one hand flying to her chest while the other clapped tightly on her mouth to forestall the scream that threatened to burst forth from her lips.

It had been just an hour since she stood in nearly this spot, held in his embrace. It was perhaps this recollection that made it so natural—once she had recovered from her fright—to take one small step forward and put her arm around his neck, pulling him down to receive her kiss.

He stiffened initially, no doubt surprised by her actions, but he made up for it in a fraction of a second, pulling her against him and kissing her with a hunger he had not shown on the roof. "You came back to me," he murmured against her neck.

She was nearly too breathless to reply and certainly too insensible to speak as a rational creature. "Yes, I...I...I missed you."

Her words, as innocent as they were, seemed to inflame him. He fumbled behind him, opening his door and her letter was trod upon as they stumbled over the threshold into his chamber.

His kisses moved more slowly then, and his hands touched her gently, almost delicately, but she was concerned. Her only thought was worry that he had misunderstood her intention in returning to him, which, given her present occupation—kissing him ardently, touching him, and permitting him to touch her— was a valid concern.

Anxiously, she pulled back and searched his expression in the dim light afforded her by the early hour. She whispered, "I do not wish to anticipate our vows. I did not want you to think that was my intent in coming back."

His eyes did not show the disappointment she might have expected from such a declaration.

He chuckled, but then his eyes grew soft, and he reached out his finger, drawing it lightly down her cheek. "Have we vows to anticipate?"

She dared not speak. There was too much within her—too much emotion, too much love—and it threatened to burst forth with the least syllable uttered. She settled for a nod, quick but conveying the agreement of every fibre of her soul. His eyes were dark as night, penetrating her in a way that made it difficult to even draw a breath.

"Do you love me, Lizzy?"

"You have never called me that," she said, feeling oddly shy. She had tasted his skin and had revelled in his lips upon her, but in saying her name—the name no one but her family ever called her—he had seen into her very heart. It was fiercely intimate.

"I shall always call you Lizzy when we are in my bed," he promised softly. "Because to say Elizabeth will require me to remove my lips from you for far too long."

She laughed a little, partly embarrassed and partly thrilled by his bold statement. She sobered then, her hand caressing his shoulder as she told him with as much gentle earnestness as she could, "I do. I love you."

"I love you too," he whispered. Drawing her back to him, he cuddled his face into her neck and kissed her, gentle kisses that worshipped her. "Every day, I fall in love with you, and every night, I sleep, certain that my attachment to you cannot grow further—until a new day dawns, and I am love's fool once more."

It was a beautiful moment, and Elizabeth wished to remember it forever. She impressed upon her mind the pearly hue of the light in the room and the feel of his arms, hard and warm around her body, a contrast to the gentle caress of his lips as they moved across her face.

"And after all these misunderstandings and strife," she said, laying her head against his chest and filling her ears with the sound of his beating heart, "the wisest and best ending of all."

"The very best," he murmured into her hair.

"I suppose we need not tell anyone of our engagement. They all think they know it already."

"We are not betrothed," was his startling reply.

Her head flew back to look at him. He had a hint of a roguish smile on his lips and deviltry in his eyes.

"Teasing, teasing man," she scolded. "What do you mean, saying such a thing?"

"You, madam, are owed a proper proposal. One that will make you swoon—one you may remember fondly. I daresay, none I have done so far would suit. What say you to tonight when I return?"

"I say that sounds fine indeed," she replied, but then she understood what he had said in full. "But where are you going?"

"I must be away for a brief time this morning. Some business. It should not take me too long to dispense."

"Oh." She was rather more dismayed by this news than she might have anticipated. It removed some of the ebullient happiness she was feeling and replaced it with a burgeoning melancholy. She tucked her head back against his chest.

Darcy rubbed her back as he kissed her head. "I promise to return before dinner. Will that do?"

"Forgive me," she murmured, holding him more tightly. "I know there are many demands upon your time."

"You may demand anything you wish of me. That you are disappointed in my absence is the gladdest thing my heart might know."

"At least you will have my letter to take with you." She bent to retrieve it from the floor and handed it to him.

"Would that I had one for you as well!"

"Do not think of that," she said with a smile. "I only hope that you will enjoy mine."

ALTHOUGH DARCY COULD NOT REGRET EVEN ONE MOMENT OF THE night prior, he did hope the delay would not lead to ill consequences for his friend. It was Bingley who had sent the express, bidding his urgent assistance. Inasmuch as Darcy was disappointed in his friend's recent behaviour, he would not see him suffer.

Darcy arrived in Sheffield just at dawn. The place designated for the meeting was the Noose & Gibbett, which was scarcely two miles from Norton Lees, the seat of the Staley family albeit for only a generation. Darcy looked about with a critical eye as he entered the town. It was every bit as dirty and crowded as it was reputed to be. Sir Albert stood outside the place, evidently awaiting him. Darcy dismounted his horse and tossed the reins to a sleepy and bedraggled-looking stable lad. "Where is Bingley?"

"He will be along in a moment. Perhaps you and I might make a plan for him while we wait."

Darcy followed Sir Albert up a narrow staircase, dark and shrouded in dust and cobwebs. He winced as he inadvertently kicked some small animal lurking in the shadows. The two gentlemen arrived on the upper floor, Sir Albert leading him into a small, dingy room and closing the door. Darcy looked around for somewhere to sit, finally settling gingerly into a chair that gave up a cloud of dust along with an alarming creaking noise.

"Bingley's note was rather scarce with details."

Sir Albert sighed, looking concerned. "A young lady, who may or may not have a full belly, and a young bachelor of newly made, moderate wealth, friend to her brother. I daresay, you might be able to fill in the rest yourself."

Darcy shook his head and uttered a soft oath. "I told him not to—"

"Aye," said Sir Albert. "As have I. Rather likes a good time, our Bingley. The question is—how can we keep him from making this temporary error a permanent one? I daresay, you might prefer to see him married to…Miss Bennet, is it?"

Darcy nodded.

"I believe Staley set this whole thing up. Rumours say the girl loves someone he finds unsuitable—rather a conceited man for such a new fortune if you would like my opinion. Claptrap, I assure you."

It was a relief to see that Sir Albert seemed to have some mind in the matter. Darcy leaned towards his unexpected ally.

"So what has been done?"

"Staley wants twenty thousand pounds for her."

"Good lord. And Bingley is—"

"Unwilling to pay it. Claims he has already given Staley too much at the card tables."

"It is a rather large sum," said Darcy, shaking his head. "I should balk myself at such a sum. Oh, that he had merely exercised prudence. But he has danced the tune, and now the piper must be paid."

"Honour is what is important here," said Sir Albert. "Do you not agree?"

Darcy pinched the bridge of his nose. What could be done? Bingley had dallied, and it perhaps would break Miss Bennet's heart for good. He wondered idly how much Abell liked Miss Bennet and whether Miss Bennet might find living at Lessing Grange agreeable.

"I do agree. I think, Sir Albert, we are of like mind in this and now need only to induce our young friend to do what must be done."

"I shall drink to that," Sir Albert replied.

The door opened, and Bingley entered bearing three mugs and an easy grin that nearly made Darcy groan aloud. "Have you gentlemen fixed this yet?"

He spoke blithely, and Darcy longed to punch him for treating lightly such a serious subject. "Yes," Darcy snapped. "We have."

"Pass those around, Bingley," said Sir Albert. "I think we must drink to your health."

Darcy leaned back, thinking of the muddle his poor friend had just made of his life. He was not in the habit of drinking at such an hour, but it was an extraordinary circumstance.

"The specialty of the house," Sir Albert said as he pushed a mug towards Darcy. "I am told it is as fine as may be had anywhere in England."

Darcy looked at his portion dubiously. "Only for you, Bingley, would I gladly imbibe such alarming-looking ale. To King George then."

23

THERE WAS POUNDING, LOUD AND PERSISTENT, ACCOMPANIED BY muffled shouts. The noise pulled him through the swampy mire of his dream, and he struggled, grasping the dim bursts of light and trying as best he could to pull himself into wakefulness.

When he did, he sat immediately. He had been undressed. Or had he undressed himself? In such an establishment, one could only imagine what sort of servants might be about. His head pounded, and he was unbearably thirsty.

Then it came to him. As his eyes moved around the small, dirty room and he heard the words being shouted over the pounding, he knew. He understood immediately that he had been gulled. That Bingley, of all people, had gulled him.

Naturally, the girl was present, crying and acting the part of the maiden caught in a tryst with her lover. Doubtless, the pounding on the door was from her brother and probably several other people who would try to hold him accountable. His teeth gritted and he rose, swearing before all that was holy that he would not permit this to ruin him.

HAVING AWOKEN EARLY, JANE BENNET DECIDED TO DRESS, AND

although she was not much in the habit of walking, she decided a little stroll in the garden might be nice. Knowing her sister often enjoyed such amusements, she went into Elizabeth's room to ask whether she would like to join her.

The first things Jane saw were her own slippers, tossed carelessly to the corner of the room. She scowled. She was very particular in the care of her clothing and did not like when Lizzy wore her things, much less had the cheek to wear them and then toss them about. She picked up the shoes on her way to her sister's bed.

Elizabeth was soundly asleep, her face pressed into the pillow and her hair wild around her. Jane clucked softly: Elizabeth would regret she had not taken more care with her brush.

Jane laid her hand on her sister's shoulder and shook her gently. "Lizzy? Lizzy, it is past eight."

Much to her amusement, Elizabeth only turned over in her sleep, uttering some half-intelligible words sounding like she was calling for Mr Darcy. Once she recovered from her surprise, Jane giggled. Elizabeth's eyes opened a tiny crack.

"Jane," she said sleepily. "What are you doing here?"

"Waking you, my sleepy sister. It is eight o'clock, and I hoped you would join me for a constitutional."

Elizabeth closed her eyes again, flinging her arm over them. "Eight," she groaned. "Unnnghh."

Jane took a seat on the bed. "Yes, eight. Come walk with me, please?"

It took Elizabeth several moments to reply. Jane peered at her, wondering whether she had fallen asleep again.

At last, Elizabeth mumbled, "Sleep more. Wake me when you return."

Such behaviour was strange indeed. Lizzy never slept late, nor did she forgo the chance of a walk.

Jane decided to try again. "Lizzy, Mr Abell is coming here today, and I wanted to tell you a little about him so I could have your opinion on the matter."

Elizabeth did not reply. Her mouth had fallen agape again, so it was reasonable to think she slept once more.

Jane shook her, a little harder. "Lizzy, are you ill?"

Elizabeth's only reply was a breathy snort.

"Goodness," said Jane. "I begin to think you were awake all night."

Elizabeth mumbled something and turned again, snuggling deep into the coverlet.

"I suppose I shall go and think about Mr Abell on my own then," said Jane firmly. She rose. It was not her habit to walk out alone—nor to think of gentlemen or how much she should like them—without first talking it over with Lizzy. This time, however, she supposed that she must.

So resolved, she departed her sister's room only to find Miss Goddard had just entered the hall. The two ladies smiled with all the awkwardness inherent in two rather shy ladies who have just realised they will be made to converse with someone they scarcely know.

"It looks like it will be a fine day," said Miss Goddard.

"Oh yes. I must say our weather during our stay has been excellent. I have nothing of which to complain."

"That is good to know." Miss Goddard gave a little nod. "I do have every hope of continued good weather."

"Yes," Jane agreed. "I believe we may depend upon it."

There fell a brief silence, each lady lost in her musings. In Jane's case, her thoughts were directed towards Mr Abell. She believed she was wearing her nicest dress, but would it be nice enough? Mr Abell was no doubt accustomed to ladies who wore much finer.

"We anticipate callers this morning," Jane said. "Mr Abell and his sister."

"Have you met them already?"

Jane started and, against her inclination, blushed. "Yes, yes I have met him…them, that is. Mr Abell and his sister. Both are amiable people. I liked them very well." Knowing she was babbling, she forced herself to stop.

"They are my cousins."

"They are?" Jane exclaimed. "I did not know."

"My mother was the cousin of their mother."

"I see." For some cause unknown, it made Jane blush more to hear of this connexion.

Miss Goddard was watching her closely. "My cousin Robert has been, of late, disappointed in love."

"Has he?"

"Oh yes. The lady received his attentions gladly, and I believe he was quite taken with her and on the verge of making her an offer. But the whole thing went off when she received an offer from a man who was titled."

"That is a shame." Jane knew not how best to understand this. Was Mr Abell too lovelorn to court another? Was he put off by the notion of matrimony entirely?

"Have you danced with him?" Miss Goddard asked. "Or have you not been to any balls since you were in the county?"

"I danced with him at an assembly. He is a pleasant dancer. I believe he honoured my sister as well. I also spent a bit of time with him at a recent gathering they hosted."

Miss Goddard looked at her sidelong, appearing pleased. "He wishes only for a devoted lady, one whose affection he need not doubt."

They had reached the first landing. They would soon be in the part of the hall where they might encounter servants or other guests. Thus, Jane, on an impulse, said to Miss Goddard, "I had a mind to take some air before breakfast. Will you join me?"

"With pleasure, Miss Bennet." Miss Goddard smiled.

Miss Goddard was the first to speak when they had gained the out of doors. "You have been crossed in love, or so I have heard."

Jane laughed in an embarrassed manner. "Lord Saye leaves little unsaid."

"He is an unrepentant gossip," Miss Goddard said with a little laugh of her own. "Never tell him anything you would not like his most intimate friends—a number of only fifty or so—to know as well."

"I see! Yes, it is true that, for some months now, I have lamented the fickle attentions of Mr Darcy's friend Mr Bingley."

At Miss Goddard's questioning look, she added, "There is nothing of which I need reproach him. It was naught more than an error of fancy on my side."

"But not less painful for it." Miss Goddard patted Jane's arm. "I know, believe me, I do."

It was now Jane's turn to give a look.

Miss Goddard nodded. "'Tis true. Another man with all the dash and flair I had always hoped to find. He was handsome, charming, and quite unsuitable. My mother urged me to accept Saye just to get me away from that man, though Saye has his own tendencies towards wildness. Still, it broke my heart to give up on the man I believed I loved."

"It did?"

Miss Goddard nodded sagely. "Oh yes. But, Miss Bennet, what you have to comprehend is that not all men are made for marriage. It requires a certain fortitude, I think. It is why my mother has made Saye wait so long to marry me."

"She has?"

"Oh yes, indeed—a year complete as my betrothed to see whether he will remain constant. After all, a broken engagement may be risky, but it is nothing to the pain of a faithless husband."

Jane stared at the path thoughtfully. "I see."

"I think what you truly need to know is whether or not you *could* love a man, not whether you do already. After all, we are permitted so little before the engagement—it is nearly impossible to sufficiently know a man."

"You are suggesting that if I know a man well enough to apprehend something of his character..."

"And to know his family and friends," Miss Goddard added. "Know what principles he has been raised with and what expectations a lady might have of him."

"...then there should be no scruple in accepting him provided one has a long engagement to come to know one another."

"Precisely," said Miss Goddard with a little smile.

The two ladies continued quietly on their way.

Suddenly, as if it had just occurred to her, Miss Goddard added, "To be married to the sister of Mrs Darcy would be something. My cousins have sought a nearer connexion to the Darcys for some time."

"What have you done to him?" Bingley cried. "Is he dead?"

"Of course not," Sir Albert snapped. "You promised you would do as I said, now go do it."

"Darcy will despise me forever!"

Sir Albert sighed heavily. "Mr Darcy will have no cause to repine. A nice little sleep and, when he wakes, a little spot of trouble he will be required to wave his purse at. Have you not noticed that nothing sticks to this man? Some are born lucky, that is all."

Bingley anxiously peered into his friend's face, wishing for reassurance that somehow, some way, this whole thing might be forgot.

"Darcy's circle has a different set of rules, my friend. A little money and a word or two from his uncle, and the whole of it will be dismissed as nothing. All will be well!"

"But what of Millicent? What will become of her?"

Sir Albert was not inclined to worry overmuch for Millicent, and he spoke of her with impatience. "The same that happens to every lady who finds herself with a bellyful—a secluded cottage somewhere or a hasty marriage. Once Staley has his pockets filled by Darcy, 'twill be a simple matter to find a willing gull, I am sure of it."

"But Darcy is going to know he did nothing," Bingley said anxiously. "What if he dismisses the whole of it as nonsense?"

"He will still wish to pay the girl to avoid the blemish on his reputation and to take care of things quickly."

Bingley raised his hand to his mouth and nibbled at his thumbnail. If Louisa were there, she would box his ears for such a vile habit, but she was in London and Bingley was nervous. "He will be angry with me."

"What should that matter to you?" Sir Albert snapped. "Darcy has been exceedingly disrespectful. Ruined your courtship of Miss Bennet—all but tossed you from his carriage. No—Darcy is a poor friend. And he has never liked me! Do not think I am unaware of how he speaks of me!"

"You are right, of course, you are right." Bingley was much relieved. For a moment, he had nearly felt guilty.

"Now, if I were you," his friend advised, "I should be long gone before any of this happens."

THE SECOND EXPRESS FROM SHEFFIELD, THIS ONE DIRECTED TO THE attention of Colonel Fitzwilliam, arrived just as the man himself finished a second cup of coffee. He had indulged in a hearty breakfast and, many hours later, would be glad he did, for it was the last he would eat for some time. In the moment, however, it did no more than prove challenging for his digestion.

He opened the express, hoping it was not from his general, for he was not due back with his regiment for another week. He dearly hoped his respite would not be cut short.

What he read caused him to grow immediately pale. He then reread it, studied it carefully and, moments later, went to find his father, stopping just briefly to talk with Darcy's valet and Mrs Reynolds.

BY NINE IN THE MORNING, THE SUN SHONE BRIGHTLY IN THE GUEST chamber inhabited by Elizabeth. She tried mightily to pay no attention, pulling her pillow over her head. But it was not long after that Elizabeth concluded more sleep was impossible and pulled herself from the bedclothes. *It is for the best, else I shall find myself unable to sleep tonight too.*

For a moment, she contemplated that. Perhaps it would be for the best after all? A smile played at her lips as she thought of her desire for another night on the roof with her almost betrothed. *Would you risk death for the cause of more kisses?* She knew well the answer was yes—unquestionably and unhesitatingly, yes.

But no, a proper lady and good guest would rise and prepare for the day, and so that is what Elizabeth did. She descended the stairs at ten in the morning, much later than was her wont but not such a disgraceful hour that anyone would suspect something amiss.

LORD MATLOCK WAS READING THE NEWSPAPERS AND SIPPING coffee, when his son entered the salon. Fitzwilliam was feeling rather distressed and could only imagine how plainly evident it must be to his father. "What is it, Son?"

Wordlessly, Fitzwilliam handed the express to his father.

Lord Matlock opened it and began to read. Moments later, incredulous, he sputtered, "What! What is this nonsense? Who would—?"

Fitzwilliam sank into a chair in an excess of weariness despite the early hour. "From Darcy's friend Bingley. He claims Darcy left Pemberley last night, went to Sheffield for a gathering of young gentlemen, and found himself in a liaison with Miss Staley, sister of one of Bingley's friends."

"Impossible!" Lord Matlock declared. "He was with us the entire night!"

"Except when he was not," Fitzwilliam said. "He left after dinner if you will recall. I know not where he went."

"Well his man would know whether he slept—"

"Fields has already confirmed that Darcy did not sleep in his bed last night."

Lord Matlock shook his head and softly cursed.

"Miss Elizabeth was not looking well at dinner," said Fitzwilliam. "She scarcely ate two bites. Perhaps they argued?"

"She is rather the spirited sort. Could they have argued so violently as to send him into the arms of another lady?"

"No, he would never do that, but it is entirely possible he went to Sheffield at Bingley's request and fell into a situation not of his own making. He could have sought to drown his sorrows and overshot his mark."

"So he found himself alone with this Miss Staley..."

"And Mr Staley is demanding justice for his sister or a meeting on a field of honour."

"Blast it to hell," Lord Matlock said under his breath. "This is not what Darcy needs."

"No." Fitzwilliam shook his head. "Not in the least. I assure you, it is likely a trumped up bit of nonsense. Alone in a room or something similarly silly. Darcy would not have ruined the girl, no matter how upset he might have been."

"This whole thing might even have been contrived," Lord Matlock said, his fingers steepled under his chin. "For money, possibly?"

"If money is their object, it will be easy enough, but they may wish to see this girl settled in marriage for reasons we do not yet know."

"Reasons we might not know for certain but can likely guess." Lord Matlock groaned.

"Let us hope it is not as bad as that," said Fitzwilliam although, in truth, he believed it likely was.

"If they want to entrap him, they will have already blackened his name," his father warned. "Mark my words."

Colonel Fitzwilliam rose and went to the window, looking to see whether his horse had been brought around. It had not, but he had no doubt it would be there shortly.

Lord Matlock watched him. "Should Miss Elizabeth be told of this?"

Fitzwilliam returned to his seat. "What is the likelihood, do you think, of us being able to manage this without it coming to her attention?"

Resting his chin on his fingertips, Lord Matlock thought a

moment before admitting, "Not likely at all, but I think we must do as we can."

"Saye and I shall do our best to dispense with it all."

"I would like to join you. Darcy may need me."

"He very well might, but pray, come in the carriage if you must. Our aim is to ride hard to get to him as quickly as we can."

"I suppose it is left to me to speak to Miss Elizabeth, then?"

"I can do it with you if we send for her now."

24

ELIZABETH'S STOMACH GURGLED LOUDLY AS SHE ENTERED THE breakfast room, reminding her that she had not eaten much the night prior. She was reaching for some eggs when the door opened, and Mrs Reynolds looked in. "Miss Elizabeth, Lord Matlock requires an audience with you as soon as may be. He is in the green salon."

There was something in her countenance—it looked a trifle pale and rather grave—that alarmed Elizabeth. *He knows. He knows I was up on the roof with Darcy all night.*

She set down the spoon. "Of course. Now? Or shall I—"

"Immediately would be best."

Did she seem disapproving? Scolding in some way? *It is just your imagination. Who could know?* Elizabeth rationalised as she followed Mrs Reynolds. But her reason was not sufficient to stop her heart from pounding or her hands from growing rather clammy.

This is silly. What is the worst he could say? Immediate marriage? Very well, I shall agree.

Moments later, she entered and saw not only Lord Matlock but also Colonel Fitzwilliam, both appearing rather distressed. She searched their faces, anxiously looking for signs of anger or disapproval but could perceive nothing more specific than distress. Even that showed only in their eyes; both had carefully blank faces.

"You wished to speak to me?"

"Your uncle will join us in a minute."

This was serious indeed, but Elizabeth refused to be alarmed. Mr Gardiner might be disappointed in her behaviour, but it mattered not. She and Mr Darcy were in love, and they were to marry. To stay up all night kissing on the roof was perhaps not the most proper thing, but surely, it was a minor offence under the circumstances. She patted her palms lightly against her skirt to blot the moisture that had arisen on them.

"Forgive me." Hurried and a bit out of breath, Mr Gardiner entered the room. "I was at the stables. No one is sick, I hope?"

"Not at all." Lord Matlock directed him towards a chair, and with a nod of thanks, Mr Gardiner sat. "Richard and I needed to speak to Miss Elizabeth and wished for your presence."

"Very well." Mr Gardiner gave her a quick, appraising look. "Are you well, Lizzy?"

"I am well," she affirmed quietly, looking at her lap. She raised her head. "We are all here, your lordship. What did you wish to say?"

Brusquely, Lord Matlock asked, "Did you and Darcy argue last night?"

"Father!" Colonel Fitzwilliam hissed. "Miss Elizabeth, do not feel you need to answer that."

She was so stunned that she responded. "Argue...um, no... not exactly, no."

"Well did you? Or did you not?" Lord Matlock demanded.

"I—" She began, but Colonel Fitzwilliam interrupted.

"Miss Elizabeth, we have learnt some troubling news this morning."

"Oh?" Elizabeth's heart began to pound, and her mouth felt as dry as her hands were moist. "What is it?"

"I received an express from Mr Bingley, who, as you might know, is staying with friends nearby in Sheffield, and he invited Darcy to go to them. Apparently, he left Pemberley shortly after you retired last night and went to a party in Sheffield where… where he was…caught, or perhaps induced, in a sort of…a…"

"A situation with a young lady," said Lord Matlock, his head turned away from the group. "A situation that affects his honour."

Elizabeth glanced at her uncle who was leaning forward, his eyes intent on Colonel Fitzwilliam. The colonel moved to kneel beside Elizabeth.

"Miss Elizabeth, pray forgive my familiarity, but I beg you to believe we shall sort this out as best we can. I know how Darcy feels for you, and there is not the least question in my mind that this is some sort of…scheme or something to entrap him. If there is some way out, we shall find it."

"You think it is true then?" Mr Gardiner asked. "I should not have believed it of him."

"Nor do we," said Lord Matlock. "But the missive came from Bingley who is his good friend, someone he trusts."

Mr Gardiner sighed.

"We could not give credence to it otherwise," said his lordship. "But the circumstances of it are rather damning. I think it likely that this argument with Bingley has had him a bit overset, and when he was summoned to join his friend, he went and found himself in an untenable situation."

"Bingley has not been much a friend in recent weeks though, has he?" She spoke confidently, hoping Colonel Fitzwilliam would assume Darcy had taken her into his confidence.

Colonel Fitzwilliam looked at her warily. "Bingley has

always been a good friend to Darcy though, and Darcy has always taken good care of him. I have not the least doubt that, if Bingley summoned him to Sheffield, Darcy would go as quickly as his horse would take him."

"It is interesting you should say that Mr Darcy has always taken care of him. You have said so before."

Colonel Fitzwilliam had an odd expression on his face as if he were trying to decide whether to be amused or alarmed by Elizabeth's accusations. "Have I?"

"You have. When we met in London, you told me how Mr Darcy had spared Mr Bingley from an imprudent attachment. You said Mr Darcy was 'forever doing favours' for Mr Bingley."

Colonel Fitzwilliam reddened. "I did not realise until later that I spoke of your sister, and knowing her as I now do, I am mortified—"

Elizabeth waved her hand to stop him. "I have often wondered why you said it like that—that he was *forever* doing favours for Mr Bingley."

"Bingley is the kind of young man to get into scrapes from imprudent attachments and so forth."

"There had been others before Jane," Elizabeth conjectured.

"Well…yes. Yes, there had." Colonel Fitzwilliam spoke reluctantly. "Bingley is often in love, and he freely shows his affection. I do not doubt he had some attachment to your sister, but his attachments are many and varied."

"Yes," said Elizabeth. "Yes, I do believe that." So much was making sense to her now, so many of Mr Darcy's actions seen in a more benevolent light. She cursed her former stupidity, her naivety in her understanding of Mr Bingley, and her insistence on his reunion with her sister. But there was no time for that now. Now, she must gather her courage and be the true friend her beloved needed.

"Miss Elizabeth, to what does this analysis of Mr Bingley tend? We must be off to find Darcy and see what can be done to extricate him from this situation."

"There is no possibility that Mr Darcy was in Sheffield last night." She raised her chin and clasped her hands tightly in her lap. She hoped she would not tremble or falter, but she dared not look at her uncle. "I think this is, as has been seen before, a ruined attempt for him to save Mr Bingley. He has taken on himself yet another of Mr Bingley's mistakes. I daresay, it is Mr Bingley who has ruined the girl in question."

"I know that is what you would like to believe," said Colonel Fitzwilliam gently. "I think you might be correct but—"

"But nothing." Was her voice always so loud? "It is true, and I know it because…because I was with him last night—all night —until the early morning. He was with no one but me."

Surprised silence blanketed the room. Elizabeth thought she ought to blush, but strangely, she did not.

"Lizzy," said Mr Gardiner quietly. "Your reputation, dear, let us not forget—"

"Forgive me, sir, "I do not see that it harms my reputation at all. It is perhaps not entirely proper but hardly unusual for a betrothed couple to seek time together outside the eyes of their elders."

"So you were with him alone last night?" Lord Matlock asked, rather loudly.

"Yes," said Elizabeth. "From midnight until about five in the morning. On the roof." Now came the blush she had missed previously. She was trying to be candid and brave, but it did not follow that her maidenly sensibilities were entirely forsworn. To admit to his relations that she, in essence, had spent the night with Mr Darcy on the roof would still cause a blush.

"How did you get on the roof?" Fitzwilliam asked.

"We used the holds. He told me you and he had chipped them into the wall long ago."

"To get down, you would have to—"

"Enter his bedchamber," she replied, blushing even more furiously although her voice was steady, "through the window."

It was at this moment that Saye entered the room, looking uncommonly harried. "The horses are ready. I have my comb and Darcy's best brandy. I daresay, I am well prepared for whatever we might face."

He looked around the room then asked. "What is it?"

Elizabeth refused to be ashamed and spoke with as much confidence as she could muster. "I have just told your brother and father that I was with Mr Darcy last night. Thus, he simply could not have been in Sheffield."

Saye permitted a broad grin to overtake his face as he leaned against a table. "You surely did. Saw you myself, in fact, tiptoeing down the hall just afore dawn. I must speak to my cousin, however. I have always found it more gentlemanly to visit the lady's rooms rather than to subject my lady to the need of skulking the hall."

"I think it must have been past five," said Elizabeth. "Quite impossible for him to have been in Sheffield before daylight."

"Five? Perhaps. But not yet sunrise for when the sun had indeed risen, I was"—Saye grinned wickedly—"not engaged in any activity suited to the hall."

Lord Matlock scowled at his son for a moment before turning his bluster to Elizabeth. "I think no matter what times we assign to this nonsense, the point remains that you spent the night with him! You will have to marry him now, for when a lady enters a man's private rooms, you can be assured she will be made to—"

"You need not fear any argument from me on that score," Elizabeth interceded. "I intend to marry him post-haste, and therefore I beg you to go recover him at once. This is Mr Bingley's scandal, not his."

"If he has not been there the night, then the girl's reputation may still be saved," Mr Gardiner said. "Hers as well as Mr Darcy's."

"Quite right," the colonel said, rising immediately. "Come Saye, let us go. There is no more time to waste."

FOR ALL HER ASSUREDNESS, ELIZABETH WAS NEARLY QUAKING WITH anxiety by the time she left her interview with Lord Matlock and Colonel Fitzwilliam. How cruel, how unjust, that such a mean situation should arise just as she knew her mind for Mr Darcy! Yet above that was fear—fear he was in danger or in some way suffering. She prayed he would not grow angry and fight with someone less principled than he—someone who might think nothing of bringing him to harm.

She was saved from a day made long with anxiety by visitors: Mr and Miss Abell. Their presence was sufficient to produce diversion enough to still her mind—particularly as she saw Jane so agreeably engaged with Mr Abell—but it could not be denied that Elizabeth did nothing more than mark time until Darcy returned from the business that had called him away earlier that day.

Her mind would wander, particularly later in the afternoon when the party had moved to the garden for refreshment. She was nearly ill with worry as she wondered what was happening in Sheffield.

Her aunt and uncle joined the little party in the garden. They talked, laughed, and were in every way the good company they always were, but Elizabeth knew they, too, were upset beneath their serene countenances.

"And how long do you intend to remain in the county, Mr Gardiner?" The question arose from Mr Abell who, judging by the look of things, might have had his own interests in mind.

Mr Gardiner set down the teacup he was holding and cleared his throat before answering. He did not look at either of his nieces. "This might come as a surprise as I have not yet been able to inform my hosts, but I am afraid I shall have to depart on the day after tomorrow. Business calls me back to town."

It required every ounce of Elizabeth's fortitude to refrain from crying out in shock. She did not doubt that her uncle was removing them from Pemberley in response to her behaviour, but she thought it unjust nevertheless. Fortunately, Jane gave voice to similar thoughts.

"That is a surprise, Uncle," said Jane demurely. "I had thought we would remain another week complete at the very least."

"Forgive me." But Mr Gardiner did not sound sorry. "It is as it must be. A few days more and we must be on our way."

Shortly after her aunt and uncle excused themselves from the party in the garden, Elizabeth followed, intent on seeking a private audience with them. To her good fortune, she found them together, and alone, in the drawing room.

"Why are we leaving? We have scarcely been here a fortnight."

In sedate tones, her aunt said, "On the contrary—it is nearly three weeks."

"But not since Mr Darcy's arrival. We had been a se'nnight before he came!"

"Be that as it might, we are still going to leave." Mr Gardiner looked at her sternly. "The plan is quite settled."

"Why?" Elizabeth knew she sounded like an irascible child but could not bring herself to mind.

"Because I feel we must. Your father entrusted me with your care, and inasmuch as I find Mr Darcy an honourable young man—"

"He is!" Elizabeth leaned so far forward she nearly fell from her seat. "He is the best of men, and this bit of nonsense cooked up about him will—"

"Will lead to a great deal of trouble," her uncle concluded. "I understand how ridiculous this is, but I do not need to tell you that the damage to his reputation could be significant. He might feel he needs to marry this girl—"

"No!"

"Elizabeth, please hear your uncle," Mrs Gardiner admonished gently.

"He might," said Mr Gardiner. "I hardly know what will come of it. What I do know is that it may have been extremely unwise for you to be so frank about your…your interlude on the roof."

Elizabeth met her uncle's look squarely. "I have done nothing of which to be ashamed. Indeed, I should be far more ashamed to see my beloved hang when I know he is innocent."

"So you will sacrifice your reputation for his? Lizzy, you just told an earl that you spent the night with his nephew."

"Outside!"

"Outside of marriage! In any case, your precise location hardly signifies. You were alone. You entered his bedchamber willingly."

"To avoid certain death in descending from a roof!"

"Irrespective of your reasons, it should not have happened. I am done speaking of this. We shall be away the day after tomorrow. Please make your preparations accordingly."

Chastened by the knowledge that she had embarrassed her uncle, Elizabeth allowed her face to drop into her hands. "I am sorry."

"Just please understand that I do what I must for your reputation. Until you marry, it is nearly all you have."

"I know," she said, her tone muffled by her hands.

Mrs Gardiner spoke more gently than her husband. "It is my hope that all will be set to rights and soon, and if after that, Mr Darcy wishes to court you—"

"Then I shall be at Longbourn," said Elizabeth, her tone wooden. "I shudder imagining him staying at Longbourn."

There was a brief silence.

"That is ungenerous, Lizzy," said Mrs Gardiner. "For you, I daresay, he would gladly spend some time with your family."

At length, Mr Gardiner, trying to sound cheerful, said, "You will come to us at Christmas. Stay with us in town and then—"

"Christmas?" Elizabeth exclaimed. "In December?"

"That is traditionally when Christmas is held," said Mr Gardiner with feigned joviality.

"I cannot imagine being apart from him until Christmas."

"I know this is not what any of us wish, but we must do what is right." Mr Gardiner reached towards her, holding out his hand. "You will see it is for the best this way. Allow him time to sort out this business of Miss Staley."

"And what if he cannot?" she asked, pleading with him to provide her some comfort.

There was none to be had. Her uncle merely offered a false smile and a brief squeeze of her hand. "We must hope for the best."

DARCY SOON COMPREHENDED THAT STALEY WAS LIKELY PARTY TO

whatever scheme Bingley and Sir Albert had laid out. Staley wanted to see Darcy married to his sister, and the truth of what had occurred the prior night did not concern him. He was perfectly willing to go along with Bingley's deception in the cause of seeing his sister married to a wealthy man. Bingley would have done nicely, but Darcy was even better.

With this in mind, Darcy reviewed his alternatives. Truth and reason were out as Staley had no interest in either. Money was another possibility, but Staley required an unreasonable sum. An amount, Darcy surmised, that would induce some other fellow to marry her with a bastard on the way.

"She is increasing?" He spoke abruptly, interrupting whatever stream of lunacy Staley was spouting at the time.

Staley stopped a moment and drew up, just staring at Darcy.

"Your desperation to see her settled is plain, and I shall know the cause of it."

Staley considered him a moment, then spat on the floor between them and answered grudgingly, "Yes, she is increasing."

"And her lover?" Staley did not answer immediately, so Darcy impatiently said, "Come now, out with it."

"I believed you—"

"No, no. Enough of the lies. You know as well as I do that I have never seen her before today. Was it Bingley?"

"Yes," said Staley, but in such a way that made Darcy doubt the veracity of his word. "See here, sir, no matter what has come before, one cannot deny that you—"

"Yes, I can deny it," Darcy snapped. "I can deny it very well."

And so it went, round and around while Darcy searched his mind, ever certain that, in the end, he would be made to fight for his honour even as Staley sought to restore his.

By the time his cousins and uncle found him, Staley was gone even though no resolution had been reached. What Staley wanted, Darcy refused to give, and what Darcy was willing to give would not satisfy Staley. The truth was irrelevant, and all that was important was the brief moment when Darcy, dosed to insensibility with laudanum by the man he once called friend, was found in bed with a strange young girl.

It was the work of a moment to fully apprise his relations of the state of the scandal gathering around him. They had surmised most of it already.

"Where is Bingley?" Fitzwilliam took a seat on the dusty bed beside his cousin.

"Likely as far as his horse could take him."

"Who could imagine Bingley would be so disloyal?" Saye asked.

"As the weakest of men do," Fitzwilliam said warmly, "he left another holding the bag and scampered away. It takes courage to own up to mistakes."

Disgusted, Darcy rose, his movements impatient and angry. *Happiness was just at my fingertips, yet when I long to grab hold of it, it is wrenched from me.* "I shall fight if need be. Fitzwilliam, will you second me?"

"Darcy, no." The protests of his cousins came immediately, and Fitzwilliam added, "Any man who would engage in such a hoax as this would not hesitate to fight unfairly. It is not worth the possibility of injury."

"Who is Staley that he should have the power to darken the Darcy name?" asked Lord Matlock.

"A nothing and a nobody," Saye rejoined.

"You tell me what else might be done," Darcy entreated, pacing about the small, dark room. "Truth does not matter, and Staley wants her married."

"But it is nothing to do with you," said Fitzwilliam. "We know that for certain."

"Your faith in me is heartening. Alas, it is useless."

Lord Matlock spoke up. "We know from Elizabeth where you were last night."

"I was in my bed," Darcy snapped.

"Elizabeth told us everything," Fitzwilliam told him, "in the presence of my father and her uncle."

"I am exceedingly disappointed that I have never considered the roof myself," Saye interjected. "I can only imagine how delightful it must be to feel the fresh air on your—"

"Stay off my roof, Saye."

"What? Darcy, that is ungenerous."

"You have your own roof. In any case, I shall not have Elizabeth subjected to this scandal."

Patiently, Fitzwilliam said, "You were with your intended wife in your home all night, not in Sheffield and not with Miss Staley, and Miss Elizabeth is willing to have it be known."

A mix of emotion coursed through Darcy, and the weight of it had him sinking onto the bed. Dismay that Elizabeth knew of his predicament but also warm tenderness. He imagined her coming to his aid, bravely telling his uncle—his formidable uncle!—what they had done.

Reality intruded as he imagined what she must think of it all, and he groaned. "Just when we had reached an understanding between us."

"You are not listening to us," said Fitzwilliam. "She does not care. She is happy to have it known she was with you, if only for Staley and Bingley to be proven frauds."

Darcy lay back on the bed. "I cannot bring her into this."

"She has brought herself into it," Lord Matlock insisted.

"Have I not done enough to her, to her family? She—"

"Then what?" Fitzwilliam asked, frustrated. He sat, taking a place next to his cousin on the bed. "So you will preserve her reputation only to see her into a different sort of scandal? The talk will be that she was set aside in favour of some Miss Staley no one has ever heard of. Is that better?"

Darcy did not immediately respond. At length, he said, "There must be another way, but I am too tired and in too much distress to think of it. I must find Bingley, first of all, and in some way prevail upon him to clean up his own problem."

"What you need to do is call Bingley out," advised Saye. He opened the bottle of brandy he had purloined from Pemberley and took a hearty swig. "Then turn him into the magistrate for assault on a gentleman. I despise a coward." He passed his brother the bottle.

Darcy sighed and stared at the floor. "I wish I could despise him, but the truth is, I feel rather responsible for him. If I had not begun by separating him from Miss Bennet—"

"Good God, Darcy! Enough of this—it is not your fault!"

Darcy shrugged. "I wish I could feel so."

There was more arguing and more pacing done by all four gentlemen. Darcy could not permit Elizabeth to be drawn into the situation, no matter what they said. In the end, it was decided they would petition Staley for a bit of time to locate Bingley, and if they could not find him, then Darcy would meet Staley on a field of honour.

DINNER WAS A QUIET BUT PLEASANT AFFAIR, AND ELIZABETH MIGHT even have enjoyed it had she not been excessively worried by Darcy's absence.

The gentlemen arrived back at Pemberley just as the rest of the group retired to the drawing room. All went to their respective bedchambers to refresh themselves. Colonel Fitzwilliam was the unlucky fellow who went downstairs first. Elizabeth, unable to stay herself any longer, fairly pounced on him.

"Please tell me," she begged. "I cannot bear waiting."

"You should hear it from Darcy," he said, unable to meet her eye.

"It is bad then." She swallowed hard against her emotion.

He beckoned her into a corner, lowered his voice, and placed his back to the room. "It is a right predicament. Bingley has never been high in my estimation—I require more than an easy smile and happy temper to really like a man—but now, he is fully sunk. He has done badly by Darcy and has importuned on his friendship in the most grievous way imaginable."

Fitzwilliam shook his head. "Darcy has all the appearance of sternness, but in truth, it takes a great deal to turn him against someone he really loves."

Elizabeth looked down, murmuring, "So I have learnt."

"He will do all he can, but what he will not do—what might save him—is to spread the word of where he truly was last night and whom he was with."

"But I—"

"I know you did, and he was pleased to know of your sacrifice. But he feels he has done too much against you and your family already. He will not put a mark against any of you again."

Briefly, Elizabeth covered her face with her hands. "This business with the young lady though, it is lies, and surely, once it is known—"

"Bingley laid his trap well. I shall spare you further details, but it was persuasive in the appearance of debauchery. Word has been spread in London already. It is a right disaster, and Darcy is left with it. His hope is that he might find Bingley and prevail upon him to do the right thing."

"There seems a small likelihood of that."

"There does indeed."

CAROLINE BINGLEY THOUGHT JULY WAS THE ABSOLUTE WORST OF all months to be in London. It gave new meaning to the word "ennui" and made her almost wild to be anywhere but town. Anyone who was anyone had already left or soon would, the shops were nearly empty, and the potential for amusement was non-existent.

She absently fanned herself with a newly arrived letter, wondering whether she should open it immediately or save it for later when the tedium would truly overcome her. There was a fly buzzing about the room, and she needed something to distract from the sound, so she decided she would open it. Moments later, her eyes flew wide, and her hand rose to press against her bosom in shock.

"Well then!" Caroline cackled gleefully as she used her other hand to wave the letter at her sister. "There is some news!"

"Who is it from, Caroline?" Her sister looked up from her indifferent attempts at needlepoint. Louisa was once again stitching baby clothes, and Caroline hoped it would be for some purpose this time.

"Our brother." Caroline licked her lips, savouring the anticipation.

"Oh." Louisa's mouth twisted with disappointment. "He never knows anything of use."

"I beg your pardon, but this time, he does."

"What?" asked Marston's sister, who was visiting with them. Eugenia was a fashionable girl, rail thin, and possessed of an air of confidence that added to what was only a middling handsomeness. She was one of the noted gossips of the *ton* and prided herself on being the first to know things. Caroline smiled warmly at her.

"It is a rather interesting development in the life of a certain wealthy bachelor from Derbyshire."

"Darcy?" Louisa kept frowning at her needlepoint. "No one cares about Darcy anymore. He is nearly married."

"Is he? I think not."

"No?" Eugenia and Louisa looked at her with rapt attention. Louisa even set down her needlepoint. "What does that mean?"

"He was caught," said Caroline, her eyes wide and her mouth a parody of shock, "in a liaison with another lady!"

The other two gasped and immediately asked, "Who?"

Caroline sat back, fanning herself with the letter vigorously. Then she squinted at it. It was not necessary, for she already had it almost committed to memory, but she did it for effect. "We know her," she informed Louisa. "Quite well in fact. Handsome girl, good fortune. Eliza Bennet is nothing to her."

Who is it?" Louisa cried out, the needlepoint falling beside her. "Who?"

"Millicent Staley."

More gasps ensued, along with a request from Eugenia to tell her of this lady since it was someone she did not know.

"That, my dear, is because she is full young," Louisa informed her. "I am sure she is not out."

"Darcy will not marry her! No matter what, he will not jilt Eliza."

"He might have to."

"I heard her father signed the articles."

"No, I am sure he did not."

"No, no, I heard he did."

"It is of no consequence, for I am sure they would accept a payment for his release."

"It is clear," Caroline pronounced, "that his infatuation with Miss Eliza is quite ended. I should not wish to marry any man under such circumstances."

"No, nor I," agreed Louisa, seeming to forget that her own husband could scarcely remain conscious in her presence.

"But did she not go to Pemberley for the summer?" Eugenia asked. "How positively dreadful. I am sure I could not bear the shame."

"Evidently, he got what he wanted from her," said Caroline. "And thus ended his fever. It happens. I am not so much a maiden that I do not understand such things."

She pressed her lips together primly. "After all, once the milk is had, the cow does tend to look a bit shabby, does it not?"

25

THE TRIBULATION OF THE DAY WAS CLEARLY MARKED ON DARCY when he appeared in the drawing room. He walked stiffly, his eyes were shadowed, and lines that had not been there the prior evening marked his face. He greeted his guests with bare civility, and although he tried to smile at Elizabeth, he produced only a faint grimace.

Warmth flooded her as she beheld him, and a strange desire to protect him came over her. Odd really—she imagined that only gentlemen would feel this impulse to fight to protect their loved ones, but she felt it stirring within her. She loved him deeply, truly, and fiercely, and there was but one thought in her mind.

Mine. He is mine, and I shall be damned before I allow the likes of Bingley to take him from me.

After all, had they not suffered enough? Had he not suffered enough? True, some of it—most of it—had been by her hand, but no matter what her mistakes had been, it did not follow that she would permit another to trifle with him.

Who is Millicent Staley to me? Who is Mr Bingley? I do not care two straws for whatever predicament they have made for themselves.

As soon as the gentlemen had something to eat, Lord Matlock called his sons and nephew into the study for a conference. Darcy regretted it even though he understood the necessity. Elizabeth seemed quiet and watchful, and he wished he understood what she was thinking.

"Bingley has likely made for London," he said. "He has a few family members still in the north, but my guess is that he will most likely be found in his usual haunts. In any case, his sister may know something of his whereabouts."

His uncle laid an arm on his shoulder. "Your family is behind you, Darcy. Saye will attend you."

Darcy nodded. "Fitzwilliam's leave will end in August, and I think it best for him to rest here rather than chase Bingley about the country."

The men talked for a while, but no matter how they twisted and turned it, one thing was clear: Darcy could not fight; it was too dangerous. They must find Mr Bingley and force him to face his fate.

The others had retired by the time the men emerged from Darcy's study. With regret, Darcy resigned himself to speaking to Elizabeth on the morrow. He was reaching for the handle to the sitting room adjoining his bedchamber when it opened for him. He gasped with surprise but then smiled when he realised who awaited him, and he stepped eagerly towards her.

Elizabeth went into his embrace as easily as if she had been formed there, clasping him tightly, just as tightly as he held her. The moment was long but too short as he pulled himself away to look at her.

"What are you doing here?" he whispered.

"I could not sleep until I talked to you," she replied in the same low voice.

Her reply took all felicity from him. They did have a great

deal to speak of, and none of it was happy news. He stepped back and took her hand. "Come," he said, leading her to a little couch by the fireplace.

He sat and she curled next to him, watchful and anxious. "This is entirely my fault," he said, beginning in the middle. He told her all that had occurred between Bingley and him, including Bingley's growing anger that had caused him to take up with Sir Albert and his group. Although he could not detail to Elizabeth everything Bingley had done, he did tell her some of what had been said in the carriage on the way to Pemberley.

"So he was on his way here?"

Darcy nodded. "Until I asked him to leave."

He raised Elizabeth's hand to his lips, touching them lightly. Then he rose, leaving her on the settee. He could not face her for the next part of the story, so he leaned on the mantel, looking at the empty fireplace. "From what I know, it seems Bingley had a liaison with Miss Staley. Miss Staley is with child. I do not know whether the child is his, but her brother believes it is—though the brother is willing to lay it at my feet as well."

"Why you?"

Darcy shrugged. "Money? My known wish to protect the Darcy name? I know not. But what they did was…"

He could go no further. Regret choked him and he stopped, his head bowed and his fingers pinching the bridge of his nose to stave off the pain in his head.

"Make it appear that you were with her last night?"

She sounded remarkably calm, and he turned back to her. "Yes. Elizabeth, I swear to you on all that is holy, I never saw the girl—"

"I know you were not with her," she said with a little laugh. "You were with *me*. Do you think I could have so easily forgot?"

"But never. I have never been with her, ever. I never met her before today." He went to her and took her hands. "Upon my honour."

She tugged one hand free, laying it on his cheek. "I do not doubt it."

"Staley will challenge me. I shall agree to it but not before I have some weeks to find Bingley. I do not deny that I have contributed to this, but neither am I responsible for his misdeeds."

"Of course."

"Nevertheless, there will be scandal. Word has already been sent to London of my indiscretion, and things of this nature do spread like wildfire."

The irony of his statement struck him as Elizabeth replied, wryly, "So I have heard."

The dim lighting of the room could not overshadow the majesty of her eyes as they gave him a look of tenderness he had only before dreamt to see. He gave her a faint smile, the best he could muster.

"It will be resolved, all of it. I am determined. And when it is, we shall marry, but in the meantime, you should go back to Hertfordshire to your family."

Again, she touched his cheek, caressing him delicately. She smiled kindly, reassuringly, at him, and he longed above all to sink into the comfort of her embrace. "In retrospect, it seems providential that Jane and Bingley should be apart. He could not be under your direction forever, and what sort of family might they have made with so malleable a form at its head?"

His head drooped a bit, seeking more of her touch. "He is young. He might have grown into a better man."

"He might have," she agreed. "Or he and Jane, by virtue of being each so complying, might never have resolved on anything, exceeded their income by every turn, and had every servant cheat them."

This made Darcy laugh although he thought she might be right. Two easy tempers made for an agreeable home but not necessarily an orderly one.

He put a kiss on her hand. "You will forgive me then? Or at least forgive me enough to await my addresses at a more auspicious time?"

"You are already forgiven. But as for awaiting you, I fear I cannot."

IN SHEFFIELD, MISS MILLICENT STALEY WAS WHOLLY AWAKE AND longing for something sweet. Since learning of her impending motherhood, she could not have nearly enough dried apricots. She would have them all day long if possible, but her brother could scarce afford them.

She was not entirely certain of this idea for her to marry Mr Darcy. Mr Bingley had been much more to her liking—agreeable and kind and such a dancer! Why, she believed Mr Bingley liked a country dance more than any gentleman she had ever known. And he was quite handsome, dashing in his blue coat. She liked Mr Bingley very well.

Now Mr Darcy was another man altogether. He looked rather dour, even in repose, and his clothing, while fine, was far too much like she saw on older country gentlemen. She wanted to be in town and meet the Prince Regent and the patronesses of Almack's, not be stuck on some estate even more remote than her brother's. It did not suit her at all, the life of a mistress of a grand estate. Quite dull.

Suddenly, she heard the sound of rain on her window. It was a hard rain, tossing the droplets like pebbles against the glass.

Then she realised that she was a silly thing, for it was not rain at all, but pebbles, and where pebbles were being thrown...

She giggled with eagerness and ran to the window, throwing open the sash.

He stood beneath her window, barely visible in the scant sliver of moonlight. "My darling," he called.

"Shh!" She scolded him at once, secretly pleased with her power over him. "You will wake the neighbourhood."

"Come out here then, and I shall whisper as quietly and sweetly as you please."

She made haste to join him, throwing on as little clothing as she needed to greet the out of doors. She nearly ran to his arms, and as expected, he immediately swept her into his embrace.

They had been apart too long and had wished too much for one another, and their liaison quickly grew heated. Millicent uttered, "Stable." He knew her mind at once; it was not a scene uncommon to them. He carried her there, half walking and half running across the lawn, the moon blessedly obscured by clouds to shield them.

It was not until sometime later as she lay back on the soft old blanket admiring his form that she realised he was not wearing his regimentals. She enquired about it immediately.

He beamed at her broadly, offering a bit of snuff from the box he had procured from his trousers. She accepted, and he took a generous measure for himself along with a nip from a flask in his coat.

"Millie, I have come into a bit of good fortune."

He was not a wealthy man nor was he well placed, but evidently, an aged uncle had obligingly died at this most convenient of times and left him with a house and a flourishing business to go with it. Together with Millie's portion, they would make a fine pair.

And a handsome couple, Millicent thought gleefully. She studied his form, admiring his taut muscles and the thickness of his hair. Much preferred to Mr Darcy or Mr Bingley, to be sure!

"Will your brother approve my suit, do you think?" He had just cause to worry. He was not a gentleman, his uncle having made his fortune as a mill owner, and he was expected to tend his uncle's business. Further, her brother did not approve of men from the military, thinking they grew far too wild during their times of rest.

She smiled at him. "We shall not offer him the opportunity to refuse."

"You would rather not await me?" His distress was plain for a moment, but he roused himself, and a shade of something like his usual hauteur came to rest on his countenance. It made her smile.

"I am an exceedingly impatient lady. Having come to know that I love you, I fear I shall be unable to find contentment in waiting to have you."

"I do not understand. What is it you want of me?"

Elizabeth pressed her lips together a moment. Her insides were quaking, and she was cold all over, but she forced the words from her lips. "I want to marry you."

Darcy's mouth dropped open. Whatever he thought she might say, she had clearly surprised him.

Given no symptom of his regard, her anxiety could only increase. "If we marry, then we shall endure together whatever may come, and no one could cause you to marry another. Then we might freely tell those who wonder about the night in question that you were with me and not Miss Staley. That will make it infinitely better, do you not think? For it would not be quite so alarming for those about to marry to spend an evening out upon a roof—perhaps a tiny bit ill-advised but not so dreadful and certainly not nearly scandalous."

She paused and asked again, "Could we marry first?"

His apparent relief was sudden and profound as he swept her into his arms, holding her so close she could feel his heart beating beneath his shirt. "I cannot. You may not bear this burden for me."

"Is that not what it is to be married? To have someone to stand with you no matter what trials may come."

He shook his head. "You are too good, but this is not what you deserve. You deserve far better than to marry under scandal and gossip."

"I care nothing for that," she said fiercely. "It is nothing to me so long as I have you."

This seemed to astonish him. "Do you truly feel this way?"

His amazement touched her more than mere words could have. He doubted her, doubted the strength of her devotion, and with good cause. Elizabeth had not given as much encouragement as another lady might have. Her love might have appeared shallow on the surface, but the roots within her heart had grown strong and deep.

She nodded, keeping her eyes on his. "I love you. Do not doubt me in this. I might have been excessively slow to recognise it and wholly stubborn in acknowledging it, but you, sir, have come to own my heart."

She laid her hand on his heart. "Pray, do not ask me to leave you."

He closed his eyes a moment. "I have made two disastrous proposals to you and now cannot even offer you a proper wedding," He shook his head. "I cannot ask you to elope with me."

"Ah," she smiled. "But it is not an elopement, is it? Did not my father sign the articles? Did he and my mother not give their blessing to our union?"

"Well…yes, they did."

"Do you still have them? Signed by him?"

He ran his hand over his mouth. "I do."

"It occurs to me that a man who has done so much might have also purchased a licence. Did you?"

"I might have…but I pray it has not expired. They are valid for ninety days only."

Elizabeth nodded. "Is it here?"

He looked at her for a long moment and finally admitted, "In my study."

They went down the servant's passage, quiet and clandestine, eventually arriving in his study. He had brought a lamp, darkness having fallen quickly, but despite the dim light, it was short work to locate the papers he wished to find.

He stared at the licence for so long that Elizabeth grew anxious. "Has it expired? Are they difficult to obtain? How long do you think—"

"Tomorrow." A smile, broad and happy, came over his countenance. "Tomorrow is the last day it may be of use to us."

Her smile grew to match his. "It is an omen. All is as it should be. We have signed articles, a licence, and a bride and a bridegroom who love one another. What more is there?"

"Your father ought to be there to give you away."

"My father will be just as happy to hear the news from his study."

"What of your mother?"

"Jane will marry Mr Abell and distract my mother from her misery."

"Jane wants to marry Mr Abell?" He looked at her in surprise. "Truly?"

Elizabeth laughed. "She likes him very well, and he plans to come to Hertfordshire. That is all for now, but we shall certainly see. He seems a good sort of man, but this time, I have learnt to let Jane shift for herself in matters pertaining to her heart."

"It is likely for the best that way," he agreed.

"So there you are. All is in order. There is no impediment."

"I loathe scandal."

"I have been the subject of scandal for some months now," she said with a little smile. "One grows accustomed to it."

"It is a great comfort to know that, no matter what, all attempts to marry me to Miss Staley must fail. Bingley will have no choice but to own whatever it is he did—presuming I should be successful in my efforts to find him."

"Oh, dear." A horrid realisation struck Elizabeth. "Will it make Mr Bingley more determined to avoid your notice if he knows you have married?"

There was a silence as both considered her worry and found themselves unable to dismiss it.

"It will," she said. "It surely will. He will know his scheme has failed, and he will be more determined than ever to run. The Staleys may then make greater effort to discredit you or call you out."

Happiness was drawn from Darcy's face in a trice. He looked down at the marriage licence in his hand as if hoping it had some answer to this newly recognised difficulty to their happiness.

"So we shall keep it secret," Elizabeth said, speaking briskly and in a determined fashion. "No one will know and then—"

"No. No, we cannot do this."

But Elizabeth knew her power now, and although she could

not abide the notion of being the sort of female who used arts and allurements to bid a man to do her will, in this case she believed she might permit the exception. She put her hands on his chest, caressing him lightly. "Do you not wish to marry me?"

"It is my greatest wish."

"Mine too," she whispered, her eyes for him and his for only her. "Truly. That is what matters to me and nothing else."

"Now this is a difficult spot in which to find myself." He ran his finger lightly on her cheek. "To deny you is impossible, yet I fear to acquiesce will eventually cause you misery."

"As Mrs Darcy, I am certain I shall have no cause to repine."

"I shall see to it you do not," he vowed firmly, following his finger with a little kiss.

"Then what impediment is there?"

Another short pause ensued. "I shall send word to the parson."

Elizabeth felt the wide smile that came over her countenance. It was short work until her cheeks ached with the broadness of it, but she did not attempt to disguise her joy. It was soon mimicked on the countenance of her betrothed, who grinned in a way she had never before seen.

"So we shall be married from Kympton tomorrow," he said.

"At the earliest possibly hour."

"Who will attend us? Clearly every one of my family is ineligible—too much given to gossiping."

"Jane cannot be trusted. She will become worried over something or other and end up telling someone of it."

"The Gardiners?"

Elizabeth shook her head. "My uncle is liberal in many ways, but in this, I fear he will take the side of propriety. Let us not risk it. If we cannot have all our family with us, it is better by far to have none. To choose is to inevitably cause offence. I can hear my sisters now asking why this sister was allowed while this one was not, or why your cousin stood for you while another did not."

"I am marrying a wise woman." He laughed. "Yes, you are quite right in this. What then of Mr and Mrs Reynolds? I pay for their silence, and heaven only knows, it would not do to upset the new mistress."

"Quite right! It seems we have settled it, sir."

He said nothing, his dark eyes locked on her face. She met his gaze with one of equal emotion, realising the enormity of what had been decided: tomorrow she would become Mrs Darcy.

"You are certain?"

"Never more certain of anything," she answered honestly.

He ran his hand through his hair. "I arrived home thinking all was lost, and instead, I find I am to have my heart's desire— and sooner than I ever dared dream."

"It is perhaps not as I expected when I came to Pemberley, but having so decided, I must say it feels...just as it should."

"Oh yes." With that, he pulled her into his arms. "For the first time in a long while I must agree: things seem to be happening just as they should."

26

THEY REMAINED IN HIS STUDY, AND FOR THIS, ELIZABETH congratulated herself. Her clothes were in disarray, but her modesty remained. This, too, was a source of pride, for it was no easy accomplishment to have it so. Having at last reached an understanding, their passions rose accordingly, and both felt their restraint should be commended.

They were curled into a chair meant for only one, and they had been kissing for an eternity. "I have not even proposed to you properly," he said in a low voice.

"I believe I understand your feelings and wishes well enough," she teased. More seriously, she added, "As I hope you do mine."

"I understand them." He pulled away to look at her. "But believing them is another matter entirely. It seems like a dream having you here in my arms and saying you love me. I am afraid that whatever Bingley put in my drink remains with me still."

"I am sorry." She touched him tenderly on his cheek.

"For what?"

She ran her hand into his hair, playing with the curls around his neck. "It is not easy when a friend disappoints us."

He pushed his face into her neck, kissing it. His voice was

muffled when he replied, "I am particularly unlucky in my friendships. Some might say I choose poorly and adhere to my choice with great obstinacy."

Bingley had hurt and betrayed him as much as Wickham ever had. The pang that smote her at that thought was considerable.

"What are you thinking of?" he asked.

"I am wondering how well I might do if I were given the chance to thrash Mr Bingley for what he has done."

"If nothing else, the element of surprise might allow you quite a few punches." He kissed her before adding, "Yes, for his disappointment of your sister, I have no doubt you would like to exact some vengeance."

"I am as responsible for Jane's prolonged misery as anyone else. Once she realised it would come to nothing, she was rather quick in putting it aside. It was the months of uncertainty that did her ill." She moved her fingers through his hair in a light caress. "No, it is on your behalf that I would like to punish him. You deserve far better than he as your friend."

He studied her with a tender look in his eyes, and she knew her words had affected him. "I believe my finest hour was when you allowed me your friendship."

"And I offer you much more than that now. My friendship, my love, my everything—they are yours, forever and always."

He did not speak, but she did not doubt he felt it deeply. Rather than say more, she shifted her position on his lap, kissing him in a way she hoped would show a measure of her regard. They continued for some time. Serious conversation was forestalled in favour of whispered nothings of love and promises for their shared happy future. There was the occasional notice of the time and the need for some sleep, but these were mostly disregarded for the more pleasurable pursuits at hand.

"I must go," she whispered for what must have been the tenth time.

"No," he murmured against her lips. "I am nearly your husband, and I command you to stay."

She laughed. "So that is the way of it then?"

His voice was as authoritative and commanding as ever it had been. "Yes."

Sometime later, she mentioned, "If we do not sleep, we shall be too tired to marry."

"The service is not long. We shall manage."

Soon, she noticed the room was bathed in a pearly grey light, weak but gaining steadily. "Surely it is not the dawn?"

"No, no, it is not."

She laughed at him again. "It is, sir. I fear we cannot avoid the break of day."

He moaned a little bit but then said, "But it is a rather good day, is it not? I suppose I should be glad to see it arrive."

"It will be a wonderful, perfect day. Though I am still loath to see the end of this night for it has been rather wonderful too."

"You will not regret the absence of your family at your wedding?"

She shook her head firmly. "I wish to be married to you with no further delay or difficulty. That is my only wish."

She knew it must be a test to his honour to marry in such an irregular fashion, but these were irregular circumstances. "This way we shall know that, no matter what may come, we are together, and we are married. Nothing and no one can put us apart."

There came the sounds of servants stirring. "I must speak to Mrs Reynolds," Darcy whispered, "to secure her assistance in our wedding."

"Make haste," Elizabeth whispered back, her words in

contrast to the languid and lingering manner of the kiss she gave him.

"How will you leave without anyone taking note of your absence?"

"I frequently walk in the mornings. No one will think otherwise if they see I am gone." She considered it a moment and sighed. "I suppose I should dress as if I had walked."

"We shall be a fine pair, then, for I must wear riding clothes." He smiled at her. "I admit, as beautiful as you were when I saw you dressed for the assembly, the most lovely I have ever seen you was the morning you walked to Netherfield."

"You like muddy petticoats, do you?"

"I adore muddy petticoats," he growled, attacking her neck for some last kisses.

With a laugh, she said, "Shall I see whether I can find some puddles on our way to the chapel?" He agreed it was a fine idea. At last, they rose, leaving each other with a promise to meet within a few hours.

THE VICAR RECEIVED THEM JUST AS THE HOUR OF EIGHT WAS STRUCK and by half eight it was done. Miss Elizabeth Bennet was no more, and in her place, stood a Mrs Darcy. Darcy believed he had never felt such pride as this, to look on such a lady and know she was his by her choice and inclination. She had chosen him. He could hardly contain the emotions within him. They pounded within his breast, making him want to laugh and cry and shout.

Mr and Mrs Reynolds had wisely travelled in the servants' conveyance and melted away from their newly wedded master and mistress without ceremony or notice. In their own carriage,

Darcy gazed at Elizabeth across from him. "Mrs Darcy, you are too far away from me."

She reached her hand towards him. "Come join me please, Husband."

He moved across the carriage, settling in beside her and pulling her close. They would not have much time. Soon, they would be back at Pemberley and forced to behave as two people in love but unmarried. He suddenly recognised what a cruel predicament that would be.

"Fie on Bingley," he murmured into her neck. "I do not suppose I shall be able to behave as if I am not married to you."

She moved her head so she could kiss his jaw. "Yes, I do not think..."

"What?"

She smiled up at him, her hand caressing his arm. "I was not prepared for how the depth of my feeling has altered. Feeling myself bound to you and knowing you have bound yourself to me—it is rather astonishing. My love for you has changed, has grown, just this morning. I should not have thought it possible."

That she so accurately described what he felt, and to hear she felt it too, amazed him. He pulled her more tightly against his side. "It was rather wonderful, was it not?"

She sighed. "And now we must be in the company of the others and pretend we are not secretly longing to steal away."

He chuckled, more from surprise than amusement. "Do you long to steal away with me?"

His words ended with a hitching of breath as she turned her face to his with a look in her eyes he had not seen before. "After the last nights we have been together, can you doubt it?"

There was absolutely nothing he could think to say. He stammered like the greenest of lads, feeling heat wash over his body that had nothing to do with embarrassment. "I...I did not know whether... Our marriage has had unusual circumstances...but—"

"But you will come to me, I hope?"

He closed his eyes against the rush of desire breaking upon him at these innocent, charming, and undeniably enthralling words. "My uncle and the others believe I am to be gone this morning in pursuit of Bingley."

"Oh."

Was there disappointment in her tone? How he hoped there was! And what fool would leave behind a newly married, disappointed, beautiful, and loving bride? Not he, to be sure!

"But I shall tell them otherwise," he said firmly. "Hang Bingley. I have far more important considerations today."

He bent forward so he might take her lips in a deep kiss, one that would assure her of the power of his wish and his love. It was different from the way he had kissed her before. This was the kiss of a husband, not a suitor. She was pink and breathless when he pulled back.

"Ah yes, that is it, exactly."

"What is?" She looked a bit dazed.

"That shade of your skin. I believe it will match very well."

She touched her fingertips to her lips, still somewhat dreamy in her aspect. "What? What will match?"

"This." He pulled from his pocket a necklace he had purchased with her in mind. He had begun with pearls but returned them, not wishing for the association with his failed proposal in London. No, this he bought just before coming to Pemberley, full of hope, love, and ardent longing, knowing she had arrived before him and praying he could make her love him.

She gasped when she saw it, and although he did not believe

her unduly impressed by baubles, he knew she liked it. She touched it gently with her finger. "It is lovely! A pink—"

"Pink topaz." He reached to fasten it about her neck. "And the very shade of your lips and cheeks when I have finished kissing you."

His hands still occupied around her neck (Blasted clasp, how was he to make it fasten?), he was quite unprepared for the manner in which she leaned forward with her hand resting on his leg to kiss him.

"Thank you," she said softly. "I love it. How kind of you to give me something I may wear, rather than this"—she gave a little frown at her hand bearing the ring he had just placed upon it—"which I must remove."

"And not to bear bad tidings," he said, having at last completed his task of attaching the necklace. "But I fear the time is now upon us."

They were at the stables, having asked to be delivered there instead of to the house. Elizabeth sighed and removed her ring, slipping it into her pocket with another little pout.

Darcy exited the carriage and extended his hand to help her down, noting that, although she had worn it for mere minutes, her hand within his already felt quite strange when her ring was absent. *Blasted Bingley. Pray that I do not find you, sir, for if I do, I am likely to rend you to bits for this.*

ELIZABETH STOOD A MOMENT BEFORE THE DRESSING TABLE IN HER bedchamber, looking at herself in the glass. So much had happened; she was rather astonished to see that she looked the same as always. With so material a change within, one expected some outward mark. *Married!* She was a married woman now. She could hardly credit it. It was why she had—quite boldly, she thought—urged him to come to her as a married man should. She wished to be in all ways married even though the thought of it did rather disconcert her.

"I am a wife," she whispered to her reflection. "I am Mrs Darcy now." It was not wholly real to her yet; nevertheless, the knowledge made her smile until her cheeks ached with it. It was a delicious secret she held to herself.

"Well then, Mrs Darcy," she said quietly. "I suppose you must be off to your breakfast."

Elizabeth took stock of those in the breakfast room as she arrived, noting her husband had preceded her along with Jane, Georgiana, and Mr Gardiner. Her uncle had evidently just finished as he rose, kissed Elizabeth on the head, and asked whether she had walked that morning. He had left the room before she replied, his mind apparently on other matters.

"I can scarcely credit it is your last day at Pemberley!" Georgiana cried in dismay as soon as Elizabeth had taken a seat next to Darcy. "How fast our time has gone! It seems only yesterday that you arrived."

"For me as well," said Elizabeth, feeling the touch of her husband's hand on her knee beneath the table. "How soon since I arrived, yet how much has happened."

Georgiana glanced anxiously between her brother and her friend, then leaned forward and placed her hand on Elizabeth's. "I know I do not fully understand all that has happened..."

A strange chuckle-like sound came from Mr Darcy, but he quickly lifted the newssheet to cover his face. Georgiana did not appear to notice.

"...but I am quite sure it will be settled for good."

"Thank you, dear Georgiana." Elizabeth smiled warmly at her unwitting new sister. "I feel just the same."

Colonel Fitzwilliam entered the room. "Darcy, I believed you would be for London this morning."

"I cannot leave until tomorrow. I have business to attend before I go."

The colonel picked up a letter that lay next to Darcy. "So, there it is then." Opening it, he scanned quickly before tossing it back.

"I expected it," said Darcy, his tone suddenly grave.

"Did you reply?"

Darcy nodded but said no more. He quirked an expressive look towards Georgiana, and Fitzwilliam understood immediately.

Jane was finishing her breakfast, and Elizabeth took the opportunity to enquire after her plans for the day. With cheeks stained crimson, Jane told her sister that she would go to Lessing Grange. "My aunt wished to accompany me, but she is not well this morning."

"So Mrs Annesley offered to go with her," Georgiana interjected.

"Lizzy, you are most welcome to join the party," Jane proposed.

"Elizabeth has offered to assist me," Darcy announced, using his most imperious voice.

That is a useful voice in times like these—times when no one would dare ask precisely what I shall assist him in doing.

Darcy ate heartily, she noticed, though she could not. The subject of his discourse with his cousin had intruded on her more pleasant musings. *All will be well,* she assured herself silently. *No matter what, he will be well.* Surely knowing he had a loving wife who awaited him would prohibit him from undertaking too much danger.

Everyone was soon finished with their meal. Jane left first, followed by Colonel Fitzwilliam. Georgiana slipped out soon afterwards.

Darcy caught Elizabeth's hand as they were leaving the room, pulling her close and whispering, "Mrs Darcy, it is a horribly long time until we retire."

"Exceedingly long," she murmured. Then, a fit of daring seized her. "But it is not quite so long until we are meant to dress for dinner."

She glanced up at him, seeing his cheeks had gone ruddy. With a quick look around her, she kissed her fingertips and pressed them to the reddest bit of his countenance. With a swish of her skirts, she left him.

In Sheffield, Staley received a letter from Mr Darcy. Darcy repeated his unquestionable innocence in the matter, telling Staley he had been drugged—a fact Staley already knew.

He rubbed his face. Blast, but sisters were a great deal of work. He had truly wished for nothing more than to see Millie settled then learnt there was to be a merry-begotten child! What a black day that was.

But here was Darcy offering to help find Bingley and persuade the man to do what was honourable and good. Staley was not certain he wished to see his sister married to Bingley— he had turned positively libertine—but Darcy was unlikely to yield.

He feared that the rumours in London would be slow to catch. The problem was that nearly everyone of importance had already gone away, and those who remained would be rightly dubious. Darcy was known for his moral character and had a young sister himself. Staley felt he had little in the way of power over the man, and he had begun to fear he might instead find himself on the end of Darcy's blade.

He supposed it could not hurt to enlist Darcy's assistance. Let the man see what could be dug up and think more on it from there.

THE DAY WAS PASSED IN THE WAY OF A ROMANCE NOVEL. THERE were private moments afforded them, and although no one could have imagined the truth, their relations and friends did appear to recognise a change. Nevertheless, any private moments were too scarce and quickly interrupted.

Elizabeth was determined to put aside thoughts of Mr Bingley and directed herself to these few happy hours she had remaining with Darcy. Darcy had evidently decided to do the same. He teased her by whispering, "I love you, Mrs Darcy," whenever he had an opportunity. She countered with as many flirty-eyed looks as she could, including a mouthed, "I love you, Mr Darcy," when she was not being watched.

They attempted to make good on their plans to go fishing in the early afternoon but were foiled by Saye and Miss Goddard, who came to the river soon after. Miss Goddard engaged Elizabeth in conversation while Saye and Darcy stood on the bank.

The fish were well inclined towards being caught, and Elizabeth found Miss Goddard an agreeable companion—but it was not nearly how they wished to spend the day. The finest moment of it was when Saye asked his betrothed to walk down the path a little ways. Darcy was upon her nearly as soon as they had gone around the bend, kissing her hungrily. He pulled back just in time for their companions to return.

When the afternoon sun drew long, Elizabeth nearly ran to

her bedchamber, filled with equal parts trepidation and anticipation.

Once safely enclosed in the room, she paused, gazing into the looking glass, smoothing her hair and straightening her dress. Both silly and likely wasted actions—but she simply had to do something. She wished herself able to speak to her aunt to gain some advice. This was her only regret in the whole of the affair.

She first sat on the bed but then felt too conscious of the fact that it was the bed. She alternately stood by the window and the fireplace then sat in a chair. A sound outside the door made her heart leap into her chest. It proved to be nothing, and she soon calmed herself.

The minutes dragged by, and she wondered whether he had misunderstood her. Perhaps he would not wish to go to her now, preferring the dark of night. Perhaps she had been too forward, too bold? She hoped not.

A small, quiet knock interrupted her anxious musings. "Come in," she called softly, rising at once from her chair.

He entered the room looking grave. He went to her immediately, taking her hand and kissing it gently. "Did I misunderstand you before?"

Suddenly shy, she shook her head. "No, but I...if you do not wish..."

"Oh, I wish it, I assure you. I want you as my wife so badly it is almost a sickness. But you...perhaps you need more than this..." He gestured around the room.

She knew not what he meant but decided to reassure him. "What I wish is what I said before: I want to be your wife. Unquestionably and irrevocably your wife."

This made him smile faintly, and their eyes locked together. "Then we are agreed."

"Yes."

Neither one was inclined to move until at last he leaned in, softly kissing her cheek. She took his hand as he did, and held it tightly. He reached for her, drawing her slowly into his embrace and moving his kiss to her lips.

It astonished her how much his kiss was already familiar and dear. The shape of him over his coat was known to her now, and the feel of his hands tracing her figure was expected but not less thrilling for it.

"Do you know...?" he began. "Someone has told you...?"

"A little," she admitted. "I shall need to rely on you for the truth of it."

This made him laugh a little, as much as he could with his lips pressed to hers. He murmured, "I shall do my best to be a diligent instructor."

"It is to your own benefit if you do," she teased, retreating behind her humour for a moment to allay her nervousness.

He removed his cravat while continuing to kiss her, and she thought him rather clever for his ease in doing so. Then he begged her assistance in removing his coat, and afterwards, she, of her own accord, removed his waistcoat and enjoyed the feel of him so strong and muscled beneath the thin lawn of his shirt.

It was her turn to be undressed, which once again raised her anxiety. Needlessly, it would seem, for Darcy was tender, kissing her on the back of her neck as his hands fumbled with the buttons of her gown. He insisted on removing her stockings while she sat on the edge of the bed, gently untying and rolling them down her legs.

There was much to surprise her in the events that led her from maidenhood to being Darcy's wife. She had no notion that he would wish to kiss her breasts or that she would enjoy it so much when he did, and she surely did not anticipate that the pain of their first joining would be so inconsequential in light of the pleasure it afforded her to be as one with him.

She watched his face as he took his pleasure in her. It was an oddly sentimental feeling as she considered him in light of their extraordinary journey to get where they now were, husband and wife. He lay on her for a moment afterwards, heavy and warm and still, gentle kisses dotting her brow as he gained his breath.

"Are you well?" he asked in a low voice.

"Very well," She gave a little kiss to his chin in return.

"The pain...?"

"It was not so bad and very brief." Her fingers moved lightly up and down his back. "And much overshadowed by all there was to enjoy."

He began to move away, and she clutched at him. "Wait...do not..."

"I fear I am too heavy for you," he explained and turned so his weight was removed, but instead, she rested on him. They lay in silence for a moment, caressing each other absently.

"I do not know if I can do this."

She understood exactly what he meant. "You will find Mr Bingley ere long and prevail upon him to do what is right."

"I shall have thoughts of you urging me to complete the unpleasant business quickly."

"And Mr Staley...?" She enquired hesitantly.

"I told him I would not answer his challenge for a month. By then, I shall have found Bingley, and the truth will be known, though I suspect Staley knows the truth already. But let us not speak of such things, not now."

Too soon, they were required to end their time together, brief as it was. It was still more astonishing to have the man she once thought so proud assisting her as she dressed, tugging determinedly at her corset until she laughed and told him he had done well enough. When both were prepared to face the rest of the household again, he paused, drawing her into his arms.

"I cannot think I have ever been so happy," she told him, tilting her chin to look up at him from within his embrace.

"Truly?"

She nodded. "I am exceedingly glad to be your wife." She squeezed him hard to emphasise her point.

He began to speak but stopped…and started once more but did not continue.

"What?"

He shook his head. "No, I…you have not had much sleep these past few days."

"That is true. I have not." After a short pause, she added, "I expect I shall sleep very well in my uncle's carriage."

"It does pass the time, does it not?" He still seemed uncertain.

"Fitzwilliam?" she whispered. "I do not wish to sleep during what might be our last private time together for some weeks."

"So I may come to you tonight?"

She smiled. "I would be dreadfully disappointed if you did not."

PATIENCE SUFFICIENT FOR A WEEK WAS REQUIRED OF MISS STALEY, soon to be Mrs Erskine. Samuel Erskine—her beau, her lover, and soon to be her husband! She could scarce believe how well it had all worked out.

She was sure he would be delighted once he knew about the babe, but there was one small problem—the matter of her liaisons with Mr Bingley and Mr Darcy.

Mr Darcy maintained his innocence, and she thought that was likely just as well. Her dear Samuel was not a big man, and if he was required to fight one of them, she would rather it be Mr Bingley. Mr Bingley was rather a slight gentleman, and from what she had seen of him, not too muscular. Samuel could tear him to shreds; she had no doubt, and in any case, it was Mr Bingley with whom she had dallied. Mr Darcy was nothing more than a little game.

She believed she did rather well in the telling of it. She was unsure how it came about that Samuel believed Mr Bingley had forced himself upon her, but so it was. His rage was rather an exciting thing. To have a man so protective of her and willing to fight for her was exceedingly romantic, and she longed for the thrill of a proper duel, her two lovers meeting at dawn to avenge her honour.

She determined she would wear her lightest, whitest muslin. A maid-in-the-meadow look with some curls falling about her shoulders and the breeze just so. It would be elegant and all things charming.

She could scarcely wait.

27

Inasmuch as Elizabeth believed the mysteries of the marriage bed had been revealed to her following her delightful afternoon with her husband, when night fell and they were together once more, she realised there was more—much more—to be known.

He came to her again, remarking lightly on the odd circumstances that brought him to unite with his wife in the visitor's wing of his house. He teased her by saying the unexpected location, along with the clandestine nature of their marriage, had given him a sense of adventure.

"More adventurous than scaling the wall to reach the roof?" She laughed. "I am not certain I can tolerate more in the way of adventure, sir."

"Oh, my love, I believe you can." His voice turned serious and richly deep; the sound of it brought a slight shiver over her, though she had no idea why. Soon enough, however, she did know why, and she liked his sense of adventure very well. They spent nearly the whole night long in one another's embrace. Occasional dozing and conversation were the only respite from their passionate interludes.

It was all rather extraordinary, Elizabeth mused as the first true beam of sunlight entered the room, casting a warm glow on the sleeping face of her husband. Darcy, the man she had once been loath to even admit into her society, was now firmly entrenched in her heart and soul. She had never been so close to another, not even Jane. It was this confession that brought tears to her eyes, even as she swallowed back the small sob caused by the thought of leaving him.

This is silly. You will be parted no more than... In truth, she hardly knew how long. Would it be a week? A month? Just how resourceful was Mr Bingley when it came to evading his duty?

"How can I leave?" she whispered. It seemed such a loss to suspend her status as a married lady—even if her status was known only to Darcy, herself, the parson, and the Reynoldses—and return to Longbourn pretending to be a maiden.

Yet leaving was precisely what was required. Mr Gardiner wished to depart at first light, so it was not so long after her musings that she was required to gently wake her husband, urging him towards departure. From his plainly evident reluctance as well as his many lingering kisses, she had to believe he felt the same way she did.

Nevertheless, there was nothing for it. Too soon, they were aboard Mr Gardiner's carriage after offering thanks and hugs and all the necessary cries of a visit cruelly cut short. Darcy offered her a correct bow and a kiss on her hand, but his eyes said much more. In them, she saw his remembrance of their past days and the promise of many more to come. She supposed it would need to do for now.

THE WHITE HART IN HARROGATE WAS THE PLACE OF THEIR rendezvous, but Sir Albert did not join Bingley as he had plainly said he would. Bingley found himself with a most uncommon sensation as the days of waiting passed. It was some time before he understood it was loneliness.

The trouble was that he had not the least idea what to do. Darcy would certainly be searching for him, but he would not look in Harrogate. No doubt, Darcy would go directly to London. Bingley was sure it was best to remain where he was— at least, he believed he was sure. The problem was that he had no one to tell him whether he should or not.

WITH HIS COUSINS BY HIS SIDE, DARCY WATCHED THE CARRIAGE move away from Pemberley, travelling down the lane that would take them southwards through Leicester and Northampton to get to Hertfordshire. It was, in Darcy's estimation, the route affording the greatest comfort in terms of posting inns and good roads.

Darcy would also travel but did not attend them, intending to ride hard and fast to make up for the day he had spent with his wife. A day well worth the spending, he thought, and he momentarily became lost in pleasing recollections of the time spent in her bed.

He set out for London with Saye no later than an hour after the Gardiner's carriage had departed. He first had a diversion near his home—a visit to Lessing Grange.

He had considered carefully this visit. Although he could not say he knew precisely Mr Abell's intentions towards Miss Bennet, he believed he had a fair idea. He also felt it was in his purview—and therefore not officious interference—that he should speak to Mr Abell of the scandal touching himself and, by extension, Elizabeth's family.

He and Saye were shown into the drawing room of Lessing Grange where Mr and Miss Abell sat with their mother. After some time politely conversing, Darcy asked to speak to Abell privately on a matter of some delicacy.

They walked out into a small parterre that had statuary and a fountain. Saye walked with them but lagged a bit behind.

"You are kind to receive us," said Darcy, beginning with politeness as he struggled to determine how best to introduce what needed to be said.

Mr Abell smiled warmly. "It has been pleasurable to spend these recent days in company with you and the Miss Bennets, sir. I hope I do not speak amiss when I say that I have fond wishes for many more such times."

Darcy grimaced unintentionally. "Yes, well...I..." He knew not how to continue.

Mr Abell seemed to take a dim view of his response, or lack thereof. "Sir, if there is something you need say to me, pray, speak directly. I shall not faint. I have learnt it is best to know these things outright."

Surprised, Darcy did not immediately comprehend his words. He stopped and looked at the man who met his gaze squarely.

"If you think I have developed a tender regard for Miss Bennet, you are certainly correct, but if you have come to tell me my suit would not be welcomed—"

"No, sir, I assure you, I did not come here to say any such thing!"

"Oh good!" Abell laughed with relief. "I must say, I could think of nothing else that might put such worry on your countenance."

"No, that is not it, not at all."

"Then do not keep me in suspense. What should I know?"

Looking at the man's guileless expression, Darcy took a deep breath and began. He started with Bingley, telling him briefly of his recent behaviour and the arguments between them and continuing with the occurrences in Sheffield. "So there is a bit of tattle, some talk...none of it true, not even the least bit. Nevertheless, it is marring my...Miss Elizabeth and I, and I have no doubt that...that—"

"So we are off to London," offered Saye. "To find Bingley and cause him to own up to his mistakes."

"But nothing is certain," Darcy said. "And until the matter is settled, there is likely to be a bit of talk."

Abell looked to be deep in thought. The three men continued their stroll as they circled slowly about the parterre.

"If this will affect your pursuit of Miss Bennet," said Darcy at length, "I thought it best you should know now. I also wished you to have the facts of the matter as I am sure you will hear various stories in Derbyshire, in Hertfordshire, and likely in London as well. I do intend to clear up the matter as quickly as possible."

Abell gave a small shrug. "I suppose there is always some sort of gossip going about, but I am glad you told me. It makes no difference to my courtship of Miss Bennet, but at least when I hear whatever I do, it will not be a surprise, and I shall know how to respond."

"So you will go to Hertfordshire as you have planned?" Saye apparently had some foreknowledge of Abell's intentions.

Abell nodded. "Within the fortnight, I intend to be there. I have written to a friend in that county in hopes I may visit him, but"—he grinned—"I do believe he has some idea of my true purpose there, and it is not to see him."

"Splendid," said Darcy. "I pray I shall see you there ere long."

SAYE AND DARCY RODE TIRELESSLY, COVERING AN UNPRECEDENTED number of miles, until they arrived near collapse at the inn where they intended to put up for the night. Darcy spent the miles thinking over and over again of his time with Elizabeth. Innocent remembrances had given way to the less innocent ones many, many miles past, and he was rather of a mind for a cold bath. He had glanced longingly at more than one stream as they passed.

Saye had been rather quiet throughout the ride. No doubt, it was partly from exertion, but he had a look of contemplation about him that, in retrospect, Darcy thought he should not have overlooked.

Saye spoke lightly as the two men strode towards the rooms set aside for their use. "You seem well, Cousin. I admire your equanimity in this business. I am sure I should not have managed it half so well." Saye followed Darcy into his room and dropped into a comfortable chair.

"Thank you."

"You have an uncommonly sedate temper. I do not know that I have ever seen you this much at ease."

Darcy went to the washstand and poured water from the ewer into the bowl. He noted it was pleasantly cool. "I do not know what you mean."

"When I am with Lillian," Saye began with a broad grin, "particularly after a separation, I am nearly wild with it. I have seen that same wildness in your eyes when Miss Elizabeth is present."

Darcy bent, splashing his face. "I am not wild. I am under good regulation, thank you."

"*Now* you are."

Darcy took up a cloth just rough enough to give his face a good scrubbing. It had a rather pleasant feel, and he extended it back along his neck, wishing Saye would just leave so he could retire.

"Or shall I call her just 'Elizabeth' now? I think Miss Elizabeth has been resigned, has it not?"

Darcy's head jerked towards his cousin who sat with a broad grin, looking over at him. Darcy said nothing, thinking frantically for some explanation as he reached for the towel to dry his face.

Saye kept grinning, crossing his ankle over his leg. "You married her."

Darcy opened his mouth then closed it again, carefully laying the towel next to the bowl.

"Avowed and a-consummated, that is my expert opinion, and the latter bit many times over, I should say. Or at least as many as could be done in one night, but you are young and have a wild, albeit suppressed spirit that should—"

In a trice, Darcy was towering over his cousin, placing his hands on the arms of the chair and leaning in close to Saye's face as he hissed, "It is of utmost importance that you keep your mouth closed in this matter for—"

"If you do not lean back in the next four seconds," said Saye calmly, "I am going to kiss you, and then you will be plagued by the sorrowful realisation that the last lips on your own were not hers but mine."

Darcy pushed away from him at once, nearly leaping backwards, while expelling his breath in an indignant huff. He turned back on his cousin, looking out the darkening windows.

"Darcy elopes!" Saye crowed gleefully. "This scandal grows ever more scandalous."

"I did not elope," Darcy replied, as icily as he could. "I had her father's permission and blessing and was married by licence in my own parish. How is that an elopement?"

"Because I did not get cake," Saye replied blithely. "I under-estimated you, sir. I had decided you would have her to the altar by Michaelmas, but you have beaten that by a good many weeks and trumped Bingley while you were at it. That's a good man."

"I married her because I love her, and she loves me. Bingley affected nothing more than the timing."

"Of course." Saye waved his hand. "Rather a stroke of genius actually, and there is nothing so invigorating as a dose of marital bliss"—he paused to wag his eyebrows in case Darcy had missed his meaning—"to clear a man's mind."

"There is nothing blissful about marrying and then being forced to leave your wife the next day."

"And is that why we delayed a day?" Saye's chuckle soon moved into a heartier laugh. "When you said you had business you must attend to, I had no idea you meant the business of bedding your wife!"

Darcy disregarded him; Saye was too near the truth and thus was best unacknowledged. "In any case, the sooner this matter can be dealt with, the better for us both. Are we agreed? Let us form our plan to locate my errant friend."

On arriving at his house in London, Darcy had the pleasure of finding a letter from his wife.

> *My darling husband,*
>
> *I am quite daring to be addressing you as such, but I am simply unable to resist. Georgiana said something to me once of the pleasures that might be had in merely writing the name of your heart's desire, and I am finding it to be true. I have covered another page with variations of your name and mine. I shall*

enclose it to make you aware of what a silly lady you have married.

Darcy paused, looking at the attached page. It was indeed covered: *Fitzwilliam Darcy, Mr Fitzwilliam Darcy, Mrs Elizabeth Darcy, Elizabeth Darcy, ED, FD,* and his personal favourite, a little monogram that wound both of their initials together.

I wondered, as we journey southwards separately, how often your mind was turned to me, and just as quickly, I realised you might have wondered the same of me. So I shall tell you that you are quite constantly in my mind. I think of the week spent together at Pemberley with great fondness, and in particular, I recall the last days many times over. You were fearful that I might regret the absence of my sisters and friends at our wedding, but I assure you, I do not. To me, it is that much more wonderful because it is something we two alone have shared. It is, and will always remain, our private moment together, the time in which I bound myself to you for all eternity, and I am glad there is no one else to think of but you in that recollection.

I pray that you will not think me wanton if I confess that my mind often wanders to other private moments we shared afterwards. Nay, I should confess, it is exceedingly often that I think of these things and anticipate many more nights spent in your arms.

I suppose I must write of something else, for I am using my aunt's little traveling desk, and she will no doubt wonder what makes my cheeks blush so! Alas, there is little else I wish to say save that I love you most ardently. You need never doubt that.

Your wife,
Elizabeth Darcy

P.S. I think that looks rather well, does it not? It does take a bit of time to grow accustomed to a new signature, or so I have found. I think I must write a great many letters to you to practise it and become proficient.

Much emotion was stirred within him after reading her words. He was made joyful by her sentiments and sorrowful by their separation, and yes, he had to own that her veiled references to their limited time in their marriage bed inflamed him nearly instantly.

"My Elizabeth," he murmured. "No lady in the world is like you."

He permitted himself a last moment to long for her before determinedly setting the letter aside, knowing many re-readings were ahead of him. The temptation was to answer it immediately, but he knew he would do better to continue his quest.

"And when I find you, Bingley," he growled to no one, "prepare yourself, for I shall thrash you soundly for making me endure this."

The plans had been laid. He had hired men in the north as well as in town for the purpose of aiding his search, and he made continual rounds of Bingley's friends and acquaintances, seeking any sign of him. It was tedious work and had not yet been fruitful, but he remained at it, driven by the yearning to resume his married life.

"Well, at least he writes to you," said Mrs Bennet with a

severe countenance, tossing a letter Elizabeth's way. "That is something."

Mrs Bennet was not pleased to find that, when she returned to Longbourn, Elizabeth had no set plan to marry Mr Darcy. It amused Elizabeth at first until her mother's harangues grew tiresome. On this, her second day at home, she was resolved to endure.

Mrs Bennet, having heard the entire tale of the terrible Mr Bingley, was wholly convinced Mr Darcy would not be able to extricate himself from his duty to Miss Staley. That Darcy had no duty to Miss Staley went unheard. Mrs Bennet chose to berate Elizabeth for failing to marry him in April when he proposed, saying none of this ever would have happened if Elizabeth had only done what any other lady would.

In some sense, her mother was correct, and Elizabeth knew it was this more than anything that struck her most painfully. For in retrospect, Elizabeth *did* wish she had accepted him in April. Knowing what she did now, her ignorance and wilful blindness to his true character cost her a great deal.

Elizabeth took up the letter her mother had tossed to her, her eyes moving slowly over the pen strokes of the direction. She would savour this—and not in the presence of her mother. She forced herself to eat what remained of her breakfast, barely hearing her mother's voice as she scolded as if from afar. When at last she could excuse herself, she fled to her bedchamber, nearly ripping the letter into shreds in her haste to delve into it.

My dearest, loveliest Elizabeth,
Such pleasure it gives me to write those words and know they are true—you are dear, you are lovely, and you are mine. I can scarce believe it, not when so many obstacles have been set

before us. I do not wish your spirits low although it comforts me
to know you feel my absence as I do yours.

The most grievous of the obstacles to our felicity remains, and I
have little progress to report in my search for Mr Bingley. Saye
and I called on Miss Bingley and Mrs Hurst yesterday, and
they had little of use to tell us. They last knew their brother was
in Sheffield but heard nothing of him since. He has not been to
the rooms he keeps at the Albany for nearly a month, and his
friends have not heard from him. They were neither inclined to
worry over him nor to be of any assistance to me.

Mrs Bennet's voice came floating out a window, interrupting
Elizabeth's reading. Evidently, Mrs Philips had come to call, and
her mother was again rehearsing the great tragedy that had
befallen her courtesy of her daughters.

"...and I am sure that Mr Darcy has thrown her over! Oh,
Sister, how shall I bear such shame! It is entirely likely she spent
her time at Pemberley roaming about the fields and plaguing
him with those absurd opinions of hers..."

Mrs Philips muttered something indistinct, but Elizabeth
thought she might have heard both "hoyden" and
"bluestocking."

"I should have made her marry him in April. But now, he
will go off with this Miss Staley, and that will be that. You watch
and see whether I am right."

With a sigh, Elizabeth pressed a finger into the ear closest to
the window, hoping to block some of the sound.

Some day, I must try your forbearance and prevail upon you to
account for having fallen in love with me. For I confess, having

never believed such a thing would happen, I must know how
it did.

Even when she had finished with the rest of the letter, her eyes would return to that sentence. Although this language was no different from the rest, she believed she could read in it some insecurity of her affections and attachment to him. This would be easy enough to dispel, for it was something upon which she spent a great deal of thought.

Elizabeth set aside her letter with a little sigh. Her mother and aunt had moved on to a discussion of her figure. That she was too thin was an opinion shared by them both. They also felt she had grown too tan during her travels, and Mrs Philips recounted a recipe to her mother that Elizabeth must use to restore her complexion.

Elizabeth gritted her teeth against their criticisms and rose, intent on writing a response to her husband.

STALEY WAS TIRED, VERY TIRED. THERE HAD BEEN PRECIOUS LITTLE in his life except worry and fear since the day he suspected his sister of being with child, and he was exhausted with it.

It was his fatigue more than anything else that caused him to hear out Mr Erskine.

He did not wish to see his sister married to a soldier or to a man of business; a man of property was much preferred. But Darcy proved steadfast in his claims of innocence, going so far as to offer witnesses as to his location the night before his discovery with Millie.

Further, there was something in Erskine's demeanour that persuaded Staley he would not be gainsaid. The man laid out his case nicely. He had a house and the means to support them, and by whatever means Millie had gotten with child, he would claim it as his own.

"And if it is a son?" asked Staley rather dubiously.

"It will be my son," Erskine replied firmly.

Staley pursed his lips a moment considering. "Could it be your son?"

Erskine shrugged. "Certainly."

Heaven only knew it might well be. There was no risk in it being a tall child with dark curly hair. No, if Staley knew his sister, the child would be slight and bear a mop of a gingery hue like Bingley or Erskine—or like the muscular young footman he had dismissed in the spring.

"She cannot have her fortune until she is of age," Staley said. "Terms of my father's will. I am sure you understand."

Erskine nodded, impressively unmoved.

"So what is it you stand to gain in this?" Staley asked. "To go so far as to claim what could be the issue of another man as your own?"

This was Erskine's cue to rattle on endlessly about love, abiding affection, and other equally tiresome notions. Staley was done hearing it within half a minute but permitted the man to go on for nearly five. When he had run out of descriptive terms for his love, Erskine said, "No, there is only one thing I wish for —a wedding gift of sorts, if you will."

Staley peered at him suspiciously. "What is that?"

"What I wish for more than anything is to know the location of that scoundrel, Bingley."

"I do not know where he has gone. His home is in London."

Erskine stared at him.

Staley cleared his throat. "Why should I know the where-abouts of Bingley?"

"Millie told me of your little scheme."

"'Twas not my scheme. The scheme was made by Bingley and his friend Sir Alfred, or whatever he calls himself."

"You were a party to it," said Erskine. He then waited silently.

"What is it to you?"

"He had congress with my Millie, and she was not willing. A rake such as that needs a lesson, and as Millie is now mine in word and deed, if not yet by law, I shall be glad to give it to him."

There was a veiled insult in this, and Staley bristled accordingly. "I was taking care of it."

Erskine sneered. "Yes, with your gentlemanly airs and imposed upon ways, I suppose you were. But I am not a gentleman, nor do I pretend to be."

He rose and approached Staley. "I shall avenge her quickly; be assured of that. Swift and decisive—that is my way."

Staley shrugged. Why should he protect Bingley? "Last I knew, he was put up at the White Hart in Harrogate."

Fitzwilliam,

So you wish for me to account for having fallen in love with you? I am happy to do so today, tomorrow, and every day that you should wish to hear it, though I fear my answer will be something of a muddle.

I had been long in the middle of falling in love with you even though I could scarce account for it at times. It did not strike me as a lightning bolt as some have often described, but rather a series of little shocks—small steps towards a greater understanding of myself and what I truly felt. I had many prejudices against you, designed to conceal the frightful truth of my feelings but in Derbyshire, I could not hide behind them. Each day, with each excursion, game, and dance, I learnt that I wanted to talk to you more than I wanted anything else, I learnt that I admired you more than any man I have ever known, and I learnt that we have much more in common than I ever knew. I had not ever imagined I would find a man who could replace my Jane as my confidante and friend, but you, my love, have already done so.

What I mean to say is that I think I have loved you forever and will continue to do so forevermore. We wanted only for my ill humour and vain partiality to be set aside for me to love you fully. How happy I am that you forgave me and persisted in loving me when anyone else would have tossed me aside! Mr Abell has been in Hertfordshire by some design formed while we were in Derbyshire. Jane has not yet confided any happy news to me, but I daresay, I shall find my new neighbour in Derbyshire much to my liking.

Since writing the last, something has happened of a somewhat alarming nature—I hope you will not be cross with me when you know what I have said to my mother.

As you might have imagined, my mother has been rather vexed with me for failing to secure you while in Derbyshire. This was a source of amusement to me at first, but I must admit my patience has been tried as the days and her ire have continued. Her slights against my person and my behaviour, I have learnt to tolerate from a young age. However, as she began to claim certainty in her belief of your tryst with Miss Staley, I found I was quite unable to forbear.

And so it came out quite unexpectedly that it was I and not

Miss Staley who spent the night in question alone with you. In the event she doubted me, I urged her to apply to my uncle and your cousin, both of whom saw me as I returned to my bedchamber.

She urges my father to go to London and make you marry me. I find I am almost of a mind to encourage him to do so myself.

DARCY FINISHED HIS THIRD OR FOURTH READING OF ELIZABETH'S most recent missive as his carriage returned him from his club to his home. He dearly hoped that Elizabeth had not created a greater problem for herself than she realised, for if her mother was indiscreet and her tongue as unbridled as he knew it could be, Elizabeth would be the subject of much talk in Meryton in the next days. He did not wish that for her, not when they must prevent it being known that they had already been married for a fortnight.

He gave a quiet little growl of frustration. Nothing was coming of his searches for Bingley. He had even hired several men to trace Bingley's steps, and they had placed him as far as the White Hart in Harrogate but no farther.

Darcy had sent letters to as many of Bingley's associates as he could locate, and he visited almost daily with the Hursts and Miss Bingley. He heard endless gossip about himself and Miss Staley, though in truth, it was less than he might have expected. In any case, it seemed nothing would result in locating Bingley.

In another fortnight, he was due to rendezvous with Staley to either answer for his believed offence to Miss Staley's dignity or offer the girl his hand. As he knew the latter to be impossible, he was nearly tempted to put aside all the business of Bingley and simply fight the man and be done with it. Let them gossip about him, and let them say what they liked. He found he was growing less and less concerned.

But he could not—not truly. He would not besmirch his name, not when he had spent so many years living as he had, and not when he had Elizabeth and the family they would one day create and his sister to consider.

Whether he liked it or not, his musings kept coming around to the same thing—he must find Bingley and force him to muck out his own stall, so to speak.

28

Samuel Erskine had not distinguished himself overmuch during his brief time in the militia, but if he had learnt one thing, it was that fortune favoured the prepared. So he kept himself ready to meet his lately sworn enemy, the nefarious Bingley, who his dear Millie swore had behaved so brutishly to her.

Bingley was gone from the White Hart by the time Erskine arrived in search of him, and he had not left word as to his next destination. "London," said the innkeeper helpfully. "I believe he is from London."

"Course he is," growled Erskine. He had met Bingley only once in a brief sort of way, but he thought even then that he looked like all the gentlemen of London: soft, useless, and more concerned with the style of their snuffbox than anything else.

He set out, vowing Bingley would not evade him, and when he came upon him at a posting inn in Worksop, it was so much the better as it saved him from travelling the whole way to London.

But he was no fool, and Worksop was bustling with far too many people for the likes of what he had planned for Bingley. He would wait until the opportune moment presented itself, and of course, it did.

THE STRAINS OF THE CHORUS TO A SONG MOST SUBLIME ECHOED through his consciousness, eventually causing the organist, Mr Brydges, to wake. He lay for some time, the notes and phrases echoing in his mind until dawn, and he deemed it not only prudent but needful to take himself to the church and transcribe his divinely inspired creation.

Although it was not yet six in the morning, nothing but the splendid instrument within the sanctuary of the Church of St. Mary Magdalene would do. Despite the early hour, the ancient vicar, Mr Pennell, had preceded him and was at his morning hour of prayer when Brydges entered the church's side door. Seeing the man bowed in supplication, Brydges thought it best to touch him on the shoulder as he passed, notifying the minister of the presence of another. Since entering his ninth decade, the vicar heard little and perceived even less.

It was the usual way for Mr Pennell to utter distressed grunts of shock when his morning was interrupted, but for him to reach out and grasp Brydges with surprising strength within his withered appendages was rather uncommon.

"Oh, Brydges! Ain't you a sight this morning for such a fright as I could never imagine!"

"A fright?" Brydges sighed. Even more tedious than the vicar's loss of hearing was his rather acute perception of many spectral sounds he was sure were ominous but, on investigation, proved mostly benign—the chirp of a bird, the passing of a carriage, or in many cases, nothing at all.

"Such thumping and groaning!" The old man shook his head, his aged hands trembling even as he held them clasped to his bosom. "I was sure it was Satan himself come to claim me."

Brydges smiled kindly. "When it is your time, sir, 'twill not be Satan who comes, I assure you. Now where were these sounds? Herein?"

Then he heard the noise coming from the back of the church, thumping and groaning and even the uttering of oaths. It sounded to Brydges like something of a schoolboy scuffle had happened, though he hoped the local lads had more piety in them than to fight in the churchyard. Nevertheless, he would investigate.

With Pennell trembling behind him, Brydges strode to the rear door of the church. He exited into a vestibule where the parishioners would gather to greet the vicar following the service, and it was there that he found the body of a man.

With Pennell gasping and muttering prayers behind him, Brydges approached cautiously. The man was nearly nude, wearing no more than his breeches, and from the appearance of his body, he was somewhere between the ages of fifteen and thirty, though he had been beaten too severely for Brydges to know more than that.

Brydges knelt by the man, lowering his ear to his chest to listen for his heart beating, and he thanked God when he found it. The man groaned violently when Brydges attempted to move him a little, so Brydges let him be. Greatly concerned by the state of the young man, however, he was quick to summon a surgeon to attend him.

Mr Osgodby was the surgeon summoned. He showed all proper concern for the injured stranger and was most fearful of an infection given the man's condition and the place where he had been found. He did as well he could to tend to the wounds, after which the injured man was settled into the parish house. Mrs Badisford, recently widowed and glad of the occupation, would nurse the stranger over the next weeks.

It was a testament to both the skill of Osgodby and the youth of the victim that it took naught more than three days until the man woke, crying out and in considerable pain but awake nevertheless. A slight fever plagued him beginning on the fourth day, but Mrs Badisford was ready with her draughts, and by the time a week had passed, it had been conquered.

When the fever broke, the man awoke and gave his name as Bingley. Although the beating he had received was severe, he thankfully recalled nothing of it—not the reason nor even who had done it. His carriage and his money were gone; thus, it was presumed he had been set upon by highwaymen. The local magistrate promised to look into the matter.

He proved a pleasant, amiable man, and Brydges and Mrs Badisford agreed he likely was a gentleman, for his air and manner of speaking proved him so. "And," added Mrs Badisford, "his hands is soft like a gentleman's."

The invalid made himself agreeable no matter the society presented to him. Those who cared for him presumed someone would be looking for him, but as the days continued, no one appeared. For his part, Bingley remained remarkably disinclined towards having them summon his people. He was enjoying his time being cared for in Newark-on-Trent and was ill prepared to see it ended.

"But he must have someone," Mrs Badisford said to Mr Brydges one day. "Some relations. He told me his parents were both passed, bless them, but surely someone else would come and return him to his home."

As he was nursed back to health, Bingley spent a great deal of time thinking of his recent missteps, beginning with leaving Jane Bennet behind him in Hertfordshire. His only true failing in that matter was to listen to Darcy and his sisters, but it did him no good to think more on that now. Jane Bennet was fated to be his true love, and he must do all he could to win her.

He spoke of her often and at length to his caretakers, careful to avoid mention of her last name. "Such an obliging lady! So well favoured. I am sure there is no one like her, no one at all. I once loved a lady from York that was…well, never mind her. I believed her rather charming but then she became a bit shrewish, and in any case, she was nothing to my dearest Jane, nothing at all."

"Aye, well, she must be your wife, then. Like to be worried for you too. Shall we write to her then?"

Bingley paid no attention to the suggestion. "A sweet temper," he told his nurse. "An angel in truth as well as appearance."

He would wax poetic describing her to Mrs Badisford, remembering her perfections as he went. "I never saw a cross expression on her face nor heard an unkind word," he said enthusiastically. "My dear Jane is always possessed of the gentlest smile."

"I daresay, she is not his wife," teased Mr Pennell in a rare display of humour. "Such sentimentality as this is commonly seen in a suitor but rarely in a husband."

Mrs Badisford gave him a little frown in response to his jest although privately she agreed.

"Let us encourage him to tell us more of this Jane person," said Mr Brydges. "She is likely betrothed to him and out of her mind with fear that he is gone forever."

THREE WEEKS, DARCY THOUGHT, RETURNING TO HIS HOUSE AFTER A morning spent with his secretary and solicitor. *Three weeks with no sign of Bingley and nothing to show for my searches.*

He had sent countless letters to innumerable acquaintances, intimate and not, who might have information on Bingley's whereabouts. Anyone who knew anything of him had information woefully out of date, and all trails began and ended in nothing.

The hearsay had proven too daunting for Marston, and he was steadfast in his determination to avoid any mention of Bingley. As a result, Bingley's sisters remained unconcerned for their brother's absence, insisting he was visiting friends or travelling. Darcy was disgusted with both of them, for although he despised Bingley for his weakness and for what he had attempted against a friend, he pitied him nevertheless.

His stomach rumbled angrily as he went towards his study and paused a moment before proceeding to the breakfast room wherein he summoned Mrs Hobbs. After requesting a light meal of the good lady, he settled in with the newspapers. For a moment, he did not so much as glance at them, instead turning his head to gaze blankly out the window while he searched his mind for inspiration.

He did not know his next steps. He had no notion where Bingley might be and had begun to fear that the reappearance of his friend—his *former* friend—would be only at the instigation of that friend himself. *Unless he is dead!*

The unwelcome thought intruded itself with greater frequency. Bingley had not been seen nor heard from by any who knew him. Even Sir Albert denied any knowledge of him, having written to Darcy with the information that they had parted ways in Sheffield.

Given Bingley's most recent occupations and associations, it seemed reasonable to portend he might have come to some harm. As angered as he was with him, Darcy nevertheless felt a deep pang of sorrow at such an idea.

Intent on chasing away such glum notions, he picked up the

newspaper and turned to the society pages for amusement and diversion. It was there that he saw it.

Married…Thursday se'nnight, Mr Samuel Erskine, mill owner, to Miss Staley, both of Sheffield, by common licence at St James Church, Norton.

Darcy was so stunned that he read the simple announcement more than thrice before he could allow the meaning of it to penetrate his thoughts. Even slower was the elation that slid over him like raindrops on a hot day, relieving and soothing, beginning slow but soon overtaking the parched earth.

He was quick to pen a note to Staley.

Dear Sir,

Having just read the notice in the newspaper of your sister's marriage to Mr Samuel Erskine, I believe I may safely conclude that this business between us has reached its just end.

Please accept my wishes for good health and prosperity for yourself and Mr and Mrs Erskine.

F. Darcy

He had just sanded and blotted it when the sound of whistling echoing through his house drew his notice. Moments later, Colonel Fitzwilliam was in his study. His superior officer required his presence in London, and he was residing with his parents for the duration of the assignment.

"Lady Catherine is in town," he informed Darcy. "So I have decamped."

Darcy chuckled, and without a word, he rose and handed the

letter to his cousin who scanned it uncomprehendingly. He read it through twice before raising his eyes. "She is married?"

Darcy nodded. "Evidently so."

Fitzwilliam shook his head, cursing softly. "Better him than me. I can scarce imagine willingly leg shackling myself to such people as these, but he has done it, and you, my friend, may go forth in felicity."

"As can Bingley," Darcy said drily. "His misdeeds, at least as far as this lady is concerned, will be unpunished."

Fitzwilliam shrugged. "Yes, well, this is as it goes most of the time. Did not Wickham go free? After all, his attempt on Georgiana led to no more than a bit of extra weight for his purse. Who knows how much other brothers and fathers have paid him for his silence. Bingley will follow much the same path."

"If I can find him. He is more sly than I ever could have supposed, unless he is..."

"I hope he is dead," Fitzwilliam said. Darcy gasped, and Fitzwilliam added, "Well, I do. For what he did to you, he should be hanged. I should not mind tugging on the rope myself."

"Do not speak so."

"I speak as I find," said Fitzwilliam impatiently. "He is undeserving of your condescension, and my strongest recommendation is that you should just let him go. In whatever disaster he might find himself, leave him to it. He is not your responsibility."

Darcy said nothing, tapping the blotter on his desk with a finger.

"Darcy."

"I know, I know. Believe me, I do know."

"So, what now?"

Darcy leaned back and crossed his legs. His immediate

conclusion was to put the whole of the calamity behind him and rush to Hertfordshire to claim his wife. However, once it was known she was his wife, Bingley might stay gone forever. Then again, that might be preferable.

It was the way of the dissolute after all. He had seen it many times before with George Wickham. They appeared just long enough to vex everyone and make a hash of someone's life and then they were gone again.

"So, you will be off for Hertfordshire in minutes, I shall assume? Off to propose to Miss Bennet, I daresay." His cousin grinned at him fondly.

Darcy grinned back. "Who?"

"Miss Bennet," said Fitzwilliam, his grin slipping a bit.

"No, I do not love Miss Bennet. That would be Abell, and I believe he is already there."

Fitzwilliam rolled his eyes. "Beg your pardon. Miss *Elizabeth* Bennet then."

Darcy affected a bemused air, laying one finger against his lips in an attitude of pensiveness. At last, he said, "I am not sure I know who you mean."

Fitzwilliam stared at him, astonished but undoubtedly aware of his teasing. Darcy allowed him a moment to think about it and then said, "Oh! You mean my wife?"

Fitzwilliam's mouth dropped open.

"Mrs Darcy went to stay with her parents temporarily while I took care of this vexing business, but yes, I have felt her absence keenly. I shall be on my way as soon as may be."

"You did not... you... Did you...?"

"We were married in Kympton." Darcy smiled fondly at the remembrance of the day.

"So she accepted you." Fitzwilliam shook his head slowly, still heartily surprised.

"Hmm…" Darcy again affected a pensive attitude. "No, I would have to say it was more along the lines of *I accepted her*. She would not be gainsaid in the matter."

Fitzwilliam looked as though he wanted to say something, but he was too caught in absorbing the astonishing news.

"Well then." Darcy rose, a broad smile on his face and a lightness in his step that even he himself noticed. "I am off to Hertfordshire."

JANE WAS PALE AND TREMBLING BUT ATTEMPTED TO KEEP A SERENE countenance when she went to Elizabeth. "Lizzy, walk out with me please."

"Of course." After a brief delay to fetch bonnets and gloves and to inform Hill where they were going, they set out. Jane, who commonly kept herself to the gardens, immediately led towards the lane. Elizabeth, surprised, followed her, noticing the letter in Jane's hand.

The day was hot and close, the sort of August day that makes one long for the crispness of autumn. Flies buzzed around them and dust soon covered their shoes, but the two ladies continued a determined path down the lane.

After ten minutes complete, Elizabeth asked, "Jane, are you well?"

"I do not even know." Jane shook her head, staring at the ground and seeming lost in her musings.

"Who is that letter from?"

"A Mrs Badisford in Newark-on-Trent."

Surprised, Elizabeth laughed. "What? Who is Mrs Badisford? Do you know this lady?"

"I am sure I do not." Jane stopped abruptly, and Elizabeth nearly ran into her. Jane turned to face her sister.

"It is she who has been nursing Mr Bingley back to health. Evidently, he was found in a churchyard, quite beaten."

Elizabeth gasped, her hand flying over her mouth. "Beaten? By whom?"

Jane shrugged. "They do not know, but...but he has asked for me. According to this lady, he speaks of me quite often."

"May I see it?"

It was Elizabeth's turn to be silent and pensive, strolling slowly beside her sister while reading the letter. The lady presumed Mr Bingley had been set upon by highwaymen for he had nothing when they found him—no purse, no carriage or horse, and not a stitch on his back. He said he had no family, and the only person whose name he mentioned was Jane.

Mrs Badisford's purpose in writing was to inform his family of his condition, which was now deemed well enough for travel. The unspoken purpose, it would seem, was to have someone fetch him home.

"Shall I give it to our father?" Jane asked anxiously.

"Obviously, you cannot go yourself to retrieve him," Elizabeth said in a weak attempt at jest. Her astonishment soon turned to anger. "That he should speak so of you is quite bold."

"Bold?" Jane thought for a moment and then said, "Yes, yes it is bold. Brazen too."

"Brazen and rather...rather..."

"Desperate," Jane concluded sadly, her kind nature overtaking her. "He must know how grievously he has erred, how he has turned his friends against him."

"Yes," said Elizabeth warmly. "Including his dearest friend, the friend who has been by his side, who cared for him as a brother, and whom he thanked by betraying him without a thought, all so Bingley need not face the consequences of his actions."

Jane made no answer to her sister's impassioned remarks.

Elizabeth watched her walking slowly, her face angled downwards to the path before them. "Jane."

Jane did not answer.

"Jane."

"I know what you are going to say."

Elizabeth pressed her lips together. "Surely you do not...you would not..."

"I would not what?" Jane stopped and turned to her sister.

"Does this change your mind?" Elizabeth whispered, almost afraid to hear the answer.

"Change my mind? About what?"

"About husbands and the way you feel about Mr Bingley and Mr Abell."

To her excessive relief, Jane laughed. "Change my mind about that? Oh, Lizzy, no, not at all. Is that what worried you?"

With a loud sigh of relief, Elizabeth smiled. "Yes, yes it was. You seemed so dismayed and uncertain...I did not know what might plague you except the remnants of the love you once had for him."

"You could not be further from the truth. If I am conflicted, it is only because I do not know whether I should tell Mr Darcy where he is. Mr Bingley begs that I do not—that I should send someone else for him. Indeed, he did not even wish me to tell you, but I could not withhold this from you, not when you are hardly a disinterested party in the matter."

Jane smiled and reached for her sister's hand. "We have never had secrets between us, and I have no wish to begin now."

The guilt that she heaped on Elizabeth's head with such a guileless statement could hardly be borne, but Elizabeth forced herself to smile—a wavering, weak smile but a smile nevertheless.

"So Mr Bingley thinks you can send someone? How could you do so with no word of explanation?"

"I hardly know. He has placed me in an impossible situation, but then again, it seems to be his particular talent." Jane shook her head. "I am grieved, sorely grieved, by the fate that has befallen him, yet I could not be more angered by his presumption. To suppose that I, who was abandoned by him these many months, should go to his aid and keep his secrets! What he must think of me! Does he believe me witless? Artless? Without scruple?"

"I am sure he thinks none of those," Elizabeth soothed. "It is, as you said, his desperation."

"I am most ungenerous and will no doubt shock you, but I... I am not sure I would like to help him. He is no friend. He is just like his sister, willing to use anyone to further himself but overlooking everyone who has nothing to give him."

"I congratulate you, Sister."

"Congratulate me? For what? Being hard-hearted and uncharitable?"

Elizabeth shook her head. "No, my dear, this does not mean you are hard of heart nor uncharitable, for it is one thing to have compassion and quite another to be a willing fool."

"Perhaps you are right," said Jane half-heartedly.

That Darcy should be told of the location of Mr Bingley was not in doubt in Elizabeth's mind, but before she did that, she felt the weight of the secret she kept in her heart. Jane should know, and Elizabeth could not keep it from her any longer.

She stopped in the lane, laying her hand on her sister's arm. "There is something I must tell you, and I beg your forgiveness that I have not done so sooner."

Jane turned, her gaze clear and wondering.

"I love him," Elizabeth began, somewhat nervously. "I love

him too much to…I could not bear the thought that I might lose him…"

Jane waited.

"And I knew he was grieved and worried and…I wanted to relieve those sufferings, inasmuch as I could."

Jane gasped, her mind flown to a different sort of male suffering. "Lizzy! You did not…did you…at Pemberley that night on the roof, was there…"

"No! No, you mistake me!" Elizabeth gave a little laugh, feeling herself flush deeply and hotly. "That is…I did not anticipate my vows."

Jane laid her hand on her bosom, closing her eyes a moment. "Oh, Lizzy, I am glad, and you will be glad too, I am sure, for when—"

"I married him and then we…I am his wife."

Jane's eyes went wide. "Married?"

Elizabeth nodded. "We had the papers signed, the articles, and he had obtained a licence so we married in the chapel at Kympton our last morning there."

Jane stood stock still for a moment, her mouth agape, then she laughed. "Mama will kill you."

"Yes, she might," said Elizabeth with a laugh of her own. "And that is why you must do your best to secure Mr Abell so that she may be distracted by your felicity and forget about her disappointment with me."

Jane had to congratulate her sister properly then, and she drew her into a hug to express her joy. True to her sweet spirit, she could not be angry that Elizabeth had withheld such important information. She could only be happy for her.

A moment later, Elizabeth continued, "You do understand it, do you not? It might be seen as selfish on my part, but in truth, I did it for both of us."

"I shall admit, I have wondered how you could be so calm through all of this." I thought perhaps there was less feeling on your part than I had supposed, except at times, you seemed to be longing for him. I could not make it out, but this explains it."

"I wanted him to be assured of my affection and the promise of our future. We had too much uncertainty between us already without having something more."

Jane reached for her, pulling her sister to walk with her arm in arm. For a moment, she laid her head against her sister's. "It is a little sad. You are no longer a Bennet."

Elizabeth laughed a little although a slight pang entered her heart as well.

They had returned to the lane approaching the house, and there was a movement by the door that drew their attention. A carriage, large and elegant, was being taken around to the stables by their boys.

Elizabeth's heart quickened when she saw it.

"My new brother," Jane announced, "who I believe has come to reclaim his bride."

29

WHEN THE CARRIAGE WAS MOVED, ELIZABETH SAW HIM WALKING towards the house. Her heart leapt into her throat, nearly preventing her from calling out to him. "Fitzwilliam!" came forth in a gasp of heartfelt delight but, unfortunately, rather quietly.

But if his ears could not hear her, his soul did. He turned, and she knew the expression on his face—a joy unlike anything she had yet seen from him—as it mirrored her own. She could not have stopped smiling nor slowed her running footsteps, and to do less than leap into his arms was unthinkable. Ideas of dignity were discarded in favour of greeting her love with every bit of ardour she could possibly show him.

Her leap into his arms was not unwelcome. Indeed, he held her so that her feet dangled by his shins, grasping her so tightly that she gasped and laughed as she uttered his name over and over again. Their greetings were punctuated by kisses. They were made clumsy by their eagerness to love and be loved and to be known to each other once again.

"I love you," he whispered into her ear.

"I love you more," she replied.

He smiled and shook his head. "No, you could not."

"But I do," she insisted, kissing him again on his cheek.

"I cannot see how that is possible, madam."

"Oh, I assure you it is. It is. Pray, let us never part again."

"Never," he vowed. "Not even for a day."

"This is charming," said Jane, who had arrived beside them unnoticed. "Though it does bear mentioning that Kitty and Lydia are looking out the window."

Darcy immediately set her on her feet. They looked to the window and saw it was blessedly clear. Elizabeth gave Jane an accusing look.

Jane was unrepentant. "Well, they might have been, and the pair of you were completely insensible."

"My apologies, Miss Bennet," said Darcy, his more common, formal demeanour returning to him.

"Miss Bennet?" Jane asked with a little smile. "Sir, I have recently learnt that you and I are better acquainted than that."

Darcy looked at Elizabeth quickly, and she confirmed the unspoken question: Jane knew. With a little smile of his own, he took her hand and said, "Very well, then—Jane."

Jane offered her congratulations, and Darcy accepted them, bending low to kiss her hand and claim all the felicity of being a brother. Elizabeth could do nothing but smile at the two people she loved best in the world forming a kinship.

"Does anyone else know?" Darcy asked.

"No," said Elizabeth. "Did you tell anyone but Saye?" (Darcy had told her in one of his letters about Saye forcing a confession from him.)

"Fitzwilliam also knows, and they have undoubtedly made Lord and Lady Matlock aware by now. I think we may be assured that most of London will know shortly."

"That appears not to trouble you," Elizabeth observed.

"I came into some surprising intelligence this morning: Miss Staley has married."

Jane inhaled sharply, and Elizabeth's hand flew to her mouth. "Did Mr Bingley—"

Darcy shook his head. "No, some other man, a man called Erskine. I do not know his connexion to it all, but he came in at the last hour and provided me a happy resolution."

"Was it he who beat Mr Bingley?" Elizabeth asked.

Darcy turned to her at once. "Bingley? Beaten?"

Jane held out her letter to Darcy, who took it and quickly scanned the words, his expression one of utter disbelief. He read it through a second time, but what he thought of it would be unknown for a while as Mr Bennet, informed of their visitor, came outside to greet him.

Mr Bennet bore on his countenance a look of watchful anticipation that Elizabeth knew well. He was undecided whether to approach the situation as a wit or a father. The wit was most likely to emerge, and Elizabeth said quickly, "Papa, Mr Darcy has just arrived from London and is no doubt in need of some refreshment. Let us all go into the house."

As the group moved inside, Elizabeth felt a brief moment of alarm as she realised the task ahead of them was formidable. The Bennets were due a shock, and although she did not doubt their eventual pleasure in the news, she did fear what must occur until then. Her family was not at its best when surprised or taken unawares.

Hill came at once to take their things. Jane began to speak to her quietly while Elizabeth, following a quick glance at her husband, said, "Papa, Mr Darcy and I have a matter of some importance to discuss with you and my mother. Perhaps we could all meet in the drawing room."

Mr Bennet retrieved his wife from the sitting room, and she

greeted Darcy with almost comical deference. Elizabeth hoped it boded well for the visit. Mrs Bennet rattled on, apprising him of all the fine accommodations in Meryton as they moved into the drawing room. "Of course, Netherfield is...well never mind that. Who gives two straws for Netherfield! Not I, I assure you! Why, do you know there are those who travel all the way from London to stay in the Red Lion? As fine as any you will know, I can assure you of that!"

"I thank you for the recommendation, madam—"

"But the Old Swan is just as well too. Very fine, very fine indeed. You will not go wrong with either of them, I promise you."

They arrived in the drawing room, and Mrs Bennet hissed, her whisper as loud as a shout, "Lizzy! Get tea!"

With a sigh, Elizabeth rose and went to summon Hill. Behind her, Mrs Bennet went into a long discussion of the differences between the Red Lion and the Old Swan.

"...rooms are rather small," she was saying as Elizabeth returned to her seat, "but very elegant and so prettily situated on the top of the hill! Why, Lady Lucas told me just the other day that—"

"Mama, Mr Darcy will not be staying at either of the inns."

Her statement surprised Mrs Bennet into silence for a moment. Elizabeth could almost hear her thinking that Mr Darcy intended to leave immediately. Her lips pursed, her eyes narrowed, and she looked him up and down.

Darcy leaned forward. "I hope you will permit me to trespass upon your hospitality, madam, for my wish was to stay at Longbourn."

The shock was nearly too much for Mrs Bennet. Suspicion gave way to delight and more astonishment.

Mr Bennet could boast no claim to the latter; his first feeling was evidently suspicion. Peering at Darcy over the top of his spectacles, he said, "Here, Mr Darcy? I am not certain Longbourn is like anything to which you are accustomed."

"Longbourn is wonderful," said Darcy. "You have a fine home, and I have always thought it so, but it is more particularly dear to me now…"

He reached blindly for Elizabeth, who had unwisely taken a seat apart from him. She reached, sliding her hand into his. He squeezed her fingers gently and finished his statement, "…because it is the childhood home of my beloved wife."

The silence was thunderous. Mrs Bennet broke it with a squeal as she launched herself towards Mr Darcy, fluttering a lace handkerchief at him even while proclaiming foreknowledge of the marriage. Mr Bennet stared ominously as Mrs Bennet spewed forth a myriad of questions, assuring Darcy all the while that she would sit Elizabeth down straightaway and speak to her about being a proper wife for a man as great as he.

From Mr Bennet—who spoke when his wife had eventually calmed herself—an explanation was insisted upon and duly given. When they finished, it was clear to Elizabeth that her father was not mollified. He said rather sarcastically, "I believed the current mode was to permit a father to give his daughter away."

Elizabeth replied, "Has not a father who signed the articles and the affirmation, and wrote to his daughter's betrothed urging haste in matrimony, already given his daughter away?" While Mr Bennet did not admit she was right, he abandoned any notion of sardonic pique thenceforth, and Elizabeth counted it a triumph.

Chief among Mrs Bennet's concerns was the fact that Elizabeth had no gown befitting Mrs Darcy when she married. She was aghast when she heard what Elizabeth had worn.

"Your yellow spotted muslin," she gasped, her face gone pale. She closed her eyes a moment and leaned her head against the back of her chair. "No!"

"It is my prettiest walking gown and—"

"It is two years old if it is a day! I cannot think it was even worthy to be taken to Pemberley!"

"I thought she never looked lovelier," offered Darcy.

Mrs Bennet did not so much as afford him a glance. "What of your ivory silk?" she cried. "Or the pale blue!"

"I could not wear an evening gown to walk out," Elizabeth said calmly. "And we wished to keep it a secret."

"A secret! I do not see why it had to be a secret!"

"We wished to keep it a secret so that I might have greater expedience in locating Mr Bingley," Darcy explained.

"Mr Bingley!" cried Mrs Bennet. "I am sick of Mr Bingley."

"As am I," replied Darcy.

This discussion was abruptly ended by the appearance of a blushing Jane, who announced that Mr Abell's carriage had just arrived.

DINNER BEGAN IN THE USUAL MANNER OF THE BENNETS. LYDIA HAD forgotten something in her bedchamber and promptly quit the table. When she returned, she insisted Kitty had eaten her soup. Kitty cried she had not, and Lydia teased that Kitty was growing fat. Kitty ran off to her bedchamber, tearfully insisting she would not eat again.

Mr Abell blessedly missed the entire exchange as he had been immediately taken under Mrs Bennet's wing for a thorough discussion of the startling news about Elizabeth and Darcy.

"You would not like to be married in such a way, I hope, Mr

Abell. A lady marries only once, and to do so in a common old walking dress—"

"A woman," said Mary, "will always do best to array herself in wisdom, humility, and dignity. The finest pearls and the richest silks are nothing to piety and honour."

Mr Abell glanced at her for a moment; he was as yet unaccustomed to Mary's sermons. Fortunately, Mrs Bennet had a ready supply of other inanities to distract him.

"Yellow spotted muslin," said Mrs Bennet. "Why, even among her walking dresses, it was an exceedingly poor choice. Did I tell you about the gown Charlotte Lucas wore when she married? A blue silk but so dark! I declare she looked like she was in mourning—or perhaps half-mourning—but with her colour—"

Mr Bennet interrupted. "Mr Abell is far too good a gentleman to marry in sprigged muslin."

Mr Abell laughed a genuine hearty laugh at Mr Bennet's gibe. "No sir, you will not see me marrying in yellow spotted muslin!"

Elizabeth sighed, wishing the dinner were finished but realising it was far from over. It was a relief, however, to see that Mr Abell's tendency to find amusement in Mr Bennet had not yet waned.

Kitty returned, filled with righteous vexation and two spots of colour high on her cheeks. She had changed her gown, donning one that belonged to Lydia. Her first object, it would seem, was to prove that Lydia was the more stout one.

"See, Mama! See how it hangs on me!" She shook the material near the bodice demonstrating it was quite loose.

Lydia snickered. "She considers a lack of bosom something to be proud of! She'll not find a husband with that pair of nothings!"

A serious row looked set to erupt when Elizabeth rose from her seat. "Excuse me," she said with as much grace as she could muster. At her husband she dared not look, but she managed to remove her young sisters from the dining room. After a brief scolding and a threat to ban them from her house in London, they returned and settled nicely.

Elizabeth noted Darcy's obvious distraction from the moment she re-entered the dining room. She took her seat beside him, touching his leg briefly. He gave her a little smile but immediately turned his attention inward again.

There was one item of interesting news related at dinner: a purchase offer had been made for Netherfield. Mr Bennet had learnt it earlier that day from Mr Morris himself.

"It is not yet settled. Mr Bingley retains the right of first refusal, but if he agrees to give up the place, the new owner intends to be in by Michaelmas. A naval officer with some prize money and a little fortune from his mother's side."

"And is he married?" This was Mrs Bennet's first question.

"Aye," said Mr Bennet. "He brings with him three sons."

"Three sons!" The rapturous cries were raised around the table.

Mr Bennet nodded, but Elizabeth noted the telltale twinkle in his eyes. "How old are the sons, Papa?"

"I believe the oldest is a lad of nine or ten, but given the silliness at my dinner table, I should think the boy a perfect match for either of these two." He gestured at Kitty and Lydia. Lydia opened her mouth as if to protest, and Kitty, after seeing Lydia's pique, did likewise, but Jane was swift to interrupt them.

"Is it certain, Papa?"

"Nothing is certain. It seems Mr Morris has also been unsuccessful in seeking Mr Bingley, and Mr Bingley has first rights to it."

"I should not see why!" cried out Mrs Bennet. "Pooh on Mr Bingley. I am sure that man is not needed around here."

"Because it is his house, Mama," said Jane. "He has a legal right to it."

"And very undeserving of it he is!"

"Undeserving or not," said Mr Bennet, "it is his. He may use it as he chooses."

With this, Mrs Bennet began to cry at the unfairness of it all, claiming Mr Bingley should not be permitted to purchase it and thus lead the whole neighbourhood into ruin. She had a great many imaginative things she believed would happen at Netherfield—routs, debaucheries, cock fights, and the like—under Mr Bingley's mastery.

Mr Bennet made sporadic attempts to mollify—or possibly inflame—her with explanations of the legalities of the matter, which Mrs Bennet found incomprehensible. Jane spoke when she could, offering her certainty that Mr Bingley would straightaway seek to re-establish his character in the neighbourhood. The younger Miss Bennets did not care who owned Netherfield so long as they gave frequent dinner parties and balls.

And on Elizabeth's side of the table, her husband was eerily silent on the matter.

DARCY WAS SIMILARLY PREOCCUPIED AFTER DINNER IN THE DRAWING room, appearing entranced by the rather prolonged sonata Mary insisted upon plodding through. When she had finished, a walk was proposed by Mr Abell, and Elizabeth quickly volunteered herself and Darcy as chaperons.

Much to Elizabeth's frustration, she soon learnt that Jane and Mr Abell were terrible lovers, at least by her estimation. They remained within earshot of Darcy and Elizabeth, and Mr Abell continually glanced behind to ensure he and Jane would not outpace them.

"Mr Abell is very proper," she told Darcy. "He shows no inclination to leave us."

"Mm," he agreed absently. "He is known for being rather strict. He avoids the very appearance of impropriety at all costs."

Elizabeth sighed, and her husband smiled at her. "Do you prefer some rogue coming to steal her away and kiss her on the roof?"

"No," she said with a little grin. "Though it did quite appeal to me. I just hope he does like her."

"He would not be here if he did not," Darcy assured her.

"Here is not an easy place to be." After a slight hesitation, she added, "Dinner was trying to your patience, I am sure."

"Not at all."

She looked at him uncertainly. "It is not the sort of dinner you are accustomed to. Things were rather..." *Stupid, silly, undignified...* The words ran through her head, but she could not bring herself to speak them.

Darcy drew her hand into his arm. "You have forgotten, I think, Saye and Fitzwilliam's thumb war under the table at Pemberley?"

She could smile a little at that. "I suppose I had."

Darcy took her hand to his lips for a moment. "No one should be held to account for the behaviour of their relations. I would not wish for that, and in any case, it was a family supper."

His sentiments, expressed so forthrightly, could only serve to make her love him more. He had changed a great deal for her, and it was most evident in times such as these. She pressed into his side and wrapped her arm a bit more tightly in his. "Your compassion is endearing."

He chuckled under his breath. "It is interesting that you should use that word."

"What word? Compassion?"

He did not speak for a moment, staring at some point ahead of them. Mr Abell and Jane were intent in conversation, but she did not think he truly saw them.

"I have been thinking of Bingley, beaten and left alone to depend upon the kindness of strangers. I know it has been said I take too much on myself—and perhaps I do—but I am deeply regretful of the series of events that led him to this state."

"It is distressing, but he does have family to care for him."

"And if they seemed in any way inclined to do so, I would not worry—but I do worry." After a few steps more, he added somewhat sadly, "They would not even believe he was missing. They kept telling me he would appear when he wished to, and all the time, he was in a parish house sickbed."

Elizabeth walked several paces before she would admit, "I should not like to depend on either Miss Bingley or Mrs Hurst for assistance."

"I think I should go to him." Darcy gave a little nod of resolve. "Go to him, and if he may be moved, bring him back to London or perhaps Netherfield."

Elizabeth did not know how to respond. Bingley deserved nothing at all from her husband. Indeed, Bingley was fortunate that her husband did not wish to beat him himself. But Darcy would not be Darcy if he did not do the noble and good in even the worst of circumstances.

"I must go to him," said Darcy. "As you have granted me a second chance, so must I give one to him. I shall help him one last time."

Darcy and Elizabeth, rather unused to being acknowledged lovers, privately thought nothing could ever be more awkward than to retire together at Longbourn.

To be fair, the Bennet family had precious little time to become accustomed to the reality that Elizabeth was wed. The announcement was made at dinner, and it was scarcely two hours later that Mr Bennet left them, and the wordless signal to go to bed was thus given. It was Elizabeth's thought to try and outlast her sisters, but Darcy was fatigued. She could see it in his countenance and posture. She weighed the potential for some awkwardness against the possibility of private time with her husband, and the latter naturally won.

Jane, bless her, hit upon the idea of asking Hill to direct one of the upstairs maids to make a hurried cleaning of the finest of their guest apartments. It was a pretty room, large and comfortable, and it had been fitted up in the latest style only a few years past. The dressing room was well appointed, and there was a small sitting area with a number of books that Elizabeth suspected Jane had put there. *Bless her heart. Does she truly think we might read?*

It was also rather unfortunately close to the bedchambers of her younger sisters, and as Elizabeth prepared for bed, she heard them plainly. Their conversation was at first fixed on the usual subjects—a forthcoming assembly, a party, this gentleman and that lady—but soon enough turned towards more mortifying topics.

"Think of it Kitty! Even now Lizzy is likely lying in bed with Mr Darcy." Scandalised giggles ensued.

Kitty murmured something that was blessedly inaudible to Elizabeth. Her relief was temporary, for Lydia loudly replied,

"No, I know she is not, for she had her monthlies just last week, same as I."

More murmurs before Lydia snorted and laughed, sounding every inch a donkey. Elizabeth resolved to get her husband out of the room long enough to permit her sisters time to retire or at least tire of speaking of her husband and her marriage.

Just as she thought it, he appeared from the dressing room, and her breath caught a little.

It seemed extraordinary after all that had passed between them—the vexations and grief followed by their time at Pemberley, a time she knew she would always treasure—that they should be here now, man and wife. She gave him a smile that she knew could not match the incandescence in her heart.

Much to her delight, she discomposed him. He reddened rather charmingly and leaned against a small table that immediately and traitorously toppled over. He bent to straighten it, and she had the uncommon pleasure of seeing his backside covered only by thin, fine lawn aimed in her direction. She admired it because she could.

When he rose, she had the misfortune to be caught by him. Her eyes jerked away a fraction of a second too late, and she blushed. He chuckled, and she laughed at herself. "Forgive me, I have…"

He raised one eyebrow, trying to look stern although his amusement remained apparent in the twinkle of his eyes. "You have what?"

She did not answer straightaway, and he pressed her. "What? What have I caught you at there, Mrs Darcy?"

When she again was silent, he shrugged, pretending to careless indifference. "It is just as Saye said."

Elizabeth despised her curious nature for it was at such

moments as these that it forced her to betray herself. After only the slightest of pauses, she asked, "Saye said what?"

Darcy had the most egregious sort of teasing manner about him. He joined her, sitting on the bed and giving her sidelong glances. "He observed that you liked..." A little quirk of his brow and a slight gesture of his hand served to complete his sentence.

"What? Pray, tell me he said no such thing!" Elizabeth blushed so hotly that a faint, dewy sweat broke out on her. "I cannot think why he would say such a thing!"

"Never be misled by Saye," Darcy instructed her. "When he appears the most languid, the most disinterested, then you may be assured you are in trouble. He sees through closed eyelids, and his hearing is beyond anyone's I have ever known. He also has a tendency to appear when and where he is least expected."

Elizabeth merely pressed her lips together in some semblance of disapproving propriety, but it could not last.

Darcy reached over and put his hand on her hip, pulling her closer to his side. His hand remained there, hot and large, his fingertips curled just lightly into the side of her buttocks. His thumb began a slow, lazy caress.

"Perhaps I did, on an occasion, glance at...at..." She could not look at him. "Did Saye truly notice?"

"Oh, he did. And how grateful I was to him for it. It was when we went to the assembly in Derbyshire, just before you came down to the vestibule to meet us. He naturally informed me in the most vexing way possible—and of course he insisted that his posterior was superior—but I was glad to know it."

"Why?" Elizabeth asked. She shifted a little, the caress of his hand already pleasing her in a manner she knew was just the beginning of what she might anticipate.

"It taught me to hope as I had scarcely allowed myself to

hope before. If that was all you liked of me, at least it was something."

"It was not all I liked of you even then. And in any case, I believe we should do our best to forget all of my past stupidity, for now, I am quite in love with every bit of you."

She turned her face, kissing him ardently. There passed some time when they did not converse. If syllables were uttered—and indeed they were— they were not the sort from which one could assemble rational discourse.

THE FIRST MILES OF DARCY'S JOURNEY TO NEWARK-ON-TRENT SPED by quickly, too quickly for miles that took him away from his beloved. Then again, the more speedily the miles were dispatched, the sooner he would be returned to her, so he supposed he was glad.

His mind returned to their parting. Elizabeth had shocked him by weeping.

He had not even known it was happening. The Bennets had kindly melted away just before he was to board his carriage, and they were left alone. She went immediately into his embrace, holding him tightly with her face in his shoulder, so buried in his coat that he wondered whether she could breathe.

He had almost begun to pull back from her when he heard it, a sad, high-pitched, little hiccup of a sob. It nearly undid him. He pressed his lips to the top of her head. She held him even tighter as he reassured her. "Only four days there and back with no delay." Her only answer was a shuddering breath as damp-ness began to seep into his coat.

It was still a source of pleasure—much as he thought it dreadful to admit—that she would be so affected by his depar-ture. He felt in equal measure sorrowful and glad, and he could do no more than kiss and comfort her, trying his best not to weep himself.

At last, she pulled back, her eyes red and her cheeks rosy and damp. "It is very good of you to show Mr Bingley such kindness. It speaks well of your character. However, for my part, he has a great deal to answer for."

The remembrance of it was sweet, and he returned to it often in the two days spent travelling. Other, less innocent recollections also made for diverting travelling companions, but these were an impolitic indulgence. It was humiliating to arrive at a place in a state in which no stranger should see him. And he was forced to carry on his business as though he had not the most lewd images so lately in his mind.

He made excellent time on his journey and arrived at Newark-on-Trent well before dinner on his second day of travel. After making himself comfortable at a nearby inn, he went directly to the parish house where Bingley stayed.

Mrs Badisford, the lady who had written to Jane, answered the door and informed him that Mr Bingley was taking a morning constitutional with Mr Pennell, the aged vicar.

"Poor dears," she clucked. "Mr Bingley with his bad leg, and Mr Pennell being over eighty years old—why they can scarce make it round the root garden afore they needs be coming back!"

Darcy bowed, feeling unable to summon the sympathy—at least for Bingley—to make an appropriate remark.

They went outside, having proceeded through a house that was rather substantial for a parson's residence. Darcy saw Bingley immediately, but it took a bit of time before Bingley saw him.

When he did, his shock was immediate. He stopped in his

tracks and went pale, doing no more than staring at his former friend for some moments. Then he bowed.

Darcy bowed in return, and it gave Bingley sufficient courage to draw nearer.

"D-Darcy...this is a surprise...did you...did Miss Staley...ahh—"

"Miss Staley is now Mrs Erskine," said Darcy sternly. "And I have no more to say of that matter, for it is not a good remembrance and not something I care to recall. You need assistance, and for the sake of our former friendship, I came to provide it. Let us settle your accounts and get together whatever things you might have. I need to get home to my wife."

He turned sharply and began to stride back towards the house, knowing Bingley would follow.

30

It was a small matter to settle Bingley's affairs. He had gone to Newark-on-Trent bearing none of his possessions as someone had taken all that was on his person. Mr Pennell had written to the proprietors of the inn in Sheffield where Mr Bingley remembered staying, and the magistrate had made his enquiries. Alas, these efforts yielded nothing. Even Bingley's carriage was gone. Darcy wondered whether Erskine had taken it all. He did not suppose they would ever know.

Mr Pennell and Mrs Badisford felt a genuine attachment to Bingley. Mrs Badisford even shed a tear at the thought of his leaving. Darcy offered them a generous sum for all their efforts. They resisted it at first, but he eventually prevailed for the good of their parish if nothing else.

He and Bingley departed the place at sunrise the next morning. Bingley was mostly recovered, or so said Mrs Badisford, but he tired easily. Darcy rather hoped he would sleep the days away rather than plague him with conversation.

An hour complete of travel elapsed before Bingley dared to speak. "It is good of you to come to me."

"Yes, it is."

"I do not deserve such condescension from you."

"If you would like me to protest, you will wait a long time."

Bingley shifted uncomfortably in his seat. "You despise me and rightly so."

"No, I pity you. I fear you have had but a taste of what is to come."

Bingley looked stricken. "You think someone else will beat me?"

"I have no doubt you likely deserve it, but no, that is not my meaning."

"Then what?"

Darcy just shook his head. "Why did not Hurst retrieve you?"

Bingley shrugged. "I suppose he is otherwise engaged."

"And your good friend Sir Albert?"

"Deuced if I know what became of him! He was meant to meet me at... Well, never mind that. He must have been diverted."

"On to the next soiree no doubt."

His sarcasm was lost on Bingley. "Yes, he is an exceedingly sought-after man."

"Perhaps he is, but a man with a large acquaintance is not the same as a man with many friends."

This time, Bingley was astute enough to understand him. "I know, and I do appreciate that you should overlook—"

Darcy raised one eyebrow. "I have overlooked nothing. You made an attempt to take from me the thing I hold most dear—my Elizabeth, and in her, my happiness."

"You misunderstand me. I intended no such thing."

Darcy gave him a cool stare. "Then, pray, what did you think might come of tossing a young girl into my bed?"

Bingley leaned forward. "With all your connexions and fortune, I believed you would be easily able to extricate yourself, more easily than I could. I did not for a moment think you would be bound."

"I am a gentleman," said Darcy with a fierce frown intended to censure. "And if I believed my honour engaged, then I would do as I should, unlike you apparently."

"I never meant—"

"I am mightily disappointed to learn that, whatever value I placed on your friendship, you placed little or none on mine."

Bingley, chastened, leaned back in his seat and lowered his gaze to his hands.

It was nearly an hour later when he said, "Darcy, I pray you will forgive me for—"

In a tone that brooked no opposition, Darcy replied, "I do not wish to speak any further on this most reprehensible and disgusting subject."

"Very well." Bingley turned his face to the window.

The ride was long and nearly wholly silent. They did not speak again until they stopped at a coaching inn. They took a meal as they awaited fresh horses, and Darcy thought it might look odd to be utterly silent as they ate. Casting about for a moment, he hit on the subject of Netherfield.

"Mr Morris has been trying to reach you. There has been a purchase offer for Netherfield."

"But I should buy it!" Bingley exclaimed immediately. "If I have any hope of…"

He stopped, leaving Darcy staring at him dubiously. "Hope of what?"

Bingley hesitated for but a moment then, in all earnestness, said, "It does not escape me that my life seems to have gone awry from the moment I turned my back on Miss Bennet.

Darcy rolled his eyes. "And so you suppose renewing your attentions to Jane will set your life to rights again?"

"Perhaps not...not immediately maybe, but with such a wife I could—"

"Good lord, man!" Darcy hissed, permitting some of the disgust he felt to come forth. "When will you learn to stand for yourself?"

Bingley stared.

"My advice to you has gone amiss. Do not think I am insensible of the part I played in all of this. But surely you must apprehend that, if you cannot care for yourself properly, taking care of a wife will be impossible! You should be the strength, not the weakness, in the marriage."

Speaking slowly, Bingley asked, "Has she fallen in love with someone else then?"

Darcy threw back his head, closing his eyes against the stupidity of his former friend. "Bingley, do as you wish. My duty to you has been discharged, and I do not intend to have any connexion with you beyond this. But do understand me"— he opened his eyes to look at Bingley sternly—"Miss Bennet is now my sister, and as she is dear to my wife, so is she dear to me. I would not tell her what to do, but in this case, I do not think I shall need to."

Darcy hoped rather than believed that Bingley understood he did not intend to continue their friendship. Change was possible in any man. Darcy knew the truth of this from his own mistakes and experience. Bingley, however, showed no sign of alteration in his character. Indeed, he showed no sign that he even understood a change was needed.

Bingley was blessedly silent for the rest of that day. He began the next day whistling a happy little tune in the carriage, which Darcy immediately quelled with only a look. After a second excessively long and silent day, Darcy found Netherfield a welcome sight.

"How long do you intend to be at Longbourn?" Bingley asked as he prepared to remove from the carriage.

Darcy pulled his watch from his pocket, noting with pleasure that an excess of six hours of sunlight remained. "If Mrs Darcy has done as she intended and prepared herself to leave, we shall be gone within the hour for London."

"London?" cried Bingley, sounding dismayed. "You are leaving today?"

"As quickly as I can."

"But what about…"

He has at least the good sense to stop himself. "What about what?"

Bingley offered a small smile. "I hoped you might be able to look over the books with me tomorrow or the next day. I am considering purchasing Netherfield, and your opinion on the matter would be welcomed."

Unbelievable. Darcy shrugged. "My opinion is that you should do as you like."

"But do you think it sound?"

"Maybe."

"But perhaps I would do better in another county."

"Possibly."

"The fields of Netherfield are somewhat…" Bingley gave Darcy an expectant look that went ungratified. He tried again, "But the house is…"

Darcy offered nothing but a blank look. After a long pause, he said briskly, "The apothecary will be in to attend to you later and see that your injuries are healing. I must depart now, but I offer my best wishes for your good health and prosperity."

A knock on the roof signalled the footmen outside to open the door, and Darcy instructed them. "See that Mr Bingley is helped inside. He is not well."

Thus, Bingley had little choice as two men leaned in, took his arms, and removed him from the carriage with very little ceremony. He was ensconced in bed in the master's chambers almost before he knew what anyone was about.

DARCY FOUND WITH GREAT PLEASURE THAT ELIZABETH WAS WELL prepared to leave. Her belongings were ready; all she required immediately was in a portmanteau near the doors. Any other particulars from Longbourn would be sent later.

"I need only to say goodbye to my father," she told him hurriedly and disappeared down the hall to do just that.

Darcy was glad for he wished for a moment alone with Jane. He beckoned to her, asking the rest of the family who had gathered to see them off to excuse them for a moment.

"I have only a moment to speak, and perhaps I speak out of turn, but I want you to know I shall support anything you might wish in terms of your further association with Bingley."

"With Mr Bingley?" Jane's eyes flew wide.

"For your sake, I would forgive him. I shall not influence you —either of you—but do know that I shall accept anything that comes. If you wish to marry him, I shall not stand in your way."

Jane's jaw dropped. "I hardly know what—"

"I told him as much." Darcy paused, thinking he heard Elizabeth's voice. He stepped closer to Jane. "But do know this as well—you need not marry anyone you do not love. You can make your home at Pemberley, and do as you wish. Do you apprehend me? I am saying that if you want to marry Bingley, do so. We shall be a family circle as we ought. But if you do not wish to, do not. Either way. Entirely your choice."

Jane gave him a little nod and whispered, "Thank you, sir."

With that, the conversation had to end. Elizabeth appeared,

her eyes bright and eager, and within minutes, they were bundled into the carriage. "We shall reach the London outskirts before night begins to fall in earnest," Darcy assured his young wife.

"And then home," she said. "I can scarcely imagine it. I think I should have taken Georgiana's offer to show it to me when I visited, for now I can barely recall how to find the drawing room."

He smiled faintly at her jest.

After a few quiet moments, she spoke again. "Mr Abell was called back to Lessing Grange. Evidently, his father is ill, and they needed him immediately. Jane had hoped he would speak before he left, but alas, he did not."

"I am sorry to hear it. But it does make me glad that I spoke to her of Bingley."

"Of Mr Bingley?"

"I have reason to think he might attempt to renew his attentions towards her. I told your sister that if she wishes to marry Bingley, I would not stand in her way. I shall be a brother to him for her sake—if she so wishes it."

Elizabeth laughed until she realised it was no laughing matter. Then she fumed. "I shall *never* forgive Mr Bingley for trying to hurt you! He betrayed your friendship and sought to bring you harm. My good opinion of him is, I fear, lost forever, and if he thinks he can simply walk right back in where he was months ago, he will need to answer to me."

"Then you will be glad to know I made certain she understands that she can make her home with us—that she need not marry Bingley or Abell or anyone else she does not truly love."

"Thank you." Elizabeth gave his hand a gentle squeeze. "You are too good. I hope she remains steadfast in her resolution to avoid him."

"Bingley could…he might be made into a good husband for her. It would not be my choice, but…if she wishes it, I shall do what I can for them."

"I think you need not worry. Jane has taken the true measure of Mr Bingley and understands what evils must come with such a weak nature." She kissed him before adding, "The more I know of you, the more I am impressed by your goodness and the strength of your character. You are truly the best man I have ever known. I could not wish less for my sister."

"Thank you. I do not know whether I deserve such—"

"Such adoration?" She began placing kiss after kiss on his jaw. "Adoration and admiration and the most violent, ardent sort of love—you do deserve it and more."

MR BINGLEY, UNDER THE MISTAKEN NOTION THAT HIS CALLS WERE welcomed at Longbourn, became a regular visitor in the days after the Darcys left. Jane realised she would need to put an end to it, but she knew not how. In truth, a bit of her hoped it would not come to that, but one fine day when a storm had cooled the air, he invited her to walk. She accepted with dread, seeing in his eyes there were weighty matters to be discussed.

As they began to walk, Mr Bingley spoke of his personal dilemmas and tribulations. He found himself in somewhat straitened circumstances. "Nothing to worry over," he assured her warmly, "nothing a bit of retrenching will not mitigate. I need only to exercise prudence for some time."

Evidently, Mr Bingley had been quite unaware of how much his debauchery cost him, but his man of business had been to Netherfield and apprised him of the situation. His father had left him a fortune of one hundred thousand pounds, but somehow in the past year or so it had been significantly reduced—and the bills were still coming.

Mr Bingley went on at length about his plans to re-establish his credit and restore his fortunes. Jane recognised she ought not listen and tried to demur, but he blithely paid no attention. Soon, she realised that he wished for her advice or, failing that, the advice Darcy might give him if only Darcy would speak to him.

The cost of purchasing Netherfield and all of its grounds and farms was rather beyond Mr Bingley's touch due to his imprudence. He felt it would not be impossible for him to buy it if he could persuade the current owners to agree to a lower price, but it would leave him rather bereft of funds to live on. Mr Bingley did not think Darcy would count it wise to deplete his ready capital in such a way, particularly as the prosperity of the estate under Mr Bingley's management would be uncertain for the first few years.

"But what say you to that?" he asked. "Do you think Darcy would think it sound?"

"Mr Darcy?"

"Yes. In such a circumstance, what do you think Darcy would do?"

"I am sure I do not know."

"You must have some notion. What do you imagine Darcy would do?"

"I suppose I must say Mr Darcy is unlikely to have gambled his money away in the first place."

Mr Bingley appeared disappointed but nodded in agreement and asked no more.

By this time, Kitty, their unnecessary chaperon, had fallen back, and Mr Bingley took advantage. "Miss Bennet, I have been most eager to speak privately to you. I pray you will indulge me for a moment."

Oh lord, here it comes. Jane gave him a small smile and a little nod.

"These months we have been apart have been...enlightening for me, I must say. I have learnt much of my flaws and my tendencies. I have seen so much in myself that I must correct and change to be a man worthy of the love of an exceptional lady."

He seemed to want something here, so Jane smiled again.

"My illness has proven valuable in this regard. It required me to spend time in contemplation and in improving my character. Why, I have even read three books! Complete!"

Another pause ensued before Jane murmured something to the effect of well done. She wondered whether it would be presuming too much to stop his speech now.

He appeared satisfied for a moment, and his countenance wore an earnest appearance. "But one thing has emerged in my study of myself, and that is my love for you, dearest Jane. I love you as I have no other. Your sweetness, your goodness, and your beauty... I could search the whole world and not find another who compares to you."

Now what do I say? "You are too kind, sir," Jane murmured with her eyes downcast demurely.

He went on, saying all the things she had longed to hear over those long, lovelorn, winter months, but she scarcely heeded him. She instead busily searched her mind for just the right words to discourage him.

As he spoke of his attachment to her, it was all she could do not to roll her eyes, but she managed to remain complaisant.

"Pray, tell me your wishes and feelings have not changed," he urged. "Pray, tell me I am not too late."

"Well...ah," Jane stammered idiotically, feeling her skin flush. She did not want to be cruel, but the truth was cruel. *He is much too late, and in truth, I believe it must be a mercy, for I cannot think what I was about, loving such a silly man in the first place.*

"You are not attached to another, surely?" He waited, fixing her with those blue eyes that once seemed so charmingly guileless but now seemed shallow.

"I truly do not think...I want...there is something..." Jane sighed at her stammering, finally saying, "'Tis not you, 'tis me."

She could feel his eyes upon her as she kept her own fixed on the ground. "What is you? Or me? Or not me—what did you say?"

Jane looked heavenward a moment. "We are not well suited."

"But we are!" He cried out.

"No."

"I think we are eminently suited to one another."

Jane stopped walking and gave him a kindly smile. "I think we would do better as friends than as lovers."

"Friends?" He stared at her, slack-jawed. "Men and women cannot be friends. What—would you like to shoot with me or something of the sort?"

I think I might rather shoot at you than with you. "If the man I loved wished me to shoot with him, I would go happily."

"Good! If you would like me to take you shooting, I shall."

"That is not what I said."

"Then what did you say?"

He seemed to have extraordinary difficulty in comprehending her, but then again, she did not know how severe his head injury had been. Perhaps he was now an idiot, or perhaps he had always been an idiot.

"I am sorry." She turned her back on him, intending to make her way towards the house. "We should return."

Jane began to walk away at a steady pace. After a pause, she heard Mr Bingley's footsteps behind her.

His tone undeniably bitter, he said, "So Darcy was right."

She stopped immediately, turning to face him. "I beg your pardon?"

"You never did love me." His expression was hard, but his eyes were wounded. "Darcy had the right of it after all. Your attachment to me was no more than a wish to entrap a wealthy man."

She flushed again, this time with indignation. "Think what you will."

"Can you deny it?"

"Yes, I can deny it."

"Then what?" He placed his hands on his hips like a scolding governess.

"I believed I loved you. Clearly, I was wrong."

"Believed!" he roared accusingly. He pointed a finger at her. "You silly woman, you did not even know your own mind!"

Jane thought she was a forbearing soul and could tolerate many things. What she would not tolerate, however, was someone calling her silly. It grated and was perhaps the reason she snapped back at him. "Well, I had no idea that the Mr Bingley I knew was no more than Mr Darcy's puppet, did I?"

"Excuse me?" He glared at her.

"I mean," she said, speaking slowly, "that when Mr Darcy was telling you what to do, you behaved like a gentleman, and yes, I did love that gentleman. However, time has shown that is not really who you are, is it? I used to wonder why you were so very different from your sisters, and now I see you are not. You were merely under different influences. You permitted Mr Darcy to turn you into a man who was honourable, wise, and good—just as he is—but the moment his back was turned, you became someone else altogether. I have no use for such a man as you."

Jane could scarcely believe she had expressed her anger so freely; that was Lizzy's way, not hers. Mortification flooded her, and she burst into tears, fleeing his accusing glare and running the rest of the way home. Thankfully, he did not follow.

31

August 1812

THEY WERE IN THE BILLIARDS ROOM ALTHOUGH NO GAME WAS played. Instead, the two Fitzwilliam brothers, unashamed and unrepentant, listened eagerly to the row ensuing between their father and Lady Catherine. It was an old habit from their days as schoolboys when renovations to the Matlock house yielded the delightful arrangement of a shared wall between this room and their father's library. It was uncommonly useful as they grew from boys to men, and they had used it often to overhear that which should not have been heard.

In any case, both men doubted there was a soul present in the house who could not hear Lady Catherine's share in the conversation. That included old Thomas, the aged, almost-deaf manservant who had been in the Matlock's employ since his lordship was a boy.

"...sat there in Derbyshire enjoying Darcy's grounds no doubt and all the while right beneath your nose—"

"Yes," their father replied calmly. "Pemberley was quite enjoyable, I must admit. Darcy bought our niece a new instrument, and she played it delightfully."

"And what of your other niece? What of Darcy's duty to Anne? Where were thoughts of Anne when all of this enjoyment of Pemberley and frolicking about with tradespeople was taking place?"

There was a brief silence until Lord Matlock replied evenly, "I do not recall any formal engagement between them, and thereby, he has no duty to her."

This led to some near-apoplectic shrieking on the part of Lady Catherine, most of which was difficult to interpret.

Fitzwilliam cursed softly. "The old bat is really taking it hard. This just might be the end."

"Do not speak so," Saye warned. "For then Anne will be under our care."

"No," said Fitzwilliam, horrified. "Is that true?"

Saye nodded solemnly. "And it would be to you and me to see her settled. Of course"—he grinned at his brother—"you are not attached. I could see you both settled in one fell swoop with precious little inconvenience to myself."

He stroked his chin as one might a beard. "Yes, yes, a fine idea. I am surprised I had not thought of it before."

Fitzwilliam cursed again, more loudly and pointedly this time. "You will see me making love to Napoleon first."

The men laughed before returning their attention to their father's study wherein Lady Catherine was opining that Miss Elizabeth Bennet was a practiced seducer of good, upright gentlemen. Her arts and allurements had clearly confounded Darcy into doing what he knew he must not. Lady Catherine was rather explicit in her description of what precisely she believed Elizabeth Bennet had done to secure Darcy.

"To hear Lady Catherine's speaking of these things makes me shudder," Saye murmured. "Who would think she even knew such things existed?"

"You did not think she gained Sir Lewis's hand by her wit or vivacity, did you?" Fitzwilliam replied with a devilish grin. "And she was surely never pretty so..."

Saye paled as a wave of nausea struck him, considering what he had not before imagined about his aunt. "What a notion! How could you even think of such things?"

"Time in the army comes with many a lonely hour that must occasionally be filled with the consideration of strange notions."

In Lord Matlock's room, the battle continued to wage between the earl's view of Elizabeth and Darcy at Pemberley and Lady Catherine's belief that Elizabeth Bennet was the sort of female commonly going about as a despoiler of good men.

"Mrs Reynolds, I believe, has bed linens that speak to the contrary." Hearing their father make such a pronouncement caused both brothers to gasp with scandalised delight before bursting into hearty laughter and falling on each other even while Lady Catherine raged on the other side of the wall.

"Shall we tell him the bedchamber in question was in fact Darcy's marriage bed?"

Saye was too busy laughing. "I hardly know. This is just too much fun."

"For the sake of Mrs Darcy's honour perhaps?" Fitzwilliam persisted.

"Oh. Yes, I suppose there is that to be thought of. It is rather ungenerous of Lady Catherine to speak so of her own niece."

Fitzwilliam replaced his cue stick in the holder in preparation to quit the room. "But do we have Darcy's leave to spread the news?"

"I believe we must. If only so Lady Catherine will know she must abandon this idea that Darcy will marry Anne."

Moments later, two gentlemen entered their father's library after a brief scuffle at the door to determine who should enter first. Fitzwilliam believed Saye's precedence meant he should have to, and Saye thought Fitzwilliam should go first because Saye told him to, and as the elder brother, he must be obeyed.

At last, both men were in the room and uncomfortably situated on a small settee that boasted the advantage of being located farthest from their aunt.

The countenance of Lord Matlock showed that the calmness with which he had earlier spoken was no more than a disguise. His red face and clenched fists indicated his true anger at the unwanted intrusion of Lady Catherine.

Lady Catherine would not sit, it seemed. Her gown and her face were both the colour of claret, prompting Saye to announce, "Lady Catherine, that is a lovely gown, and I believe I saw one very much like it on Lady Jersey at the theatre one night in June. Hers was trimmed in gold, which I rather liked. Did you consider gold for yours as well?"

Lady Catherine scowled at him, one bejewelled hand clutching at her walking stick as if she wished to prevent herself from striking him with it.

"Boys, you had something of importance to say?" Lord Matlock enquired.

"Yes." Fitzwilliam hurriedly took the lead in the conversation. "We could not help but overhear some of your"—he glanced at Lady Catherine—"concerns regarding Darcy and Miss Elizabeth Bennet. This may be something of a surprise, but Darcy has married her. She is no longer Miss Elizabeth Bennet but Mrs Fitzwilliam Darcy."

Saye added, "So any further conversation about engagements of infants, arts and allurements, or even bed linens at

Pemberley are quite beside the point. It is finished, and they are married."

Lady Catherine opened her mouth, and her complexion grew, remarkably, even more purple with rage. However, her feelings on the subject must be left to speculation as she did not have the chance to utter so much as a syllable before they overcame her. A dull thud was all to be heard as she collapsed on the floor in a faint.

FOLLOWING HER INELEGANT SWOON, LADY CATHERINE WAS immediately taken to bed in the best guest apartment in the Matlock's home. It was an exceedingly fine chamber, and the servants of the house offered every due courtesy, but she was unappeased. Every feeling within her revolted against the connexion to such a woman as Miss Elizabeth Bennet. And to further imagine the grievous slight to her own daughter! It was too much to be borne.

She could no longer deceive herself as to her daughter's prospects. Never mind what that simpering fool Collins had to say of her, Anne was a disgrace. She had no accomplishments, no beauty, no conversation—and she was now jilted. Darcy and the trollop who had confused him into taking her as his wife had thoroughly done her in. Anne would surely not marry now.

As she lay there, having just terrorised Lord Matlock's personal physician into submission, there was but one thought in her mind: vengeance upon Miss Elizabeth Bennet.

For to Lady Catherine, Miss Elizabeth Bennet she was and Miss Elizabeth Bennet she would remain. She would never dignify the girl by attaching the name of Darcy to her, no matter what her stupid nephew had done.

Her other nephews and her idiot brother had proven remarkably helpful in the matter, giving her ample information to succeed in her cause. She had fallen silent, but while her tongue rested, her mind had not, and she knew now just how to act.

In a swirl of nightclothes, she emerged from the bed and went at once to her daughter's bedchamber. Anne was in the middle of preparing for sleep and shrieked when her mother threw open the door, but Lady Catherine was of a mind to speak to her and could not be gainsaid by such a minor thing as privacy.

"Go," Lady Catherine barked at the servant, and the girl quickly disappeared.

Anne struggled to pull the gown her maid had just undone up over her chest. "Mother, are you well?"

"Of course, I am. I had a shock, that is all." Lady Catherine waved away her daughter's concern as she took a seat on her bed. "I have been plaguing myself, wondering what I could have done to prevent you from being jilted in this manner."

"Oh. Not really jilted, for I—"

"Jilted. And your reputation will suffer for it; make no mistake. It is unfortunate enough that Darcy has let things go so long until the bloom is long gone from your rose…"

Anne frowned and looked at the glass on her dressing table.

"But I have found the answer, a beautiful scheme that will not only rescue your reputation but will also serve Miss Elizabeth Bennet the revenge she deserves."

"Cousin Elizabeth?" Anne asked in a small voice.

"Never call her that!" Her mother roared in response.

Anne, abashed, looked down at her unimpressive bosom.

"Now, hear me on this. There is a man called Bingley…" And so Lady Catherine outlined her masterful, brilliant plan of revenge. Mr and Mrs Collins, although both rather stupid, were often in possession of useful information, and they had told

Lady Catherine that Miss Jane Bennet, dearest sister of Miss Elizabeth, had been of late disappointed in love by a man called Bingley. Saye and Fitzwilliam had all but confirmed it.

"And she loves him still," Lady Catherine crowed. "So, this is your part, my dear. You will marry this Bingley."

"What! But I do not even know—"

"Marry him and, through your marriage, so destroy the hopes of the Bennets for an alliance of their daughter with another wealthy man! Miss Elizabeth will be sorrowful on behalf of her sister, and her sister will be unlikely to have another offer—"

"She is the sister of Mr. Darcy and very beautiful, I am told. I do not think—"

"Hush!" Lady Catherine glowered at Anne who shrank back. "Miss Jane Bennet will be utterly downcast, but I am known for my beneficence, and I shall save her. I shall find her a place with a good family, and in so doing, Darcy will be embarrassed to be connected to a very low family, cousin to my parson, and brother to a governess. Maybe even more! Perhaps I might be able to place all Miss Elizabeth's sisters."

Lady Catherine chuckled with glee at such a notion, warming to her idea. "What is still more perfect about this plan is that Darcy must despise Bingley for what he did to him, yet I shall force him to accept his enemy as his relation just as he has forced me to accept mine. Too perfect, too splendid by half." Her own superiority of mind amazed her sometimes.

"If this is the same Mr Bingley who has long been Darcy's friend," said Anne, shifting to cover her bosom more thoroughly with her gown, "I must tell you, Mama, it cannot be."

"Cannot be? Why not?"

"Fortune from trade." Anne knew well how her mother felt

about that. "Would you have the shades of Rosings thus polluted?"

Lady Catherine waved her hand. Such ideas could not disturb her now. "You are an aged spinster who is jilted by your cousin. It is not certain you can even bear children. Your chance to attract a man suited to your station is long past, thanks to that no-good Cousin Darcy of yours, and you must take what you can get. Mr Bingley's fortune is good—Fitzwilliam thought it near one hundred thousand pounds—and he is handsome besides."

"Cannot bear children? I am only six and twenty," Anne protested. "In any case, I am not even acquainted with Mr Bingley, and I have heard tales of his—"

"Do not think of that," said Lady Catherine. "I shall arrange it all, and as for Mr Bingley's proclivity for indulgence and debauchery, well, I shall take care of that too. A good scolding is all the boy needs."

SAYE LOATHED LONDON IN AUGUST. LONDON IN AUGUST WAS HOT, boring, and smelled strongly of horse leavings. Anyone of consequence had long since departed to parties in the country. It was a degradation merely to appear on the streets, much less act the pretence of amusement.

However, someone needed to be there to attend to the vital task of silencing the rumours about the Darcys' engagement, their marriage, and the unfortunate business with Miss Staley. As was the common way, the task fell to him.

"Everyone wishes to seem as if they stay in London because they choose it," Saye mused aloud as he waited for his coachman to open the door. "Because the real reason—that they have nowhere else to go—is simply too pitiable."

His hostess was someone whose invitation he would never accept for any reason other than his holy mission. However, his foul humour was dispelled in an instant when he entered the drawing room where the forty or so others had congregated before him. She was here: Miss Caroline Bingley, attended by that pinkish beau of hers. At once, he had an excessively amusing notion: he would see Miss Bingley hung by her own rope, so to speak. *Absolutely providential that I am here.*

Miss Bingley and Marston had the good sense not to approach, but he saw how she watched him, no doubt wishing to gauge what he knew and how much he held against her. Saye observed her throughout dinner, his eyes carefully hooded, his expression deceptively sedate. She gave him little glances on occasion, but his evident disinterest seemed to persuade her that he was either unknowing or uncaring of her brother's crimes against Darcy. Little did she know that he loved Darcy like a brother and had already made his new wife a favourite.

Marston was located across the table but two seats down from Saye, an ideal location for eavesdropping. Saye sat up, smiling at the lady to his left—Miss Sarah? Miss Susan?—and said, "You are a friend of my cousin Darcy, are you not?" He made sure to say the name Darcy with slightly more volume than the rest of the sentence.

It worked. Marston made his best attempt at sangfroid, but he was interested. Saye could read it in the unnatural stillness of his form and the slight tip of his head.

Miss Sarah (for he had decided she was much more a Sarah than a Susan) was blessedly timid and spoke her reply to her lap amidst a deep blush. To wit, she had not been introduced to Darcy, ever.

Saye chuckled as if Miss Sarah had just said the most charming thing. Replying in a low voice, he said, "I was certain we had been introduced before by"—he cleared his throat, permitting his voice to become loud—"Darcy."

Another quick glance came from Marston. Saye remained outwardly unaffected but inwardly crowed his triumph. It was enough to set a bit of tattle going at Marston's area of the table, and he did not doubt everyone expected to hear some new bit of gossip. *I am like a regal bird, an eagle or a hawk, and by the end of the night, they will all be my squalling chicks, beaks wide for whatever worms I choose to drop on them.* The thought improved his mood considerably.

There was one gentleman in the party whom Saye did not think was completely intolerable. His name was Armstrong, and he had been at school with Darcy and Fitzwilliam, though in the year between them. When the ladies had withdrawn, Saye moved closer to him.

The usual enquiries after his family were made. Armstrong was recently married, and Saye pretended to be interested in hearing more of his lady, hoping Armstrong would follow suit and ask after his family.

Armstrong did not fail him. "So what of these stories I hear of Darcy?"

"Darcy?" Saye said loudly. By now, it was a matter of course that Marston would look, but it pleased him nevertheless. His gaze slid around the table noting the posture of several gossips sitting nearby. Oh yes—all were listening although some feigned disinterest.

"Yes—some young miss in Sheffield?"

Saye acted bemused. "I cannot think what you mean. Darcy in Sheffield?" He laughed loudly. "Who on earth would leave Pemberley for the likes of Sheffield?"

Armstrong chuckled a little. "I thought I had heard—"

"No, no, with Darcy married—"

Armstrong straightened in his seat. "Darcy is married?"

"You did not know?"

"No, I... Was it in the papers?"

Saye looked like he was considering that for a moment. "Of course, it was. They married while we were all at Pemberley."

"I had heard he was very much in love."

Saye sighed and rolled his eyes. "I am sure I never expected it of him, but dear lord! One can hardly speak to the man these days! It is all about Elizabeth. Elizabeth, Elizabeth, Elizabeth! I am sure I should never hear the end of his effusions."

And Armstrong, recently married and in love himself, liked the idea of this quite well. The men went on to speak of other things for a little while until it was decided they must join the ladies. As they entered the drawing room, Saye clapped Armstrong on the back and said, "Ah! I see what is happening here."

Armstrong looked at him enquiringly.

"There has been something of a falling out between Darcy and some of his old friends. You have heard what some of them have been up to." He permitted his eyes to rest on Miss Bingley, who was on the other side of the room and quite unaware of him.

As it happened, Armstrong had not, but the details were not important to him. "So there is a breach then?"

Saye gave a large shrug. "A married man must always decide which friendships to keep and which to let languish, I suppose. If the breach happens during his courtship, well, so much the better. A married man has nothing to do with the wild young bucks, does he?"

Marston, without seeming to hurry, hurried across the room to his intended wife. He stood behind where she sat with her friends until they moved away from her then whispered, "He says there is a breach."

"What?" Caroline asked. "Who?"

"Lord Saye," Marston bit the words out through clenched teeth. "He is saying there is a breach between the families."

Miss Bingley lifted one shoulder in an elegant, supercilious shrug. "Well, with Darcy gone so utterly debauched—"

"Darcy is married," Marston hissed.

"What? Married?"

"To Elizabeth Bennet."

Miss Bingley went silent for a moment until offering a weak protest. "I am certain you are wrong."

"Darcy married at Pemberley," said Marston firmly. "I just heard it from his own cousin."

"When?"

"It does not matter. We need to be certain of it. Else, this notion of a breach will gain hold. Do not allow it to be known that you are surprised by this. Why, you must have known it for weeks—mayhap a month or two. Hang your brother and his foolish intrigues. He must sort them out himself."

HANG THE ARMY. THE TRUE POWER OF THE EMPIRE RESTS IN THE tongues of London. For once they begin to move, anything can be accomplished.

Following his conversation with the gentlemen, Saye hung back. It was visible, the astonishing news that Darcy had married travelling from group to group, everyone talking about it while attempting to seem like they already knew. Quite amusing, yet Saye wished for more.

It was a shock to all four ladies when Saye quite precipitously tossed himself in the middle of Miss Bingley, Miss

Marston, a lady who was not handsome enough to interest him, and another who was pretty but smelt dreadful. Her name would be Frowzy, he decided, as her cologne was presently failing her. Blast, but he despised August. When the time came to take his father's seat in Parliament, he would not rest until it was passed that a daily bath should be required of those remaining in London in summer!

"Ladies," he said by way of a greeting. After a brief moment of shock, mutterings of "my lord" were heard, then silence. Saye said cheerfully, "So what news, Miss Bingley? How is Mr Bingley? I have not had the pleasure of seeing him in town."

"Ah, no. No, he is not in town." Miss Bingley had the grace to look embarrassed and uncertain. "And, alas, there is little news to be had. We were all saying how dull town is right now.

Frowzy, bless her soul, added, "We were asking Miss Bingley of the marriage of Mr Darcy. Being that her brother is such a good friend to Mr Darcy, we thought she might know what to make of all the talk that is going about. First, Mr Darcy was engaged to a Miss Elizabeth Bennet and then we heard he was to marry Miss Staley, but then some others have said he is already married."

"I am sure you know all about the truth of that, Miss Bingley." Saye's warm smile in Miss Bingley's direction belied the true sentiment in his words. "All of Darcy's friends do."

Miss Bingley hesitated for a scant moment. "Of course I do."

"Because naturally anyone who claimed a friendship with Darcy must know the truth of the matter."

"Yes, indeed," she agreed. "And we have long been intimates of Mr Darcy's circle."

Saye twisted his mouth into a little pout, wordlessly

disputing her. It made her anxious and did not go unnoticed by the others in the group.

"Your brother was meant to be at Pemberley with us, and he did not come. Whatever became of him?"

Frowsy whispered something to the girl next to her, and Saye decided that despite her unfortunate odour, he just might ask her to dance some day. Not soon, but some day. He knew not what she said until Miss Bingley responded to it.

"Who said that?" She laughed a high, brittle laugh. "There was no disagreement between my brother and Mr Darcy. 'Tis patently untrue."

Marston heard her laugh and, sensing distress, joined them. Saye looked up coolly from where he sat. "Marston, you knew that Darcy had married."

"Certainly," said Marston smoothly. "Caroline, you sent a note of congratulation, did you not?"

Miss Bingley opened her mouth and closed it again.

Saye waved his hand. "Never mind that. Mr and Mrs Darcy have gone to Hertfordshire to see her family. The congratulations from their friends in London can be sent later."

"When did they marry?" Dear Frowzy and her questions. He would certainly dance with her sometime.

"Oh, it's been some time. In truth, it has been so long now that I can scarce recall it. Quite romantic, it was."

"The wedding?" Frowzy asked.

"All of it. The time he spent courting her at Pemberley, all of us just having so much fun. And then one night they had a picnic on the roof…"

"On the roof…" Frowzy sighed to her plain little friend.

Saye nodded. "Darcy did such a fine job of it that they did not wish to wait to marry."

The ladies were in rapt attention, and Saye smiled at each of them in turn. He looked around to ensure Miss Marston, a noted gossip, heard him clearly. "Miss Elizabeth had by then fallen quite in love with him too, and it was there that she agreed to marry him—but there had been so many months of an understanding by then! It seemed a shame to wait any longer. Trust me; I suffer a long engagement myself. It is a poor business for a man.

"So off to the vicar they went, with Darcy having his licence and a letter from her father in hand, and so it was. Miss Elizabeth Bennet no more, and instead, she is my new Cousin Elizabeth. I am excessively fond of her."

The murmurings went about again, each saying how lovely she seemed and how much they wished to be acquainted with her.

Saye levelled a look at Miss Bingley, his deliberate levity gone. "It was while your brother was in Sheffield. But you knew that, intimate as you are." His meaning was clear to her.

"Of course, we knew," said Marston, who still had hopes of gaining entry into the Darcy's circle. "Quite pleased for them, indeed."

Gossip was a strange and wonderful thing. No one ever heard things quite right, and it was the details that were so often shaded. By the end of the evening, some thought the Darcys had been married in early July while others believed it was the middle of the month. Saye even heard one person who was certain they had married back in April. That gave him a sincere laugh.

And even better was to see Miss Bingley at the heart of it all, attempting to deny her own rumours. There was at least one person who asked her in genuine confusion whether Miss Bingley had not told her news quite to the contrary just the day prior. Her face carefully blank, she denied any such statements.

When he had enough and was ready to leave for the night, he asked Marston to attend him to his carriage. Marston rightly understood that his lordship wished to speak to him alone.

The two gentlemen stood in the heavy night air, and Saye, inhaling the fetid odour of the street, spat. Marston was all smiles and tried to offer some inanity of conversation, but Saye stopped him with a raised finger and a quick shake of his head. Any pretence of good humour was gone, and he spoke quickly, "See here, Marston. I know full well what that woman of yours has been saying, and I also know the truth of the matter. I know you do too."

"Ah, my lord, if you please—"

Another quick shake and a frown. "If I have my way, no Darcy will ever receive any Bingley or anyone connected to a Bingley ever again."

Marston went rather pale at this idea. He spoke slowly, his mind evidently racing. "Pray, forgive her, sir, for I do not think there was ill intention behind her—"

"—vicious slander?" Saye shrugged. "Her intent is not of interest to me." He sniffed, meaning to sound as haughty as he could. "A gentleman cannot break his engagement, but there are ways to induce the lady to do it herself."

Darcy, you are welcome, thought Saye as he made his way home. He gave a self-satisfied sigh, thinking what a burden it was to be the one always going about fixing things for everyone else.

32

November 1812

"HERE IS A BIT OF NEWS YOU NEVER COULD HAVE IMAGINED," SAID Colonel Fitzwilliam, "no matter how wild your flight of fancy."

Darcy greeted him with pleasure. His wife was, as she often had been of late, with his aunt and sister at the dressmaker. He knew she required a great many new things in her position as his wife, but was it truly needful that she be gone so much? How often did a gown need fitting? "What is it?"

"Our cousin Anne is betrothed." After a short pause meant to tempt Darcy's curiosity, he added, "To your former friend, Bingley."

"What? How on earth...?" Darcy exclaimed.

"I have no notion how it all came about," said Fitzwilliam, "but Lady Catherine, against all expectation, considers it a triumph. Her letter to my father instructed us to inform you most particularly of your need to congratulate your new cousin, and she also offered to aid you in the placement as governess of any or all of Mrs Darcy's sisters."

This made Darcy laugh. "I have been accustomed these many years to seeing Anne on one occasion per annum, which was Easter at Rosings. Now, as she is wed, I cannot suppose even that is necessary. Bingley can take over the responsibility of the estate and his new family, and I shall content myself with occasional letters of duty."

"And to the positions of governess?"

Darcy laughed again, rising to take his leave and go to retrieve his wife. He was a little early, but he did not suppose she would mind. "Do tell her I appreciate her consideration, but should Mr Bennet pass, I do think Pemberley will be sufficient for the support of my younger sisters."

Twelfth Night, 1813

THAT LADY MATLOCK WOULD HOLD A PARTY IN HONOUR OF THE new Mrs Darcy went without saying. It was of utmost importance that the family show all the support they could to the couple. Her inclination had been to host a crush, but her son persuaded her to do quite the opposite.

"What is important in any party," opined Saye, "is not who is invited, but rather, who is not. Let us have a party marked by exclusion, but"—He raised one finger in caution—"we must take care that this party positively reeks of the sublime. We cannot be content to have people regret their banishment—they must be crushed by it. If I do not hear of at least three people threatening to commit suicide over their exclusion, then I have not done as I ought."

It was the work of no less than a fortnight to determine who would be among the fortunate partygoers, but for this affair, it was decided mere notes of invitation would be woefully inadequate.

"Miniature Twelfth Night cakes," Saye had decreed. "Delivered during morning hours."

"But will it not place an extraordinary burden on her ladyship's cook to be required to make so many cakes?" Elizabeth protested.

Saye gave her a withering glance. "You, my dear, have a great deal to learn about making a splash in this town."

"A splash?" Elizabeth asked with a twinkle of impertinence in her eyes. "I have never learnt to swim, sir, much less splash."

"You are in the pond," Saye replied. "Either you splash or you drown, and as I have grown quite fond of you, I would prefer that you splash."

The first such cake was delivered to Lady Harrington one morning early in December as she sat in her salon with no less than ten callers. Lady Harrington was a dear friend of Lady Matlock, so both knew what they were about in having the cake delivered at such a time, and they had cackled with glee at creating such a spectacle.

The carriage arrived with great fanfare. Two handsome young footmen, liveried, starched, and powdered to within an inch of their lives, entered and bowed with a degree of deference appropriate to royalty. One then extended a silver tray with a domed lid. On Lady Harrington's nod, the other removed the lid to reveal a parchment scroll and a cake—a small but exquisitely decorated confection of palest rose boasting two sugar paste crowns on top.

Her ladyship smiled and took the parchment, unrolling it with painstaking care. She permitted herself a faint smile as she read the missive, well aware that the eyes of the room were upon her. When she had finished, she raised her eyes to the footmen then nodded, saying, "Leave the cake there if you will." After they did, she dismissed them.

The other ladies in her salon wondered at such a display, darting curious glances between the scroll, the cake, and Lady Harrington, who took a sip of her tea as if nothing extraordinary had just transpired. No one spoke, and it seemed that no one would until Lady Harrington offered some word of explanation, so she said, "An invitation to a party honouring the new Mrs Darcy. I confess I am quite eager to meet her. Lady Matlock is unreserved in her recommendation of the lady."

And that was that. Everyone in London was soon wild to receive one of Lady Matlock's famed cakes. It required a fortnight complete for all the cakes to be delivered, but by the third day, anyone who reasonably supposed they might be included in the party had taken to staring out their windows, praying to catch sight of the Matlock carriage. When it was seen, there was excessive exultation. When it passed by, there was dismay.

Most of London was due to be disappointed. In all, only fifty-three cakes were given, and of those, all but one were accepted. That one invitation refused was by Lady Rivenhall, whose husband had been injured during his exertions on a horse one afternoon in late December. Although his lady considered leaving the good gentleman to attend the party, she reluctantly concluded it would be unseemly.

Elizabeth had rather dreaded the event though she was grateful to Lady Matlock for her kindness. There seemed too much that could go amiss, particularly as her parents had arrived to attend it. Mrs Gardiner and Jane both assured her they would stay close to their mother, but Elizabeth worried nevertheless.

Most of the usual Twelfth Night traditions were done away with in favour of a dinner, which was a testament to opulence and excess such as Elizabeth could not have imagined. And Lady Matlock had hit upon a rather strange idea for the evening.

Between courses, the gentlemen changed their seats, granting them a new partner to talk to. It was a mercy of sorts for Elizabeth in that she found herself seated next to her husband, which would not have occurred under usual circumstances. It came with its evils too, however, in that she soon saw her mother seated with Saye, and both Jane and Mrs Gardiner were far, far away from them.

"Elizabeth."

Elizabeth started. "Forgive me, love, have you been trying to draw my attention?"

"I have. What occupies you so?"

She sighed. "Fear of mortification." She gestured towards Mrs Bennet and Saye.

"From which one?"

That made her laugh. "My mother, of course. You have forgotten the Netherfield ball, I think."

"All I remember about that night was how beautiful you were," he replied gallantly.

With that, she reminded herself there was nothing she could do about her mother's behaviour, and she should enjoy her evening with her husband. Under the table and hidden by the linens, she slid her hand into his.

"Have I told you how beautiful you are tonight?"

"In a manner of speaking," Elizabeth replied archly. She had appeared before him in a different gown earlier that night, one made particularly for the evening. It was designed to display her bosom to its advantage, and her maid had done her hair to be enticing as well, with one long curl trailing over her shoulder.

It had been too much for Darcy, and his attentions were, in turn, too much for her. They had made a wrinkled jumble of that gown, much to the distress of her maid, who was forced to resign herself to a much simpler arrangement of Elizabeth's hair (for some knots simply would not untangle themselves) and a less-revealing gown. Mr Darcy had declared that no one would be permitted to see so much of his wife but himself.

Halfway down the long table, Saye and Mrs Bennet were engaged in conversation. It was alarming, but Elizabeth determinedly turned her face from them, deciding that whatever damage might be done was beyond her control.

"WHOEVER TOLD HER SUCH A NECKLACE WAS FLATTERING SHOULD be hanged," Saye remarked, as much to himself as to his dining companion. In truth, he was not pleased to find himself entertaining Mrs Bennet. He had enough to do with his own future parents-in-law; he did not need to undertake the flattery of Darcy's.

Mrs Bennet proved a pleasant surprise to him, immediately apprehending the matron of whom he spoke. "Plainly designed to hide the loose skin around her neck," she murmured. "But the dress on *that* one is a far greater crime."

Saye looked in the direction she indicated and chuckled beneath his breath. "So noted, my dear. But what do you think of *him*?" He used his spoon to make a slight flicking motion at one of the gentlemen.

Mrs Bennet raised one brow in a manner quite like her daughter. "He looks rather well for a man of his years. Is your mother much alarmed that he appears to have brought his mistress with him tonight?"

Saye nearly laughed aloud at that. The dinner improved markedly for him, and he delighted in it. These Bennets were not wholly bad, he decided by the end of the evening.

February 1813

THERE WERE TWO EXCEEDINGLY JOYOUS OCCASIONS HELD IN February. The first was the marriage of Miss Jane Bennet to Mr Robert Abell. Jane was married, as Elizabeth suspected she would be, in Meryton. It was a joyful occasion with the breakfast attended by many persons from Hertfordshire and beyond.

"You know not what you avoided, marrying as you did, Darcy," Saye grumbled. "Five hundred people! I can scarcely imagine being civil for a long enough time to greet them all."

"I know precisely what I avoided," Darcy replied. "And that is why I avoided it."

The two gentlemen had found a rare moment together during Saye's wedding breakfast and enjoyed a glass of the brandy Darcy had given his cousin as a separate little wedding present. "Has a rather nice flavour," Saye told him. "Not so much of the burn."

"Quite nice for the ladies," said Darcy with a little wink.

"You drink brandy with Elizabeth?" Saye laughed heartily. "Yes, if there was a lady who would drink with a man, it is your wife. But I do think she is having an effect on my Lillian! Just the other day, she teased me in the most impertinent sort of way! I could scarce believe my ears."

"Ah, but I wager you liked it."

With a sheepish grin, Saye admitted, "Aye, I did."

There was a sound of a throat clearing. Both men turned at once, shocked to see Mr Bingley had approached them.

Darcy supposed he should not be surprised to see his old friend there. By virtue of Anne's strange proclivity, he was now their cousin, and it was proper that Bingley should have brought his wife to see her cousin married. The gentlemen all made awkward bows to one another.

"Congratulations, my lord." Bingley was first to speak, offering the required sentiments on Saye's nuptials.

Saye gave him a tight little grimace and turned to Darcy. "Think I shall be off to find my bride. If I am to endure all these people..." His voice trailed away as he set off towards his lady.

Darcy turned back to Bingley, taking a large swallow of his drink to forestall conversation for a moment.

Bingley had altered a bit. As a result of his earlier injuries, he had undergone a surgery that left him a bit weak. Even now, months later, he remained thinner, paler, and a great deal more sombre than he ever was. He was dressed in the latest fashion, with a cravat defying anything Darcy had ever seen before. His hair was elaborately arranged in curls in a halo around his head. His jewellery was fine but excessive, and it appeared his boots were designed to make him taller.

"I have not seen you at our club," said Darcy at last. "How long have you been in town?"

He meant it as a general sort of pleasantry, but Bingley looked away, seeming skittish.

"Lady Catherine does not like White's. She feels it more dignified to belong to Brooks's."

"Why does Lady Catherine care which gentlemen's club you belong to?"

Bingley seemed about to say something, but his attention was immediately distracted. Darcy followed the line of his diverted gaze and saw Mrs Abell had just entered the drawing room. She was on her husband's arm, and everything about the pair of them bespoke newly wedded love and harmony. One could not look at them without smiling, so plain was their felicity.

Bingley did not smile. He instead looked a bit ill.

"Bingley." Bingley did not answer. "Bingley."

"What? Oh, we have changed our name."

"What?"

Bingley shrugged. "There is nothing of nobility or distinction in Bingley, so I am Mr de Bourgh now."

Darcy was so surprised that he emitted an incredulous bark of laughter. He sobered immediately, seeing there was nothing of humour in the situation. "Forgive me. That is…that is good, I suppose."

Bingley nodded, his eyes still watching Mrs Abell, whose husband had just given her a loving kiss on the hand, causing her to blush prettily. "That way, a de Bourgh will still have Rosings. Congratulate me, Darcy. My dearest Anne is with child even now."

"Is she?" Darcy madly calculated the time the de Bourghs had been married and wondered whether a quickening was even possible by now. "My sincerest congratulations. I had not heard."

"She is a jewel, Darcy. My wife is a jewel, and I am exceedingly fortunate to have her. You know not what you overlooked all these years." The words were recited as if from a catechism.

Darcy hardly knew what to say. "I wish you well. Excuse me."

July 1813

"Mrs Darcy didn't take strawberries yesterday," said one of the younger maids.

"Not hungry for them," said her companion.

"P'raps not. But Mrs Darcy always takes the strawberries."

"My sister didn't eat any strawberries, and that's why her children have such pretty, fair skin."

The young maid nodded sagely. "'Tis when you eat the strawberries that your children be such nasty, freckled things."

"Now that would not be borne, not when the Darcys always be such handsome folks. No, Mrs Darcy would do all she could to make sure her children were just as handsome as those before her."

The two ladies shared a look of suppressed eagerness. A baby would be an exceedingly fine thing, and surely all of those in the house would rejoice to hear of such news.

Mr Waltham, the valet of Lord Saye, had been sent to the Darcy's town house to procure from Darcy's valet a certain remedy for use on stained trousers. He happened to come upon the two young maids just as they finished their conversation. Although he heard only a part of it, he knew the meaning at once, and good man that he was, he hastened to inform his master what he had learnt.

"ABOUT DAMN TIME," WAS HIS LORDSHIP'S BORED RESPONSE. "I WAS nearly tempted to make sure Darcy understood how it all worked."

Lady Saye had fallen with child within the first month of her marriage. Some tongues wagged about the timing of things, but he cared little for that. He would have a strapping little lad or a darling little miss, and that would be that.

And now Darcy too! Saye, who had grown much more fond of domestic pleasures in his brief time as a married man, closed his eyes to better think of it. Two young cousins, the dearest and most intimate of friends, or if they were male and female, perhaps more, some day long from now.

He clapped his hands just as his wife entered the room. "What do you think would be better?" Saye asked her. "If

Darcy's child were the same as our child so they could be dearest friends for life? Or if one should be male and the other female so that they might marry someday?"

It was a subject of much conversation between them, and they could not quite decide which would be preferred. Lady Matlock entered as they were discussing it and gave her opinion on the matter.

"But is it certain?" She asked much later. "Darcy said nothing of this to me. Surely they would announce such glad tidings."

Saye shrugged. "I would imagine he soon will."

"I confess, I am hurt," said Colonel Fitzwilliam. "How is it that you and Lillian know, and I was not told?"

"I suppose it is because he likes me better."

"He most certainly does not. I have always been his dearest friend, and you were nothing more than the tediously aggravating elder brother we were made to endure."

"But now I am more fun," said Saye with a tormenting grin. "And, like Darcy, a happily married man. We, neither of us, have any use for a wild and uncivilised soldier such as you."

"I still should have been told."

"I am sure you would have been. Eventually."

Colonel Fitzwilliam made a disgusted noise. His brother would take any cause to gloat, even Darcy's impending fatherhood. In any case, he knew Darcy esteemed him. It did not truly matter who told whom or when...did it?

"Elizabeth is not increasing," Darcy told Fitzwilliam patiently.

"No?"

"No."

"But I heard—"

"I would think I should know if I was to be a father."

Colonel Fitzwilliam, perched on the end of Darcy's desk, considered it. "Sometimes a lady waits to tell her husband until matters are certain."

"You think Elizabeth would not tell me?"

"She would not wish to see you suffer disappointment. For that reason she might not."

Darcy considered that. It was true: Elizabeth had seemed uncommonly tired of late, and she showed little interest in her breakfast plate, making a little face when the coffee drew near or the egg plate was opened.

A thrill tore through his chest. *Could it be?*

He leapt to his feet at once. "I need to get her a present."

ONE YEAR. CAN IT TRULY BE?

Elizabeth's preparations for the celebration of their first wedding anniversary were nearly complete. The dinner had been planned, and her present for her husband was coming along nicely. There was little to be anxious for and little to fear but the climb to the roof. *That* she had not yet learnt to anticipate, but she would. For this night, she certainly would, for where else but under the warm summer sky could she tell him of their felicity?

Of course, if they had been able to get to Pemberley, it would have been much preferred, but they had been forced to remain in town awaiting Georgiana, who was visiting with friends in Tunbridge Wells. A succession of rains had delayed her return, and Elizabeth was required to revise her plans. In any case, it was much easier to get onto the roof in London, a stair having been built for just such a purpose.

The roof had become a favoured place for the Darcys. In such a home as Pemberley, or even in town, one would imagine there were ample places for solitude and privacy; however, it was not so. Someone was always about, and even if they were not directly in the room with them, they were walking down the hall or closing a door somewhere or the like. Only on the roof could they enjoy the feeling that it was the two of them alone in the world.

But he was late for dinner. Where could he be? He had departed quite hastily after a brief meeting with his cousin in his study and had left no word as to where he had gone.

THE MORE DARCY THOUGHT OF IT, THE MORE EVIDENCE HE FOUND that his dearest, loveliest Elizabeth was likely expecting his child —*their* child. He was nearly a dervish on Bond Street, buying her anything that caught his eye: a fan, several new books, a parasol—two parasols!—and a length of fine lace. It was not until Fitzwilliam recalled him to the time and the likelihood Elizabeth would expect him for dinner that Darcy stopped himself and moved towards home.

His man was yet attempting to make him presentable when Elizabeth entered his bedchamber. "Shopping, Mr Darcy? I hear you had more than one man who attended you struggling under the weight of your purchases."

He smiled when he saw her. Indeed, he thought he had never smiled as much in his life as he had in the year since marrying her. Just beholding her lightened his spirits. "I would have you know my purchases were all on your behalf, my love."

"For me?" She tilted her head. "But I am in need of nothing."

"When does need have anything to do with a man wishing to spoil his beloved wife?"

She went to him and wrapped her arms about his waist, laying her head on his chest. "I am already quite spoilt, sir. Any more so, and I may become insufferable."

He kissed her head gently. "Never."

"So were these presents in celebration of our anniversary?"

"Perhaps. Unless you can think of another thing we should celebrate?"

She tilted her head up to look at him, resting her chin on his chest. "I cannot think of anything better celebrated than the deepest and most abiding love such as we have found with one another."

"Deep and abiding love is worthy of celebration," he agreed, looking at her intently. "But other things too."

Her eyes took on a particular little twinkle he had come to know well. "Other things? Like what?"

"I am sure I cannot say."

She pretended to consider it. "I suppose I might say there are many forms of love that must be celebrated."

"Quite so." He gave a little nod. "Brotherly love, for example."

She made a displeased little frown. "I know nothing of that, so I must trust your authority. To the wonder of sisterly love, we might both attest."

He nodded. "Yet there is one love that never fades."

"Are you saying you fear your love for me might one day fade?"

"Of course not," he said quickly. "But can anything compare to the love a parent has for his or her child?"

She said nothing in reply, but the teasing glimmer in her eyes became the tender shine of heartfelt delight.

"It is true?"

A little gasp of breath escaped her, and tears collected on her lower lashes. "Yes, I...he quickened just two days ago."

Darcy tightened his arms around her as his eyes closed, and he bit his lip to refrain from shouting his glee. A child would be given to them, the incarnation of their love and the fulfilment of their wishes and hopes for the future. He could scarcely believe it.

She pulled away, pressing him to move to the roof with her so they might dine. He, concerned for her nourishment, immediately acquiesced. They arrived on the roof, and he quickly set about ensuring that she was comfortably situated on a pillow, was warm but not too warm, had plenty of all the foods that tempted her, and did not stir too near the edge of the roof. She bore his solicitude well.

It was not until later, as she lay in his arms and stared at the sky, that she asked, "So I daresay you are...but still I shall ask. Are you pleased?"

"Am I pleased?" He laughed. "Pleased cannot begin to describe me. I am a contrariety of emotion. I am proud but humbled, courageous but afraid, strong but weak. There is no describing this feeling. It is sheer bliss."

"We have settled it then," she said from within his embrace. "We three shall be the happiest people in the world."

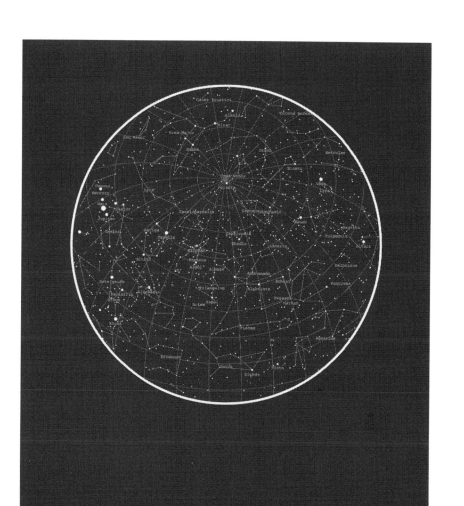

SKY ABOVE PEMBERLEY
DERBYSHIRE
JULY 1812
53.2152° N. 1.67617° W

ACKNOWLEDGMENTS

My first acknowledgement needs to go to my dear friend and business partner Jan Ashton. With her by my side, idle chatter has turned into an exciting business venture and I definitely couldn't do, wouldn't have even thought of doing it without her!

I have the most amazing team of editors in the world. Gail Warner and Ellen Pickels are revered in the JAFF community and their regard is well deserved. Also to Linda D'Orazio for being a willing and able proofer, making sure the book is polished to a shine! Thank you all for all you do; mere words can't thank you enough.

I owe many, many thanks to the wonderful readers, commenters, and beta readers from A Happy Assembly. Particular thanks to Linda Beutler, Janet Foster and Sheryl Weisbuch for their assistance in the development stages of the manuscript.

I also want to thank the people who have left reviews on my prior books (and thank you in advance to those who will review this book). Whether you love/loved or hate/hated it, the time you spent acknowledging it was important and deeply appreciated.

Lastly, all my love and appreciation to Tom, Allie, and Lexi. Love you all very much.

ABOUT THE AUTHOR

Amy D'Orazio is a long time devotee of Jane Austen and fiction related to her characters. She began writing her own little stories to amuse herself during hours spent at sports practices and the like and soon discovered a passion for it. By far, however, the thing she loves most is the connections she has made with readers and other writers of Austenesque fiction.

Amy currently lives in Pittsburgh with her husband and daughters, as well as three Jack Russell terriers who often make appearances (in a human form) in her book.

For more information about new releases, sales and promotions on books by Amy and other great authors, please visit www.QuillsAndQuartos.com.

The Best Part of Love

Avoiding the truth does not change the truth.

When Fitzwilliam Darcy meets Miss Elizabeth Bennet, his heart is almost immediately engaged. Seeing the pretty lady before him, a lady of no consequence or fortune, he believes he should not form an attachment to her, unsuitable as such a woman is to be his wife.

What he cannot see, however, is the truth, that the simple country girl harbours a secret. Before she meets Darcy, Elizabeth has spent two years hiding from the men who killed her beloved first husband. Feeling herself destroyed by love, Elizabeth is certain she will never love again, certainly not the arrogant man who has offended her from the first moment of their acquaintance.

In time, Elizabeth surprises herself by finding in Darcy a friend; even greater is her surprise to find herself gradually coming to love him and even accepting an offer of marriage from him. As the newly married couple is beginning to settle into their happily-ever-after, a condemned man on his way to the gallows divulges a shattering truth, a secret that contradicts everything Elizabeth thought she knew about the tragic circumstances of her first marriage. Against the advice of everyone who loves her—including Darcy—Elizabeth begins to seek the truth, knowing she must have it even if it may destroy her newfound happiness with Darcy.

A Short Period of Exquisite Felicity

Is not the very meaning of love that it surpasses every objection against it?

Jilted. Never did Mr. Darcy imagine it could happen to him.

But it has, and by Elizabeth Bennet, the woman who first hated and rejected him but then came to love him—he believed—and agree to be his wife. Alas, it is a short-lived, ill-fated romance that ends nearly as soon as it has begun. No reason is given.

More than a year since he last saw her—a year of anger, confusion, and despair—he receives an invitation from the Bingleys to a house party at Netherfield. Darcy is first tempted to refuse, but with the understanding that Elizabeth will not attend, he decides to accept.

When a letter arrives, confirming Elizabeth's intention to join them, Darcy resolves to meet her with indifference. He is determined that he will not demand answers to the questions that plague him. Elizabeth is also resolved to remain silent and hold fast to the secret behind her refusal. Once they are together, however, it proves difficult to deny the intense passion that still exists. Fury, grief, and profound love prove to be a combustible mixture. But will the secrets between them be their undoing?

Printed in Great Britain
by Amazon